Tom House
Spies & Sacred Lies

For Mike
Hennessy

With Best
Wishes

Tom House

Tom House

Spies & Sacred Lies

edition fischer

This is a work of fiction. Names, characters, places and incidents either are the product of the author's imagination or are used fictitiously, and any reference to actual persons, living or dead, business establishments, events or locales, is entirely coincidental.

Bibliographic Information published by Die Deutschen Bibliothek
Die Deutsche Bibliothek lists this publication in the Deutschen Nationalbibliografie; detailed bibliographic data is available in the Internet at http://dnb.ddb.de

© 2007 by edition fischer GmbH
Orber Str. 30, D-60386 Frankfurt/Main
All rights reserved/Alle Rechte vorbehalten
Type/Schriftart: New Century 10°
Printed in Germany
ISBN 978-3-89950-302-9

About the Author

The author was born in Scotland. He was a member of the British Security Services working in central Europe during the Cold War. After leaving them, he spent a couple of decades working in Research & Development, as an analyst and systems programmer, initially with German and American computer companies in Europe and later on with his own company in Germany. He has retired and is now dedicated to writing, setting scenes and actions capable of happening in our everyday life, and some of them do.

About the book

John Jameson, a Scot – ex British Intelligence Services, now working freelance as an anti-terrorist specialist for the government and an international security agency, gets involved, not only with an international murder investigation of one of his own agents and some Jews in Germany and Britain, but also with two beautiful women. His enquiries also lead him to secrets of great interest to the Vatican Secret Service who don't stop at murder and destruction in order to get their hands on the information and documents.

Secrets held by the Vatican in Rome, internal conspiracies and incompetence amongst the allied intelligence agencies come to light – sacred lies dating back to early days of Christianity and so-called direct incited sabotage amongst the intelligence agencies. A massive plot to disrupt governments using the tools of fear is uncovered.

Terrorism is predominant, anarchistic movements and Nazi organisations are involved – working under the mask of a powerful worldwide business organisation – their purpose – to gain political power and world control. Information also points to international involvement in 9/11 – others with strong motives – the ones who pulled the strings – well planned over the last two decades.

In the midst of all this, evil minds are planning to detonate a dirty bomb and instigate the use of small strategic 5 Kt atomic warheads.

Manui dat cognitio vires

Foreword

The use of spies and agents for the passing of information is thousands of years old. Today, government-, commercial-, and private espionage networks form our daily basis. The automatic exchange of personal information is fed into a worldwide spider web where individuals are shaped into pre-defined cocoons – personal information and movement no longer remaining a private matter.

The world is a small place – somebody you may meet casually, no matter where, maybe even a stranger in a bar who just so happens to be under surveillance – your tough luck – now you're under suspicion too although you're innocent. Or maybe you send a seemingly harmless cyberspace message to a friend who just happens to be under suspicion – the consequences are sometimes grave... ☦ These are just two examples of everyday encounters in the worldwide network labyrinth of information gathering – there are thousands more...

Lies are not only common in modern politics but form the basis of the New Testament – namely, not telling the whole truth may also be expressed as sacred lying.

Acknowledgments

Deepest thanks to my wife Erika – with lots of love and everlasting respect.

Most thanks go to my brother Will, for giving me the best possible guidance from the very beginning – my best friend and critic.

Exceptional thanks also to my very special friend Christine who gave me many inspirations and raised my spirits with her positive appraisal and helpful remarks.

Thanks also to my other relatives and friends for their kind help and judgement. A special note of thanks goes to my German friends Burkhard and Stefan, and to Parveez, from Karachi.

ISIA

(The organization is Fiction and purely for this book, but it could become Fact)

Terrorists are capable of choosing their own moment of where and when to strike. Therefore, governments have no other choice than to build stronger defences. Most European countries have been doing that. New laws, more controls, such as biometric passports containing fingerprints or iris scans, are in process. In some countries they are being implemented. In others they have to change the laws first. It's a long and mainly bureaucratic enterprise, and in the end, George Orwell, God bless his soul, just got the year wrong.

EU Interior Ministers faced calls for much more extensive melding of Intelligence. This was the forum of an emergency meeting in Brussels, middle of March 2004: *Guy Verhofstadt, the Belgian Prime Minister, was pushing for a vote for a European version of the CIA, an Intelligence Centre able to "share and exchange and, most important, reach a common analysis of the terrorist threat."*

Owing to the devastating structures of the police and intelligence organizations throughout the EU, this would appear to be ***wishful thinking*** and an impossible adventure.

See also appendices (back of book) for further information on:

- Jesus of Nazareth (a short true life's itinerary)
- Notes on James, Jesus' Brother (fact not fiction)
- Archaeology in the study of the Bible & New Testament
- The Bible – Torah Code (a theory)
- General Remarks – Glossary – Book Characters
- Family trees of Stern & Zuckenic on last page

Introduction

Palestine – AD 67

It is dusk as Hermes struggles up the goat's path nearing his goal – his mouth dry and eyes sore from the wind blasted sand and dust. Not long ago the journey was easier. He was able to travel on normal paths and use the wells to fill his water bag. The Romans are purging Palestine ever since Nero blamed the Christians for burning down Rome. The Zealots are retaliating and all travellers are regarded with great suspicion and treated badly. Thus, his journeys have become extremely difficult and more dangerous, having to climb many a mountain to avoid the valleys where cohorts of legionnaires are strategically placed to catch any messengers such as he. If apprehended, death and violence from ignorant pagan Roman legionnaires would be his fate, but first, oh dread, they would torture him.

Having reached the mountain ridge, he crouches behind a rock to peer at the darkening silhouette of the City of David. The shouts and sounds of distant swords beating against shields, as legionnaires patrol the city and people hurrying to get indoors before the curfew begins, fill him with great awe. He mutters a prayer,

'Oh, God, give me guidance – lend your servant good eyes and ears that he may reach the house of Magdalena's daughter safely.'

The main harvest over and having filled the tradesmen's ledgers with his meticulous script and finished his copying of scrolls at Secacah near the Dead Sea, he now looks forward to his next task, the most honourable – acting as a courier – to collect important documents left by Jesus' brother James, once the central figure of the Jewish-Christian faith in David's City after Jesus' crucifixion, and proceed to Tyre on his next precarious journey to find the Greek philosopher Dion, better known as Gold-Mouth and hand over the precious documents.

At Secacah, he enjoys the copying and the occasional translation from Aramaic to Greek awarding him with an extensive political and historical insight. He hates the interruptions caused by Hellion, the mathematician responsible for the coding of some passages with tetragrammatons and abbreviated forms. Being a Greek-Christian he is trusted by the Essenes. He has been sworn to secrecy, as some of the information he has to translate contains current Zealot activities.

Opening his food satchel he eats the remaining dates and bits of unleavened bread – more sand and grit to grind. He lets the last drops of water trickle into his mouth from his water bag, trying to wash this sandy dish down his throat. His thoughts wander for a moment, thinking about bravery and cowardice. Am I a coward being afraid of capture hence to give away my secrets under torture? I hope to God I never have to find out.

Remaining squatted, he lifts his tunic above his knees and holds it in the middle to avoid telltale stains whilst relieving his bladder – knowing the coming tension will make any thoughts of urinating near the city endanger his situation.

Letting out a soft sigh, he stands up to his full height – not much more than that of a donkey, including the ears. Being small though, has its advantages.

Making his way over the ridge and halfway down the other side towards the Valley of Hinnon, keeping the low shadow of

Golgotha on his left, he walks stealthily along goat tracks running along the sides of the valley making his way around the city until he reaches the Valley of Kigron.

Leaving the goat track, he moves down towards the city and some olive groves to a small dwelling where he hopes to pick up his guide who will take him to the secret meeting place.

Moving silently through the grove to an olive tree near the hovel, he leans against it, watching, listening and waiting for his guide, aware of his precarious situation. To trust is something he has learned since becoming a Christian, yet there are still some Jewish-Christians in the community who would probably denounce him, given a few silver pieces and he loathed the thought of being stoned to death like Jesus' brother James only five years ago.

A figure emerges from behind the leather hide covering the entrance – moving out towards him. He lets out a sigh of relief upon recognising his guide.

Two days later he starts his longest journey to Tyre with a heart full of sorrow. Magdalena's daughter has given him James' documents that are of great importance. He shall bring them to Gold-Mouth who will carry out the instructions contained within. He is now adorned with new clothes – a robe of heavy doubled cloth, shoulder wrap and sash, where the sealed documents are sewn in at various places. He also has some very important personal messages to convey to Gold-Mouth, who he calls in his own language, Chrystostomos.

He revels on memories of his fellow countryman. He admires him as a Greek philosopher and writer who has travelled the region – a major link with the Romans. Dion was born in Prusa, a city in the district of Bithynia, where he has also met with one of Jesus' apostles, Peter. Hermes envies him for that. He is a lot younger than Hermes, yet is such a wise man. He is not without opposition in Rome, but has a few influential friends. Hermes feels a bit like Dion, although his philosophy qualifications and orator qualities are somewhat pitiful in comparison. Dion travels widely throughout the empire and meets other travellers whose impressions he uses at leisure. He is able to get away with a lot being a philosopher and orator. Hermes sadly recognises that he himself would be treated as a spy, although he sees himself as an important courier or agent, making sure the right people are informed of all the wrong doings in the empire.

On his way to Tyre he meets up with Josephus, accompanied by some tough looking Zealots. He finds Josephus a fascinating character and most welcoming companion. Many a tale has he to tell of great happenings. Hermes had already heard many stories of his adventures. The best tale was of Josephus, the trained Pharisee and priest, who went to Rome in 64 AD with a Jewish delegation to secure the release of some priests who'd been sent to the capital on a false charge by Procurator Felix. Hermes knew he was the same Felix who held Paul captive at Caesarea. To hear this tale from the lion's mouth was a great personal experience – one he will tell word for word on his own travels. Josephus was now travelling incognito and knew of Hermes' mission. Hermes guessed he'd been sent to secure him a safe passage to Tyre.

Hermes, on arrival in Tyre, is utterly dismayed to find his mission of handing the documents over to Dion, foiled. A Roman galley left some weeks ago with Dion on board who is being escorted to Rome for a hearing.

Josephus tells him not to fret as he, Josephus, has been instructed to take over the documents should anything happen to Dion. He produces a skin of authority written by

Magdalena's daughter with the holy seal and secret marks, which Hermes recognises.

Hermes exchanges clothing – reluctantly handing over the comfortable robe and garments containing the documents – before bidding a sad farewell.

Josephus leaves his group sometime later between Cana and Giscala on their way to the Sea of Galilee and hides the documents in a safe place with the intention of picking them up when the time would be appropriate.

Having already joined the Zealots who've been revolting against the Romans, he eventually becomes a commander of their forces in Galilee. He fights many a battle, and in one particular fight on horseback near Bethsaida, he is captured and sent as a candidate for execution when he has a brilliant idea – he predicts that his captor, the Roman general Vespasian, will become Emperor. It is a fair fifty-fifty chance. Without this wager, the likelihood of his survival would have been zero. To almost everyone's surprise, Vespasian takes the Emperor's throne in 69 AD and leaves his son Titus to finish the job of destroying Jerusalem and the Temple and of mopping up the Jewish insurgents. Josephus becomes the emperor's adviser on Judaism. He lives the life of a pampered courtier, living mainly in Rome.

He assumes the name of the imperial family of the Flavians and is henceforth called Josephus Flavius. He writes a series of historical and semi-autobiographical books, among them the 'Jewish War' and the 'Jewish Antiquities'. Both these writings contain innumerable details about Jewish life, culture, politics and religion from ancient days to his own time. Even people mentioned in the New Testament play a role in the 'Jewish Antiquities' – John the Baptist, Caiphas (High Priest of the Jerusalem Temple, bitterly opposed to Jesus), Pontius Pilate (Procurator), the Herodians, Jesus and his brother James. Josephus, it seems, knew the Essenes quite well – in any case, he claims having spent some time with them before he decided to join the Pharisees instead. Perhaps he didn't like the idea of celibacy. He remains in Rome and dies in 98 AD.

Shortly before his death, he makes a sketch and a written reference pertaining to the place where he hid the documents given to him by Hermes so many years ago, which he hides in the back cover of the first volume of his original copy of the 'Jewish Antiquities'.

Some years later, Dion, sent into exile having opposed Emperor Domitian, is eventually rehabilitated. Previously he'd been well appreciated as an outstanding philosopher and orator by Domitian's successors Nerva and Trajan. On his travels one day, he is accosted by Hermes, now a venerable old man and asked about the documents once entrusted to Hermes. Dion knows nothing about them, and hence, Hermes eventually dies of a broken heart.

Constantinople – 330 AD

It is the year of the Lord, 330 AD, and the Greek-Christian priest, Christos Kyprianu, relaxes behind his high desk in the adjoining vestry of the new church of the Holy Wisdom, Hagia Sophia. He has just returned from the new senate house, now called the Curia, housed in a basilica on the East side of the Byzantine metropolis Constantinople. He is highly honoured and rejoices in his good fortune, having been favoured by the Emperor Constantine to continue his collation of the numerous manuscripts, many of which are copies of the originals, and to create the first holy book of the Apostles, including all Christian authors and other honourable authors relating to the period. It is to be called *The New Testament*. He also realizes the pitfalls of such an undertaking and must be careful to exclude any writings that may attract the wrath of the Bishop councils. He is still secretly mourning his fellow Donatist Christians. Constantine is capable of persecuting Christians if they are deemed to be the *"wrong type of Christian"*. His brutal enforcement of the decision reached by the Bishop council of Arelate whereby Donatist Churches were confiscated and the followers of this branch of the Christian faith were brutally repressed is still embedded fresh in his memory.

He looks forward to his next study of the first book of the 'Jewish Antiquities' written by Josephus Flavius and the enormous detailed descriptions therein. But first he must fill his empty stomach, after all, Constantine's personal Bishop had him waiting eight hours.

He takes wine, cheese, grapes and unleavened bread from the vestibule cupboard and places them on the table adjoining his high desk. He shoves the documents and 'Jewish

Antiquities' aside and relishes in the pleasant taste of the food and wine and his own ego. Absent in thought, he places the half-empty cup of wine onto the table, or so he thinks, and lets it go. Unfortunately, it is slightly resting on a document, so that wine spills onto the back of the 'Jewish Antiquities'. Aghast at his extreme folly, he mops up the spilled wine from the book and other documents with his garment.

Having dried them as best as he can, he sits back hoping the additional stains will go unnoticed, especially on the 'Jewish Antiquities'. After all, this volume has seen so many hands and it was fortunately only white wine. He moves over to the vestibule cupboard and pours himself another cup of wine. This time he remains standing, with the cup in one hand, picking bits of the food with his other. He eyes the book and decides to inspect it more thoroughly to make sure he really has dried the pages. He drains his wine cup, puts it out of reach and opens the back cover. He finds some dampness gathered in the top right hand corner. Fetching a clean cloth from the cupboard, he dabs the corner. Removing the cloth after pressing the cover, the backing is partly pulled off with it. He can't believe his eyes that perceive a thick document laid in a hollow part of the cover. His hands now shaking with excitement, he removes the document and unfolds it.

He recognises the holy seal of James on the first document. The other is a map of sorts. He realizes he is holding something of great importance to the Christian faith. His hands shaking, he reads the letter – dread and anxiety overcome him and a moment of dizziness whereby he has to hold the edges of the table tightly to prevent himself from falling off the bench. It is indeed from James and explains the latter's fear of forthcoming betrayal and possible death and the necessity for the last Testament of Jesus that is hidden, to be retrieved from its hiding place and be made public to all Christians. A map is included explaining the site.

Fearing his own death, knowing such a find be detrimental to the present pursuits of Christian teachings, he decides to place the documents back and renew the cover, making sure he uses thick paper and strong glue. Being wily and having a good Christian conscience, he decides to leave some clues in other worthy books but only referring to a hidden map showing the whereabouts of Jesus' Testament.

SPIES AND SACRED LIES

Passau, Bavaria – South Germany

Albert Schneider, a land surveyor currently working on a project with the town building authorities situated on the Haizingerstrasse in Passau, is annoyed. His wife, Silvia, has left him with the task of seeing his two children to school, having commandeered their only car and gone to visit her sick mother. Fortunately the school's not far and more or less on his way, just a few blocks short of his destination, the *Bauhof* on the *Millererstrasse*.

Having seen them through the school gate after loving hugs and kisses, especially from his youngest daughter, he waits until they enter the main school doors after farewell waves. He catches himself still waving long after they'd disappeared into the shadows of the opened doors. Secrets of the past lay behind those heavy doors that haunt him occasionally in his sleep. He turns away acknowledging the smile and knowing look of a young mother shooing her son in through the gates.

It is not without reason that his memory is juggled again at the sight of a group of five skinheads across the road – wearing the customary jackboots, black bomber jackets and dark trousers – Nazis, he decides. Their attention seems to be drawn to the school gates where he is standing. He immediately recalls similar characters vividly during his school days. They used to accost and intimidate him on his way to and from school. They were called *the Vikings*, a group similar to the

Hitler Jugend who believed in the *Fuehrer* principle. Well backed by many right wing parties and worldwide organisations with unendless money resources, they were able to uphold a modern training camp outside of Passau where members from all over the world were sent to be brain washed. Thank goodness the German law banned the group in 1994 – alas, only to be replaced by other Nazi groups, some of whom still secretly call themselves *the Vikings* – the last of the master race.

He moves up the *Millererstrasse* crossing over to the other side, shrouded by a strange feeling of dread, hoping the Nazis stay put and don't follow him. The road bends toward the *Spitalhofstrasse* where he is confronted by a large van with sliding doors parked a few meters away. It registers because it wasn't there when he passed here a few minutes ago with his children.

He feels trapped – the warning mechanisms of his brain signal danger, urging him to walk around the vehicle onto the other side of the road. However, his mind remains rational and his feet keep up momentum carrying him along the pavement between the van and the walls of a building.

Two skinheads move onto the pavement from the front of the van. The sliding door is swept open to reveal a bony middle-aged skinhead, grinning wickedly, his mouth revealing dark stained teeth and a ring through his tongue that he waggles at him, mouthing words from the past he'd hoped never to hear again,

'Well if it isn't our little Berty boy. How's it goin' you twerp.'

Albert turns around to escape and is faced by the group of five skinheads now closed in on him. He registers Nazis with flick knives and swinging chains and one with a baseball bat in his hand. He is grabbed from behind. The one with the baseball bat rams the end of the bat in Albert's stomach. His vagus paralysed, he tries to double-up to ease the pain but is held rigidly – causing him to gasp fervently for breath.

'How's that for a starter Berty? Now, you're wonderin' why we picks on you, eh?' said the ring-tongued skinhead, with a sneering grin, adding,

'All we wants is the number of your brother in the Vatican, that's all.'

Albert is totally confused, and gradually regaining his breath, he wheezes out, 'What for?'

Ring-tongue slaps him hard across the face causing his eyes to water and his nose to bleed – a knuckle-duster having left its mark. Ring-tongue's dark baleful eyes penetrate Albert's brain, forcing his thoughts of defiance aside – leaving him paralysed with fear. He remembers him now – Kraus, his nightmare from the past.

'Now, now, Berty – we asks the questions, not you. Now you give us his number, or we're gonna work you over so's you get to feel the pain, then we're gonna ditch you in the river. So if we don't get the number from you, your kids are next, one after the other and Smitty here', he points to a big-bellied, jelly-faced, eunuch type skinhead who is holding a chain, 'likes little girls, don't you Smitty?'

Smitty grins, his nostrils widen and his eyes convey his evil mind. Albert realizes ring-tongue's not exaggerating. He tries to think hard but knows he's no choice as they're going to beat him up anyway, so he gives them the number, thinking he might get out of this damaged, but alive.

The secondary school janitor is cleaning up after the mess the kids leave every morning. He curses and swears at the low upbringing of the current generation of German kids. He is now concentrating his efforts near the main entrance doors when he hears a vehicle screeching as it races around the corner. He registers a bundle that's thrown out of the side doors in front of the school gates. The vehicle does a handbrake turn and burning its tyres, accelerates fast, moving back the way it came.

Vatican City

The daily routine of Father Frederick Schneider, a Jesuit priest and important member of Cardinal Tatzinger's team of restorers is disturbed. The phone call he received this morning from a ghost of the past called Kraus, who used to waylay him and his brother in his primary school days, told him he'd just killed his brother Albert and dumped his body in front of the school, but not before he'd tortured and beaten him, and personally cut his throat.

Father Schneider has tried in vain to ring Norbert's wife who still resides in his beloved hometown of Passau. What should he do? Should he try the Passau police? Kraus told him he would get to know, because many of them are friends of his who sympathize with his cause. Kraus wants a map that's hidden in the back of a treasured book safely guarded in the Vatican Secret Vaults and has given him five days to get it. Kraus has given him a number to ring where he'll be given instructions to hand over the document.

He is shaken at the brutality uttered by Kraus who says he will rape and kill the remaining members of his brother's family one after the other if he doesn't get the map.

Father Scheider's work is mainly restoring and categorizing the many unregistered books and documents still held in a secret storeroom. He knows he can make any number of excuses to gain access to the book in question. The only snag would be the CCTV-cameras that watch over every movement. He decides to call the Monsignor in-charge, Henry Bush, and inform him of a slight indisposition – he'll not be coming in until later. He will work a bit longer that evening to make up for lost time. He needs to think now and to tune in his small pocket radio to the Bavarian news broadcasts.

Father Schneider is one of the privileged Jesuit workers in the Vatican allowed to possess and use a cell phone. Having made his call to excuse his absence, he switches on the radio and tunes in to the ten-o-clock Bavarian news. After the main political news, items of local interest are broadcast,

'...and now to the brutal killing of Albert Schneider, a land surveyor currently working on a project with the town building authorities in Passau. After accompanying his children to school he was brutally beaten up, mutilated and had his throat cut. The killing is described by a local reporter as the most beastly murder he has ever seen. Apparently the victim was beaten and killed near the school on the Spitalhofstrasse. The killer or killers cut his throat and drove the stolen van with the side doors open, pumping the blood onto the street, back to the school where they dumped the body. The reporter reckons the trail of blood is a warning to someone. One witness, reports seeing a group of skinheads hanging around at the time of the murder. Another witness who saw her son off to school is so shocked and frightened she was admitted to hospital. Other witnesses purportedly at the scene of the crime, deny seeing anything...'

Father Schneider turns off the radio. He is devastated. Dropping onto his knees, he falls into prayer, asking for guidance and begging the Lord for mercy and forgiveness should he, Father Schneider commit a sin and pass on this map. It is for the sake of the innocent, he prays, knowing full well, had he not held this post in the Vatican secret vaults, his brother would still be alive.

He has an early lunch and resumes work in the antechamber of the secret storeroom below the Vatican secret vaults. He knows where to find the book in question. He studies the layout carefully and works out a plan how he can retrieve anything hidden in the back cover without being seen. He has to rely on the shadows cast by the light under his worktable. He drops a sharp letter opener onto the floor and ignores it for the moment. After a while he manoeuvres it under the table with his foot until it hits the wall. It is not unusual for him to have books and documents piled up on or around the table. This afternoon he adds a few more books to the ones already deposited.

After evening prayers he fetches the key to the secret storeroom and looks out for the first volume of the 'Jewish Antiquities', which is one of the treasures due to be repaired. Having found it, he makes an entry in the registry book and proceeds back to his working table in the antechamber carrying the precious book. Once there he places the book on the floor slightly under the table and proceeds with the restoration of an old bible he'd been working on for the past week. An hour before the CCTV watch personnel change shift, he begins pushing the book under the table with his foot, cm for cm at a time. His next movement will have to be swift, he decides. He drops a pencil on his lap and manoeuvres his habit – forcing the pencil to fall under the table towards the back. He shoves his chair aside and drops down under the table, picking up the letter opener to open the back cover of the book as instructed by Kraus. With a swift cut the lining is freed. He prises the lining of the back cover aside and removes the contents from a hollow. He stuffs them through a small slit in his habit front pocket into his underpants. Closing the book, he picks up his pencil from the floor, moves back from under the table and straightens up. Holding it up high to inspect, and for anyone looking to see, he tests the tip, nods his head and resumes work on the bible.

The next three hours he concentrates on restoring the bible, pushing all other thoughts aside, otherwise the CCTV watch personnel would become suspicious.

Back in his room he falls onto his knees in prayer and is suddenly overcome with the shakes. He holds his hands to his face and weeps inwardly. Knowing he has to get a grip of himself, he seeks guidance from the Lord and gradually calms down.

He takes the documents from his underpants and opens them gently. After digesting the information left by Jesus' brother James, now held in his unworthy hands, he declares quietly,

'Why, oh why, Lord, have you chosen me to carry out this unworthy task?'

He thinks carefully – maybe if he destroys the letter and just hands over the map then only minor damage is done, after all, without the instructions contained in the letter, Jesus' testament cannot be found by just using the map. He knows though, at some time or other he'll be asked by his Monsignor why he chose to remove the first volume of the 'Jewish Antiquities' in the first place. Maybe he should make a copy of the map and just hand over the copy. Yes, he decides, that is what he shall do.

He opens his desk drawer and removes a suitable piece of ancient parchment paper and begins to make a copy using writing utensils and inks comparable to those used two thousand years ago. Having finished, he decides to put the original back the next morning and under the same pretext as tonight, replace the map without the letter and glue back the inset cover. He examines the letter once more and decides to destroy it. He tears it up and flushes it down the toilet feeling pleased he has protected Jesus' testament as best he can under the circumstances.

The next morning, having replaced the map and sufficiently repaired the lining cover, he returns the book to the secret storeroom and makes an entry of return in the registry book.

Saint Peter's Square

Shortly before lunch he calls the number Kraus had given him. He is told to hand the map to the officer in charge of the Pontifical Swiss Guard at the *Prefettura Pontificia* just before the changing of the guards at 1 pm. He is told the officer in charge has just as much to loose as he has.

He decides not to go to lunch and to make prayer instead. At the given time he hands over the document to the officer of the guard whom he knows by sight. His worried look tells Father Schneider the officer is also concerned about loved ones. He accepts the folded map and retains it in the palm of his hand. Without further ado, Father Schneider carries on past the portal on his way back to work.

At 3 pm Father Schneider is summoned to Henry Bush, the Monsignor in-charge of restoration. He dreads this moment, hoping his misdemeanour in the antechamber or the handing over of the map has not been reported.

He knocks on the Monsignor's door that is followed by a, 'Come in,' from a deep baritone voice.

Henry Bush comes forward to greet him with a compassionate look about his face. A giant of a man, not good-looking at all, more like Frankenstein's features without the bolt through the forehead, thought Father Schneider.

'Dear Arthur, have some very sad news indeed for you. Take a seat. Drop of brandy will help.'

Henry Bush moves over to a beautifully restored renaissance cabinet and pours out brandy into two cognac balloon glasses. Henry Bush swivels around, holds one out for Father Arthur Schneider and drains his in one swig.

Father Schneider having sat down – remains seated, cupping his full glass, hoping he doesn't crush it.

'We'll have to send you on leave for a few weeks, Arthur,' says Henry Bush, striding to and fro, 'Bad news from the home front, I'm afraid. Your brother's been murdered – just been informed by the Vatican Police,' he says point blank and stops in front of Father Schneider.

Father Schneider drains his glass and stares up at the Monsignor. Stupid American, he thinks, how unworthy and impolite of a Monsignor to tell him so bluntly in army jargon. How should I react he thinks – how would an American expect me to react? He decides not to say anything, just sit there and stare upwards.

'You hear me, Arthur – your brother's been *murdered*,' he repeats, louder – nearly shouting.

Arthur guesses he's now under shock having heard it

spoken out officially. All he can do is sit and stare at the hulk of the man rearing over him. It's just been too much for him and he is now starting to realize the implications. He feels the strain loosen and a few tears trickle down his cheeks.

'Now, now, Arthur – pull yourself together,' says the hulk, now anxious of being the cause of this burst of weakness through his brusque approach.

'I'm afraid I don't know the details,' he tried to say more gently, 'you'll have to go to the *Prefettura* to get the official story.'

Father Schneider wipes away his tears and stands up.

'It's all right Monsignor. I'm okay. It's just the shock. I'll be okay in a jiffy.'

'You need any help, let me know,' says the hulk, stiffly, knowing he really feels like saying, *get stuffed.*

He adds, accusingly – his eyebrows – raised,

'Bye the way, what was it you were after, taking the first volume of 'Jewish Antiquities' out of the secret storeroom?'

That's it, I'm finished, thinks Father Schneider and I haven't even had time to antiquate the newly glued lining cover. He conjures up a quick answer,

'Oh, just a cross-reference I came across in the bible I'm restoring. I felt like checking out its originality, that's all,' he replies, thinking maybe he should have left out the last two words – makes the excuse sound suspicious.

'Ah, thought it was something like that,' says the hulk, eyeing him closely.

'Better be going then, hadn't I,' says Father Schneider hurriedly.

'Is there anything you wish to tell me?' asks the hulk.

'No, why should there be,' answers Father Schneider, guardedly.

'Oh, no reason, just thought you might know something about your brother that got him murdered,' he replies wickedly, adding,

'Well, then, you'd better go and get packed. Let me know when you're coming back?'

The hulk, or rather Monsignor, held out his hand. Father Schneider gripped it. The Monsignor's hand was sweaty, which he thought was out of the ordinary.

He left the office and made his way back to his room to get his things packed. He isn't going to waste his time by paying a visit to the *Prefettura* that's for sure.

The Monsignor, the *'primus inter pares'* of the Opus Dei, who already knows why Father Frederick Schneider removed the first volume of 'Jewish Antiquities' out of the secret storeroom, waits a few minutes before he picks up his telephone.

Leipzig

He stood on the fourth step at a side door of the Federal Supreme Administrative Court at *Simonsplatz*. Henri Walker's viewpoint covered the stream of demonstrators arriving from the *Nicholas Church*. He was waiting for his target to appear.

This was his first proficiency test. If he succeeds, Helga had told him, he would become one of them.

The training at Passau had been extremely hard to start with, but Helga had always been there, edging him on – giving him encouragement when he thought he wouldn't make it. After the initial four weeks of physical training he began to enjoy it. After 12 weeks he was now a man to fear, a natural talent, proficient at the martial arts and a marksman with rifle and small arms. He could kill a man with his bare hands.

He was 198 cm tall – his blond crew-cut hair, and blue-eyes – trained to stare without falter under pain and physical hardness during training, gave him the appearance of a person to avoid. With 110 kg of bone and muscle, he was the best recruit they'd ever had – feared by other recruits and trainers, some of whom had ended up in hospital with a tag – discarded.

He spotted his rabbit. Its features and build were well imprinted into his memory. He moved slowly and casually down the steps, melting into the crowd. He stopped now and again to avoid drawing attention. He was within 3 metres of his lovely bunny rabbit. He watched her intensively for a few minutes knowing the sacrifice was for one Henri Walker – a good choice, he thought. She was a Jewess and was hurting the cause – reason enough.

He had developed a thing about bayonets. His choice for today was a 1900 German Mauser, one of the hardest bayonets to use as a dagger because of its length.

He moved closer, looking away, until the group he'd approached resumed talking. She was only just under a metre away. He put his hand under his jacket, pulling the Mauser from its well-oiled sheath. With one move of his right arm, he shoved the bayonet into the rabbit's stomach and upwards towards the chest, leaning forward to balance on his victim, looking her directly in the face, then pushing himself off her – at the same time turning and extracting the bayonet. He moved away casually, opening his jacket and shoving his weapon back into its sheath, bloody as it was. He flipped his jacket to and made for the middle of the throng in front of the Federal Court – swallowed up by the main crowd.

How easy it was – he was one of them now – Helga will be pleased.

Henri Walker recollects how it all started:

The psychiatric hospital for in-patients living in the catchment area between Stuttgart and Lake Constance situated near Rottweil. A cluster of archaic buildings, some of them red-bricked, four stories high called *Red Minster*. Like most institutions of this nature, the past still has its hold at the bare mention of the name *Red Minster*. Patients with minor ailments who are generally hospitalised there, even in our modern day and age, are marred for life – *"been in the lunatic bin, have you?"*

The whole complex has a menacing history passed down over the last century by the locals as a place where the really barmy are locked away. An institution also misused during the Nazi period where many mentally ill patients, even slight cases of depression, were gassed in special lorries. It's also one of the few medical institutions where catholic nuns are still working. Not all of the wards are highly secured against unwanted patient exit, but all the windows are fitted on the outside with bars, grilles and high tech security devices. One section of the hospital is fortified as a secure area to hold dangerous inmates.

Henri Walker spent three years in a special part of the hospital called *'Abteilung S'*. The day he entered the ward he swore to himself to be out within three or four years on good conduct. He accepted the medication over many months, knowing he was being doped. They monitored his medication many weeks and months.

'Open your mouth? Stick out your tongue? Turn your tongue to the back of your throat? Show me your hands, back and front?'

Once they saw he was fully cooperative and accepting his medication the checks were mainly carried out by new nursing staff. In such instances, he swallowed the tablet or fluid and waited until the nurse moved on out of sight before making for the toilet to regurgitate. He tried missing out every second or third day. His aim was to regain self-control. He had to take a tablet now and again, mainly on the weekends, because they checked his urine on Mondays. There was less staff on weekends too, meaning patients were to be kept well subdued. After about a year, he asked for a dose reduction and got it. That, he hoped, would explain his well-planned activeness, fully concentrated on early rehabilitation.

He partook in group and single therapy, outwardly with great success. Their pursuit of alluding to his deeds caused by a bad childhood and his apparent acceptance of why he was locked-up, led to his premature movement to a half-open ward. He pulled the wool over the eyes of the young female ward doctor who really thought she'd cured him. Maybe he'll go and visit her privately, one day.

Henri Walker remembered vividly the first day he was admitted and why he was sent there in the first place. He knew he was different and didn't mind being as he was.

He hated hairy women, especially those with hair under their arms or hair on their tits. He was lucky the female doctors had long white gowns and trousers on – otherwise he would have been in permanent upheaval. He hated them even more, especially if they were Jewish.

He was German, born in Berlin. Both his parents were killed in a car accident when he was eleven. He has vague recollections of the incident, as he was sitting in the rear seat of the car when it happened.

He was put in the custody of his only known relative, a

distant, half-Jewish aunt in Bregenz, Austria. She treated him as though he was a cuddly Dudley.

He remembered how she embraced him that summer's day in June when a social welfare woman handed him over to her. His aunt wore a sleeveless white bodice. She was big, ugly, and extremely obese. She grabbed him fiercely, engulfing him in her huge breasts. He tried to free himself and ended up with his head buried in her sweaty and horrifyingly hairy armpit. He took an immediate dislike to her. It also brought on a general rejection of hairy women. He couldn't hide the disgust he felt for his aunt, especially the long black hairs under her arms, her hairy forearms, legs and moustache, not to forget the mole on her chin where three long bristles stood out that poked like toothpicks when she gave him a slimy kiss. She took affront at his attitude, so it wasn't long before she packed him off to a boarding school.

Albert Krem was his favourite tutor at the boarding school – an Austrian Jesuit priest who taught him to hate the Jews, because they crucified Christ.

Henri became an altar boy and remembers the day when Albert Krem asked him to sit down next to him in the vestry after mass to have a chat. He'd finished the chores he'd been given – more than usual. He also noticed the other alter boys had gone.

Father Krem told Henri he really liked him and after chatting for a while said they ought to change. When Henri started pulling his habit over his head Father Krem told him to hold it a minute. His arms were in the air, his head covered by the habit. He felt Father Krem's hands moving under his arms and over his breast. He felt them undoing his belt. His trousers and underpants were pulled down. He was so surprised it took him some time to realize what was happening. He struggled desperately and unfortunately fell over whilst fighting against this aggressive molestation. The side of his head hit the bench and made him dizzy. He tried to free his hands but somehow couldn't get them out of the end of the habit that was in a tangle by then. Father Krem pushed him between the shoulder blades down onto the trestle. His forehead hit the trestle hard. He shouted and started to scream. Father Krem struck him on the back of his head. His forehead hit the trestle again – this time with such force, he can't remember anything after that – it must have knocked him out.

When he came to, he found himself alone in the vestry. His pants were back in place and his own pullover had replaced the habit. There was nothing to show anything had ever happened other than a wet and painful feeling and a need to go to the toilet. He had a terrible headache and felt a big lump on his forehead. Blood and snot was dribbling from his nose. Anger, shame and disgust overcame him. He felt used and dirty. He will avenge himself that's for sure.

His chance came the following week on a hiking tour. Father Albert Krem was last in the line of boys on a hike. They were climbing up a narrow path on a steep mountainside. Henri kept to the rear of the line and could feel those gloating eyes on his back. He could feel the cold breath of Father Krem burning a hole in his spine. Henri stooped quickly and undid his shoelace, pretending it was loose. He loosened the other one too and took his time tying them up again. Father Krem was irritated and told him not to dally. He waited until Father Krem overtook him. Henri thought to himself – you bastard, you'll never do what you did to me or to anyone else, never ever again. Henri caught up with him and shoved him off the mountainside on a long fall down on the next sharp bend. He was thirteen at the time – his first kill. They don't know about that one though.

He was admitted into the head doctor's office in July 1996, handcuffed. He'd been charged with the murder of a teacher. There was no mention she was half-Jewish in the press.

He recalled his own blood surging vividly as he watched her convulsions. She was big and fat and the spitting image of his aunt – the reason why he just didn't leave it at stabbing her and slicing her jugular open – watching her gurgling her own blood. He cut off her arms, making sure the armpits with hair belonged to the joints. He was in such a blood frenzy – he forgot to leave the left arm in the flat. Covered in blood as he was, he walked down the stairs and out of the building carrying the arm like a trophy. A voice had told him, *'take it, take it.'* He didn't get far down the market street before he was arrested.

After months in jail he was put on trial. A pre-trial medical examination by experts declared him mentally irresponsible for his actions. He made quite sure they thought he had a multiple personality disorder. That meant no prison sentence in Germany. His trial lasted two days – the verdict – just as he thought, instead of jail he was given nice accommodation in a psychiatric hospital for as long as he liked.

The head doctor at the time was Professor Albert Schmidbauer, a genial grey-haired fossil with spectacles balanced on the end of his nose,

'Welcome to the Red Minster psychiatric hospital, Mister Walker.'

Henri remained standing in front of the Professor's desk and stared vacantly at the wall covered with framed certificates. The Professor motioned to one of the two male nurses standing guard to take off the handcuffs, 'Please, take a seat Mister Walker.'

Henri took a seat and rubbed his wrists. The male nurses remained standing behind him,

'I know this must be very difficult for you. We will try and do everything possible to see your stay here is as comfortable as possible. Our aim is to see you leave this place cured.'

Henri couldn't withhold a question,

'If it's possible, how long do you think it'll take?'

'Too early to say I'm afraid, but judging from similar cases it could take five or six years or even longer.'

Sounds good thought Henri, deciding there and then on his further plans.

On the 10th February 2005, a number of Doctors, nurses and nuns adjurned in the main staff room to discuss Henri Walker's release. Doctor Herbert Maier, head of the parole committee for dangerous inmates, addressed the meeting:

'We have Henri Walker on the agenda. Today's the 10th February, $15.^{00}$ hrs. We agreed the year before last to move him to a semi-open ward. He spent a year there. We agreed on six months in an open ward with freedom of movement within the compound accompanied by at least one staff member. On top of that, he has undertaken twelve excursions into town accompanied by other patients and staff. According to all of the reports he has made very good progress and has shown remarkable constraint with his aggressions. All reports agree on a parole of three months providing he is placed in supervised accommodation during this period. He should have psychiatric support at least twice weekly. Anyone disagree?'

Doctor Maier looked at the meeting, not really at anyone in particular, expecting everyone to agree. His attention centred on a corpulent nun at the back of the room who was clearing her throat,

'Ah, hem, Doctor Maier. You all know my feelings about Mister Walker. I've watched him closely since he's been out of *'Abteilung S'*. I think he's fooled you all. I believe he's still a danger to the public and should never be released, ever again. I've experienced many of them and I know what I'm saying.'

'Thank you, sister Mathilda – we all know your feelings for Mister Walker. He also has complained a number of times of your open hostility towards him. However, I will make a note in the report.'

He jotted down a few lines in the final report.

'Okay, are there any other comments? No, then the case is closed temporarily pending further reports from his case psychiatrist outside and his social worker.'

Henri Walker was released on 1st March 2005. He was given a rail ticket to Villingen and some money with instructions to report direct to the supervisor at House Abax in Bad-Duerrheim where he will be staying under supervision for the ensuing three months. He walked through the portal and stopped at the little reception cubbyhole. He didn't have to knock on the window – it was open. A friendly looking old man smiled at him. Probably disabled or a pensioner, he thought.

'Good morning! Leaving us are you? Wasn't too bad here I hope?' said the old man.

'Good morning! Yes, I'm leaving, thank goodness,' Henri mumbled.

He placed a chitty he'd been holding in his hand onto the counter. The old man wrote the time of departure and his name on it and handed it back saying,

'Hope you had a good convalescence here, son, and the best of luck to you.'

Henri nodded and walked out of the portal, past the car park and out onto the main road, *"le chemin de la civilisation"*. Funny he thought – I don't feel any different.

He took his place at a bus stop. After about a half-hour's wait a bus drove him from the hospital to the Rottweil railway station. He was surprised he couldn't experience enthrallment at reaching the first stage of his goal. Probably the drugs he was under. He had to wait another half-hour until the small local train with a couple of carriages arrived. It no sooner gained speed than it slowed down again. It carried on like that all the way to Villingen, stopping at every little platform on the way. Henri felt a bit sick. He wasn't sure if it was the train's continuous stopping that did it or the unknown ahead.

He walked out of Villingen railway station and looked towards the oversized bus shelters on the right. He checked his instructions and went to the departure board for the bus to Bad-Duerrheim. The next one wasn't due for another fifty minutes. Feeling groggy, he took a seat at the bus shelter. Maybe he's just hungry he thought. A beautiful sniff of fried chicken and pork knuckle drifted continuously from a Bistro type snack bar on the opposite side of the road, slightly to the left of the pedestrian crossing. Henri decided he'd enough time and went over, dragging his big bag with him.

He looked at the menu board above the counter and worked out how much he could afford. He ordered chicken and chips and a coke. The woman behind the counter was an Asian woman, probably Vietnamese, he thought. No welcoming greeting or smile, 'bloody foreigner' went through his mind.

'Mayonnaise or ketchup,' she mumbled.

'Ketchup,' he replied.

She pulled a lever on the coke machine and filled a glass of coke, got a beer mat from the pile and placed one after the other in front of him on the counter, at the same time saying,

'Chicken and chips coming up.'

She put a plate with his order on the counter and said, 'That'll be four-Euro-forty.'

'That can't be,' he said, 'on the board it says four-twenty!'

'Ketchup costs twenty cents extra,' she replied tartly.

'But I can only afford four-twenty! I need the rest for the bus. This is a fucking rip-off.'

'Your problem! You ordered it – you got it. Now you pay for it.'

'Bloody chink,' he muttered.

Sitting on a bar stool next to him was a slim, well-dressed woman with long nylon covered legs, crossed over in his direction. Her hair was blond and short. No hairs on the legs he noticed. The crumbs on her plate said she'd probably just eaten a pretzel and was now sipping a coffee. She placed her cup on the saucer and turned to look at him. He kept her gaze. Green eyes looked at him quizzically.

'Where do you have to go?'

She had a pleasant inviting voice. He felt his face flush up. He began to get excited.

'Bad-Duerrheim,' he stuttered.

'Well you pay your four-forty and I'll drive you there, it's on my way. I live in a village just past it,' she said.

'Thanks ever so much,' he said, 'I'm very grateful to you for your kindness,' he added, hoping it sounded posh enough and blasting himself for his swearing.

'That's all right. You look as though you're in need of something to eat,' she said, smiling.

It was the way she said it, it didn't sound insulting at all. He was fascinated.

'Yes,' he said, 'I'm very hungry.'

He picked the coins out of his purse and pushed them over the counter. Without waiting for the waitress to count it he unravelled his knife and fork from the paper serviette and began eating. In between eating and swallowing, he kept dog looking at the woman sitting next to him. She was the first woman ever, he took an immediate liking to. She must have noticed because she smiled and said to him,

'Take your time, I'm not in a hurry.'

He gulfed his food down though, thoroughly enjoying it – his first uncontrolled ordering of food – his real touch of freedom outside in years. He took great care with his manners too. He used one hand only to gnaw the bones, consciously reminding himself not to use both hands, like an ape that he's used to doing. He finished eating and swallowed the last of his coke in one gulp making him belch. He tried to hold it, succeeding slightly. Nevertheless a rude noise, somewhat reduced in volume, forced its way out. The woman smiled and said,

'Well, it seems as though you enjoyed that.'

'Excuse me,' he said, blushing – at the same time covering his mouth with his hand and giving her a shy apologetic smile.

'Looks like you're finished! Shall we be going then?' she asked, turning to look him directly in the eyes, her eyebrows frowning quizzically and her lips forming into a slight smile.

'Yes, I'm finished, thanks!' He said, wiping his mouth and hands with the serviette and adding, 'Do you mind if I wash my hands first though, they're still greasy.'

'No, not at all – you go ahead. I'll wait here for you,' she said.

Henri trusted her and got off the barstool looking around

for the toilets. A prodigious looking, well-dressed man who was shaking his head, caught his eye and said,

'You'll have to go across the road to the railway station, there are no toilets in here.'

'Eh, ah, thanks,' said Henri, turning back to the counter. His face was burning.

The woman pulled something out of a basket on the counter. 'Try these sachet tissues, they're just the right thing.'

Henri was really embarrassed now. How could he forget. He remembered his Austrian aunt now, when she once took him to a restaurant near Munich main railway station. They used such things then.

'Thanks,' he said.

He ripped open a corner of the sachet and pulled it down. Extracting the moist tissue that smelled of lemon, he rubbed his hands and his mouth free of the remaining Ketchup and chicken fat. When he was finished the woman looked at him questioningly,

'Okay, now?'

'Yes, thanks,' he replied.

'Right then, this way,' she said, 'my car's parked just outside, right next to the Bistro.'

It *was* parked directly next to the small restaurant – a silver metallic Mercedes with shiny chrome bumpers and sidelinings. He didn't know the year but it looked fairly old, certainly in very good condition, he thought.

He opened the boot and put his bag in. She was already behind the wheel as he got into the front seat next to her. A discreet aroma of perfume and the pleasant smell of old leather hit him – this new sensation confused him even further.

She steered the car out smoothly from the parking lot, turning right at the post office, leaving the railway station behind them on the left.

'Where do you have to go to in Bad Duerrheim?' she asked.

The question immediately doused all feelings of excitement that had engulfed him. He had dreaded this question all along. He didn't think she would ask him so soon. Maybe she'll stop the car and ask him to get out of it when he tells her. He gave a shrug and said,

'Rehabilitation House Abax, do you know where that is?'

'Why, of course – in actual fact I work there, so it looks like we'll be seeing each other a lot.'

She turned her head slightly towards him, smiling, and said,

'You must be Henri Walker. What a coincidence! I'm Helga Schulz, your social worker.'

He nearly fell through the floor of the car. He grasped the sides of the seat hard as though he was on a helter-skelter. This is too much he thought. It took him all by surprise. He started to sweat and felt a bit faint.

She looked at him, concerned,

'Is everything okay, Henri, you look very pale?'

'I'm just surprised, very surprised, I never expected this, honestly – excuse me.'

Quietness descended in the car. Helga Schulz concentrated on her driving and Henri looked out the side window. He felt like an idiot. He couldn't find any answers or anything to talk about. He was dumb struck. This was the first moment in his life he was sensed by the nearness of another human being. The awareness was new. It took him some minutes before his old self began to regain control. His brain echoed like lightening to the thoughts of doctors, nurses, and social workers. Suspicion – shrink heads know all the tricks, he thought.

Maybe this is all part of their plan. He'll keep things open for a while with this one he decided, at least to a certain extent. She couldn't have known he'd go into the Bistro or order something he couldn't afford. No, this was destiny, definitely something he or she couldn't do anything about, or was it?

Vatican city

Once he'd finished packing, Father Frederick Schneider tried ringing his brother's wife Silvia again. This time the phone was picked up and a voice answered timidly,

'*Ja,*'

'Hello, is that you Silvia?' he asked.

'*Nein*, this is Marion, mother's in the kitchen with a policeman.'

'Listen, Marion, this is uncle Freddy. Please ask your mother to the phone, dear, it's very important.'

Marion didn't answer – instead she put the phone aside and shouted,

'*Mama,* it's uncle Freddy.'

A few seconds later he heard a high-pitched female voice call his name,

'Freddy?'

'Yes, it's me, Silvia,'

'Oh, Freddy – you've heard the bad news?' she asked, sounding shaky, obviously trying hard to maintain control.

'I have, Silvia,' he replied, 'it's a terrible shock. Are you allright? Have you been intimidated by anyone? Has anyone tried to frighten you?' he asked, hurriedly.

'No, Freddy – why, what's wrong, why are you asking?' she

said, her voice quivering, 'you know why he was murdered, Freddy?' she added, accusingly.

'I can't tell you on the phone, it's too dangerous and you can't trust the police in Passau Silvia, so please, please be careful. Don't tell the police I told you about not trusting them. I'll be on my way by train this afternoon. It arrives in Passau tomorrow morning just after half-past seven. I'll let you know everything tomorrow. It's so terrible.'

'Allright, Freddy – I won't say anything, but I must tell you what the policeman just told me. Mother was poisoned and taken to hospital. The policeman says Albert's murder was deliberate because I normally take the children to school, that's why they poisoned mother so's I'd rush to the hospital and Albert would have to take the children to school. Who could do such a horrible thing? Oh, Freddy...'

'Listen, Silvia, you can't trust anyone in Passau, it's best you move away for a while after the funeral. I'll see what I can arrange when I get there. Please be careful, Silvia, and keep the kids away from school and indoors.'

'I will, Freddy.'

'Okay, then – bye for now, Silvia – see you tomorrow. God bless.'

'God bless, Freddy.'

He's never bitten his nails since childhood, but now he bit off a chunk of skin and nail from his forefinger and nibbled it, full of guilt and anger before he spat it out. He blasted himself for not handing over the original old map. If they don't find what they're after they'll think he made deliberate changes when he copied the map and go after Silvia and the girls. He checked to see if he'd pocketed his railway tickets – Signora del a Fonte of the Vatican travel office had made his bookings for the afternoon Intercity from Rome to Venice and a sleeping compartment on the Euro Night Express from Venice to Wels in Austria and from there with a regional train to Passau in Germany.

Venezia Mestre railway station

Fabio Lorenzi waited patiently on the platform for the incoming Intercity from Rome. He'd always been a faithful and obedient catholic, even during the four years he'd spent in the Italian Special Forces where he'd been forced to kill or be killed. His military padre forgave him many times even though in confession he admitted having no feelings of remorse after a kill.

On finishing his military service he was engaged by the Vatican to carry on where he'd left off in the army. It was extremely difficult for him at first to believe the Vatican required his services as an assassin. He was introduced to the rites of the Opus Dei and had extreme relief after a kill in flagellating himself. He was now a devout member of the Opus Dei stationed in Venice. His superior is a nun, who wears a metal flagellate garter, with pricks, that cut into her thigh.

His lust rises at the memory. When she first told him about it and showed him the garter, he couldn't stop himself from stroking her beautifully white thigh. They both got aroused when his stroking ended up between her legs. He took her there and then. Hence, she is his prize and after every kill, he has her 'till the cock cries.

He giggled inwardly at his rhyming and the double meaning. He was awaiting his next task – to rid the Vatican of a German priest who had done great damage to the Vatican. His instructions were to board the train and eliminate him. Then make his way back to Venice and claim his rights. He giggled again at these lustful thoughts.

Bad Duerrheim

Henri was on kitchen duty this morning for the last time – laying the table and making breakfast for those other dimwits, one of the tasks he disliked. Big tits Getrud was lingering around him, getting in his way.

Today's his big day. The three months are up. He wouldn't have coped with most of those other idiots if it weren't for his social worker, Helga Schulz. Always had a smile and a good word for him. No one has ever given him so much self-confidence. With her on his side he could fight the world.

'You stupid man! How many times do I have to tell you I drink black tea and not herb tea for breakfast,' shouted the unwashed, greasy haired, bulimia seeded kleptomaniac – hunched over the table as usual – her chin level with the plate. The slit-eyes focusing on him from the slightly raised head spewed hatred.

This was the part he enjoyed. He loved to get that lanky jerk worked up. Maybe she'll throw her cup at him again. What a farewell present! He thought about teasing her again about her slit-eyes. Last time she started foaming at the mouth, got real fits she did. Turned the table over and pulled a huge bunch of hair from her head. Maybe it was because he had added,

'Too much masturbation's not good for you, you'll end up blind!'

He chuckled at the thought. Why do people get so upset when you tell them the truth – just because he went into her room once – 'cause he couldn't concentrate on his book? The walls are thin and his room adjoined hers. All he wanted to do was tell her to turn her radio or television down a bit. His mistake was to walk in without knocking. She hadn't even noticed him coming in. She was sitting on an armchair her skirt over her head and one of her legs over the arms of the chair. She was shaved and he could see a huge shining wet clitoris poking out of her slit. That comes from a lot of masturbation, he guessed. Most of the clits he'd ever seen in medical books were tiny protrusions. She was moaning real loud, too. That's where the noise was coming from. He got a hard-on, so he got his dick out and started masturbating too, right in front of her. She only got the message someone else was in the room when she got covered by his spunk. He couldn't understand why she got so upset. Maybe she just doesn't like a gang wank!

Frau Schmidt, the duty nurse brought everyone to order.

'Henri will be leaving us today,' she said.

Five weirdoes banged their spoons on the table and shouted hoorah, hoorah. Only big tits didn't join in, she said,

'So soon, what a pity,' and blushed deep red at the sound of her own voice. He felt some sort of relationship with her. She was the only one who was acceptable as his equal. The others were just sick, petty criminals. He was the only one big tits would talk to. He loved to hear her telling her story. He noticed she shaved every hair on her body apart from her scalp, after he'd told her his gory story. She'd killed her dad who'd been having it off with her since she was nine. On her sixteenth birthday he came home drunk. Not even a present for her. The bum raped her and fell asleep on top of her. She pushed him off. Tied his arms and legs to the bedsteads – got a sharp, 12-centimetre steak knife from the kitchen, woke him up and cut his dick and parts off. She watched the blood streaming out for a while, deciding it was taking too long. She hated hearing his screaming too, so she went to the kitchen again and came back with a long bread knife. She wanted to cut off his tongue, but he wouldn't open his mouth, so she cut his head off instead. That was a good one, he thought – something he'll have to try sometime. Maybe he'll use something bigger, a nice Japanese Samurai sword, perhaps. One swish...! Maybe he won't cut her tits off. He'll pick big tits up one day. He's got her address. They'd make a good team, he thought.

Henri was just finishing his coffee when Helga Schulz came into the kitchen.

'*Guten Morgen, allerseits.*'

'*Guten Morgen, Fraeulein Schulz,*' they answered.

'Have you got your belongings packed, Henri?'

Henri nodded.

'Okay then. We'll meet at my car in the car park in three-quarters of-an-hour, with all your luggage, okay?'

'I'll be there,' he answered – hating to be reminded of things like a juvenile. After all, at 23 years of age, he wasn't to be treated like a kid anymore. Maybe she has to say that in front of the other staff. They don't know their secret, do they? Henri shook hands with all the goons and the staff, just as Helga Schulz had told him to do. Only slit-eyes waved him off. Being social will look good in your report she'd said. It will be closed after that because she'd put in some good words for him too.

Big tits Gertrud was waiting in his room when he went to get his luggage. She came swiftly towards him and embraced him. He hadn't realized how strong she was. She kept him held with one hand and let the other wander down his back and around to the front where she gently stroked his dick through his trousers. She kept her hand on it and whispered in his ear,

'You won't forget me will you, Henri?'

'Never, ever Gertrud,' he replied.

Henri got the biggest hard-on of his life. She felt it and moved her mouth to his. The kissing aroused him even more. She opened his belt and using both hands, pulled his pants down. She grasped his dick and moved her hand, back and forth. She took his hand and moved it under her skirt. He felt her pussy – it was warm and wet. She had no pants on. She moved her skirt back more and brought his dick to her pussy. She moved it up and down on her clit. Their kissing intensified. She didn't say a word, nor made a sigh. He realized she wanted him badly. She moved his dick into her pussy and they moved back and forth in frenzy. It was the break of a new dawn for Henri when he came. He felt her coming at the same time. It was an overflow, a flooding from burst dams. Henri remained standing, waiting for the swelling of his dick to subside. It didn't. It throbbed for more, but his legs were too wobbly. Big tits understood. She locked the door and led him to the bed.

Henri was sitting on a low wall near the car park, waiting for his social worker. His dick was still hard and swollen. He hoped his social worker, Helga Schulz, wouldn't notice the bulge that was bigger than usual. If she did, maybe she would offer to blow on it and cool it down for him, after all she's always on about his welfare. He chuckled at that, imagining her holding his dick and blowing her warm breath on it – instead of it relaxing, getting a wallop of spunk in her eye.

'Henri, Henri! Wakey, wakey, where ever you are.'

He opened his eyes and looked the object of his desire right in the face, thinking, if you only knew.

Helga Schulz was smiling. She left him and walked over to her car. Henri did the same – dumped his luggage in the boot and climbed into the front seat right next to her.

'Well, Henri – you've come a long way haven't you.'

He couldn't help giggling, thinking about spunk again.

Helga Schulz thought he was just relieved to be a free man again.

'Remember your oath, Henri – I help you out of your schlimazel and you help me?'

'Yes, Fraeulein Schulz, I do.'

'Well we are on our way to Passau now, to the camp I told you about. You do remember? The place where I used to go with my sister when I was younger – *the Vikings*?'

'Oh yes, Fraeulein Schulz, I remember.'

'Look Henri, I think it's time we got to first names, don't you? You're not in the clinic anymore, just call me Helga from now on, all right.'

'Okay, mm..., Helga.'

'You'll enjoy your training I'm sure of that. It may be a bit hard from what you're used to, but if you want to learn all about weapons you have to be fit first. You'll get to know my sister too, once she gets back from the Middle East. You'll like her, you know. Both of you have a lot in common.'

She giggled at her own statement and put her hand on his knee. He grabbed it on impulse and put it on his dick.

She looked at him softly and said,

'We'll have to wait until we get to the camp Henri, we've got a five hour journey ahead.'

Henri sighed and nodded his head thinking of those promising words.

Frederick Schneider

Shortly before the inter-city train arrived in Venice, Father Frederick Schneider went to the toilet carrying his suitcase. Discarding the priest's attire that he wore on boarding the train at the *Roma Termini* – he changed into a dark, light, polo-necked pullover with light dark green corduroy trousers and put on his favourite brown leather jacket, a remnant of his national service days with the German Paras. A navy blue baseball cap now covered his greying hair and dark Gucci sunglasses were perched on his nose. He'd moved the remaining contents of the suitcase into a lightweight rucksack he always has in the suitcase – handy for shopping and day trips. He left the toilet and said a silent goodbye to his old suitcase, which he placed on a luggage rack before moving down the train a couple of carriages. He was concerned. The fact alone that he now knew the contents of the map, that Kraus was aware of his knowledge and his figuring Monsignor Henry Bush also knowing about it sooner or later, made him decide to be on continuous guard realizing that if his brother was killed just to get at him for the map then he was definitely their next target. They weren't going to get him that easy, though. He hadn't done any close combat training for years, but he was in good condition. Like some Germans he takes pride in trying to fit physical training into his program at least two to three times a week even though he is a Jesuit priest. Squash is his favourite work out.

He waited near the exit door, allowing enough room for some passengers to get in front of him before leaving the train. He wasn't going to be first out where they could make an easier identification. In a crowd it would be more difficult. Whoever was on the lookout would be watching for a priest in the main stream changing platforms for the Euro Night Express and there were a number of clergy in priest's attire on this train. He'd decided to leave the station and make for the airport to catch a flight to Munich. He'd ring up his good friend Josh, in Straubing, from his Army days who'd remained in the Paras as a regular soldier and now had his own private security company. He would get Josh to pick him up from Munich, only just over 80 Kilometres from Straubing, once he explained his situation.

He left the platform and made his way to the main exit. He knew Venice like the back of his hand and had many friends here but decided not to involve them. He wandered about with no particular destination in mind – just stopping occasionally to check his rear. Satisfied no one was following him he doubled back and took a Vaporetto to the Piazza San Marco where he took a seat near the entrance to his favourite café, *Café Florian*. Before sitting down, he popped his head into the café, waved to the barman and shouted,

'Ciao, Sebastiano.'

The barman nodded and motioned a waiter out to serve him. He ordered a large cup of cappuccino and a tiramisu, the café's speciality. The order was delivered swiftly, which he recognised as his personal fortune in knowing the barman. With great deliberation he dipped his spoon into the tiramisu and moved the inviting load slowly to his mouth where he let the full flavour develop, forcing his taste buds into full action before he finally let it be passed to deeper regions where taste buds no longer dwell. In between passionate spoonfuls he sipped his cappuccino, thinking hard – pondering occasionally with his empty spoon hovering in the air – working out his next moves.

His possible opponents in mind, he eyed the area intensively now and again – searching for suspicious characters – a very difficult task at this busy Piazza full of tourists.

Using his cell phone, he made a call to the Marco Polo airport and booked the next flight to Munich. He sighed, having finalized his further actions – paid up and left the café, taking the Vaporetto back to the main thoroughfare – from there he took a taxi to the airport.

Venezia Mestre railway station

Fabio Lorenzi had Frederick Schneider's visage imprinted in his memory. He was annoyed at the massive stream of passengers moving down the platform towards him – especially the large groups of clergy. His dark cold eyes tried picking out the individuals in clergy attire but after a while he gave up. He became extremely disgusted at his own feeble attempt of scanning the crowd, realizing he'd never find him in this fast moving mass. Hoping Frederick Schneider was a straggler, he waited until the crowd thinned before he started walking up the train. He walked back and waited another ten minutes before he gave up. Maybe I've just missed him he thinks and relaxes, grinning – he has the details of Frederick Schneider's night sleeper, so what's he worrying about. He changed platforms and boarded the Euro Night Express.

Father Donaghue, an Irish priest, just manages to board the Night Express before the stationmaster blows his whistle. He looks up the conductor. Puffing and panting, he explains his predicament,

'*Signor*, here's fifty Euros and there's another fifty for you if you can find me a sleeping compartment. My secretary forgot to book one for me. If you're lucky to find one I'll be in the dining car.'

'Yes, certainly Sir, I'll see what I can do. Sometimes people who've booked don't turn up. I'll find out when I check the latest list. I'll see you in the dining car in about forty-five minutes, okay?'

'Splendid, that sounds promising,' he said, in deep Irish brogue. 'Gives me enough time for eats and a few drinks,' he adds, chuckling.

The conductor smiles, thinking the Irish priest reminds him of Robin Hood's Friar Tuck, and moves on.

Nearly on the dot – Father Donaghue's cheeks are reddened from his fourth whisky and third beer – the conductor passes on the good news.

'I've found a compartment that hasn't been taken, Sir.'

'That's fantastic,' says Father Donaghue and places the other fifty discreetly into the conductor's hand.

'Thank you Sir, let me show you the way,' says the conductor. Father Donaghue eyes his glass that is still half full,

''twould be a sin to leave it,' he mutters, and downs it in one go, picks up his worn suitcase and follows the conductor.

At 2.15 am just before the next stop where Fabio Lorenzi has planned to get out, he leaves his seat in the 2nd class and wanders down to the 1st class sleeper. He stops at the compartment in question and hears a loud snoring from within. He puts on a pair of tight-fitting, light jeweller gloves, and using a universal key, unlocks the door quietly. Just in case Father Frederick Schneider was awakened, he retreats back to the corridor window pretending to look out. Hearing the snoring continue from within, he quietly slides the door open, and takes in the small compartment with one sweep of his sharp eyes. Lying over a suitcase he notes a dark suit, a priest's white collar and a figure sleeping soundly in the berth – sufficient confirmation. He removes his hand from under his jacket that is now holding a gun fitted with a silencer and fires off three deadly shots. He removes the silencer, retrieves the empty cartridges, and pocketing the gun and silencer he leaves the compartment, locking the door behind him.

The train is gradually slowing down by now, so he walks a bit further down the train, putting in a couple of carriages distance from the 1st class sleeper and leaves the train a few minutes later.

Munich

A small commercial jet touches down – its twin jet engines howl as the aircraft decelerates. The jet turns off the runway. Frederick Schneider looks out the window as the plane taxies slowly towards the terminal buildings. He sincerely hopes Josh hasn't let him down and the cavalry is waiting to secure his safety.

After customs formalities, he walks out and spots Josh immediately. Keeping his cap down low he moves to the side and stops for a moment outside the ropes. He does a quick sweep of the awaiting crowd, not really sure what he is looking for. Frederick grunts inwardly at his over cautiousness and approaches Josh from the side.

'Hello, Josh,' he says nonchalantly.

'Freddy, for Christ's sake, don't ever do that again, creeping up on me like that,' replies Josh, studying him closely.

'Bloody hell though, you're dressed up like in old times,' he adds grinning.

'I wish it were, Josh, but let's get out of here quick before the crowd disperses,' he says quietly through his teeth.

'Sure, Freddy.'

Josh turns and nods in the direction of the exit. Two athletic, blond-haired, middle-aged bodyguard types with hard features fall in behind them on their way out.

'My men, just in case we experience any opposition,' he adds from the corner of his mouth.

Two black BMWs join the motley of vehicles outside the arrival terminal. Josh guides Freddy and his entourage towards them. He opens the rear door of the front vehicle motioning Freddy to get in. Freddy takes a seat in the rear and is just about to make himself comfortable when he realizes Freddy wants to get in that side too.

'Bloody hell, Freddy, move over, will ya,'

Freddy grumbles – picks his rucksack up and shifts his backside over.

Freddy has one foot in and one hand on the top of the door. He looks around and back to the other car, waiting until the two bodyguards disappear into the rear BMW before he climbs in and closes the door, at the same time addressing the driver,

'Okay, Heinz, let's go,' and turning to Freddy, adds, 'I think we have about an hour for you to tell me what the hell a Jesuit priest dressed up like an Italian gigolo is so darn worried stiff about, and take off those incongruous Gucci's, for Christ sake – you look like a bloody Italian fairy.'

'I'll take them off once we're outside Munich and not before, Josh. You'll approve my precaution of wanting to remain ingognito when I tell you what this is all about.'

'Okay, then Freddy, you're the boss,' he said, grinning like a Halloween pumpkin.

Freddy explained the whole plot, emphasizing the brutal killing of his brother Albert – the warning hanging over the rest of Albert's family and the danger they were in from the Nazis and now possibly from the Vatican Secret Service. Josh didn't comment when he told him about the map showing the whereabouts of a hidden Jesus Testament – the reason for all this. Freddy didn't mention the letter that was with the map originally that he of course had destroyed. His main concern at the moment was for his own safety and the safety of his brother's family who were still in dire peril.

'That's just about it briefly, Josh,' he added apologetically.

'Christ, Freddy, this goes damn deeper than I imagined when you asked me for protection. The first thing we'll have to do is get your brother's family to safety. We'll put them up in a safe house in Straubing for a starter. Then you'll have to think about yours and their future. I'm afraid if the Vatican's after you then your job as a priest is over. Maybe I can get you into the German *Zeugenschutzprogram* – new identities and a change of address. We'll need your cooperation as a witness against the Nazi's though when the time comes.'

Freddy turned to look at Josh.

'But what good's my testimony. I only heard a warning voice on the telephone,' he said, despairingly.

'Well, then – we'll just have to set them a trap, won't we,' replied Josh, grinning sadistically.

A thought came to Freddy on the mention of the *Zeugenschutzprogramm*,

'Tell me, Josh – just what sort of an organization is yours?'

Josh grinned and turned to look Freddy in the eyes who'd by now discarded his dark Gucci's,

'I'm afraid my firm is just a cover. We work for a government agency, that's all you need to know. You're in luck – I can pull a few strings in this particular case, because we've been after the Nazi group in Passau for some time now – splinter group of *the Vikings* – haven't been able to pin them down. We've suspected the local and regional police are involved, that's why all our efforts have been sabotaged and side tracked. When we get to Straubing I'll get my guys together and we'll sort something out. We'll need you as our decoy to lure them out, though.'

Freddy stayed the night at a villa on the outskirts of a Village near Straubing – Josh's private security company. At 6 am Josh's support troops arrived. After a quick briefing, 10 armed men left in three vehicles – two SUVs and a BMW. Their objective was to secure and protect Silvia and the two girls.

At 7 am, Freddy rang Silvia from an unregistered cell phone,

'Ja,' a voice answered,

'Silvia?'

'Freddy?'

'Yes, its me – look, I'll be arriving a little later, please stay indoors and don't let anybody in, under no circumstances, and for heaven's sake don't let the kids out, lock all doors and windows. I'll be with you in a couple of hours and don't tell anybody I'm coming, you hear?'

'I heard you, Freddy,' she said, fiercely, 'you've a lot of explaining to do when you get here.'

'I know, Silvia, it'll all work out, you'll see. Got to go now – see you later, bye.'

'Bye, Freddy and take care,' she replied, soberly.

Josh laid out his plan at breakfast and after a briefing the rest of them left at 9 am on their way to Passau – another two SUVs and a BMW. Inside those vehicles were the remaining 8 tough looking agents, plus Freddy and Josh sitting in the lead BMW.

As they approached the outskirts of Passau, on Josh's instructions, Freddy rang up the local police station using the same unregistered cell phone as before and gave the pre-arranged message,

'My name is Father Frederick Schneider. I'm the brother of Albert Schneider who was murdered yesterday. I wish to report the involvement of a person called Kraus who is responsible for the murdering of my brother. I'll be coming to the police station shortly to hand in my statement.'

He broke the connection.

'Good, Freddy – now, remember, just hand over the statement we concocted this morning to the duty policeman and tell him you're going to your sister-in-law's place. We'll take it from there,' said Josh heartedly, 'and remember, we'll be ready to move in if things get too hot for you.'

The car came to a halt twenty metres from the police station.

'Okay, Freddy – good luck.'

Freddy left the safety of the BMW and walked the short distance to the police station. His legs were wonky and felt like jelly babies – his stomach was in uproar – just short of vomiting and thinking everyone was looking at him because he was shaking uncontrollably. He went into the police station and walked up to the counter, trying his best to make a bold appearance,

'My name is Frederick Schneider, I rang earlier, and here is my statement,' he stuttered, placing the statement on the counter in front of a young policeman who eyed him questionably, 'I shall be at my sister-in-laws should you wish to know more,' he added.

'Em,' the policeman started to say, as Freddy turned on his heels and walked out.

'Wait a minute,' yelled the young policeman after him.

When Freddy didn't stop he picked up the phone and dialled a number.

Freddy started walking the five blocks to Silvia's place. At first his legs barely carried him – still scared, even though he knew Josh's men were out on the streets too, ready to come to his rescue. Inwardly he was praying, although his conscience was telling him they were all liars the whole Vatican hierarchy. Sacred, my foot, he was thinking. This line of thought seemed to calm him down a bit. Maybe it was his anger evoking such thoughts of sacrilege. No, he told himself – he wasn't the one who has desecrated the religious teachings. It had always been there he knew at heart – he, Freddy, had seen many documents that contradict the teachings of the Roman Catholic religion, the basis for all Christian religions. It is saddening to be faced with the savage truth in such a way. He had always felt he was a true believer, a stout catholic and his religious convictions had been so strong. His hand moved under his jacket – feeling the tape that held the hidden mike – reassured this was worth the effort if they managed to arrest Albert's killers.

Two blocks to go he thought, as he turned the next corner. He walked on and heard a vehicle approach from behind that was slowing down. This is it, he thought. They're going to snatch me now. His pulse now doing overtime, he felt like running as a Ford van, it's sliding doors open, screeched to a halt. He was snatched and pulled into the van. He recognised Kraus who was sneering at him,

'Now look who we've got here, eh! His honour from the Vatican gives us the pleasure, eh!'

'Haven't changed have you Kraus, still the same stinking skunk you were as a teenager,' said Freddy, knowing the provocation would get him a belting.

Kraus hit him across the face brutally, using the hand decorated with a spiked knuckle-duster.

Freddy moved his head before contact but still felt his skin tear and the blood and tears form, as his cheek was cut and his nose battered. He spat blood in Kraus' direction and managed to utter the words he'd learned out by heart,

'You got the map you bastard but how do you know I didn't change it, eh. Killing my brother hasn't helped you, that's why I made a few changes.'

Freddy tried to force a grin to emphasize his statement but it was more like a grimace.

Kraus was livid – his face reddened with fury.

'You fucking bastard – now that was a stupid thing you did. I'm gonna get the information and you're gonna suffer real bad until I get it...'

Freddy interrupted him,

'Tell me Kraus, why did you kill my brother? Don't you think a warning or a kidnap would have been sufficient to make me get the map?'

'You stupid bastard, I cut his fucking throat because I've always hated you – father married to a Jewess – you piece of shit,' shouted Kraus, white foam now oozing out of the corners of his mouth.

That was the moment Josh's men had been waiting for. His vehicles pulled out from various places near the snatch and surrounded the van. Men jumped out and converged on the van. The door was shoved open hard and Josh was standing on the pavement with three men, their weapons raised – ready to shoot and kill.

The police station at Passau was a bustle of activity. Many police and prison vans were parked outside. The German Federal Police, the BKA, had taken over from Josh and were in the process of interviewing and arresting some local officers and members of Kraus' gang. They wouldn't be able to get them all, but it was a start.

Freddy was escorted to a local doctor where he was stitched up and had his nose plastered. He would carry some thin scars physically, but the damage within was greater. Freddy has decided to accompany Silvia and the kids to a different part of Germany where they'll be living under a new identity until Kraus' case comes to court. He knows he'll always have to be on the alert because someone somewhere might be urged to take a bribe and hand over information, especially if *their* loved ones were in peril.

Berlin – Hotel, near the Old Opera House – Monday 15th August 2005 – 15⁰⁰ hrs.

The killer's sharp eyes registered every movement as he watched from the shadows of an empty flat on the third floor of a building directly opposite the Old Opera Hotel in Berlin. The weapon wasn't his choice – a hunting rifle – an insult to his profession but indeed ideal for the initial purpose of intentional confusion.

Flipping down a heavy tripod, he placed it on top of a sturdy old table layered with many a coat of paint. Balancing the rifle on the tripod, he adjusted to target position, sighted in at the given hotel window opposite and locked the swivel arm. He relaxed for a few more minutes on an old but steady chair. Like the table, a remnant of the previous occupants or possibly supplied by his client's organization – taking no chances, he figured. The table was jammed perfectly under the windowsill at the half-opened middle window. All other window blinds were down two-thirds, acceptable for an empty flat without raising suspicion. His was lowered just enough to leave room for the job at hand. He observed the hotel room opposite through his binoculars, taking them down occasionally to rest his eyes. Nodding to himself after a glance at the *omega* wristwatch claimed from one of his previous victims, he picked up the binoculars again to watch the movements of the target that had entered the hotel room opposite.

The right moment having arrived – he swapped the binoculars for the rifle's telescopic sight, taking his time and melting smoothly into the prepared position. Loosening the swivel lock, he manoeuvred the crosshair of his lens on the target – at the same time moving his forefinger to rest lightly on the trigger, waiting patiently until the target was steady and the cranium centred. The smell of fine gun oil and the feel of the hunting rifle letting his thoughts wander for a moment to the woods, his favourite hunting grounds – amused at the thought of being on a raised hide and waiting for the buck to come into full view of his sights – easy meat and ready for the recoil.

Ian Stewart was confused. His girlfriend, Martha Stern, was overdue. However, this was a personal affair, otherwise he would have left by now. Hotel room business is not his piece of cake anyway. He was in turmoil too at the sad task ahead.

He fetched a bottle of mineral water from the mini-bar, held the neck and twisted the bottle top breaking the seal. A few more twists and the top came off.

Turning to the window he looked out over the *Bismarckstraße* and took a long swig from the bottle. He could just see a corner of the *Old Opera* building on the far left. It was too quiet in the hotel room, so he opened the window. A welcoming rush of noise engulfed him – the bustle of city street sounds outside now fitting the images he'd been watching. He was part of it – he could hear and feel it. He was more than a little agitated at Martha being late – it wasn't like her. At the back of his mind he was thinking Martin Cole, his chief, who'd arranged the meeting, would've informed him of any unexpected delay. He moved back into the room and checked his cell phone – nothing new.

His stomach rumbled, a reminder he hadn't eaten since breakfast. His eyes fell on the small wicker basket on the round table in the corner – a few edibles by the looks of things. He twisted the cap back on the bottle and placed it on the table. His fingers rummaged through the basket picking out a small bluish cellophane packet with *'Studentenfutter'* written on it. He tore it open and poured some of its contents into the palm of his hand. That looks okay, he thought – mixed nuts and raisins will do for the moment.

His thoughts went back to his first encounter with Martha. It was the way she carried herself through a difficult oration at the ceremonial opening of a Holocaust memorial in Berlin some months back making her stand above the other official speakers. The bearing of a German Jewess of the new generation burdened with the past, yet very open-minded about religion and current Israeli politics, stopping just short of a reprimand for the latter. She didn't care about *kosher*, so he invited her out to dinner at a restaurant of his choice. Not only was she good to look at but very interesting to listen to. He dated her frequently after that, their relationship becoming intense and more binding as the months went by.

Eventually, and perhaps against his better judgment, he mentioned his job with the International Security Intelligence Agency – affectionately known as *the Agency* that strictly speaking, is against the rules. He told Martin about her views, particularly relating to the possibility of Mossad agents having infiltrated Western intelligence services. Martin thought it was time for him to break contact. If she'd told him, then there were likely to be others already interested in her and any links involved. His conscience was troubling him too. Deep down he knew he'd fallen in love with her and should've put her in the picture much earlier. It really hurt him being ordered to disengage from her. He thought of ignoring Martin's order, but that would mean losing his job and a fat pension. Maybe she just wanted to be friends and would reject the love idea anyway. Where would he stand then? Anyway, orders were orders and most of the time Field Intelligence Operators obey their superiors. It's easy enough declaring such instances in training but it's a different matter when you're in the middle of it. Initially, he'd asked Martin if he should write up the usual report. Martin told him not to bother – he would pass on an oral report with his request for a surveillance team.

He thought it a bit strange when he received a text message from Martin on Saturday, just two days ago, instructing him to meet Martha in this particular hotel room today. He found it particularly odd because Martha had mentioned being at a demo in Leipzig today. The message was formulated as a direct order and suggested a better ambience in the hotel room for breaking the news to her. How did Martin manage to persuade Martha to come to this rendezvous and miss out on her demo in Leipzig where she was to give a podium speech due to be broadcasted internationally? He sighed – his was not to question orders.

He moved back to the window and leaned out, his elbows resting on the windowsill. He looked down at the traffic and movement of pedestrians on the pavements. He turned his head to the left towards the subway sign. Maybe she's coming by *U-Bahn* he thought. His interest now settled on the comings and goings from the underground entrance and exit.

His well-trained eyes caught a light reflection from a window across the road. He moved his head in that direction trying to focus on the source – a momentary perception of a dark figure hunched in the corner of a half-opened window. The stance and silhouette whisked through his recognition system, taking just a split second. It dawned on him that the figure was holding what looked like a rifle, pointed in his direction. He had been too preoccupied with thoughts of Martha and Martin to notice the trap – his reflexes weren't quick enough. He was too late even to hear the pop and see the brief whiff of smoke and feel the bullet that smashed through his skull. For one second he was focusing on the movement opposite and the next thing – oblivion. Ian's head crashed back, his arms outstretched, *'Studentenfutter'* scattered and his body slammed back into the hotel room – time-out in this world for Ian Stewart, ISIA – Specialist Intelligence Operator.

A few minutes later one of the residents opposite the hotel looked out her window and saw a gathering of pigeons and sparrows at the hotel window. She called the hotel reception to complain about the thoughtless guest who's feeding the pigeons, which of course, everyone in Berlin knows, is forbidden.

Leipzig – Monday 15th August 2005

CNN correspondent Douglas Willis interviews vicar Christian Fueller from Leipzig amidst other reporters also firing their questions. Douglas Willis speaks into the microphone and faces the camera:

'For several weeks, peaceful demonstrators have been forming up early Monday evenings at the *Nicholas Church* in Leipzig. From there, they move on to the building of the Federal Supreme Administrative Court at *Simsonsplatz*. The procession gets longer every minute as more people join – moving towards the centre of Leipzig, popularly called the *Exhibition City*. Ages from all walks of life, even the very old and young families with their children walk together in this peaceful procession. That's how it is this Monday and all signs show it will be the same next Monday. Of course they are demonstrating against the new Bill causing drastic cuts on social benefits for the 6 million unemployed. One person is with them at the *Nicholas Church,* but doesn't join the march. The 61 year old vicar, Christian Fueller, who was the instigator of the Monday demonstrations towards the end of the communist regime GDR.'

'What makes the masses join such demonstrations, Herr Fueller?' asks Willis, the reporter.

The vicar responds,

'Elias Canetti wrote in his study *Mass and Might – Long masses form a procession.* In his case the goal was the Promised Land. He says the procession would remain a mass for as long as the participants *believed* in their goal.'

'You talk with demonstrators. You speak into microphones and give interviews in front of TV-cameras and above all you speak to the crowd, but why do you remain at your church when the procession starts its march? Why don't you join them?' asks Willis.

'First of all we have prayers – this has an inflating effect on the demonstrators. That was how the Leipzig model 1989 functioned. It brought down the Iron Curtain and became the starter that eventually caused the end of the totalitarian GDR regime. Total control of people and property must never be allowed, it has to be eradicated. When people hear our church bells they converge at the church. I have to be here to receive them. It functioned with the Leipzig model in 1989 like the Pavlovian reflexes,' The vicar continues, 'Let me explain – Ivan Pavlov, a Russian physiologist, did research and experimented on the nervous system. He found out that in conjunction with food, people were trained to react to the sound of a bell, whereby their stomachs reacted with an over production of gastric juices.'

'Do you allow political parties, unions and others to participate?' asks Willis.

'I would warn against the danger of peaceful demonstrations being engulfed and misused by Right Wing Socialist radicals and Leftist movements who would like to profit from the unjust treatment of the millions of unemployed by the government and use them politically in the forthcoming elections,' the vicar replies sharply.

The reporter turns to speak to the person standing next to Christian Fueller,

'Herr Hellwig, you are from the Leipzig Social Centre organization committee, who have done a lot of arranging and publicity for the demonstrations. What do you say to the participation of other parties and organizations?'

'I would certainly disagree with the vicar. The demonstrations are democratically open for all citizens, but members of political parties and organized parties are *not* allowed to hold speeches,' Hellwig replies.

The vicar takes over and speaks vehemently into the microphone,

'The church will not tolerate the participation in the demonstrations by the egoistical group orientated aims of the Right Wing NSPD, the Left Wing PDS and other obscure groups, who it seems, want to benefit and use the demonstrations for their own platforms. I will not allow that in my church community!'

The vicar continues,

'Karl Marx once wrote – History always repeats itself, the first time as a tragedy and the second time as a farce. This time the demonstrations were a bit too early.'

'Do you think the same?' another reporter asks Herr Hellwig.

'Christian Fueller already had a special peace prayer gathering advertised on posters organized for the 30th August, long before he went on holiday. His theme was justice for all. He was betting on the familiar mix of holy service and the ritual silent march. But the East Germans are fuming ever since the unemployed have been reduced to beggars. Instead of receiving work from the benefits office they've been given *one-Euro-an-hour* jobs. They wish to say: *enough is enough – no more cuts*. The nation's anger has been boiling and the first demonstrators went to the streets in Magdeburg early August. So the people of Leipzig couldn't hold back and need the vicar to lead them,' Hellwig replies.

'Yes, that's correct, that's how it happened. We had to jump on the bandwagon. However I'm somewhat concerned that small radical groups, who we know are very quick, could take over command,' the vicar counters.

Herr Hellwig, with a smirk on his face makes a cynical remark,

'Christian Fueller is a noble and sober Christian?'

'The church may not identify itself with populist talk,' the vicar counters, adding, 'what we should be talking about is the miserable morbid standstill in this country. Everything's paralysed. We have a continuous growth in unemployment, and a large part of the population is sunk in depression with a *no chance* attitude. I am very angered at the way in which fat cat directors help themselves to tens of millions in extra bonuses – the excess with which these directors stuff their pockets full. The audacity they have is what upsets me and upsets the people. The economy ethics have fallen by the wayside. This is terrible. We could use all these millions of Euros pocketed by those fat cat directors to provide for all of the homeless and socially discredited in all of the major German cities.'

The vicar cites from Genesis,

'*A nation, that has no vision, becomes wild and desolate,*'

He quotes a second citation from the Old Testament,

'*Justice enhances a nation but sin is their downfall.*'

The CNN reporter speaks to the camera:

'Christian Fueller is not a self-righteous person. The man in jeans and threadbare denim vest is a man of the people – his motives are honourable. A man with a name, though without vanity, his plans are very bold.'

Encouraged by these words of sympathy, Christian Fueller adds,

'For us, October is the month of revolution and reformation. I've been saying for years that the latter part is missing. It is only now that people are actually grasping this. The first part was to peacefully overcome the division of the two German nations. We managed that. Part two is eternal peace and social justice in Germany as a whole. That still has to happen. What pleases me too, is what Hermann Huebber, the council chairman of the Protestant Church in Germany, says – *the capitalistic market economy is not in a position of solving the people's problems*. All-in-all Germany is moving, as it should, from the bottom upwards. The saturated party landscape will soon be answerable. The impulses can only come from the East. The people have to be polarised.'

Another reporter butts in,

'Christian Fueller is an idealist and pragmatist at the same time and a reformer of Lutheran strength. So, he knows what's to be done, does he?'

Christian Fueller runs his hands through his grey short-cut hair.

'Sometimes I think we should send the people who are calling out the downfall of social support for a week to the Ukraine. They should see how the people there have to live. They would crawl back over the German border on their knees singing hallelujah.'

The same reporter butts in again,

'That view will upset lots of demonstrators.'

'I'm not prepared to say just what people expect or want me to say,' the vicar replies.

'Just a minute,' the CNN reporter excitedly interrupts, holding and pressing his hand over the mike in his ear, listening hard.

'Reports are just coming in of a bloody murder – a young Jewish woman has been knifed to death at *Simsonsplatz*.'

'May God have mercy on her and her assailant. This is a very bad blow for our peaceful movement. I hope justice prevails,' says the vicar, drawing himself back to the elemental force of the Protestant as though he is saying – here I stand, I cannot do otherwise.

'Under these circumstances I think it would be appropriate to have prayers. Thank you ladies and gentlemen,' he says.

Turning around, he disappears through the crowd standing at the entrance to the church.

London – John Jameson, early Tuesday 16th August 2005

"Early to bed, early to rise, makes a man ... yeah!"

Full of sleep, my eyes gazed at the alarm clock as I rolled over to pick up the telephone receiver. My bedroom telephone is one of those old fashioned black British Telecomm apparatus, but this one has an extra gadget – a privileged leftover from my days with the British Intelligence Services. It also has that beautiful deep mellow ringing sound. It's loud enough to wake an elephant, but I just love it. It gives me the feeling of being at home in a sane country.

It was 2.30 am. I'm usually very belligerent at this hour of the morning, so I bellowed my phone number into the mouthpiece, hoping it sounded sarcastic and angry enough.

A polite young female voice answered.

'Duty Officer, Maureen Bailey speaking – would you please press your button, Sir?'

I was awake like a spark. I don't get called-up often from my old firm MI6 at these hours. I pressed my scrambler button, heard a few clicks and scratches and then the female voice came on again.

'Thank you Sir – may I now have your identification please?'

I threw my legs over onto the floor and balancing the 'phone between my chin and shoulder, I leaned over to the bedside table, pulled-out the drawer and reached in for my wallet. Extracting my temporary security card I gave the required code.

'Thank you Sir! I have a priority one message for you.

The text is as follows:

John, Tom Atkins here. I apologize for the disturbance. We are having an all night session and something cropped up that your expertise on the Muslim/Nazi links might help to clarify. We have the okay from Jack Orlowski. I know I can rely on you, so how about popping over... ASAP?'

A slight pause, then the sweet voice of Maureen Bailey asked,

'Do you have a reply, Sir?

'Yes, I do. It's now 2.34 am. I'll be on my way in about 15 minutes.'

'I'll pass the message on. Goodbye Sir.'

'*Goodnight*, Miss Bailey.'

'Ms Bailey, Sir!' Her end of the line went dead.

By now, I was wide-awake. She was probably trying to be

polite by saying goodbye and I put my foot in it with my goodnight, or she's just quick. Ah, sad days – maybe she's an old spinster. You can't always judge the age by the voice.

I put the receiver back on the hook, wondering how the bloody hell MI6 knew I was at home? Remembering the mention of Jack Orlowski I knew the answer. I pursed my lips and deflated my lungs in a long steady sigh. I'm supposed to be on my annual holiday.

My expertise has been required officially in recent months and I enjoy the exchange with MI6. With regards to my humble person they are probably thinking

"The opportunities of bringing the alienated into the fold are not to be sneezed at."

Perhaps that's not the main reason – they just haven't got enough experts. I can judge that from their occasional debriefings.

I wouldn't describe myself as a particularly meticulous person. I just prefer to have things well organized, so I've the habit of laying out the choice of clothing for the following day before going to bed. Comes from early days as Field Intelligence Officer in the British Intelligence Service. Job timing mostly unpredictable. Except of course on the rare occasion, when I meet my old *bunch* and have a binge.

I got dressed, splashed my face with chalky water supplied by the Thames Water Company and combed my almost achaetous scalp. I really only need a comb with a dozen or so teeth, which reminds me to cut and shave-off these remaining smooth-haired strangles some day soon.

I took a long swig of soda water from the bottle – got my short stay bag out of the hall cupboard – put my lap-top in the side bag – rang for a taxi and left the flat. By the time I reached the lift, got down to street level and unlocked the hall and outside doors, the taxi was waiting. I asked to be dropped off at the corner of John Islip, Atterbury Street. I preferred walking the rest, besides it's not good for your image when you ask to be dropped off at MI6.

I walked past the old buildings of what used to be the Royal Army Medical Corps training college. Their gates sadly closed in 2000 when they moved to Gosport. The clock's still there though. I always glance at it when walking past. It reminds me of youthful days with one of the students. I can even remember her name – Helena Vakuli? – lost sight of her after she moved from South Norwood to Manchester. Her pleasant memory brightened me up as I carried on down to Millbank and crossed the road to the Thames.

It was a cloudless morning and fairly warm. No one in sight and the only sounds coming from occasional vehicles going over the Vauxhall Bridge or passing behind me and the tide lapping against the stone structure below.

I stood for a while listening and gazing at the Thames and the silhouette of famous buildings. Standing there alone, breathing in the unmistakable smell of the river, the patriotic feeling arose, even though I'm an out and out Scot. Maybe it's because I feel important doing something clandestine, but authorized. Or maybe it's because of Tony Blair's devolution for Scotland! Nothing I can relate to anyone. Maybe because the Scots were always in the front line and I get upset when my country *Britain,* is described as *England.* The English, French and Germans have a habit of doing that. Scots tend to push themselves harder than others too!

Putting these thoughts aside I turned and walked towards the Vauxhall Bridge – up a few steps and onto the bridge – on my way over the Thames towards MI6, enjoying the early morning air.

John Scarlotti – Director of MI6, early Tuesday 16th August 2005

I went in by the night door, undergoing the customary security check including biometric identity control. I emptied the contents of my pockets into a basket where they were scrutinized and placed into a locker together with my overnight bag and laptop. The only remnant was my PowerPoint CD that was registered and handed back to me.

The guard informed me I was the last one in and the director was waiting, so the security protocols were kept to a minimum. Once the checks were over I was given a necklace type plastic identity card. One of the guards escorted me to an elevator. He accompanied me in and pressed the indicator button for the lowest level. No word was spoken. Leaving the elevator, we went along well-lit corridors. We left the main corridor and continued down a short passage where another security checkpoint awaited us. The security guard checked my chip-card registration in his computer and a red light just up the passage turned to green. The guard waved me on. I was now on my own. I observed a metal door about 10 metres further on. On reaching it the door opened automatically. Inside, a security guard checked my biographics, nodded his approval and told me to carry on through the next door.

Tom Atkins, head of Special Operations, SO, anti-terrorist branch came forward to greet me. I detest his double questioning – going over material minutely and asking for details to be repeated over and over again. Very tiresome and irritating – reminds me of an instructor from my *rookie* days at the Intelligence Centre '*...pay attention to detail, that's the essence of intelligence gathering.*' Sometimes I think he's just not good at memorizing what he's being told or perhaps he just wants to catch me out. Tom and I have had numerous dealings in the past. I detest his upper-class manner and his *'we're something better'* image – typical of some in the *intelligence* branch. Mostly academics – some should never be in the positions they hold – thinking about Britain's past betrayers. One good thing came of that, the aftermath – agents and staffs were vetted more thoroughly and on a regular basis. It's bloody well high time they stopped recruiting mainly through the *old boy* net though, getting *the **nice** boys and girls from university* – mostly all brain but no guts! Not many agree with my attitude that they don't possess the intuition you get when you start at the bottom of the ladder instead of jumping in two thirds up, but that's the way it is with western intelligence agencies.

I saw the director engrossed in discussion with a group just behind Tom.

'Good to see you John,' said Tom in his affected Oxford English, 'knew you'd come!'

Tom lifted his right arm and smiled, the smugness gleaming from his face. The arm moved slowly describing a wide arc, at the same time proclaiming,

'Welcome to our *Panoply*, Britain's most advanced *high-tech* protected conference room – do excuse the extra security precautions! Most worthy of our humble abode, though, what!'

I grumbled inwardly, not letting my countenance betray my true feelings for this affectation, and put on my well-trained welcoming smile.

Justice reigned as I put the hand he shoved out in greeting into a sharply tightened vice. It must have left its mark as a slight grimace passed over Tom's face, a reminder to brace his hand next time or hating me for being so brutal. John Scarlotti, the director, gave me a brief nod as Tom forced his hand from my grip. He turned and said something to his group, which then dispersed to seats placed around a long oval table. The movement of the director to the front caused those still standing to take their seats.

Tom touched me on the arm and led the way up near the front. Without further ado he sat down. I followed suit and sat down on the only free seat left, which was next to him. King Arthur's roundtable was now complete but where do I fit in – am I *Sir Galahad*? I had a look around trying to place the nametags and faces,

John Scarlotti Director of MI6, formerly chairman of the JIC commission on 9/11, *Stephen Landers,* Director General of MI5, MI6 Chief *Richard Dearcove* – member of the JIC commission for 9/11 and an Assistant Deputy, some SIS and BIS department chiefs and a group of departmental ministers from the JIC Commission, two of whom were women. Last not least, two welcoming faces from New Scotland Yard, Assistant Commissioner *Charles Cross* and Chief Superintendent *Dave Haddock,* from Special Operations, anti-terrorist dept. I knew both of them well.

This is quite a set-up I thought – something's afoot. Has a slight political touch but on the other hand there are too many professionals present. There can't be more bomb attacks on the tubes or buses, at least I would have heard about that from my own sources. *Al Qaeda* green shoots are always up to something, but our infiltrations to their networks and cells, and the help we get in Britain from the public and most of the Muslim leaders as a follow-up from 9/11 through to 21/7 and the new amendment to the Prevention of Terrorism Act passed in the House thereafter, is a great help.

Scarlotti and *Dearcove* were damned lucky their heads hadn't rolled after their part in the WMD intelligence report that formed the basis for the war on Iraq. *Scarlotti* was even promoted to head the SIS. I thought they would have become *persona non grata* – so there seems more to this than meets the eye. Maybe his days as director are not that numbered as heard on the grapevine!

The director stood motionless for a few seconds, seemingly undecided about something. His jaw hardened, his mind made up – he broke into a half-smile and turned towards me.

'John, could we have a quick word before the session continues?' he asked.

I was taken slightly by surprise, but got up and walked over, expecting a word or two on the *need to know* principle.

The director moved to the far corner of the room opposite the technician's table. I followed in his wake. We stood near a wash-hand basin. Above that was an extremely disproportionately large mirror – a typical MI6 blunder. I immediately categorised it as *'Venetian',* wondering who was watching from the other side.

'Thank you for coming under such short notice, John,' he said.

'Before we continue our session, I'm afraid I've some bad news for you. We received unconfirmed information a short while ago, that an ex-pat working with *the Agency* has been taken out in Berlin. Another working on the same job is reported missing. We have no further information on this. I believe they're good friends of yours – Ian Stewart and Martin Cole. I understand you were FIOs together. Martin's the one who is missing.'

I was braced for the names but still felt my knees wanting to buckle under me for a moment. I closed my eyes briefly, took a deep breath and opened my mouth to say something in reply. I shut it quickly – only a few indiscernible syllables seemed to pass from my brain to my throat and I didn't want them croaking out. The director remained emotionless, his countenance stony.

I nodded after a few seconds, saying,

'Thanks Sir, for telling me personally – I appreciate that.'

'Okay, John – when you're ready let's have you bring us up-to-date on the *Muslim/Nazi* business.'

The director moved back to the assembly.

I remained standing in the corner, thoughts of Ian and Martin racing through my brain. I came back to reality and went over to the two technical assistants sitting at the side of the room and handed over my CD with the PowerPoint presentation.

The director picked up his glass and poured in some mineral water. All eyes looking, he took some heavy gulps, his Adam's apple the size of a gob-stopper on his long neck, popped up and down with each swallow until the glass was emptied. Placing it back on the table he leaned forward to Tom and muttered something, then straightening up, lifted a ballpoint pen from the table and tapped it on his empty glass. Calling for order, he said,

'Ah-hem... ladies and gentlemen... just before the break, AC *Charles Cross* brought up an interesting angle. Do we have anything concrete on *Muslim terrorists* operating within or with *ultra-right* organizations in Europe and elsewhere?'

The director continued, half-turning towards me,

'*Stephen Landers* brought your name up, John. He is quite sure you can fill in the holes on this matter. We understand you've been working on this lately on a larger scale,'

He looked at me and asked,

'Can we go on with the show, John?'

'Yes, certainly Sir,

For the next 25 minutes or so I gave an actual account of

the various verified links known, their backgrounds and whereabouts and a brief prognosis of their aims and *modus operandi*. I was glad to have something else to concentrate on. It gave me a chance not to think about my mates. I answered questions that followed until they petered out. Nobody mentioned Ian or Martin. After no more questions were asked the buzzing of individual conversations started. This was the signal for the director. He stood up and addressed the assembly,

'All right then, if there are no more questions for John, then I think we can dismiss him. We'll just have a short five minute break, so John can get his bits and pieces together,' said the director, 'John, Tom will escort you out. Thanks ever so much for coming.'

'No problem, Sir, anytime!' I said, thinking about the extra cash that would come in handy for my new boat – *pennies make pounds!*

The director's face was now a complete mask. I nodded in his direction anyway and moved over to the technicians to fetch my CD.

Tel-Aviv North – Mossad Headquarters, Tuesday 16th August 2005

Jacob Weizmann was sitting at his computer as usual in the Mossad specialist analyst department referred to as PAHA. Above his thick blond eyebrows was a broad forehead – well creased by the continuous information overload his brain was confronted with daily. He had a strong, attenuated, aristocratic nose and a mouth that curved upwards in a natural grin. His chin was formed like a ledge of granite. A broad back protruded over the rear of the chair and when he stood up, his two metres five dominated the room. Due to his blond hair and blue eyes, he was called the Northman. For some time now he's been showing signs of continuous nervousness. Some reckon his wife is the main cause.

Jacob guessed he married only because they don't let you into the Mossad unless you are married. On the other hand that's only half the truth. It was really his wife who persuaded him to join. He'd just finished university with a *cum laude* doctorate in computer science. At the time she was a young secretary, one of three who were working for Ben Israel, the Mossad chief in 1995. His wife, Sarah Gurion had famous relatives, so maybe there was some back scratching done. Jacob sensed she was using him somehow. He realized on their first night together she was something special in bed. Jewish women are known for being very sexy and extremely active in bed, but she really beat them all. As time went by and her cravings increased, he became ill. The doctor sent him on a health cure for four weeks to the Dead Sea, where he managed to get back to his senses. From then on, he did try for some weeks to douse her sexual appetite. He gave up eventually. She was the one who had a problem, he told her – she was definitely oversexed. He called her a nympho-maniac – didn't seem to upset her at all. After that, there was just sex every two days instead of five times a day. He told her he couldn't carry out his work otherwise. The whole marriage was insecure from his point of view. Amazingly, she waved his arguments aside and remained the sweet person she always was. He left it at that, but a nagging question mark remained thereafter – whom was she doing it with right now?

Something worse than being married to a nympho has been worrying him since August 2001, keeping his mind occupied –

his thoughts in turmoil – his conscience twisted – his memory of the incident repeatedly cart-wheeling back to that day:

'Hey, Northman! You doing some thinking about our decrypting or are you having a nap?' the voice of his superior had bellowed into his ear.

He recalled the incident vividly. It was one of those days in August 2001 when he'd been popping his wife half the night before. He'd deciphered an important message sent by one of their own Mossad Signal Intelligence Units. He also received a copy of an NSA message bearing similarities – apparently information the Mossad Communications Department had missed out on.

'You stupid idiot Abraham', he'd answered, 'you do that again and I'll punch you so hard you won't be in any position to put in a complaint. You bloody well know that can damage anyone's eardrums for good. Come to think of it, if anybody puts a complaint in, then it'll be me. Now what the hell do you want disturbing my precious thoughts?'

'The big boss says you should take a look at this, before you write your encryption conclusions, and it's your eyes only the boss says, so you've got to sign for it and make sure you don't let anyone else see it otherwise you'll have a Mossad annihilation team on your tail. He wants it done straight away.'

He gave Jacob a big envelope with Top Secret written on it and a big red cross across front and back from corner to corner and handed him a registry book. Jacob signed the book and went into a secure room, taking the envelope and his encryptions with him – Abraham, his direct superior, walked away shaking his head.

Jacob had already deciphered his own two messages, one was from Hamburg, Germany and the other was from Jalalabad, Pakistan. The first message from Hamburg was plain,

See you on the eleventh and don't forget, all five packages go par Avion to the addressees we agreed on.
  So God will (Allah inshaalah)

The second message he deciphered was a bit odd,

Our destination has changed. The first two groups are now to go to twin peaks. The rest as agreed. All packages par Avion.
  God is great (Allahu akbar)

His task was only to decipher, thank goodness. Let others do the rest. He opened the Top Secret envelope and took out a single sheet of white paper that would change the face of the Western world and turn him into a nervous wreck.

Tom Atkins – MI6, early Tuesday 16th August 2005

My CD had just been handed over when Tom's voice piped up near my right ear,
'Ah, looks as though we've got everything then, eh! Okay, let me lead the way up, John.'

Tom led me back through the dungeons. This time we took a different corridor, ending up in a central lift area. We got off on the fourth floor. Near the elevators was a small conference room just past the rest room. Tom headed straight for it. He must have had intelligence operation maps or strategy charts or something in that line lying about in his own office – information or even somebody I wasn't supposed to see. I have a photographic memory and my trained eyes don't miss a thing.

He's not taking any chances. So much for the working together bit with other agencies, I thought.

'Do take a seat John. I expect you realize I am informed about your unfortunate colleagues – my most humble and sincere sympathies! You're probably most anxious to get back to Berlin post haste. Before you leave, I've been instructed to give you two classified dispatches that came in this evening. One is from the ISIA and the other one's from the German BND. The Germans are specifically asking for you. My, my, they don't seem to be in the picture though – think you're still a member of MI6.'

Tom finished his vociferous rattling and moved his hand to a button just under the lid of the table that he pressed. A door at the side opened and a tall alert looking middle-aged agent, a xanthomelanous type, probably Middle East, maybe Jewish descendant, entered the conference room. The mention of the name that followed verified my first inclinations.

'John, this is my colleague Joshua Grossman. He will remain with you until you leave the building. He will see to your needs if there is anything you require, if it's reasonable and within our means of course. If you don't mind I have to get back to the meeting, so I'll leave you in his capable hands,' said Tom.

'Thanks for everything Tom – I'd just like to check out these dispatches on a safe line. One to *the Agency* in Berlin and one to the BND in Munich if that's all right?' I asked.

'Yes, of course – Joshua will see to that. Is that all?' asked Tom – his emphasis on *all* was one big vocative challenge,

It was as though that was *all* I would get anyway – maybe more requirements than he'd anticipated. I thought of saying no, just to tantalize him.

'Yes, that'll be all. Thanks again, Tom,' I said.

'You scratch my back and I'll scratch yours, eh, what!' Tom replied.

I felt my face take on a pained look that was unrestrainable. Tom didn't notice. His hand was already on the door handle. He opened the door half turning – gave a short wave, more like finger waggling and without looking back he walked out without further ado. Maybe he's gay I thought.

Joshua stood opposite waiting. No face or body movement, nothing to discern here – well trained I thought – not my cup of tea!

I read the first of the two dispatches Tom had given me. It was from the European intelligence director ISIA, a confirmation of what the MI6 director had already told me, and an order to break off my annual holiday and get over to Berlin immediately. The second dispatch contained a request from the director General of the Bundesnachrichtendienst – German Secret Service, BND, addressed to me personally. It was an urgent message. A telephone number and a reference number for confirmation purposes were given. I recognised part of the reference number – an old acquaintance from the Cold War days.

Turning to black eyes Joshua – that was how I'd categorised him for memory purposes, I asked,

'What about the safe line then Joshua?'

Not one reflex from Joshua at my impolite directness, I noted.

'No problem Sir, just press the yellow button on the side of the table.'

I pressed the button and a part of the table ascended half a metre and stopped. Bugger, I thought, he didn't even ask if I wanted on-line video conversation. I picked up the telephone that had appeared and dialled Jack Orlowski's number in Berlin. I didn't bother telling Joshua this was *need to know* to get him out of the room, as they monitor all calls anyway. It's up to me to keep the calls as short and incomprehensible as possible, I thought. It was now 4.35 am, that makes it 5.35 am in Berlin.

'ISIA, Jaqcueline du Fries am Apparat.'

'Hello Jacky, John Jameson here,' I replied in German.

'Is Jack Orlowski there?'

'Hello John, Jack's with the rapid response team, just a second, I'll try and connect you.'

After a few seconds Jack came on the line.

'Hi, John, heard the bad news?'

'Yes, Jack. I'm at MI6 – was asked to give their all night session a briefing on the Nazi/Muslim links, I gather you okayed it! Something nasty is going on, it seems. Keep your side short and to the point, all I'm informed of is – Ian's dead and Martin's missing!'

'Correct John, they rang here first to get our permission for the briefing before they contacted you! I told Tom Atkins about Ian and Martin. That's why I've sent confirmation direct to you at MI6 instead of your home address. Did you get the dispatch?'

'Aye, thanks Jack. I've just read it. I've also got an urgent request here from the BND. I don't exactly know what it's all about.'

'Okay! First of all the information about Ian is correct. It was a professional hit. Martin is officially reported missing. Otherwise we're in the dark. Your orders are to forget your vacation and return to base immediately.'

'Mm. I'll get over as soon as I can. Bye the way, who's in charge of the rapid response team?'

'Gérard van der Falk.'

'Good choice! Listen, I'll let you know my ETA, as soon as I can. Got to go now!' I said, replacing the phone on the hook without waiting for an answer, knowing he'd object to any interference.

My next call was to the BND operations department in Pullach, Munich.

'*Bundesnachrichtendienst Zentrale, Guten Morgen! Kann ich Ihnen helfen?*' said a deep male voice.

'Yes, good morning,' I replied in German.

'I have a reference number here – are you ready?'

'Yes, please carry on.'

I gave the reference number.

'I am also expecting further details from you,' I said.

'Just a minute, ... ah yes, there is a number here for you to call.'

The BND desk officer gave me a German telephone number. I recognised the pre-dialling code for Stuttgart.

'Any further details?'

'Yes, you should ring the number and tell them where you last met – you are expected to know this.'

'Okay, thanks a lot.'

I was familiar with the reference number, or at least with part of it. It had registered immediately. I knew who was trying to contact me. I knocked the cradle and dialled the new number.

'Schmidt,' a wary sounding voice answered.

'Leipzig, 1988,' I said.

'I have a message for you – *Please contact the old mill I need your help, Karl.*'

'What's the date and time the message was registered?'

'It has yesterday's date, and was made at 13^{48} hrs.'

'Okay, thanks. Should a query be made – I'll be on my way today. Maybe I'll get there by tonight. I'll contact the old mill when I get to Germany. Have you got that?'

'Yes, I have.'

'Okay then, goodbye.'

When it doesn't rain it pours – I've two problems here and I'm really obliged to both. Karl's real name is Olaf Ertl, a BND agent I met on a job in East Germany in the late eighties. We uncovered some links between Right Wing political parties, a new rising of ultra-right gangs linked to East and West Germany and the rebirth of an organization of ex-SS individuals who had used the organization ODESSA to flee from allied retribution. Otto Skorzeny grounded the organization in 1945. Skorzeny was a German Para officer. He was Hitler's special agent for sabotage and secret missions behind enemy lines and led the mission to free Mussolini in Gran Sasso in 1943. ODESSA helped 18,000 SS to escape allied justice from 1945 onwards. I remember Olaf telling me Skorzeny is a regimental hero still held in high regard by the modern German Army Para Regiment. To this day, they have a tendency towards the Right during basic training and military history in particular.

At the time the West thought they could use the Ultra-Right gangs for their own purposes but it proved to be a shot in the dark. The gangs were riddled with East German State Security informers *(Ministerium für Staatsicherheit – MfS)*. The whole thing was a set-up by the East German State Security *(Staatsicherheit – STASI)*.

ODESSA is also part of my recent research into the global Ultra-Right organizations and their Muslim links and leftovers from the Stasi.

I gathered my thoughts together – I'll see what I can do for Olaf first, once I get to Germany, then catch a flight from Stuttgart-Echterdingen to Berlin. Before I do anything, though, I'll have to arrange for help to keep my back clear. Let's see what my pals from the *bunch* can do about that.

Looking at Joshua, I said,

'Just one more call.'

He didn't show any signs of comprehension, just sat there looking in my direction, his dark irises not missing a thing. I rang up *the Agency* in Berlin. Jacky was still on duty. I told her I'd be involved with the BND for a day or two in Europe, but I'd be checking in now and again. I knew Jack Orlowski would be fuming, but I have my priorities too and anyway, the RRT are already working on Ian and Martin's case. I stood up and said,

'Well that's that! I'll be leaving now.'

I made a move towards the door, but was interrupted by Joshua.

'Just a minute,' he said, his voice sounding ugly.

I decided my first impression was right – I didn't like him. He went over to where I'd been sitting and pressed a button on the side of the table. The telephone table descended out of sight leaving barely perceivable hairlines in the table furnish. He walked around me knocking me roughly on the arm as he went passed. He opened the door, just enough for him to check if the corridor was empty. He opened the door fully and turning to me said,

'Lets go.'

Definitely confirmation there was somebody on that floor I wasn't supposed to see.

I picked up my belongings from night security and left the building. That's funny, I thought, as I started to relax again. I was glad to get out of there this time. I've never had this feeling of apprehension before that I experienced in there this morning. Maybe it's because of Ian's death and Martin's disappearance. I would like to know who else was on that floor though. I could have made some more calls from there too but I don't like showing all my cards, not to MI6. I have a feeling my umbilical is just about chewed through!

It was high time I checked my mailbox and got some more help organised. My next stop is Chris Fenton's place, a few blocks from here. But first of all, let's check to see if I'm free of bugs or any other devious tracking devices. I took out my dummy hearing aid, flipped a side switch and ran the device over my bag and clothing. Sure enough, I found two devices. Some stupid MI6 academic wasting taxpayer's money I thought, as I threw them into the opened side door of a newspaper delivery van just turning my corner. I put my dummy hearing aid in a side pocket of my bag, thinking I won't need it anymore today.

I stopped at Bessborough Gardens next to some large bushes near a water fountain and gave Chris a call from my cell phone. He was in, and as always too polite to mention the early hour. I kept the call short – told him I was only a few metres away and I'd be there in a jiffy. He would know where I'd just been and something was up.

I heard the milkman pass down Bessborough Gardens on his round just as I reached Chris's house – one of a row of stately four and a half storey Georgian buildings, not counting the basements. The buildings were fronted by a low brick wall, clad five feet high with iron railings, coated with generations of black paint.

I took the steps up to the entrance in one go and entered an imposing pillared porch to be confronted by a massive black painted door dashed with plenty of polished brass. I noticed there was no direct means of entry to the basement.

A glimmer of light showed from a lamp above the front entrance. I chuckled to myself thinking of the probable CCTV-camera and Chris watching me now. I knocked lightly on the door with my knuckles. I thought using the impressive brass lion knob would wake the whole neighbourhood and some of them may just work off Vauxhall Bridge at MI6.

Villingen – Red Cross collection for Tuzla and Tula, Tuesday 16th August 2005

Hermann Schmidt, a very jovial, two metre, brawny Russian-German climbed out of his battered and rusty old VW-Passat and walked over to the warehouse ramp.

He had an over-sized paunch – the result of age, good food and not enough exercise, but mostly due to a hypertrophic liver caused by the Russian habit of drinking too much vodka.

Miss Karen Mai, a slim, but sturdy middle-aged German spinster, was standing on the ramp waiting for him. They shook hands.

'Hello Hermann, I trust you've been abstemious with alcohol the last few days. You know the checks on the border to Poland are very strict.'

'I just had a bottle of beer and a Vodka with my *Vesper* last night, Karen,' he said, grinning.

'I hope you don't mean a bottle of Vodka?' she returned, half-heartedly. Her look though, remaining critical.

'I'm only joking Karen. I've been on herb tea the last three days. You know I'd never endanger my job. Without my licence, that's it – I'm out of a job. Besides, I couldn't let you drive all the way now could I, even though you're as good a driver as I am,' he said, chuckling.

Hermann got a couple of bags from his boot and took them over to the lorry. He climbed into the driver's cabin of the heavy

Mercedes Benz Red Cross lorry used mainly for transporting relief goods. He stowed them away in the back compartment. He noticed Karen had already tidied it up a bit and stowed her bags. He hopped onto the ramp, went to the back of the lorry and undid the tarpaulin. He pulled out the stoppers and let the back down onto the Ramp.

'What are you undoing that for?' She cried.

He turned to Karen and replied,

'We loaded the last of the boxes from the Red Cross depot last night. Peter Jacobi says there's some last minute stuff here to load.'

'There's been a change of plan Hermann. We had a call yesterday. We can pick up some x-ray equipment from the Goldenbuehl hospital. Their move to Donau-Eschingen is now complete. They've newer x-ray equipment there, so they've decided to write-off the older equipment as a donation for the hospital in Tula. We can drop it off in Tula with the other donations.'

'What about customs? Isn't that a dangerous cargo?'

'That's already been cleared. The equipment has been dismantled and put in special boxes, so I've been told. We've added them to our cargo list.'

'Well, Miss Karen Mai, it's your risk. I just hope you've got enough spare cash for the customs people, just in case. You know how underpaid they are!'

'Let's go then Hermann,' she said, annoyed – hating it when Hermann digs her with Miss.

Hermann relocked the back and replaced some of the tarpaulin stoppers.

They left the old French barracks depot in the *Unterkirnacherstrasse* in Villingen where they had a temporary storehouse and arrived a few minutes later at the recently closed *Goldenbuehl Hospital.* Hermann drove straight through to goods delivery and backed up to the ramp.

Miss Mai got out and went looking for the caretaker. The building seemed completely deserted. She came back some minutes later. Her face was one big question mark.

'The caretaker is not here. I rang him up on my cell phone. He says the equipment was picked up last night by our organization. The two men said they'd been sent to pick up the x-ray equipment for Tula. They had a big lorry with the white circle and Red Cross in the middle, on each side. He said he'd no reason to doubt their identity. He didn't even ask for their credentials.'

'This looks bad, Karen. You know as well as I do, no other organisation in this area uses Red Cross lorries for carrying donation cargo. It's easy enough to make those big Red Cross stickers and stick them onto any lorry. Seems to me, someone else has pinched our stuff. This looks like a job for the CID (Kriminal Polizei).'

'I do believe you're right, Hermann.'

CID – Regional District SW Germany, Friday 19th August 2005 (Landeskriminalamt Stuttgart) – Special Operations Department – the phone is playing Yankee Doodle!

'Chief investigation officer Stahl speaking.'

Dieter Stahl, the chief officer, held the phone, listening. He looked irritated.

'You have a what?

Oh, I understand.

Look, why don't you send us a fax?

You thought it had a high priority did you – well I think

you'll have to leave that up to us to decide. Just send a fax to our headquarters.'

He put the telephone back rather viciously.

'What was all that about chief?' his second-in command asked.

'Oh, the police division at Villingen-Schwenningen report that x-ray machines designated for donation hospitals in Tuzla, Bosnia and Tula, in Russia were stolen from different locations over the last two months by what appears to me to be rivalry help organizations,' the chief answered.

'You know the directive about such items, Sir! We ought to inform the Federal Investigation Branch in Wiesbaden (Bundeskriminalamt), about this, don't you think so, Sir?' said his second-in command.

'No, I bloody well don't think so. I'm not going to make myself look ridiculous. Anyway its Friday afternoon, so let's not have our weekend spoiled, eh! Let's wait until Monday when they go through the faxes. Maybe some other ops leader can decide if he wants to follow this up or just file it.'

Chris Fenton – early Tuesday 16th August 2005

Chris opened the door, and without comment moved aside to let me in, shutting the door quickly behind me. I noticed a sheet of steel reinforcing the inside of the thick panelled door. Four cylindrical steel-rod shutting mechanisms impressed me. The door edges had security hinge bolts fitted to protect the door from being jemmied-up. From the outside it looked as though curtains were pulled over, covering the windows. From the inside however, a polished steel sheet was implanted. Judging by the wiring, an alarm system was installed, all in all making burglary very difficult indeed. This was the least to be expected. Chris used to work as technical support supervisor for counter-intelligence, counter-espionage and counter-terrorism units in the field. Anything you wanted, he could arrange it. Requisitioning was more like a game to him. Although we were never close friends he was one of the few people I trusted and one of the sturdiest members of the *bunch*.

After *donkeys'* years in the BIS, I'm now a freelance *Intelligence Analyst,* working semi-official as an international anti-terrorist specialist – a privileged civvy who's worked for the establishment for so long the umbilical chord seems indispensable. During the Cold War we knew our enemy and his *modus operandi.* It made things a damn sight easier then. I still have strong ties and haven't lost a general feeling of *esprit' de corps.* After the golden handshake I couldn't settle down. Once you've been in the business as many years as I have, without much time for hobbies, retirement is difficult. Fortunately a reunion with my old *bunch* was due just as I was thinking about taking up some sort of hobby. They are a cuddle-muddle from various British intelligence agencies, including some ex-SAS, ex-Para's and ex-Marine commandos. We formed a club some decades ago and meet in an Expatriate club near Charing Cross at least once a year. Chris pops in occasionally, but keeps much to himself. They've become very much my family these days, a few of the founder members like Martin Cole, in particular. He put me on to a consortium called the International Security Intelligence Agency, ISIA, formed in December 2001 after the WTC, 9/11 – disaster. An organization supported by the USA and Britain and a few EU countries with some offices in European capitals and Washington. France and Germany were the only countries who wouldn't join. They were not against the ISIA operating in their countries though. In actual fact they were reasonably supportive on the financial side.

The last two years I've been working as CEO for Germany in Berlin. My operating theatre is Central Europe, mainly Germany. At first I wasn't too pleased to find an American as the Director General for Europe, *Jack Orlowski* – it's his southern drawl too.

I had Queen's English elocution lessons before leaving Scotland for a posh school in Tunbridge Wells as a young lad. I still like my *Robert Burns* brogue though that I turn to on occasion, usually whenever Jack's drawl gets so slow I can't remember the start of his dialogue. He seems to have gotten the message, though. If he drops out the flunkey bits, I get the meaning without yawning or falling asleep.

Maybe he has a general problem? I've noticed the occasional stutter when he's trying hard to keep his sentences short or perhaps there's another reason?

Sadly, the reunions have slowly diminished. The *bunch* is decimating much faster as the years go by. Being a holder of some of the biggest secrets in the country I never let my hair down with any company other than with the lads in the *bunch* and even then I'm still cautious!

Chris moved on through the room, that apart from the steel sheeted windows and door, seemed to be a comfortable waiting room, with a fireplace, a big thick carpet, a long coffee table and sofa with side chairs taking up the rest of the room. A fair sized flat screen was hanging on the wall facing the windows and a beautiful Chinese carved rosewood table took up the window corner with the obligatory Chinese lamp on top. Some paintings of London buildings, the Thames and photos of various security systems covered the wall leading to the corridor.

We went through a door on the left into a corridor leading on towards the back. We passed stairs going upwards on the left. Chris took the next door on the right leading us down some steps to the basement and into a scullery. Just inside, on the right, was one of those huge fridges, that years ago, you only got to see in the States, and don't expect in a small and narrow British scullery. Nowadays, they are very much on sale in the UK. Chris opened the fridge door and pressed a button at the side, a small piece of plastic that looked like ornamentation covering a hole.

He closed the fridge door. Mechanisms moved and the fridge slid backwards on rails about 2 metres. The whole process only took a few seconds. Chris pressed a switch on his way into the gap left by the fridge. A light came on and I could see him moving to the left and downwards. Probably going under the front room, I thought. I followed him in. Chris was waiting on the top of some steps. He pulled a lever on the side of the stairs and the fridge moved back into its old position. He shoved a locking lever over the main lever without saying a word. That told me, nobody else could gain entry through the fridge. Down another thirty or so steps and a brief walk along a bricked tunnel then to the right and up another five steps. By my judgment we were under Bessborough Park Gardens. The hideout is probably an old shelter, a leftover from the battle of Britain, I thought. We entered Chris's safe rooms.

Only then did Chris turn around and grin, saying,

'Nice to see you John – what business brings you here at such an early hour? Don't tell me – got ourselves into trouble with the establishment again have we, eh?'

Chris has a weird sense of humour. But the way he just said

that reminded me of the immeasurable confidence I always had, using him as a back up. I didn't have to ask him outright, because I wouldn't be here really for any other reason. I just murmured,

'Aye, Chris, sorry about the early hour.'

Chris ignored my last remark.

'Well – you had breakfast yet? No you ain't, so we'll just get something organised before business, eh, mate, all right! I'll have some eats too, I think.'

'Yes, thanks Chris – I'll not argue with you on that. I could do with a cuppa and a bite to eat.'

Chris opened a cupboard door, where he extracted a mike and gave his instructions for breakfast.

He turned back to me saying more than asking,

'Like our eggs sunny side up don't we John, and crispy bacon was it?'

Chris has an excellent memory. I replied,

'Good memory Chris, yes thanks.'

He passed on my preferences, put the mike back in, and shut the cupboard door. Turning to me with a big grin on his blessed round cockney face he said,

'Let's sit at the table John, looks like we've got a lot to talk about 'ain't we.'

Leipzig – Tuesday 16th August 2005

Moshe Jacobs, who owns a Jeweller's shop in Leipzig and a friend of Golda Stern, Martha Stern's Grandmother, was reading the obituaries, one of the first pages of the daily newspaper he reads. He called out loud as he came across Martha's name.

'Not Martha,' he shouted.

Moshe's wife Sarah rushed into the dining room from the kitchen wiping her hands on her apron.

'What is it, what's the matter?'

'It's Golda's niece Martha, she's dead.'

'Oh, no. She's so young. What's happened?'

'It says here her life has been taken – that means she's been murdered. How many times did I tell her not to mouth her opinions out loud.'

'You and your suspicious nature – how do you know it was intended?'

He ignored her question.

'It says here the funeral's tomorrow. Look, you speak to the family more than I do, why don't you ring up and find out?'

Sarah looked at him reproachfully. Her eyes were saying, *"always me having to do the dirty work."*

Paula, a distant relative, answered the phone. Moshe listened while Sarah expressed her condolences to Paula, saying they would both be there tomorrow and asking what had happened. He nodded to himself where he thought he heard confirmation of his first thoughts as his wife has the habit of repeating things people say.

Sarah put the phone down. She was quite pale – visibly shaken.

'You were right Moshe, she was murdered, stabbed by an assassin yesterday at the Leipzig Monday demonstration. She was standing amongst the Jewish delegation. They were a group of mostly elderly Jews, so she must have been killed deliberately. They haven't found the killer yet. Paula says Martha's being buried tomorrow morning. Her body is in the morgue and you know how the mills of the justice department grind here! They won't release the body until tomorrow. No respects for Jewish traditions!'

Rottweil, Germany – the door to the Swabian Alps and the Black Forest – early evening 16th August 2005,

The taxi-driver creased his face, just the touch of a smile. I saw him watching me approach his vehicle in the taxi-queue at *Rottweil* railway station without moving an eyelid. The bugger didn't budge either. Not a sign of subservience – of good customer service, I thought.

I got into the cream coloured limousine and shoved my bag over the back seat.

'Guten Abend!' said the driver, *'Wo soll's denn hin gehen?'*

Judging by the broad accent, I put him down as a *Black Forest* local, a big well-fed German. I returned his good evening in fluent German. On his question of *where to,* I gave him my destination. I set my *don't want to talk to you face*, buckled my seat belt and settled back in the seat. At the same time I analysed what I'd just done and decided it was all a waste of effort, 'cause *Black Forest* men are not renowned for being garrulous anyway. To pass time I let my mind go – reiterating the incident. Maybe he was a foreigner? A lot of them keep you immersed in conversation so you don't notice them taking the longest possible route – acceptable on occasions when you're after information. The most serendipitous sources for information are Turkish and Italian taxi drivers. This one seems to be an original. I wouldn't ask his name though – be disappointed – probably Lenin or Skrypinski. A real *Black Forester* wouldn't be working as a taxi driver anyway. I felt satisfied with my conclusion.

I turned my head away from the front windscreen. The one and a half hour flight from Heathrow to Stuttgart-Echterdingen was comfortable enough in the business class seats. Glad too, there weren't so many air pockets. The subsequent transfer to the city with the *S-Bahn* and the train journey to Rottweil were illuminating. Gave me the opportunity to acclimatize. Take on a low profile, that's my motto – just be one of them – a grey man.

No queues here! Just elbow work, stares, and retaining the urge to remonstrate. May the strongest survive! Staring is common in Germany. Not a place for individuals suffering from an overdose of self-consciousness though, and definitely not very ideal when you're on close surveillance either. I imagined them staring like that in *Glasgow* or any other place in the UK, come to think of it. Probably why a lot of German male tourists find themselves in a punch-up in the UK without ever having said a word. A single German male is almost quiet, nearly timid and generally acceptable. In a group most of them are nauseating, loud and have the tendency to bully other people around, so the majority of 'em get what they deserve anyway. It comes mostly from their upbringing. It's usually the mothers who are left with this task – so German kids are allowed to do almost everything and that means they make as much noise as they like. They have the tendency to be socially collective, not leaving much room for individuality. Such traits are rewarded to outsiders or to those who rise above the others distinctively.

My eyes were dry and getting sore, and my stomach and intestines were playing a slow rumbling tune. I hope it wasn't the ham and egg salad sandwich with mayonnaise I had at lunchtime?

I gave an inward chuckle as a childhood memory interrupted my thoughts: *Sitting next to Dad in the front seat of the old Morris Minor, the smell of real leather dominating. Dear old Dad, cursing the weather and all the other drivers who ought not to be behind the steering-wheel of a car then blowing his head off at me for daring to fart in his car.*

It was useless trying to single-out these hailstones, I thought. They were big and flying in like bullets, hitting the windscreen and bonnet with the rapid percussion of machine-gun fire. When bullets came that fast, there was no escaping their deadliness.

It was quiet and peaceful in the car. I felt safe for the moment. The deep purring of the Mercedes diesel eventually lulled out the battering sound of the hailstones and the swishing of the wiper. I was tired anyway and dosed off for a while, my thoughts going back to my previous visit here a few years ago.

The taxi driver guided the car around the countless bends of the slippery mountainous road, casually using thumb and forefinger to move the steering wheel. His right buttock seemed to spill over onto the middle console, lying there wobbling. No wonder he didn't get out of the car to help me at the station. Despite his bulk, he manoeuvred the rear-wheel driven Mercedes with perfection. Even with the weather and the bends it was a fairly comfy drive.

The darkened sky and black clouds seemed like a herald of worse things to come. I'm sure it would've been less menacing under different circumstances.

Buchenberg was my destination for the night. It brought up thoughts of the concentration camp *Buchenwald.* What a daft meander, but again, maybe that's just how I'm feeling right now. This time, something deep has registered in my *database* – over 30 years of experience in the field and too many pointers. My antenna is red-hot, saying – *watch your back!* Brushing these floods of foreboding aside, my old pal *stomach* reminded me of the good food at the *Guesthouse,* where I'll be staying for the night.

We had no sooner arrived in what seemed the start of a village when the taxi stopped. *'Wir sind da – Café Rapp,'* said the driver.

I paid the driver off, giving him the ten percent tip expected in Germany. I picked up my bag from the back seat and walked briskly towards the café. Hopping over the front steps and entering the hall, I opened the door on the left leading into the *Café Restaurant Rapp.*

Buchenberg is a small-scattered village with ca. 1000 inhabitants. The café is also the bakery and cake shop. That part is slightly separated from the Restaurant. I had recollections of the food. An *epicure de Gourmet* would find reasonable satisfaction. The counter, also the Reception, was on the right behind the door.

A bell rang as I opened the door. I popped my head around the corner checking out the counter. Frau Rapp, who was standing behind it, broke into a big smile as she recognised me. The sight of her pleasant face and reddened cheeks made me feel welcome. She waved a hand, wiped her right hand on her apron and reaching up, lifted a set of keys down from the cupboard in the corner. She moved out around the counter towards me. I was still standing half in half out, so I moved back into the hallway.

'Mister Jameson, ah, it's been a long time, so it has. Welcome back, welcome back,' she said, as she came out, beaming all over her face. She gave me her hand, shook it, and pulled me towards her, giving me a big long hug. She let go and pushed me back a bit, like I was her little boy, although we're both about the same age and she's still a very attractive woman. For a moment she looked into my f ace reading the signs. A sadness crept over her countenance.

'Ah, but you are alone. It is so sad,' she said in English,

'Your poor wife! We thought you would never come here again. But you do not want to grieve. Let us not talk of these things. I have given you a different room. It has a beautiful view over the valley and is very spacious – here is the key. Will you be dining here tonight?'

'Yes, thanks a lot Frau Rapp – it's nice to see you again too. You're looking really well. I'll certainly not miss the chance of your husband's good cooking.'

She interrupted him.

'My son does the cooking now, he is a *star chef* you know!'

'Ah, excellent,' I replied.

'I might be having guests but I'm not quite sure. I'll have to make a call first. I'll let you know.'

'Of course, Mister Jameson – what time do you think?'

'It's 7 pm now, let's say in about an hour, at 8 pm.'

'You know tonight's dance night? We have a one-man band. He plays on the Hammond. He's very good. Has a good voice too. You will like it because he sings lots of oldies too. We get many guests from health clinics in Koenigsfeld.'

'In that case I think it'd be wiser to have a table away from the music?'

'Certainly! Until later then Mister Jameson – enjoy your stay.'

'Yes, thanks very much,' I said.

I left her in the hall watching me like a mother as I made my way through the other door leading to the stairs and the guest rooms. The room was as she'd described – spacious and friendly. Flowers were arranged on the round table in the middle of the room. The room smelt fresh and welcoming. The balcony door was ajar and I could hear the jangle of cowbells from the pasture – each one with a different tone, echoing across the small valley. A variety of birds were chirping and singing. Thrushes seemed to dominate, their sounds carried across the valley and through the forests of pine trees to others some distance away that, in turn, took up the singing. Most probably marking their areas or glad the storm was over and happy the worms are now wriggling their way near the surface. The clouds have receded and given way to sunshine and a bright blue sky, it really feels like the world outside has just been reborn.

I don't usually let emotions take control but a bit more moisture than usual crept into my eyes. It all came over me again, remembering how it was last time I was here. Perhaps I should have stopped over-night in Villingen instead.

I was on an MI6 job working together with the German Secret Service (BND). Olaf Ertl was my liaison man. We worked together on and off for over a year. Olaf had recommended the area here for its quietness and beauty. The nature walks, villages and culture, not to mention the solitude despite the numerous hikers, who seem to be swallowed up into the multitude of paths through forest and vale. I got to know the huge area well with my wife Anna. We also became good friends with Olaf and his family.

It was just over two and a half years ago! My wife and I were enjoying a week's break hiking in the hills above Schoenwald and this beautiful part of the Black Forest. Anna took the car on our final day to Schwenningen to do some last minute shopping in the mall. I hate shopping so I let her go on her own. A hit and run driver killed her just outside the town centre as she walked across a pedestrian crossing. Witnesses said the driver must have seen her but didn't stop or make attempts to drive around her. The police never managed to catch him. They got the car but that had been stolen. Olaf tried his own investigation using strong connections but nothing came of it. It made no sense. I guess that was one of the reasons I took early retirement. My life became a total vacuum in the aftermath of Anna's death. The searing ache remained for many months. Some say I'd never mourned enough. Others told me to let go, but something inside has held all that back – unfinished business!

There are four mills here, two of which still operate. I rang up the one in question from my room.

'*Ja!*' said a voice at the other end.

'Hallo Olaf, John here,' I said in German.

'John! Am I glad to hear your voice again.'

I heard relief but also a touch of anxiety. I put on my matter of fact voice knowing Olaf would get the message.

'Look Olaf, I've promised Frau Rapp I'll be eating here tonight, so why don't you join me, we can talk about old times then. I'm afraid I'm only on a stopover.'

'John, I think you'd better start without me – I've already eaten. I'll come over later. What time are you dining?'

'About eight-o-clock?'

'Yes, all right – will it be okay if I bring my sister with me? She can drive me home if I drink too much. The police are very strict here nowadays.'

'Yes, certainly, I'd be delighted to see her again. See you later then, bye.'

I hung up not waiting for a reply. That's usual in my business. Olaf knows I don't chatter on the phone – he doesn't either.

I had a long bathroom session – loosening the stress and gathering my thoughts whilst having a long shower and a meticulous shave. I put on fresh underwear and light clothing. It's informal here so I thought slacks and a short-sleeved shirt without a tie would be okay. Feeling just fine and relaxed, I slung a jacket over my shoulder just in case. The nights can cool down quickly here, which is ideal in summer. The village is about 900m above sea level and has 6 to 7 months winter and a fairly hot summer. Lots of snow and skiing in winter, mostly langlauf – thinking of the times I'd been here with Anna.

I took my seat at the table. There were still a lot of empty tables in the restaurant. That's good. I like being able to register what's going on.

The waitress was new, young and very friendly. I ordered a bottle of *Maerzen* beer to still my thirst, remembering the German rule for drinking:

'*Wein auf Bier das rat' ich Dir, Bier auf Wein das laß' sein.*'

Meaning, wine after beer is ok, but beer after wine is not – otherwise a hangover is a certainty. *Maerzen,* a difficult word to remember, is the nearest I can get to *lager* beer. The German *Pils* is a bit too bitter for my taste. I had a look through the menu. It never takes me long to order – always a matter of principle. Has a lot to do with the job – trying not to miss a thing that's going on. It also pleases the *maitre d'hôtel*.

I decided on a *1998 Chardonnay, Delle Venezie* to go with the *hors-d'œvre: Slightly smoked Scottish salmon, slightly smoked fresh trout from Lake Constance laced with fresh horse-radish sauce, crab in cocktail sauce and garnished with various fresh salads served with freshly baked farmer's bread.*

For the *main course* I decided on:

Oven-roasted breast of goose slightly pink in the middle with a light brown sauce, served with croquettes and fresh French beans. A 1999 Bischoffinger Enselsberg Spaetburgunder went down well with that.

The meal was light and I have to do some talking afterwards, so I thought I'd better not overdo it by ordering the apple-strudel with vanilla custard for dessert that I'd had in mind.

I spied Olaf and Elsa coming around the corner towards me. It was an embarrassing moment. I tried putting on my best smile but I wasn't much of an actor tonight. I stood up pushing my chair back and moved into the open to greet them. Once they got nearer I noticed grief and pain in their faces. I knew it wasn't for my sake.

Elsa took my hand and moved into the hug I offered her, but her body seemed stiff. I also noticed she wasn't dressed up as elegant as she used to, just slacks and a t-shirt. She clasped my upper arm and with a voice full of expectation said,

'I'm ever so glad you came John.'

Her grip was strong and meaningful – a beautiful one metre seventy slender woman. Her eyes met mine briefly, wide and open. She seemed like a little blue-eyed blond ..., I thought for a moment. Yes, like a Barbie doll – breakable! Her features though, just as perfect as Angelina Jolie's. She let go and moved aside – her cheeks flushing like an overdose of rouge.

Olaf came forward, his right hand grabbed mine and his left closed in on my elbow. The whole arm was shaken, up and down. He said, in a deep baritone voice – a pleasant one to hear,

'John, you don't know how glad we are you've come. Something terrible has happened.'

'Let's sit down first, shall we,' I said.

After we'd taken seats there was a difficult pause that I tried to break. I said,

'Look, it seems like we've got a lot to talk about. I didn't realize a Hammond organ could be so loud. We ought to move elsewhere. I've finished eating. What about upstairs – in the lounge if it's free or in my room? I've checked the room out for bugs – it's clean. What do you think?'

'Okay, John – we can't really talk freely here.'

'Right, I'll just get this lot put on my tab and give the waitress a tip. What about drinks? Something hot, or soft drinks?'

'John, I don't like interrupts, so I'll order something up front and we'll take it up with us, okay?'

'Yes, okay, but put it on my tab.'

There seemed too much coming and going when we got upstairs, so we decided on my room.

Elsa made for the *pouffe* and Olaf and I got settled in the two wicker armchairs. I offered to fetch another chair from the lounge but Elsa said she didn't mind.

'Let's all have a drink first. Olaf, want something stronger?' I asked. He nodded.

'I've brought a nice Scottish whisky from Oban,' I added.

'Yes, that'll be fine, John.'

'What about you, Elsa?'

'Rather not, John – I'm driving. I'll stick to my tea.'

I poured out two whiskeys whilst Elsa lifted the white teapot from the tray and poured herself a cuppa.

'Just a touch of water to let the flavour out?' I looked at Olaf raising my eyebrows questioningly.

'Yes, thanks John.'

After adding a touch of water to the whisky glasses, I sat back and let the whisky gain full flavour for a few seconds before lifting my glass slightly in their direction. Nodding, I took a sip. Olaf did likewise. Elsa cracked her lips politely. I cupped the glass in my hands.

'Okay,' I said, 'first of all let me put you both in the picture. I'm sorry I haven't spoken to you since Anna's funeral. To tell the truth, I've been trying to forget this place and everyone involved – that's the truth. The whole thing put an end to my career because I started getting weak. So I quit early. You remember Martin Cole? Well he put me on to the ISIA, you may have heard about them Olaf.'

'Yes, I have.'

'Well, I'm with them now on a regular basis, as are many ex-pats.'

They both looked at me quizzically – expecting more information. I thought that's enough about me to start with. I took another sip. Looking serious at both of them I bent forward putting my glass back on the table and said,

'Okay, folks! What's the score your end?'

'I hope I didn't cause you too much inconvenience by going through the official channels, John. I didn't know where you were. We got your last two Christmas cards but there was no return address – typical British, if you don't mind me saying so. You remember my nephew Hans?'

'Yes, I do. He's your son Elsa?' I looked at her for confirmation. She nodded. Olaf continued speaking,

'He's been studying law and has a thing about the Middle East. I've been pushing him to follow in my footsteps in the

BND once he finishes, but he's not made up his mind yet. Just over a year and a half ago he started studies at Damascus University learning Arabic during term holidays. Two months ago he went back to do advanced studies. He should have returned a week last Saturday. That's eleven days he's overdue. I rang up our Embassy in Damascus. I was told the class finished and broke up last Friday week the 6th August. Most of the students left the country.

'Have you checked the airlines?'

'Yes, but he never showed up. It looks like he hasn't left the country. But no one knows where he is. The Embassy sent someone to check his digs. The landlady could tell them nothing. He's just disappeared.'

'Did he give any inclination in his emails or calls, that he was going elsewhere?'

'No, but the landlady's son says Hans told him he was being followed. I thought that was maybe Syrian Intelligence, but my Embassy have contacted them. They deny any involvement.'

Elsa interrupted,

'Tell John about the letter to Robert!'

'Ah, yes,' said Olaf, 'there is something else that came up about Hans. I asked one of his old school friends, Robert Feldhausen, if he had any news from Hans, because Elsa said they meet now and then when Hans comes home on his holidays. He said he received a letter from Hans that may help us further. The funny thing though, the letter's not from Syria. It's stamped and posted from *Tyre* in the Lebanon. He also said he thought the context was strange, not like Hans at all. Hans writes in his letter too about things they've never talked about before. I've brought along a copy for you. Maybe you should read it before we carry on. I'd like to hear your opinion. It could be important.'

Olaf handed me the letter, which I read through twice.

Dear Robert,

I'm on my second time round at Damascus University now. Learning advanced Arabic is intensive and much more difficult than the previous university training courses. My written language and theory are above average though, especially on political subjects, but my colloquialisms remain below average – still, I do try my utmost. It was the same with the 'th' and 'wh' in English at school.

Remember your words before I came to Damascus the first time! No girls – or girls wrapped-up and guarded! Well, wait until you read this!

This time I'm not the only German. A tall blond girl with perfectly formed breasts, called Frieda Schulz from Munich, turned up on her first day in a very tight leather skirt, the cleavage of her breasts more than visible. The eyes of a few gaffers rolling over – you could see their imagination carrying them away. Maybe they were hoping she would get nervous, then breathe heavily, whereby perhaps her nipples would jump out and wave in greeting! I reckon she's at least one ninety tall. Her legs are really long, so long and smooth, 'right up to her neck', or so it seems, the skirt hardly covering her crutch. The sight of her beautifully rounded bottom, bare(ly) covered with a g-string, was absolutely damaging to all males when she went forward to write her name on the blackboard. She dropped the chalk, seemingly on purpose and bent down very slowly to pick it up. Wow! I can still see the image, especially the indentation of her pussy. Unfortunately, she's the type to look at from a slight distance, because the heinously high cheekbones, the extenuated nose and very bronzed tan (probably all over) spoil the picture a bit. She looks well trained, so I don't know what else she has up her sleeve. I wouldn't like those legs around my neck though!

One of the Brits, Ian Ferguson, commented on her appearance, just loud enough to be heard in our corner of class, calling her 'a toasted tart'. I thought that was a bit rough. Couldn't help being amused though.

I think our Syrian teacher Fatima was quite upset about Frieda's appearance as I caught the words `something less dégagé and please to cover your arms, legs and neck...' as I left class for the lunch-break on that first day.

Now I've got to know her a bit better, I would describe her as a nasty piece of work. As a German I feel ashamed.

I won't bore you with too much data on the rest of the crowd, except to mention the nationalities: two Germans, two Brits, one Dutchman, two Koreans, one from the North who always wears uniform and boasts about being a real Korean and an easy going Western type from the South. A handful of tight-lipped Asians (Indonesians, Malaysians), an American girl called Sheila Simpson (poor copy of Cameron Diaz) and three Jews who keep well apart from the rest. Under normal circumstances I would classify them as arrogant, but there again, being in Syria as a Jew must be a very tightening experience. So I guess I'll excuse their attitude.

My main concern is Frieda. She's become outwardly hostile toward the Jews. She seems to be supported in her views by the Dutchman Henrich van Gelders. They both have this thing about Arian purity. Although she appears to be intelligent she is utterly ignorant. She is loud and vulgar. I gather she spent most of her youth with the Right Wing Vikinger Jugend. She is engaged as a journalist with the Bayern Nachrichten (Bavarian News) in Munich and says her studies at Augsburg university involved Social Sciences and Germanistic. I cannot imagine her motives for learning Arabic though.

I tried to break the ice with the youngest Jew, talking about jobs after studying is over. I said something about employment – if there are no jobs in Israel. I told him the CIA would welcome him with open arms as they are in desperate need of human intelligence resources. He was visibly shaken. He replied very nervously, looking around all the time, never again to use such syllables here in Syria as the Syrian Secret Service are very sensitive regarding Americans and their various intelligence organizations. Anyway, he said, they hold continuous surveillance over each and every member of the class. So I guess I got a little titbit from that conversation! Have to keep my nose clean, eh!!

This weekend I'll be staying with the family of Achmed's aunt. Her husband, Hussein is a retired Syrian Army Brigadier. I can imagine the topics once again being chess, combined with battles of war and good old Carl.

Well, Robert it's time for a shave at the barber's, a stop-in at the café for fresh strawberries, fresh almonds, a mint tea and perhaps I'll read a bit of Lewis.

Regards to all
Your Hans Ertl

'Hm. There could be some pointers here, I'll have to think about them, so let's just put that aside for the moment.'

I noticed their anxiety and didn't want to say what I thought – Europeans were being abducted by Arab extremists who threatened to behead them if their mother countries didn't prevent their involvement in Iraq – but Germany has no involvement, so there must be a different reason.

'I know what you're thinking John. We've both thought about abduction too.'

'Yes, but Hans is German – that can't be the reason.'

'I've talked earnestly with Elsa, who thinks there may be something but she doesn't know how it could involve Hans. She's never talked to anyone about it before.'

I looked at Elsa. She moved her legs out straight then pulled them in, seemingly embarrassed. Leaning forward she pulled her arms around her knees. She talked about her time in a Kibbutz after she left college – she spent six months near Haifa where she became infatuated with one of the boys. It was her misfortune she didn't use contraceptives. She became pregnant. Hans was born in Germany. She never told Hans or anyone else who the father was. When she stopped her story I said,

'Someone may have told Hans. Maybe he's gone looking for him.'

Elsa looked up – her face was burning.

'That's not possible,' she cried, 'nobody knows, not even his father.'

'Yes, but maybe his father found him through you. That wouldn't have been too difficult. All he'd have to do is check the date of birth and then bingo!'

'But why on earth would he do that?' asked Elsa.

'Well, he knows your full name and may have come across Hans' surname in Damascus or through the Jews in his Arabic class.'

'Good God – I never even thought about that,' said Elsa.

'Elsa told me the name of Hans's father, Kenneth Woodward,' said Olaf, 'I've put his name through the channels.'

'What was the result?'

'We got a hit. The age was right and he was in the Kibbutz at the same time as Elsa.'

'What's he do for a living?'

'You're not going to like this – he's with an Israeli government agency, we're not quite sure but we suspect the Mossad.'

For a moment, I was sitting on another planet looking at this room through a glass ball. My mind was soaring. Olaf interrupted my thoughts.

'I know you've had dealings with them John. I thought maybe your connections might bring more light. I know you may not want to. Maybe it may be digging up too many ghosts of the past for you. But I remember Anna's story. I know it's some time ago, but perhaps Anna's half-brother Ben can help. What do you say?'

'I've never talked much about Anna's family before, she didn't want to either – something about skeletons in the closet. You know Anna was Jewish and I'm a Roman Catholic. Well, the feeling I got, was, they would never let me forget that fact. Her half-brother Ben said he was in the Israeli Diplomatic Corps, or was the last I knew a few years back. He never forgave me for marrying her. He also holds me responsible for her death. He wouldn't tell me the reason why he thought so. He is a strong believer in the Jewish faith. I thought he was a bit radical in his views. There was something odd about him, as though he was deliberately hiding something. But there again I get that feeling with a lot of Jews. I think I'm a fairly good judge of character and remember putting him down as someone not to cross or trust. Ben seems to dislike me, more or less told me so. I've never quite understood why he could possibly consider me such a danger for her. I wasn't that important in the intelligence scene.'

'John, I think it's high time you did some straight talking with Ben,' said Olaf.

'I think so too – arranging it could be awkward though.'

The mention of Kenneth Woodward kept buzzing me, which probably showed.

'What's up, John?' asked Olaf.

I looked at Olaf still thinking – putting in name, time and place. It took a few seconds before I answered.

'It's very strange you mentioning Kenneth Woodward a few moments ago, it brought a sudden memory from childhood days.'

'Oh, please tell us what it was,' said Elsa, her face blushing again as she caught herself – perhaps being too nosy.

'Yes, very strange coincidence – reminds me of my childhood in Dundee. My best friend for over a year was called Robert Woodward who lived a couple of houses away at number 17, Blantyre Place. We were the same age. He had an elder brother called Kenneth. What a coincidence. Funny thing is, they were both Jews too. I didn't know what it really meant. It was only when other kids started shouting names and threw stones at them I knew they were the Jews Father Brown, our religion teacher at school, told us, had crucified Christ, not that it made any difference to me. I was the only kid in the area that stood up for them – I threw the stones back. Unfortunately they moved to America soon after. Since then I guess it strengthened my judging people by character and insides and not from any labelling. I became a bit more canny over the years and became very choosy with whom I termed as *friend*.'

'That's very moving John,' said Elsa.

I brushed away her softened comment, adding,

'My thoughts keep coming back to the letter Hans sent to his friend Robert. Did Robert have anything else to say?' I asked.

'Well, I'm afraid there was nothing much more he could add. Robert thinks Hans was in some way concerned but definitely not scared. After his first studies in Damascus he did mention other students telling him Syrian Intelligence were vetting their telephone calls and mail. He also said that he, Robert, had never said anything about girls to Hans at all. The bit about long legs up to her neck was a bit unusual for Hans too, he said. In fact the whole description of the girl and other information puzzled him,' replied Elsa.

'Well, that gives us somewhere to start. What was your analysis Olaf?'

'The letter being posted in *Tyre* tells us that Hans, knowing Syrian Intelligence were vetting their mail and other communications, didn't want the letter to be intercepted. Maybe he gave the letter to someone else to post outside Syria, but only because he felt it was otherwise dangerous.'

'What we also know is, Hans knows you're ex-BND, so he'd count on you contacting Robert eventually if anything happened to him. Hence the indirect hints in his letter,' I said, adding, 'Did you give the words *'right up to her neck'* any consideration?'

'Yes, we did. We thought Hans was just telling us he really knew she was trouble,' replied Olaf.

'But, couldn't he also have meant she was planning something important enough to investigate further – like right up to her neck in bad business, meaning deeply involved?' I added.

'Maybe,' answered Olaf.

'I think from what Robert tells us the latter is most probable,' I said.

'Anyway, I had some checks done on the names mentioned,' replied Olaf, 'and we came up with the following:

The girl, *Frieda Schulz,* has quite a record. A nasty piece of work. She's a real Nazi – been charged and sentenced for disorder, assault and manslaughter. She spent six months in a correction facility in Augsburg at the age of 16. She did two and a half years of a four-year sentence as an accomplice for manslaughter charges at the age of seventeen. The Nazi gang she was with, chased and beat-up an African student just for fun. They left him lying in the gutter critically injured. He died subsequently from multiple injuries. According to other members of the gang, she was the one who did most of the kicking and stamping. She caught up on her education in prison and went straight to university whilst out on probation, where she actually did get her degrees in Social Sciences and Germanistic. Both her parents are in the Nazi movement in Germany. Her father is a leading member of a Right Wing political party called the NSPD. She spent most of her childhood with the Right Wing *Viking Youth Movement*. She hates Jews maniacally and blacks or ethnic minorities in general. We don't have any information on the Brit, *Ian Ferguson*. Maybe you could help here. Perhaps he knows something. The Dutchman, *Henrich van Gelders* is a member of a Right Wing movement in Holland. It's possible he knows *Frieda Schulz* from childhood days with the *Viking Youth Movement*. The American girl, *Sheila Simpson*, is a language expert. She's a linguist in French and Spanish and works freelance in Brussels. She doesn't belong to any organization and has no record, at least not apparent under that name. Well that about sums up our brief analysis,' said Olaf.

'What about the three Jews? Hans doesn't mention them by name, although he describes them in a somewhat suspicious manner,' I asked.

'We did think about that but have nothing to go on. Maybe *Ian Ferguson* can put more light on that matter,' replied Olaf.

'Two other people we need to talk to are *Achmed* and his uncle. That's going to be the most difficult bit. It means someone's got to go to Damascus. I think that person should be you Olaf. As you are Han's uncle I don't think you should have any problems getting a visa, that is if you need one nowadays.'

'Yes, John – Elsa and I had thought about that, but I wanted to talk to you before I left. There would be a problem from my old firm, not letting me go if I went forward officially. So I'll have to go about the whole thing privately and discreetly without involving them. That's why Elsa and I thought maybe you could help us.'

'Well, to me it sounds as though Hans is telling us outright he's in trouble.'

I pushed my chair back – looked at both of them seriously and spoke – feeling a touch of tiredness creeping into my voice.

'This is not going to be easy. We've a lot of work to do. I think you should get to Damascus as soon as possible, Olaf. I have to go on to Berlin tomorrow. I haven't told you yet but you remember Ian Stewart, Olaf?'

'Yes, I do.'

'Well, he was taken out in Berlin by a professional killer the day before yesterday. He was on a job with Martin Cole who is now missing.'

'Oh, no! John, why didn't you say something before? I mean, you have your own problems to worry about!'

'Look, Martin's an old hat, either he's dead or he's gone underground for reasons we don't know and until we find out why, I think finding Hans is more important. Ian's killer won't go unpunished, believe you me.'

Elsa slid off the *pouffe* onto her knees and in a burst of emotion, took hold of my left hand. Her other hand rested on my arm.

'Oh, John,' she said, her voice choking.

'I hope we can find Hans. I know he's still alive, I can feel it.'

'Look, Elsa. Let's be honest with each other. I can't make any promises, but Olaf and I know if we all work together and do all we can, then we'll find Hans. I know it's expecting a lot but you know the business Olaf and I were involved in. There's no room for emotions, it blinds and worst of all it can get you killed. What we have to do is try and think clearly without getting worked up. Olaf and I will be in different places, so we'll need a contact person, especially whilst Olaf is in the Middle East. I suggest you be that person. Get a friend to buy you a cell phone and for Christ's sake don't let it be registered under your name.'

'Why do we have to go to all this secretiveness?'

'Elsa, why do you think Hans sent Robert such a letter through the Lebanon instead of Syria? There could be more to this and that's why we can't afford any risks whatsoever. What do you say, Olaf?'

'Yes, I agree entirely what John has said. I would also say to you dear sister – not a word about anything to anyone, even if they come forward as friends of yours or ours. This is something between the three of us and could be a matter of life or death for either Hans or ourselves.'

'Another thing too, Elsa,' I said, 'Olaf and I ought to ring in on a daily basis. I suggest 16.00 hrs for Olaf and 16.30 hrs for myself – GMT – add an hour on for German time Elsa. Otherwise we'll try again every four hours thereafter. No calls after 1 am, or in my case 1.30 am – the next call at 16.00. If neither Olaf nor myself have called in by the third afternoon then here is the number of a good friend in London. He'll then call out a rescue team. Oh, and don't forget to give him your cell phone number. I'll give him a ring and pass on the meeting details – I've spoken to him early this morning. He doesn't know about Hans yet but he's been alerted for any possible back up I may require regarding Ian. We need a fairly neutral meeting place, somewhere a lot of people frequent. I think I know a good spot. How about the entrance to the water falls in Triberg at 11 am the following day after the call to London? With the entrance behind you, stand to the right looking towards the road as though you're waiting for someone, which you are of course. I expect there will be two of them, but only one will contact you. He will ask you the way to the two mills. You'll answer – you mean the four mills? No, the two mills, he'll reply. That way you'll know he's the right man. Tell him that's in the same direction you were going to go anyway, so you'll show him the way. You should be wearing a black blouse and black trousers with a white scarf around your neck. If no one comes, then leave after ten minutes. Go and have a coffee somewhere near or do some window-shopping. Try again an hour and a half later. If they don't come, go home. They'll only give you a ring on your cell phone if no contact can be made on the first day. Oh, and don't forget to keep your cell phone battery charged.'

'It all sounds so mysterious, but I'll do what you say.' She replied, with a slight touch of restraint.

'Okay, folks, I've had a long two days and I'm flaked out so I'll have to get some shut-eye now. I want to give my friend in London a ring too. I'll be moving on to Berlin tomorrow.'

'Yes, okay John. We'll be leaving now,' said Olaf, who stood up and put his hand lightly on my shoulder – a gesture from someone shy of showing his thankfulness.

I shook the other hand he held out firmly and nodded to him looking into his eyes, hoping mine were telling him everything will work out.

'Thank you, John,' he said.

'Good luck in Damascus,' I countered.

Olaf moved to the door making way for Elsa who slid into my arms. This time there was no stiffness. She felt warm and soft. A bit longer would have been nice but out of place. She kissed my cheek and said,

'You don't know how glad I am you've come to help.'

There were tears in her eyes as she let go, holding on to my right hand, pulling it out to its full length, as she moved to the door, letting her finger tips linger on mine just a few last seconds, making my heart jump a little.

'Cheerio!' I croaked out.

Hotel Steigenbuehler – Davos, Switzerland, Wednesday 17th August 2005

Richard Teufel, leader of the Nazi Party Germany – Holger Dietrich, one of Germany's eight highest Attorney Generals – Hans Joachim Baum, leader of the Right Wing Austrian Party NFPÖ – Detlef Holgerlein, member of the supervisory board of the German International Corporate Bank – Akram Abdul-Saad of the Saudi Investment Group, Oleyan – Harold Osborne of the British National Insurance Company, Inc., London and Muhammad Ghazi Nour of Mahmud Trading Inc., Rotterdam, were seated in the moderate sized security conference room of the Hotel Steigenbühler, used sometimes for G8 meetings. Mustafa Kamal Kassas of the Swiss Bank International was standing addressing the group:

'Comrades, we have at last some very good news. Our group has collected forty-seven old x-ray machines from different parts of Germany and Holland. Excellent material for one or two dirty bombs. We've had enormous luck, because the

German and Dutch Press gave prior news of hospitals that were closing down. They even gave details of equipment to be donated to various former Eastern Block countries making it very easy for our cell-groups to go into action ahead of the Help Organizations.

As you all know, we've been very careful since the fall of the Iron Curtain. Those of you at this table are the only ones with full insight, apart from our Fuehrer. I would therefore stress once more the importance of secrecy. Any signs of a leak will cause our specialist department to remove and seal the leak.

Our *Armageddon* for the Zionists is nearing – therefore it is of the most vital interest for us to keep a low profile. All front action, I repeat, all front action is to be carried out at cell-group level only. No links to higher levels is allowed. Anyone crossing this line will be liquidated. If we keep to this rule, no organization in this world will ever break our ranks and get to our inner circle. I will now hand over to our honourable member Richard,'

'Thank you comrade Mustafa!'

Richard Teufel stood up and addressing the group, said,

'We have again been fortunate in our foresight to obtain 105 kilogrammes of highly enriched uranium oxide (HEU), from our Russian friends through our contact in Damascus. The big payment agreed upon has been carried out through our own banking system and cannot be traced.

We can also add forty-seven x-ray machines, which cost next to nothing.

My friends, we are most fortunate that a new German government think they will be taking over soon. Their slogan *Sozial ist was Arbeit schafft* is a reminder of the *Third Reich* slogan *Arbeit macht frei,* which was over the gates of the concentration camps.

The neo-liberal politics of the government has played into our hands. Just think comrades, people out of work get *one-Euro-per-hour* wages in Germany instead of steady jobs with future prospects.'

Richard Teufel gave an affected laugh. Mustafa Kamal Kassas took up, the others joining in. Richard Teufel's countenance remained blasé. He waited until the laughter subsided.

'Why do you think I laughed? Not because of those two easy acquisitions, no I am laughing because that is what the SS in the third Reich did too – labour costs for next to nothing!'

He laughed demonically, inflated by these thoughts. The others joined in and were soon holding their sides that were soon hurting from the fits of laughter. Once again, he waited until the laughter subsided.

'I would like to bring into mind our wise decision of the past to wait for the right moment. My comrades – that moment is very near. I know some of you are angry and impatient because we have waited so long. We were not to know that those mad Zionist Mossad leaders would penetrate Osama's cell-groups. Our dearly trusted friend Osama assured Akram Abdul-Saad he had no inkling of the 9/11 targets. He tells us that Zionist agents infiltrated his organization. They were the ones that supplied the groups with target information and tactics. Comrades, we know now why everything went so smoothly. Not so if we compare with previous Bin Laden operations before 9/11. The question that many in the world asked is, who has benefited most from such an attack?

The first answer is:

The Zionists of course, because the world looks the other way to further Zionist atrocities and they get more support in their striving against the Palestinians and the rest of the Arab world. In the eyes of the world they feel they now have the right to call all Muslims terrorists.

The second answer is:

The Americans did it. We know the intrigues of the CIA, the power struggles within and other clandestine organizations in the American government. George Bush wanted to show his father he could do it better. The main reason being, the securing of the oil fields and going after Saddam Hussein.

What they all don't know is – we've been pulling most of the strings all along. We've discussed our *modus operandi* at great length, especially concerning targeting. This still remains open – that, we agreed upon. Whether we let one or more atomic bombs go off using our HEU or whether we start with some dirty bombs until the governments of this world react to our demands remains to be seen. We have discussed targets – those again dear comrades we have not yet decided upon. What we have at the moment is a great number of options. We shall have to play it by ear if we are going to be successful. We will not under any circumstances go by any one plan at all costs. Adolf Hitler made those fatal errors. A sick man, someone who let power overcome clear thinking. However, we have one exception to our strict plans. We will start by setting off a dirty bomb in a Nazi stronghold in Germany to draw attention away from us, and a 5 Kt atomic bomb at a main nuclear plant in Iran. Which one, has still to be decided upon.'

A murmur of instant disapproval passed through the group. He waved them off, saying,

'This time, the world, and especially the haughty German Government will be willing to accept our demands. Germany is the weakest – they are the only ones who will cave in after the first attack. The Iranians will think Israel were behind the atomic attack and will declare war against them and no doubt will have the support of many Arab nations. This has to be, dear comrades – this will get the remainder of our Nazi friends in Germany and Europe on our side especially as we will lay enough evidence to point the finger of guilt towards the Zionists, who are normally so good at doing the same thing. We will cause the rest of the Arab world to help us in our fight against Zionists. What we will also do is to detonate a 5 Kt atomic bomb after the dirty bomb attack, possibly in Tel Aviv.

We also know of some Zionist agents who think they've gone unnoticed in our ranks. Those we will use to help in the blaming process, which will of course be supported by other tactical blaming prior to the bombings. Don't fool yourselves to thinking our preparations will go unnoticed. For this very reason we have built a great protective organization in Europe, the Middle East and the Far East. Our brothers and sisters are in action on all continents and a lot has been done to infiltrate the security services of all nations.

One more thing before we depart. We have not invited our French, British and American organizations to partake. That is too much of a risk. In France, Broudiere, who sits in the *Palais de Justice* as judge and prosecutor, has built up an antiterrorist security network, making penetration of our organisation a constant danger. The British are too scary and watchful since 7/7, 21/7 and the numbers of CCTV-cameras have increased. The Americans too are on their toes since 9/11.

The German Interior Minister and his fellow colleagues in the Kingdom of Bavaria talk their heads off about more security measures and that's about as far as it gets. Yes, comrades, Germany, Iran and Israel are the best targets. What with the help of the hundreds of thousands of our German Nazi friends, who for years have waited patiently – a piece of cake. Not to mention the Iranians who support the Hammas in Lebanon and Israel.

Comrades, public hostility and distrust in national governments, the UN and multinational companies has risen significantly over the last two years. The global economy is growing at its fastest rate in three decades and chief executives are cutting themselves huge paychecks, whilst more companies are reducing manpower through amalgamation, forcing more people out of work. The global mistrust is forcing leaders to apply more drastic economic reforms, that in turn, give more arguments to the fundamentalists of modern society. Comrades, I could go on and on. What it boils down to is – the time is ripe. But now, I have kept the best news to the last. Our Fuehrer has information concerning hidden documents that supposedly reveal the last testament of Jesus Christ. He is in possession of a map where we think this information is hidden. In due course we will send a team to retrieve it. If we get these documents in our hands it will make our takeover bid so much easier by revealing the lies of the Catholic Church. Comrades, I give a toast to our forthcoming domination of the world – I say, fear to them all, to the depths of their hearts and the annihilation of Israel. May they all writhe and rot in their agony knowing they can do nothing against it! May we cause chaos and bedlam!'

He raised his glass and his right arm and shouted.

'Fear, fear, fear!'

The others got up and raised their right arms with clenched fists, shouting in chorus,

'Fear, fear, fear!'

Achmed – Damascus, Friday 15*th* July 2005

He was huddled over a makeshift stove sipping mint tea in the back of a store in eastern Damascus – a part of the city out-of-bounds for Europeans wanting to stay healthy. His shirt collar was turned-up and his dusty khaki outfit bore ochre patches from the walk down the sand blasted alleys. The blond hair, not covered by his cap, was bleached white from the sun, face and neck toned vermilion. At this moment anger mixed with sadness entangled his thoughts.

Despite the remaining heat on his sunburnt parts, he shivered as he tried to grasp the meaning of what Achmed, the storekeeper's nephew, had just related to him a few moments ago. He couldn't get his thoughts straight quick enough, as the multitude of possibilities crossed his mind. Benumbed, he let them unfold.

His eyes moved away from Achmed and stared at a big blister on the whitewashed wall for a while, gradually becoming aware of the situation at hand. The blister started to grow, so he shut his eyes briefly, took a deep breath and let out a long soft sigh. He straightened his back a bit, shifting his hocking position and letting his mind continue to wander in this maze.

Achmed glanced sadly at his German friend Hans, realizing the discussion was over for the present. He felt somewhat guilty for giving way to the heat of the moment and letting out so many secrets. He felt the urge to leave. He got up slowly, went to the back of the room, slid behind some heavy curtains and made a quiet departure down a narrow hallway leading to a side alley.

Hans barely took notice of Achmed's departure – his brain was doing overtime. This was the type of information that fits into the power struggle puzzle. He had never regarded Achmed as any real source of information. He's such a quiet horse. Come to think of it, what does he really know about him. From the outside he seems a simple, good-natured person, easy to converse with on general topics, asking questions at the right places. He is also an *orthodox Christian,* which seems to make him less prejudiced than a *Muslim.* If Achmed's information is authentic he thought, he'd better keep it to himself for the moment. It would otherwise jeopardize his stay here. He just hopes *Syrian Intelligence* never grill Achmed or his relatives. But there again, what's *Syrian Intelligence* compared to the Mossad? Where could he be safe from them?

The conversation with Achmed today ended up with the Iraqi occupation. That had touched a nerve. When Achmed got going he had listened carefully without budging an eyebrow.

He recalled his own heterotelic motives for learning *Arabic,* built-up over many years – the reason for his being in the Middle East in the first place. Since his first year at German university he had been trying to understand the Arabs and why they want to retain their complicated and one-sided system. Achmed accepted his thirst for knowledge and understanding. They had covered a lot of ground over the last year and a half. Being German too, helped, as he was regarded as a neutral.

He brought his mind into constraint for a while: *"Saddle the horses – get ready to jump the obstacles!"* followed by a revival of his recent relaxing experience, *"Sitting on hot tiles in Hamam, lots of hot water, soaped-up with olive soap and drinking "chai" – the world is our field – mental disconnection – retention,"* then back to the *main stream*, back to reality.

Expectations and perceptions of great strength arise as he tries to collate the images. His strong willpower, to bind himself more to the Orient and perhaps unveil this new nightmare, makes it all the more challenging. Thoughts of his studies in Germany of recent years, readings of *Keyserling, Dostojewski* and *Spengler,* which held so many contradictions, yet were so easily dissolved. *Debt and atonement*, this treasure influenced a large part of his passive spirituality during his first weeks in *Damascus* – the thoughts of debt, and atonement being the main parameters. Additional inspiration he gained from *Jüngers* thoughts about his brother *Friedrich Georg* and his search for the keys leading to the founding of the occident states – the rules that were the framework for the microcosm of life. The idea *state*, its parameters and implications becoming transparent, supported also by his studies of *Waldgang, Aristotle and Plato* in *Marburg. Friedrich Georg* became his impetus and also *Georg's* failure to find any political influence regarding the totalitarian ideas of proletarian Germans and Russians who dispersed the rights of justice. Thereby, *Carl Schmitt*, apparently a friend of *Georg's* older brother, spoke of the leader, *'der Fuehrer',* the person who **dictates** the *rights*.

His mind cleared – back to the present, to that *now*. The prediction of citizen's rights, the multiple options in international law adding more and more weight to public rights. Thank goodness we have them, he thought – but alas, they only seem to be apparent in the occident. Trying to analyse the new situation, he went over what Achmed had said,

'You know Hans – you are very naïve! The biggest crime the Americans committed against humanity was by denying their prisoners held in Afghanistan, Guantanamo Bay and Iraq basic international rights and by applying torture. They have lost their rights as a leading nation for that. *"The best country in the world and God is on our side."* All that *Georg "double-you"* bullshit makes me want to vomit! They do not differentiate between the innocent and the guilty when they go hunting terrorists from door to door. They are the kings and bash down all doors, not thinking that nearly all of the people behind those knocked down doors are innocent. Because of these incidents, the Americans make those innocents their enemies. Why don't they learn from the British who don't do these things in the South? They learned their lesson in Northern Ireland decades ago.

After over a century of British and French interference in the Middle East, lots of Arabs used to look towards America for guidance. Some had admiration for the American way of life and many go to study in America and a lot of them are now American citizens. Now, we know different. To the Americans we are just underdogs and they treat us all as such. They are just interested in our oil. Their system is so riddled by the *Jews* that their hands are tied. They will always be on Israel's side and genocide will continue. You are different. The Germans have behaved well in this conflict. *Adolf Hitler*, he was a dictator and a bad man, I know. He did horrible things, especially to the Jews. He knew they were the main problem in this world but he did not know why, except of course he hated them and Himmler hated them even more! The Jews have been the guilty ones since the crucifixion of Christ.'

'What the hell are you talking about Achmed?' he answered, adding, 'This type of talk is very anti-Semite, you know. I'm afraid, if you're going to carry on like this I'll have to leave!'

'Hans, wait please. I will tell you a true story, one I know from my other uncle who knows, because it happened to him.'

Achmed replied with such intensiveness and concern, that he decided to listen to him for a while.

'Okay, Achmed, I'm listening.'

'Yes, Hans – well it all started in 1995. My uncle *Hakim Sadeh* is a civil engineer. He worked in the Lebanon for *United Saudi Maintenance & Services Company* on a 6-month contract basis. They were repairing overland telecommunication stations and setting up new networks. The contract was nearly over when an Egyptian sub-contractor approached him offering him a job in Israel with a company called *Cairo Telecommunications Company*. What he didn't know at the time was that this was a subsidiary of *Bin Laden Telecommunications Company,* a daughter of the *Saudi Bin Laden Group, SBG*. Well, he worked there for about two months nearly non-stop before he had his first four days off. Not long enough to go home, so he decided to do a bit of sightseeing in Jerusalem. He was walking down the *Sultan Suleiman Road* one Friday evening. As he made his way into the old town he heard sirens, shouts and some shooting from the temple mountain. He decided he'd better go back and had just turned around when he was overtaken by a group of young Palestinians who looked as though they'd been up to something. That was his bad luck. Shortly after that, as he was walking back slowly, he heard a shout directly behind him. The next thing he felt was a blow in the back of the neck. That was the last he could remember until he woke up in *Ashkelon* prison. He was kept in solitary confinement for 4 weeks and during that time they kept the lights on in his room all the time, coming in every hour or so just to wake him up and shout obscenities at him, or drag him out and into the interrogation room where they accused him over and over again of terrorism and spying.

They were Mossad, he was told by one of the other prisoners when he was put into another cell. He said he would never forget one particular interrogator who made him strip his clothes off numerous times and humiliate him. They told him he would never leave the prison alive. He only got one meal a day and that was taken away from him sometimes just as he was going to eat it. He wasn't really beaten, but they pushed and shoved him making him fall and pulling him up by his hair. Once when he was in the interrogation room they asked if he was thirsty. He told them yes, so they gave him a jug of water to drink, then another. When he refused to drink any more they tied his hands, pulled his head back and put a funnel in his mouth and kept pouring in jug after jug. He was never put on trial or given access to a lawyer. One day, after about four months, he was suddenly released, just like that, no apologies, nothing. He was put on a bus with other prisoners and they were driven over to the Palestinian autonomy area.

He has never been able to get his pay or his belongings back. My uncle is a devote Muslim, not like us. He is a very sincere man. He has never done a bad thing in his life. This nearly broke him. It took him 6 years before he took up contract work again. He said he would never work in Israel again.'

'Did he ever try to sue the Israelis, Achmed?'

'Oh, he wrote lots of letters, even to the UN. Went to see Mullahs, lawyers and judges, but they all told him there was nothing to gain, as Israel doesn't recognise international law. But he did manage to get the name of the Mossad interrogator who humiliated him, *Ben Goldmann,* which he passed on to Amnesty International.'

'That's good – maybe one day he'll get his reckoning.'

'Hans, you'll probably not believe this but the horror story for my uncle did not end at this.'

'What?'

'As I said, it had taken him 6 years to get his mind back to normal. He took up contract work for an American company in Baghdad last year, wanting to help the Iraqis rebuild their infra-structure.'

'This is really difficult for me to tell you as things went even worse for him this time. Exactly the same thing happened to him as in Jerusalem, this time it was the Americans.'

'Good grief!'

'Yes, he was in Baghdad walking back to his digs from work. As he walked across a square he passed a group who started throwing stones and other things at police and military forces just outside a US camp. He ran for cover when the police and Marines retaliated by shooting back at them. He managed to huddle down behind the big wheel of a parked lorry. They must have singled him out, because they sprayed the lorry with bullets making him stay put. They rounded him up afterwards with a group of the stone throwers. He made out at least a dozen civilians around the square who were lying in pools of blood. They all looked dead.'

'Surely he managed to convince them he was just a passer-by?'

'No way.' He protested in perfect English. They just told him to shut up, he'd get plenty of time to talk afterwards, at which the Marines all laughed.'

'Couldn't he get legal assistance or ring his contractor?'

'Hans, you really are wet behind the ears. For the Americans all Arabs are suspects – they are the enemy, especially well-educated ones. Anyway that's the way they treated him.'

'This is terrible.'

'I know, but the worst is to come. They herded them all into cellblock 1A in *Abu Ghraib* prison and cut off all their clothes. Their plight was intensified by the presence of two US women

MPs and some US male MPs. The women tantalized them. They put a black smelly hood over his head and he had to put his hands behind his head. He felt a mouth close around his penis. He saw what he thought were flashbulbs going off through the bag and knew they were taking pictures of him.'

'I read about it in the papers, disgusting.'

'Yes, but the thing that really terrified my uncle was when they took him for interrogation. The first two weeks American Para-Military interrogated him. My uncle thinks they were CIA. My uncle's English is perfect, he studied in England.'

'That's probably what made them think they'd captured a high ranking terrorist,' said Hans.

'But he didn't tell them at first that he'd studied in England. Anyway, they left him alone for another two weeks. He was never charged or given legal advice.'

Achmed took a long sip of *chai*, looking sadly at the stove.

'My uncle nearly had a heart attack when he was ushered one Saturday evening to a different interrogation room. He was shackled to a big ring in the floor. In the corner a hooded prisoner was standing naked on a box with electrical wires attached to his arms and genitals. He had read about such torture methods, which Stalin and the Gestapo also used. If you fell off the box you were electrocuted. He was left there alone with the other prisoner, who was perspiring terribly.'

'This is really sadistic,' said Hans.

'Well, some time later, two MPs came, disconnected the wires on the other prisoner and took him away to another room. When they went out the door he could hear screams and shouts from all directions. He told me he'd heard about this and hoped to *Allah* it was just recordings.'

'They made him wait for many hours. He was very hungry and thirsty. All of a sudden the door burst open and two interrogators came in. Their clothing looked slightly different from the other interrogators and they spoke to him in Arabic. Because they shone the light in his face he couldn't see their faces, but he thought he recognised one of the voices.'

'Good God, it wasn't that guy from the Mossad?'

'Yes it was.'

'Goodness gracious! What are the Mossad doing in Iraq?'

'Knowing what he does now and what's been in the press, the Americans used two civilian firms to carry out some of the interrogations. He reckons one company was CIA and the other Mossad, or a mixture of both.'

'Why would they do that?'

'Because they don't have enough specialists who speak and write *Arabic* in the CIA.'

'This must have been terrible for your uncle.'

'Yes it was, and it was made worse because the CIA interrogators had told the Mossad he was hiding something.'

'Was he?'

'Yes, he thought it wise not to mention he'd been in Israel or in one of their jails, also that he'd studied in England. So you can imagine how he felt when Ben Goldmann confronted him. He managed to get a good look one day to make sure it was him.'

'Good God, it must have been a nightmare for him.'

'Well, he won't tell us what he went through after that. We think it was bad. We reckon the imprisonment in Israel had him hardened up so much that he was able to prevail.'

'Did he let the Mossad man know he knew who he was?'

'Praise Allah, no – that would've been his death warrant. He kept to his original story but let them know he'd studied in the UK, one of the bits he hadn't told the CIA interrogators.'

'Was he tortured anymore?'

'As I said, he wouldn't talk about those things after his confrontation with *Ben Goldmann*. He gave us the impression they seemed satisfied with his answers after some further weeks of questioning.'

'What happened then?'

'Again, as in Israel, after four months he was put on a bus with other Iraqis and dropped off in the centre of Baghdad.'

'Will he be taking legal action? I've read about some Iraqis who are doing so.'

'My uncle is too afraid. He says the Mossad would get him if he tried. No one mentioned the Mossad and no one is to know they were involved in Iraq. Imagine the outcry and unrest in the Arab world?'

'God, I feel angry, real angry about this. There must be some way of getting retribution or revenge?'

'It's best you forget about what I've just told you Hans. My uncle says the Mossad is everywhere and there's no escape, so stay quiet if you want to stay alive.'

Secure conference room New Scotland Yard, Wednesday 17th August 2005

AC Charles Cross and Chief Superintendent Dave Haddock, both from police special operations, counter-terrorist department, take the podium.

Charles Cross addresses a group of high level senior officers from various police departments including the anti-terrorist unit, MI5 counter-terrorist department, members of the JIC, special ops personnel and GCHQ. Members of MI6 were not present.

'Thank you for coming, ladies and gentlemen – this meeting

is Top Secret and the Zionist topic is not for discussion outside this room. Those of you from police forces will notice a couple of new faces from MI5, JIC and GCHQ. Some other faces you may have expected to be present are not here mainly due to tighter security precautions that will be explained in due course.

Chief Supt Dave Haddock will fill you in. It may be a bit dry, as we're not having PowerPoint assistance for security reasons. There'll be no notes taken whatsoever. Okay, Dave. The floor's yours.'

'Thank you Sir – all right then, first of all I'm going to start with a bit of history. Some of this is not new. We want to do a low level analysis from the point of view of the Occident, especially Christians, the Orient and Muslim world. The part about Khomeini is shoved in as a reminder what can go wrong, especially the French bungling and where the apple started to rot. The Zionist part is the most interesting and is the main purpose of our meeting. It is of vital importance.

I'm not going to argue about detail. I also don't want any comments on the banality of some of the statements – let's just look at them as common facts. You all know the game – somewhere to start looking – look again at the basics without the frills.

To start with, a few reminders about friends and allies, especially our so-called American friends:

As you all know, 9/11 has made vast changes to our lives. In World War II it took the Americans a long time to come to the aid of Europe to fight with us against the Nazis. Roosevelt in one of his many speeches to the nation directed against American involvement to help fight the Nazis, after having been asked openly for help by Britain numerous times, said, quote:

I've said it time and time, and time again, your sons will not be involved in a foreign war.

In Britain, the general census of opinion at the time, and in some cases still is, was, they only sided with us, because they were attacked themselves by the Japanese at Pearl Harbor, after which they automatically became involved when Hitler declared war on America three days later. Would they have reacted the same if 9/11 happened in the UK instead of America?

Remember Suez? Who was it forced the French and us to withdraw? Historians reckon the Middle East crisis, as it is now, wouldn't have happened if we'd been allowed to finish what we started and why did Harold Wilson say no to our involvement in Vietnam? Maybe he didn't like the idea of British soldiers only having drinks from their water bottles whereas the Americans had their automatic coca-cola machines with them in the field. But seriously it goes much deeper. Some experts advised him, and thank God, he listened to them. The American idea about counter-insurgency in Indo-China proved to be unusable then as it is today in Iraq.

Gentlemen we could go on and on and find a lot more reasons for not siding with the Americans in the Iraq war. One in particular sticks out:

During the IRA terrorist activities over a number of decades, various US Governments did nothing to counter the IRA support from American citizens when urged to do so many times by our government.

The security problems and the protective measures we have to take nowadays would urge George Orwell to say *'I told you so',* if he were still alive. These measures also swallow huge amounts of our taxpayer's money, not to mention the massive manpower support and highly advanced technical equipment required. Our main terrorist intelligence sources in the UK and elsewhere are currently from the Muslim communities.

What changed in the Muslim mentality to produce such

hatred and suicide bombers? Well, let me just go back a couple of decades to where it looked like the spark lit the tinder.

In November of 1978, strange things were happening in *Neauphle-le-Château,* a village on the outer Parisian *Banlieu.* It was so named after the owner of the seventeenth century castle and lies at the edge of the fertile *Beauce* planes where grain crops are mainly grown. Some of you who've travelled a lot in France can place it through the nearby cathedral of *Chartres,* with its renowned violet-blue church windows. Of all places, Ayatollah Ruhollah Khomeini decided to stay there for a while. A fellow Persian countryman offered him the use of his small *Maison de Campagne.* Ayatollah Ruhollah Khomeini settled in there with a couple of his faithful followers. It was quite a while before the Parisians and foreign press became aware of the presence of the *Marche persan.*

Who knew anything about Ayatollah Khomeini in those days, and who knew about the religious background of the Muslim Schia? Word spread like wildfire among the many Iranian students who were scattered over Western Europe – mainly West Germany and France. A strange signal went out from this white bearded old man, who carried the black turban, the symbol of a descendant of the prophet.

How come Ruholla Khomeini got to France to *Neauphle-le-Château* in the first place? That was no spontaneous decision. In the summer of 1975 the governments of Tehran and Baghdad had finally agreed to settle an ancient dispute, going back to Babylonian ages and the first decades of the Islam, through a *modus vivendi* that would benefit both parties. A clause in the agreement was made regarding the exile of the Mullah of Nadschaf, Ayatollah Khomeini – an Iranian the Iraqis wanted to be rid of. The Iranians didn't want him back in Iran either. He was to be exiled to a third state. The Iraqi

Mukhabarat, the secret service of Saddam Hussein, had proposed to the *Savak*, the Iranian secret service, to exile the stubborn old Shiite to Libya or Algeria. They had experienced enough problems in the past with the revolutionary Shiite Ali Shariati, who escaped from Iran and found asylum in Britain. Shariati gathered many followers at home in Iran and some say the *Savak* executed him during his exile in London. Tehran put in a veto, declaring Khomeini would have found a revolutionary platform with President Boumedienne of Algeria or Colonel Gadhafi of Libya. According to Iranian police experts he would have become a threatening torchbearer of Islamic indignation over the decline in moral standards of the Pahlevi regime. Therefore Tehran sent a message via the Iranian Embassy in Paris to the *Quai d'Orsay*, the French Foreign Ministry, enquiring whether Giscard d'Estaings' Fifth Republik would give this little known preacher from Qom an entry visa into France. In Paris, the responsible authorities, the *Direction de la Surveillance du Territoire (DST)* gave their consent. Like their colleagues in Tehran, they little suspected that by doing so they opened Pandora's box.

To be banal, one could say the French are to blame for the Islamic Revolution and the worldwide Islamic fundamentalist crisis, just as historians declared ex German Foreign Minister Dietrich Genscher responsible for the Balkan War by his recognizing the existence of Slovenia as a sovereign state without having consulted his European partners.

In Libyan or Algerian exile, Khomeini would have been one of the many ex-politicians and would-be revolutionaries from all over the world who were exiled to those two countries. Having to operate within the highly spun and paralysing network of the suspicious local security organizations there, he would have been hardly considered interesting to the international press. On the other hand, in France, in the immediate vicinity of the Parisian metropolis, Khomeini became renowned overnight. He was the target of exotic curiosity and in no time at all became an explosive political issue.

What went on from there is general knowledge. Khomeini eventually went back to Iran and with the support of millions of followers took over power. The Iranian revolution took place. After a vast purge against Iranian loyalists, they led a holy war against Iraq that caused the deaths of millions of Iranians and Iraqis. Khomeini is long deceased and was a powerful member of the *Basij,* a paramilitary force of Islamic militants. *Mahmoud Ahmadinejad* is now Iran's new president – a dangerous man thought to have been one of the terrorists involved in the storming of the US Embassy in Tehran and an extreme Zionist hater. There is still a lot of unrest and many student uprisings occur. Many people wish democracy will eventually prevail, but the religious fanatics in the system do everything to stop that happening. People are jailed and physically punished for trivialities. Wives are stoned to death for petty reasons, and so on. Iran is in a state equivalent to the medieval ages, or even before. Possessing the atomic bomb as a WMD has been one of Iran's main objectives. The chances are, the new president isn't any different. All the Iranian talk about processing uranium for peaceful purposes is a typical Arabic way of defusing Western fears.

In Iraq, the radical Shiite cleric *Muqtada al-Sadr* is striving for the same thing, Khomeini being his idol. While *al-Sadr's Mahdi Militia* represents a serious threat to Iraq's stability, an equally vexing challenge to Iraqi order is taking shape in the Sunni Muslim dominated areas North-West of Baghdad, where Sunni terrorists, Baathists and nationalists are thriving.

How does all this affect us with our own internal security problems within the Muslim community?

Well, the coordination of our intelligence gathering and counter-terrorism methods and policies in the UK, thanks to the IRA, are more advanced than the USA and have been for decades. We centralized our intelligence and criminal information computer systems years ago, so we have central access to actual *state of the art* information around the clock from any part of Britain or the globe. We work in close coordination, analysing and assessing the information from our own sources through the police, MI5, SIS, GCHQ, JIC, the recently formed ISIA and our many intelligence allies abroad. The time factor is the main problem here, due to the massive network information correlation required.

As regards to the Muslim organizations, we have some of our own people and plenty of sources in their ranks. Also, we have the better training and experience fighting terrorism. We also have the majority of the Muslim communities in Great Britain on our side that are cooperating fully since 7/7 and 21/7. We could do with more Arabic linguists, but are managing fairly well. Our major problem that still remains is the collation of original Arabic information from the vast amount of information available through national and various worldwide networks, in order to be able to use it quickly and effectively.

In comparison to other countries, we have identified and acted swiftly against any attempts of terrorism through Muslim activists in our country. We know the troublemakers and their *modus operandi*. We still have great problems ahead in identifying new cell build-ups.

We have bottlenecks concerning manpower, in order to keep them all under surveillance, until we can haul them in with enough evidence for the executive.

We are not dealing with Al Qaeda – we are now dealing with an ideology. The problems in the Middle East give fuel to agitation, making it all the easier for Muslim activists to recruit new members. Currently we have 3000 Muslims on record in Britain who have apparently attended training camps in the Arabic world, or who have physically participated in the War in Afghanistan or Iraq. The offshoot cells are comprised mostly of young Muslims born in Britain who are recruited ideologically. We suspect that at least 50 % of the British Muslims who have visited these training camps are potential terrorists. To top it off – Jihadists are now capable of recruiting new members in their ranks faster than we can keep track of them due to a grave manpower shortage in our security forces.

In Israel the religious hardliner Zionists rule with an iron heart. No compassion or a place to stay for the Palestinians from whom they stole the land they maintain they are protecting. Behind the scenes exists one of the most extreme secret intelligence organizations in the world, the Mossad. Hardliner Zionists and Mossad agents and sympathizers are to be found everywhere, especially in key positions. Zionists have lobbies in every Western country in the world. The two strongest lobbies they hold are in the USA and Great Britain.

There is great anxiety in the Western world concerning the increased radicalisation within the Israeli Government and security forces. Western governments seem to have become lame ducks. It appears that renegade elements within the Israeli Security Agencies are running amok. We have suggestions at hand of possible Bin Laden cell infiltrations that took place prior to 9/11, by a special Mossad group.

For years it was general practice to exchange information with other intelligence organizations, only when it was decided we had the same target. The general rule being – no third parties. Well that has changed since 9/11 extraordinarily. It seems as though it has become general practice to more or less pass on most classified material to other agencies as a general handout. This has got to stop.

Any President or Prime Minister in Britain or America, or any other Western country for that matter, knows not to cross Israel or politically confront them for their wanton killing of innocent child stone throwers or for building their damn wall and for lots of other atrocities.

The Western world condemned Iraq for not withholding the UN resolutions. What about the hundreds of resolutions and UN Supreme Court orders the Israelis ignored? These are the very reasons why so many young Arabs and Arabian woman volunteer for the Jihad – willing to give their lives as a means of protest. We do not condone the wanton killing of innocent civilians in this bloody Jihad process. We see it every day on television and Westerners know in their hearts that the politicians can't do anything because of the Zionist lobby, or they even fear for their positions. Some Westerners blame the Americans who have 30% Zionists in Congress, so it's no wonder why the Arab world thinks the same.

Our main problem here is that it is very difficult to discern who is a Zionist radical, bearing in mind all Jews have Israel, their motherland in their hearts.

Another problem we see as the biggest threat, are the so-called Zionist *Sayanims* who see themselves as volunteers. We call them sleepers.

What I have been saying is not to be regarded as anti-Semite. These are useful thoughts based on some highly verified facts that have come to our notice.

You all know the *modus operandi* of intelligence organizations. Some of you belong to them, others have been seconded to one type or another or have worked or are working closely with them. Well, think back how many Jewish colleagues could you have had working next to you in the police department or other sensitive working places. You may not have known they were Jewish, but sometimes their names, actions, eating habits, or religious practises may have given you food for thought.

Can you imagine what damage they could do if they changed loyalties, i.e. taking orders from elsewhere. Think of the possibility of how many sleepers are amongst them, ready and waiting for the word go!

We all know a lot of British Jews have an Israeli Passport as well as their British Passport, for security reasons. There's nothing wrong with having dual passports, but that's where it starts to eat you!

What applies to British Jews working in our police and intelligence agencies at home and abroad also applies to British Muslims. Under the current threat we cannot discard possible disloyalties and security slip-ups.

Our main problem here is key decision positions in our intelligence networks and government agencies. We have good reason to believe information is being wrongfully discarded or has been tampered with. The processing through our various channels and the verification of data with other original source agencies during the Butler inquiry brought out some discrepancies that led to further inquiries. We are in the process of making decisions to reduce any future damage in this particular area.

The question will arise in your minds:

Was this general or deliberate falsification and passing on of the false information?

The other major problem is, that our vetting system has

been changed in recent years to allow third generation immigrants access to classified information. Three decades ago not even black people were allowed that privilege. In the USA it's the 2nd generation, so I think we also have a general problem here regarding true Muslims, especially those who are regular Mosque worshippers.

Let's go now, to Bin Laden. He has very rich family roots. The Bin Ladens have companies throughout the Middle East. He knows what capitalism can do to his people especially their culture and religion. When Bin Laden was younger he had a number of visions. One of them was compassion for his fellow Arabs in Afghanistan, who were under Russian occupation. He wanted to see them freed from this yoke. He set up fighting cells and got major support from America. One of his support officers from the CIA was Donald Rumsfeld. There are a number of stories around but it seems fallible knowing a bit more about Donald Rumsfeld, that he didn't treat Bin Laden very well, in fact some say he cheated him and through his actions nearly got him killed. In actual fact in the end, the CIA did want Bin Laden removed – a good reason for Bin Laden not to trust Americans. He now hates everything the USA stands for.

Since 1998 Bin Laden has been justifying his cause due to:
– Iraqi sanctions that caused the deaths of hundreds of thousands of children.
– Controlled occupation of Palestine by Israel.
– Daily murdering of innocents in Palestine by Israel.
– Occupation of Saudi Arabia by allied troops.
– War against Afghanistan and Iraq.
– Corruption in Saudi Arabia, etc.

Bin Laden has become the *Che Guevara* of the Middle East, that's why he has so many followers. Even if he's put out of action he'll remain a martyr, thanks to both Bush's and

Rumsfeld. What we do know is *not everything* accredited to Bin Laden is his work. I want to emphasize that. Again, remember, we are now dealing with the so-called Al Qaeda ideology. We have no 100% verification, if he is, in actual fact, still alive.

Western politics will always fail in the Middle East. It is a different culture and the majority of Arabs believe in the Koran as a way of life, much more so than Westerners do with the Holy Bible. Western economic growth is based on capitalism. So any influence the West takes in the Middle East will be seen as profit gaining – especially when oil is involved. The West is anxious to secure oil production for purely economic reasons.

Now, about the religious problem – unfortunately the Mullahs take advantage by putting the Koran to their own use by making up their own interpretations in the specialist contexts. There are many of them especially regarding the Jihad. But there again doesn't the Holy Bible do the same. What about all the different Christian faiths and all their interpretations? We wouldn't let anyone interfere with our clergy, now, would we? In most minds the Western World thinks they are more civilized than Muslims. That is true to some extent from our point of view of being free to choose how we want to live.

Arabs are indoctrinated by their religious teachers, their Mullahs, to follow the codex of the Koran. This starts at a very early infant age and is carried on through to teenage and hence through adult life.

Earlier Christian teachers did the same. It has been proven that Mullahs in some cases and their religious Mosques are the centres for recruitment and cell build-ups. This has proven to be the case involving radical Mullahs. Don't forget the third generation youngsters who visit their relatives in the origin countries of their fathers. They are easy meat.

Let's go on to the Israeli/Palestinian problem, which is the central catapult. Until that's settled peacefully and to the satisfaction of both sides, there will be great unrest in the world. It is up to us all, and especially those responsible in governments, to cut out the wrongful and deliberate influence of Zionist activists within our own ranks. Before a dirty bomb or a small, atomic bomb, for instance, becomes the starter for greater damage to life on this planet. There has to be action against this happening now and not *after* it has happened like the 9/11, 3/11, 7/7 and 7/21 attacks.

We have to show the Arabs we are aware of their problems and must try and help globally to put out the fire in Israel on both sides of the Jordan River. Someone has to start and our PM is fully behind these actions. He is still angry that he's been misled by the deliberate sabotage that Zionist activists, and, or Muslims in our own ranks have been causing, that led him to believe Iraq had WMD's – if this is indeed the case. Not to mention the general blundering of the CIA and our own intelligence agencies.

Okay, folks. I have one more topic. We have information of strange happenings within the Mossad. It looks as though a killer commando is operating not only in the Middle East against terrorist leaders, but also in Europe. It has similarities to the Nakam, a Zionist group founded after the war to take out Nazi criminals.

They are not only out for the Hamas leaders – they're after Mullahs, Nazis and others. A number of Jews have been taken out in Germany of late and that's the backlash. There is definitely a connection between the Muslims and the Nazis. We'll have to do something about that before it gets out of hand.

There is one terrible factor we have to take into consideration. What if it's just a feint? What if they have a different purpose, like going for politicians supporting the anti-Zionist movement in Governments throughout the world? We may very likely see some action once culprits have been moved to less sensitive positions.

We want all information, regarding the subjects I've just mentioned, recorded and data based with our new *ISAAC* system – *Internal Security Administrational Access Computer*, with an emphasis on access. Only high access privileges will be granted.

Most of you are aware that the FBI arrested Larry Franklin, a Defence Department analyst for spying for Israel. He passed on top-secret information to them.

To recuperate – we now regard persons working in key positions who have a strong Zionist or Muslim background, a possible danger to the establishment. They should be moved rapidly elsewhere, very discretely of course. This also applies to immigrants or those married to immigrants including their spouse in key positions. Before any such decisions are made we must meet and discuss the finalities. You may think these measures an overreaction, but unfortunately the information we have make these measures necessary. There may be a number of innocent loyal British citizens amongst those moved. That is unfortunate. This is, I repeat not a long-term measure. It is purely a precautionary move until we've ousted the moles.

One thing before questions – do not, under any circumstances, mail each other electronically or otherwise on this topic or talk about it on the telephone, even if the line is secure.'

'Now for questions – yes, Jimmy?'

'James MacMillan, MI5 – Sir, I'm sorry to say this, but isn't this going a bit far. I mean, moving Jews or Muslims from their positions. If this gets out there'll be an outcry. Another thing too, what makes you so sure hardliner Zionists or Muslims haven't already thought about this possibility and have done the necessary cover-ups? I think the whole thing is a bit too vague for such hard measures.'

Dave Haddock turned to his chief.

Charles Cross took up the question.

'Thank you Jimmy – yes, from what you've just been told I would tend to agree with you. We've discussed this problem at the top. As you all know, the foreign minister is a Jew himself and very open towards free religious practicing. The prime minister has approached him with the problem. The foreign minister agrees with us. He sees great dangers forthcoming if we don't take precautionary measures. Those were his exact words. He made it quite clear this is not to be seen as punishment. It was his suggestion to take the weight off their conscience by moving possible dangerous sources to less vulnerable positions. The Secretary of State, the Home Secretary has given the go ahead.'

'Yes, Sir Miles?' asked Dave Haddock.

'Miles Docherty, JIC – are we going to issue a directive on this issue?'

Again his chief Charles Cross answered the question.

'No, I'm afraid not, Sir Miles. No one is going to hang himself in this manner. The Zionist hardliners, as Chief Haddock pointed out, are very powerful and would use it as an instrument to strengthen their key positions and oust the government. The backlash in the Muslim world too, would be extreme, to put it mildly. No, the operation must be carried out with the utmost care. What we don't want is the moving of all Jews or Muslims from their positions just to be on the safe side. The task of moving anyone at all is a filigree piece of work, to be done with the greatest caution. We will leave the decision-making in your hands when we meet to discuss the individuals involved. One other thing, you are all probably thinking, why have I been picked out? You all know the answer to that.

Any more questions – no, then I suggest we all meet here again a week today at the same time? Any queries regarding the subject of our discussion is to be referred to the Bin Laden and Iraqi problem, which is not untrue. Thank you all for coming. Jimmy, could I have a word with you before you go?'

James MacMillan nodded and moved towards the front nodding his goodbyes on the way.

'Jimmy, this is unofficial as far as the chain of command goes,' said Chief Cross, 'I didn't want to discuss this openly, but we have a problem with MI6. Until our unconfirmed information has proven otherwise we have a *mole* or what the Americans would describe as a *fox in the chicken coop* in MI6. That's why we didn't send them an invite to this meeting. We know you coordinate with Tom Atkins and we don't want you mentioning this to him. We are not certain but our info points to his department.'

'What are we going to do about that, Sir?'

'We have some people working on it. Anything of importance, we'll contact you.'

'Okay, Sir – that's all for now then, is it?'

'Yes, that's it for the time being. If nothing else turns up, we'll see you next week.'

Jimmy nodded to the two chiefs and left the room with his head buzzing with questions he thought he knew some of the answers to, but just wanted confirmation.

Berlin – 'The Agency', International Security Intelligence Agency, ISIA, Wednesday 17th August 2005

I entered *the Agency* building situated near the Berlin Olympic Stadium that used to be the Headquarters of a British Army Unit during the Cold War. An ugly building of the Hitler Arian era – the same design as the Olympic Stadium buildings, so Hitler's star architect Speer, probably designed *the Agency* building too.

I knew I was in for a hard day, as no sooner had I inserted my ID-card and the magic eye ran my Iris check, when I heard a buzzer go off in the security guard's office. Bill Reaves the security guard, a retired staff-sergeant of the British Army Para Regiment, very light footed for his size and armed with a 9 mm Browning stuck in his holster, pounded out of his office

'Mr Jameson, Sir! I have instructions from Mr Orlowski for you to report to him immediately, it's important.'

'Thanks, Bill, you can give him a ring and tell him I'm on my way up.'

I took the lift up to the third floor, got out and walked across to a corridor blocked by a huge steel grille frame with a door in the middle. I swiped my ISIA ID-card through the electronic card reader and placed my thumb on the fingerprint sensor as soon as a green light came up. The metal door lock buzzed. With a slight shove on the door, an opening mechanism took over and opened the door fully. I walked through into the main ISIA secure area. A bit out-of-date and way behind times – just what I think every time I come through here – low budget or the money flows elsewhere!

I showed my teeth to the CCTV camera on my way to Jack Orlowski's office, knocked on the door, and walked in.

I got the usual natural smile from Susan Hanson, Jack's

secretary – a mouth full of bleached teeth that closed, forming seductively pouted lips. No matter what trouble's brewing, she always gives me that friendly Hawaiian beach smile.

'Good morning Mr Jameson, welcome back,' she said, in her clear, drawn out, New England dialect – beautiful just to listen to.

'Hi, Susan, nice to see you.'

'Just go through, Mr Orlowski is waiting for you.'

I would like to have stayed for a chat but Bill's message still rang in my ears. I don't think my name has ever been entered into the building access entry file. I tapped lightly on the door and walked in.

'Ah, John, glad you didn't dally. We have a real emergency on our hands. Take a seat and let me fill you in.'

I took the leather armchair from the corner of the room and shoved it sideways to the desk, ignoring the two plain chairs placed in front of it. If I was going to listen to a long liturgy then I would prefer to be comfortable should I nod off, which was highly likely with Jack's slow southern drawl.

'First of all Ian's funeral is on Friday – I think it would be appropriate if you could do the oration, seeing he was one of your closest friends.'

Jack looked at me quizzically, obviously expecting an immediate answer. I had gotten the message why my presence was urgently required! I put on a poker face and remained stubbornly silent, staring Jack out. He didn't budge an eyelid. People may be right about the unsmiling mandroid some people make Jack out to be, I thought. But nevertheless, he was the first to give in.

'I gather from your silence you are not particularly keen?' He said dryly.

'Jack, thanks for offering me the privilege. I know you may

think it's my prerogative but I'm definitely not the right guy for Ian's oration. We were friends going back a long time. Under these circumstances it's definitely not going to be my show.'

'Hmm! Well in that case I guess I'll have to do it myself then. We'll get together tomorrow afternoon. I expect you to help me?'

'Yes, of course, Jack. I would've suggested that anyway.'

'Okay, that's settled then. Now about our progress – the RRT have been working closely with the Berlin police department. They've set up a special murder commission in LKA 11. I've arranged with the German police high commissioner to have a constant German liaison police officer here during the investigation and if needs be, I'll find a way to hang on to him for a while. They sent us a guy called Marcus Anderson, from LKA 651. He's working under Gerard van der Falk in the RRT. We've given him medium access privileges to our international computer system and have established a link to the German Police Criminal Information Database. Marcus has retained his special access privileges that may be useful. We are not allowed to update the German criminal record database – that remains his privilege. Apropos, access privileges! Well, as soon as we found out Martin Cole was missing, all ISIA codes were changed and a system check carried out. Special logging and report warning mechanisms were built around Martin's access data and working files. The super-user and administration codes have all been changed. We ignored the instructions in the emergency safe and introduced new access codes to avoid disturbing any Trojans that may have been in the system, which is highly unlikely. We've kept the main system going, apart from a brief system shutdown to copy the back-up disk. With all our extras we may catch up on any intruders, should there be any. For general security and working purposes we shut down the complete system, retracted the data base hard disk from the back-up system and made a physical copy, re-inserted the back-up disk in the system and re-booted. Using the copied disk, we've established a separate subsidiary stand-alone system with a new security software package. We didn't find any bugs or Trojans. We're using duplicate data files, databases and programmed some new alarm mechanisms. The new temporary system is an in-house stand-alone operating system with a special security firewall and no hardware or software communication facilities. It is situated in a protected room in this secure area. There are only three access working terminal units within that room that have been designated to five people. I have a list of those persons and would prefer to keep it on a need to know basis. During this investigation we'll be using the cached back-up database now situated on the stand-alone system. All specific documentation during the investigation is to be entered into this system only.'

I stifled a yawn, thinking how ridiculous he was overdoing the handling of the situation – got his priorities muddled – typical Langley touch. Jack carried on, seemingly in his element,

'The RRT have been searching through Martin's computer files, any files from cases left at home and in his office. Various other possibilities have been checked without result. We've found no indications pointing to his disappearance or his involvement in Ian's death. That may be good, but it all looks too clean. Apart from a few personal photographs, mostly involving the crowd here, there are no indications of a private life. As far as Ian is concerned, we have reason to believe Martin is in some way involved. We found a text message on Ian's mobile telephone directing him to meet a person called Martha Stern in the hotel where he was murdered. The message text was sent from Martin Cole's cell phone. Either he sent it himself or someone is holding Martin and did it or it was sent from a cloned cell phone with Martin's number. We now know Martha Stern was a Jewess and was murdered in Leipzig at about the same time Ian was taken out. She was involved in an Israeli/Palestinian help movement and was very critical of the current Israeli Government and the doings of the Mossad, which she has openly stated on an international platform. She was due to speak on a public platform in Leipzig on the day she was killed. I've spoken to Ian's direct colleagues. Other than Jacqueline du Fries, no one else knew about Ian's relationship with Martha Stern. How does she know? Well, Martha Stern rang up Ian once in the office. Jacqueline overheard Ian's part of the conversation. Afterwards, Ian explained to Jacqueline that he was very fond of Martha but was capable of keeping his private life apart from duty. Fortunately Jacqueline is a good listener and got Ian to tell her more about Martha. She managed to get a clear picture. Jacqueline tells me Ian reported all his movements concerning Martha to Martin Cole. There is nothing on records though, which is highly suspicious. It was because of this information from Jacqueline and Martin's disappearance that I took drastic security precautions.'

I stifled another yawn and thought I'd better boost Jack on that statement.

'I agree entirely Jack. That was the first and most important move for the RRT set-up under these circumstances.' I said, doing my utmost to keep my face rigid and poker-faced.

Jack nodded, looking closely at me to see if I was having him on. Satisfied he found no signs, he carried on,

'Now, about the weapon used. The ballistic report shows the bullet was calibre .308 Winchester. Hotel personnel and guests present at the estimated time of death, report not hearing any gunshots, so a silencer must have been used. The German LKA forensic laboratory experts have run searches through ballistic records. There's a suggestion a Mauser M 03 hunting rifle could be the weapon used. At 3.8 Kg, unloaded, without even telescopic sights, it's a fairly average weight for a hunting rifle. The killer must be used to animal hunting to use a rifle like that for killing people, if it is that type. The team is working on a number of possibilities. At this point we can't rule out any organization or persons.'

'What about Martha Stern? How was she murdered, Jack? What weapon was used?'

'She was stabbed whilst waiting in the middle of a crowd during a demonstration in Leipzig. From the reports it appears the killer was a young blond haired youth with an everyday German face and build, who was swallowed up by the crowd immediately afterwards. A cool calculated execution, over and done within seconds. No one near the victim could even describe the killer accurately. He knew what he was doing. A clean thrust under the ribs straight into the heart. With such force, he must have had direct facial contact. After the thrust, he pulled the knife out and put it under his jacket. It certainly couldn't have been an ordinary kitchen knife.'

'Due to the timing and distance between Berlin and Leipzig I guess we've got two separate killers and a major link to both victims.' I said, shaking off any personal feelings concerning Ian, now to be described as one of the victims.

Talk about killing! I thought I might be able to kill two birds with one stone, so I added a question,

'Jack, have you got anyone checking possible Arab-/Israeli or Nazi involvement, either in Ian's or Martha's case?'

'I suggest you talk to Gerard, I know you have some powerful Arab and Jewish contacts and the Rightist movements are in your field. Perhaps you could ask around? Oh, and bye the way John, what was the BND after?'

'Oh, nothing much of importance.' I said, wanting to keep my other involvements out of this for the time being.

Jack remained quizzical, expecting a follow-up explanation that I reluctantly gave,

'An old friend from the BND wanted some advice and help reactivating some of my old contacts. Nothing that will disrupt current operations.'

'Glad to hear it – now you go and talk to Gerard, you've got maximum clearance and don't forget tomorrow afternoon – Ian's oration.'

'I won't. Oh, and what I wanted to say earlier, but I didn't want to interrupt your train of thoughts was, I think with all due respects, we owe Ian the full works, – oration, a British guard of honour with a firing salute and bagpipes playing, preferably by a Scottish piper – a real Scottish farewell.'

Jack scowled, obviously displeased.

'I'll see what can be done,' he grunted, immediately lowering his head to the table to some paperwork – the signal to leave.

I know when it's time to put the right question for ending a session with Jack point blank. First thing though, I'll have to make sure the *bunch* from Charing Cross know about the funeral. I'll put Chris Fenton in the picture too.

The RRT office was a bustle of activity. The whiteboard that covered the long side of the room was in need of a few more non-permanent marker pen notations. As most of the information was second hand – from the German CID – I guess we had to make the most of it.

The victim board was reasonably filled with the crime scene photographs. It's very helpful at the start of a murder investigation getting to 'feel' the crime scene. All neon-ceiling lights were on, including a few spotlights. The blinds were down. Gerard was on the phone and the other three in the room didn't bother to look up when I came in, all of them staring at their terminals with their hands splayed on their keyboards. Two were talking into headphones. They were probably scouring the Internet or downloading files – or going through official databases, gaining useful information, I hoped. I know they'll get good results, after all, most of them have degrees in crime science and *the Agency* has sent some of them on various follow up analyst studies to the Jill Dando Institute of Crime Science in London. Terms like SARA (Scanning – Analysis – Response and Assessment), Crime Analysis Triangle, POP (Problem Oriented Policing), and Intelligence Analysis are in common use in the Crime Intelligence Analysis Department, when they get the chance to use it.

I followed the sparse notations, lines and links on the whiteboard – nothing Jack hadn't filled me in on. I had a look at the crime scene photographs. Putting my personal feelings aside, I studied Ian's forehead wound. The thought of the Winchester as the murder weapon got me itchy. I recalled everything I'd picked up on Martha. The photographs tell their own tale. Even in death she looked very pretty despite the look of surprise and pain etched into her face. I was stunned by the coroner's report on Martha. The stab wound depth measured 20 cm and the width of the cut was about 3.5 cm. The weapon had been half twisted in the wound too, before extraction. The type of weapon was described as most likely a bayonet. I immediately thought of a Nazi killer, a Jew hater – someone who'd gone through military training perhaps – a sadist as well. No killer in his right mind would use such a weapon in public. He must be immensely strong too, I thought, or his hatred gives him the extra strength. Both murders, it seems, point in the same direction, especially the time factor and both knowing each other. Unusual weapons too, for professionals, that's for sure. Going through the flipcharts, one in particular caught my attention – the distance from the hotel window to the shooting point – 60 metres, at an angle of 15 degrees. A professional killer would never have used such a rifle. I had a look at the printout of the crime mapping and analysis program. I picked up the marker pen and wrote a few of my own conclusions on the white board:

Killers:

- Not the general professional / assassin type in either killing – or are we being led astray?
- Ian Stewart – probably an expert hunter used to hunting with the Winchester and not the first time he's killed a person with that rifle. No inkling to any person or organization, as yet.
- Martha Stern – must be in fairly good physical condition - most likely a Right Wing militant Jew hater.

Very meagre I thought – *it's a long way to Tipperary!* Gerard van der Falk came over and laid his hand briefly on my shoulder just as I put the marker pen back. I'm not really particular about such body contact, but seeing he's a Dutchman, I let it go.

'Short holiday, eh? But it's nice to see you again John – good points!' he said, looking at the board and nodding his head in approval.

'Aye, it's good to be back, things were getting boring in London,' I replied cynically.

'Sorry it had to be Ian,' he said, sadly.

I didn't comment. I picked up the ballistic report and autopsy reports and turning to Gerard, said,

'Let's have a seat and go through what we've got.'

I left half an hour later, but not before I rang up the Stern's in Leipzig to arrange a visit that evening.

Olaf Ertl – Damascus, Wednesday 17th August 2005

Olaf Ertl entered the hotel room. It was reasonably quiet and smelled surprisingly fragrant. Probably recently squirted from an air freshener, or maybe they've just modernised the air-conditioning, he thought, as he put his case on the rack behind the door. He moved automatically to the bay windows and opened the balcony door. Turning back into the room, he picked up a chair from under an oriental table and placed it at the opening. He sat down and marvelled at the panorama of the old city of *Damascus*, the noise and bustle and the unmistakable smell of the Orient wafting its way into the room. His thoughts wavered for a few minutes, a brief smile appearing on his face – reminiscences of the past.

The call for late afternoon prayer from the minaret opposite released him from revenant history. He spotted the entrance of a huge bluebottle – big enough to decimate with a .45 revolver. Picking up the fly swatter from the table he hit it hard, too hard – leaving a bloody stain.

That brought his mind back to the business at hand. He got up quickly to shut the balcony door. At the door, he had second thoughts. He decided to go outside first and check out the neighbouring balconies. Satisfied, he shoved the door to and turned the handle into locking position.

He went back to the small table and lifted the phone from the cradle. The noise from the air conditioner was barely noticeable – plus points for the hotel, he thought. He gave a number to the receptionist and waited. A male voice answered in Arabic, asking him his business.

'My name is Olaf Ertl from Germany. I'm here on private business in Damascus and would like to speak to Mr Munir Gholam,' he answered, in his best Arabic.

'One moment Sir, I will see if His Excellency's available,' a voice at the other end answered. Probably a servant or secretary he reckoned.

He was put into space for a few minutes and listened to some lulling Arabic background music. The music was interrupted. He half expected Munir wouldn't be available.

'Allah be praised! It is I, Munir speaking. What a wonderful surprise, Olaf!'

'It's nice to hear you again Munir. I'm sorry I couldn't give you prior notice, but I wasn't aware myself until yesterday, of my coming. I'm afraid I'm here on a very delicate and urgent personal matter, nothing official. I thought, perhaps you might be able to help with a few suggestions?'

'Yes, of course – I understand. If it's so urgent then we can meet now if you like?'

'That's splendid Munir,' he answered.

'Look why don't we meet at Percy's – you remember?'

'Yes, I do. Thanks a lot Munir. I've just arrived, so I'll freshen up and be on my way in about ten minutes.'

'Okay, Olaf – I'll see you there.'

He put the phone down and made his way to the bathroom. He'd made up his mind before he left Germany, that Munir, a

Lebanese, who was involved in international cargo container transportation between Europe and the Middle East, would be the right person to contact. They'd both met during an international inquiry into weapon smuggling in Hamburg, where Munir was the contact person for a French company called *Forship* with links to the BIN LADEN GROUP, who were very interested in having the matter cleared rapidly. Olaf wasn't sure how far the links had grown since then, but knew he could possibly get to the right people through Munir for a start. Munir, he remembered, during the investigation in 1998, was very pertinacious about the innocence of the BLG that in the end became the official version. At least nothing defamatory could be found. The evidence against BLG was found unsubstantial. Munir, though, he thought at the time, had all the appearances of a well-trained intelligence operator.

He put on some light clothes and using the stairs, made his way down to the hotel lobby. Ignoring reception, he walked out into the evening air of Damascus that was still quite stifling.

He walked down the steps past the doorman giving him a slight nod. He turned to the left and walked briskly towards an alleyway that he knew led eventually to the *Kasbah*. Some time later, after dodging through several alleyways and making innumerable turns, he stepped into a teashop, a meeting place from early days given the pseudonym *'Percy's'*.

Olaf squinted his eyes to focus on the darker interior of the teashop and spotted Munir eventually. He was grinning all over his face, someone who obviously enjoyed being on the other side of the fence, or for a change, didn't have to play the role of underdog, or maybe he's just pleased. Arabs in general are very friendly and receptive when meeting people. The Oriental smile is like the Asian smile. Most of the time it's put on. The Americans have a similar habit with a tendency to over-exaggerate. Difficulties arise on differentiation, so it's always best just to make a try. The Europeans seem to do it best and stay courteous at the same time. Olaf thought, *'I do it my way!'*

Under normal circumstances Munir would've been the last person his old company would have let him contact officially. Not being in the BND anymore has some advantages though.

Berlin – Jan Hellstern, ex overt Mossad agent, Midday Wednesday 17th August 2005

I sat down again behind my briefly vacated desk at *the Agency* and dialled a number in Bernau, situated in the north-eastern outskirts of Berlin, where an old pal of mine from overt embassy days was now living in retirement. Waiting for the phone call to be answered, I recalled those memories of the past:

It used to be a sport amongst Intelligence agents during the Cold War, especially the CIA, to do the embassies and gather as many visiting cards as possible. The CIA regarded the card owners as potential clients, that is, sources, which was utter nonsense, but that's what they got paid for. We used to have a laugh and give them a run for their money by setting up teams to block them, butting into conversations and such like.

What a blow now though for such an organization after having been at the top for over 60 years, just because Bush is sore at them for giving up under White House and Pentagon pressure. Bush forgets he's the one that pushed them, together with the others in the White House, and above all the Rumsfeld maniacs at the Pentagon. ·

They all persuaded the CIA to produce just something, so

they could go to war in Iraq. The CIA should have stood their ground. Unfortunately George Tennett gave way to the threats about the uselessness of the CIA. Some say he was told they would break its back if he didn't bring up plausible information. Well they've done that anyway. Maybe now they've got the Patriot Act – Americans spy on Americans, they'll get wiser. It wasn't the CIA's uselessness – it was the arrogance and ignorance of a world power and a lousy President who just wanted to show his dad he could do it better – that's what caused 9/11 and its aftermath. History will show Bush the cowboy, who bullied his men to forge documents so they could go gun-down all them badies, just like in the good old days. The USA under Bush is becoming the world's most ruthless and hated government and that's the word in all agencies throughout the world. The world's eyes are all on Guantanamo too – that's enough to piss anybody off.

I was working as an overt agent, so called Military Attaché in Moscow when I came across Jan Hellstern from the Israeli embassy. He caught my eye once at one of those receptions where I appeared for the first time with my wife Anna. We'd just been married a couple of weeks earlier. Jan apparently knew Anna from Leipzig and came over to us. He introduced himself and gave Anna a hug. I wasn't too fluent in Hebrew, so I missed out on the burst that followed. When they'd calmed down, Jan apologized and changed into English. We all had a laugh watching the CIA agents doing their number that was so obvious at the time. I got the impression Jan knew a lot more about Anna's past than I did myself, but there again Jews do tend to be uppity and secretive at times. Anyway, it was something neither of them wanted to share with me, if indeed there was anything.

I was just about to put the phone back on the hook when it was picked up at the other end. A female voice with a Swiss German accent repeated the number I'd just dialled and cautiously asked my business.

'My name is John Jameson. I'm an old friend of Jan's. This is his number?'

'Yes, it is.'

'Can I speak to him?'

'I am so sorry, but Jan is in the city. If you like I can give him a ring and pass on your number?'

'That would be great, maybe I can meet up with him this afternoon?'

'Well, I don't know where he'll be – I'll just have to try and see if he answers my call.'

'Well, thanks a lot, here's my cell phone number.'

I gave her the number and said goodbye,

'Aufwiederhoeren.'

'Aufwiederluege,' she answered.

As I was about to be on my way to Leipzig I thought it wiser to have given her my cell phone number that under normal circumstances I wouldn't have done. I just didn't want Jan ringing up *the Agency* and his call being transferred to Jack Orlowski's secretary. I made a note to exchange the cell phone for a new one when I get back from Leipzig. Less than five minutes later my cell phone buzzed.

'Yes!' I barked.

'Hello, John, this is Jan speaking.'

'Hi, Jan. Thanks for ringing back so quickly. I'm in Berlin on my way through to Leipzig. I wondered if we could meet this afternoon?'

'Well, John, what a surprise! I've just finished some business here and was about to go home for an early lunch, but we could meet somewhere in the city and have a meal and a chat?'

'That would be great, Jan. What about Borchardt's, it's between the *Gendarmenmarkt* and the *Brandenburg Gate*. I know the *maitre* so we shouldn't have any trouble getting a table. Be my guest.'

'Well, thanks John, I know Borchardt's but getting a table is extremely difficult, so this'll be a real treat. I've heard so much about the restaurant. You know you can bump into almost any politician or celebrity there! Just like the old days, eh.' Jan sounded really enthusiastic now. I felt pleased with my choice.

'What about twelve mid-day, is that all right? It's eleven thirty-five now, so that should give us both enough time to get there.'

'Yes, that'll be perfect, John. See you there then – bye!'

Borchardt's is a Berlin classic that first opened in 1853. It was mostly destroyed during World War II and left to decay during the reign of the East German Communist regime. Re-opened in 1992 it's a real magnet for Berlin's political and social life. I needed Jan's help and this was going to be a starter in return.

Jan was waiting in a doorway, a couple of doors down from the restaurant. He slid out onto the pavement and made his way towards Borchardt's. His timing perfect, from the moment he saw me arrive in the taxi and move to the entrance. We shook hands casually, his grip a bit tighter than usual. We walked in without having said a word.

The *maitre* recognised me, having been here on a number of occasions, mostly with UN Security Council delegates. He directed us to a table in the corner. I had a brief glance around the room, noticing Joschka Fischer the German Foreign Minister and a few of his Green cronies stuffing themselves silly. No signs anymore of Joschka's jogging escapades judging by his corpulence, even though the press say he's taken it up again. He's certainly come up in the world, I thought. From throwing bricks at policemen during demonstrations and wearing plimsolls in parliament and now representing the German Government, he's really done well. No sign of Cameron Diaz or DiCaprio today. Jan will have to make do with Fischer, I guess.

We both ordered the classic Wiener schnitzels that are pounded flat nearly to the size of a dinner plate. We had French fries and salad to go with it and a bottle of 1985 Château Mouton Rothschild 1st Cru Class. I would have preferred a cheaper wine because at 545 a bottle I guess I'll be overdoing my meagre expense account and cause pandemonium at *the Agency* cashier's office, not to mention Jack's reprimand. I thought it maybe worthwhile giving Jan a treat.

We did some small talk, mostly asking the whereabouts of old embassy colleagues and acquaintances and recalling some hilarious events. We both avoided talking about Anna. Jan didn't mention the German Swiss woman who'd answered his phone either. After the main meal we had some fresh fruit salad and ice cream and finished off with Espresso. Jan knew this was the last place on earth to talk about their kind of business. I suggested a walk to the *Brandenburg Gate* and through the archway down *Unter den Linden* to *Alexanderplatz*. I thought that would give us plenty of time for a chat on the way and then we could split and take the tube from *Alexanderplatz* to wherever we had to go afterwards.

We walked under the archway of the *Brandenburg Gate*. I shuddered inwardly at the thought of how it used to be during the East German reign. I remembered numerous occasions, standing on the Western side eying the Vopos, seeing and feeling the evil, oozing from the concrete walls and barriers that separated the same nation. Thank you *Solidarnosc*, thank you John Paul, thank you Gorbi for *Perestroika*, thank you Ronnie for giving Gorbi the tip *tear down this wall* and thank you East German Monday demonstrators – all of you together brought that wall down.

We stopped at one of the many benches *Unter den Linden* and sat down. A chilly wind had come up. The sun was hiding under thick blankets of cloud too – fat chance of eavesdroppers.

Jan sighed and half-turning to me, said.

'We're in for some bad times John, really bad times from what I've heard in the grapevine.'

'I've been hearing some troubling stories about renegade Mossad Kidon teams here in Europe. Is there anything in that?'

'Not only in Europe John, there seems to be worldwide take-outs. No one in his right mind would talk about this anywhere so let's change the subject. I'd like to enjoy a few more years of my pension, thank you very much,' he grinned laconically.

'Then it seems I've looked you up at the wrong time Jan. I was after some information about certain characters. It's probably too dangerous even to ask around *ad lib* at the moment.'

'It depends who you're after John.'

'What about Martha Stern, Anna's half-brother Ben and a certain Kenneth Woodward.'

'You really are sadistic John. That's definitely turning the thumb-screw, you know.'

'I know you were fond of Anna, Jan. There was some secret bind neither of you wanted to talk about.'

Jan ignored my comment.

'I can tell you about Kenneth Woodward. He's in the Mossad and responsible for Central Europe. I'm not aware of his speciality. Anna's half-brother's name is Ben Goldmann. You'll find him in the Mossad liquidation department or somewhere equivalent that's really gory. Martha Stern was in some way connected to Anna. It has something to do with Anna's childhood. That's all I can tell you.'

'Jan, you know I wouldn't be putting you at risk by contacting you if there wasn't an emergency. Even after Anna's death I left you alone, although there were a number of things unclear. At the back of my mind I always thought you'd be able to supply the answers. Anyway, at the moment I need to know how I can get in contact with Ben Goldmann and Kenneth Woodward? I've tried through normal channels but had no luck.'

Jan stared at me without expression. I thought he was going to stare me out, but after some seconds he broke the silence and said,

'John, I'll give you two inside numbers, that's all I can offer. The first one is for Ben Goldmann and the other is for Kenneth Woodward. You realize, that by contacting Ben through official channels may have brought both him and yourself in dire danger. The numbers I've given you should get you through to both parties directly. When you call them, don't go into any detail, just demand an appointment to see them on neutral ground and don't forget to protect your rear – that is vital! I don't have to tell you not to meet them on your own!'

With that, Jan tore a page from his notebook and wrote down the numbers. He handed me the piece of paper and pressed it into my hand. I started to say something, but Jan grabbed my arm in a vice grip and said,

'Enough has been said good friend. Let us depart now without solace – Shalom, John and good luck.'

Jan got up, and without a handshake or a glance back, he disappeared in a group of sightseeing tourists just passing by.

I waited a few minutes before I got up and walked the rest of the way to *Alexander Platz,* my mind set on the two calls I'll make soon.

Tel-Aviv – Mossad, Wednesday 17th August 2005

David Silverman, head of the Mossad *Liquidation* department, picked up the phone. ' Yes, what is it Judith, you know I'm not to be disturbed.'

'I'm sorry sir, but you did say any more public mention of the name Ben Goldmann was to be reported to you immediately.'

'And?'

'Well we have an enquiry through an overt line from the ISIA Berlin requesting a meeting with Mr Goldmann.'

'Well!'

'Sorry sir, it was requested by a Mr John Jameson.'

'So, so, he's coming out into the open is he?'

'I beg your pardon sir?'

'I'm just thinking out loud, Judith.'

'Oh!'

'Did he state the purpose of his request?'

'Yes sir, he did.'

'Well, what the hell was it you stupid woman?'

'Hmm! He states it is an anti-terror matter that can only be clarified by Mr Goldmann.'

'Well, put the message in my in-tray and bring it to me with the rest of the mail later on this afternoon and don't disturb me anymore – do you understand, Judith?'

'Yes, sir!'

Judith Salomon placed her phone back on the hook. Her hand was shaking and her face was as red as a beetroot.

'That bad was it,' said her colleague Sarah, who was sitting behind the opposite desk.

Judith Salomon got her breath back and fumed out,

'What a despicable person! I wish I were back in the Human Resources Department. At least they've good manners there. Have you seen how he sits in that office, Sarah? – Like a big fat menacing toad spitting out gall. He doesn't even shave properly, not to mention those gorilla hairs sprouting from neck and chest and above his collar. Have you seen the hairs on his face, hanging out his nose and ears? It's disgusting – eee... git!'

A voice bellowed from Mr Silverman's office – the door was slightly ajar,

'You do know the purpose of this department Ms Salomon?'

Complete menacing silence descended on the office and Judith Salomon's complexion changed from deep red to chalk white as she realized the folly of her outburst. She was now shaking convulsively. She logged herself out of the computer and switched it off. Opening her side cupboard, she took out her bag and without further ado left the office. Her colleagues, still under the influence of the threat, watched her actions in amazement. Sarah's looks were more like admiration. Judith knew she was in for trouble.

One of the reasons they had Judith working for the *Liquidation Dept.* was her photographic memory. She remembered Ben Goldmann's address and telephone number because it was only last week she had to deal with an official charge against him from the UN Human Rights department. Knowing the telephones were monitored she decided there and then to confront Mr Goldmann personally and inform him of the awaiting doom. She knew he would be put on the hit list now – at least that's what she heard Mr Silverman say to the *Kidon* chief if any more public mention of the name Ben Goldmann was made.

Ben Goldmann was on lay-off after an assignment in Iraq. He was busy writing a lengthy report on his computer when the doorbell rang. He went to the door and stood at the side observing the visitor through the CCTV-camera placed above the entrance. He recognised the new secretary from fat boy's office and opened the door.

'This is a big surprise Judith,' he said.

Noticing the worried expression on Judith's face, he added,

'Is something up? I can see there must be. Come in – let's go into the sitting room, we can talk in there.'

Ben Goldmann led her into the sitting room. She still stood undecided. He went over to her, took her by the arm and led her to the settee. He placed his hands on her shoulders lightly, forcing her to sit down. He took a seat opposite and said,

'You seem to be very worried indeed Judith, but it's all right – it's safe to talk, I check the room out daily.'

Judith explained the reason for her visit and her concern that he, Ben Goldmann has most probably been put on the L-list. She told him about her stupid outburst and her fear she too was now on that list.

Ben Goldmann studied the situation, realizing Judith was still very traumatized.

Judith relaxed slightly, but still had an uncertain feeling if she'd done the right thing.

'Okay, now tell me exactly what was in the message to Mr Silverman.'

Judith repeated the context word for word.

'Okay Judith, what I want you to do is not to go home for the next four or five hours. Go to the museum for the rest of the day. I'll go to the office and clear things up. Go back to work tomorrow as though nothing has happened – okay?'

'Okay, Mr Goldmann – you're sure I'll be all right, I mean I won't be put on that dreadful list, will I?'

'Certainly not, Judith, not if I can help it. You just leave things to me.'

Ben Goldmann showed her to the door, trying hard to hide his impatience. He knew he'd have to work fast before fat boy got the word out.

He left the flat shortly afterwards. On his way out, he sent a coded text message to two colleagues to meet him at the corner of *Sderot Dizengoff Street* and *HaMelekh George Street*. Ben Goldmann knew there was still time as fat boy doesn't sort his mail out until the afternoon. It was lunchtime now and he knew where to find him.

The following day Judith went back to work as usual. As she went through security control the guard stepped up to her. Judith thought – she's a goner now.

'Feeling better today are we, Miss Salomon? You looked very unwell yesterday.'

'Uh, oh, yes! I'm feeling much better today thank you.'

'You still look very pale. You ought to see a doctor, you know.'

'Yes, thanks, maybe if I've the time I'll do just that.'

The guard shook his head knowingly.

Judith pulled her card through, moved to stand at the feet markings and waited for iris control. The green light showed and the stile-bar-lockage buzzed giving her free passage through.

Most of her colleagues were already there. Judith went over to her desk, put her bag away and sat down, dreading the moment when Mr Silverman gave his morning shout. She turned on her computer and logged herself in, relaxing as she realized she still had access. She settled back in her chair and glanced across to Sarah who was staring at her with an expression Judith had never seen on Sarah's face before – a mixture of amazement, disbelief and wonder.

'What's up Sarah?' she asked.

'Have you read the papers yet Judith?'

'No, not yet – why? Is there something special?' she said innocently, not knowing.

'You'd better read this yourself Judith.'

Sarah handed her a copy of the HAARETZ newspaper and moved around the desk to her side.

'There, look at the statement from the restaurant in the *Sderot Dizengoff Street.*'

Sarah read the article and felt her heart thumping. She caught the faint in time and took a deep breath. Her mind was working very quickly as she realized that hers and Mr Goldmann's problem had now been solved. She just hoped she wasn't next on Mr Goldmann's private list.

Sarah talked excitedly,

'No wonder he had a heart attack with all that fat he carried around. Serves him right, bloody bastard. Good riddance, that's all I can say. I expect we'll all have to attend his farewell party,' she said, giggling at her joke.

'I wonder who's going to be our new boss?' asked Sarah innocently.

Judith's mind was now doing summersaults.

The Sterns, Wednesday 17th August 2005

I gave Elsa a call from the train. She sounded worried, as Olaf hadn't made his check-in call at the agreed time. I tried to calm her down. I told her she knew Olaf was in Syria. I told her to wait until my next call was due and if he hadn't checked in, then I'd do something about it.

I arrived at Leipzig *Hauptbahnhof* shortly before 7 pm and went straight for a taxi. I gave the address to the driver who made a face when he heard it. Without further ado he jerked the taxi from the curb into the moving traffic.

The taxi stopped at a row of tenement buildings in East Leipzig that hadn't seen much paint in the last 60 odd years. Chunks of the façade rendering were missing, showing the uneven rows of bricks underneath. Looks like some of the rebuilding work of the *Trümmerfrauen* just after World War II has been brought to the light of day, I thought. Some workers were unloading scaffolding from the side of a lorry, so it looked like something was going to be done at last to stop the building from collapsing.

I pressed the buzzer once for Stern and waited. I stepped back a bit from the door and looked up when I heard someone calling. I realized then they didn't have an intercom. I shouted my name up and the door lock buzzed. I pushed the door open and climbed the stairs. Inside, it was very clean. The wooden banisters were worn but shining. The smell of disinfectants, polish and the lack of dust, gave a sense there were a lot of elderly folks living here. The young and middle aged usually don't give a damn nowadays. I reached the fourth floor where an old man with hard, squinted, steel blue eyes that stood in contrast to his aristocratic nose, was standing near the banisters. I'd noticed someone looking down at me whilst climbing the stairs. He remained staring as I reached his landing. I held out my hand and said,

'John Jameson from Berlin – I rang up at midday.'

'Ah, yes – Jameson the Scottish man.'

He ignored my outstretched hand and pointed to the opened door.

I was annoyed at myself for forgetting to say good evening. I wonder how the old man knew I'm a Scot because my German is so good I usually get mistaken for a Black Forester or a Schwab.

The old man led me into the main sitting room. Black clad figures in mourning attire were sitting at a settee group. Judging by the heavy odour of alcohol and the reddened cheeks, they'd already had a few. It smelled fairly familiar. I guessed they were sipping *Abtel*.

I stopped just inside the doorway to the living room. The old man grabbed me fiercely by the arm and pulled me to the front of the group.

'This is Mr Jameson the Scottish man,' he snarled, harshly.

I wondered for a minute, whether the old man had Alzheimer's or something. A slim woman, about forty, I figured, stood up and came towards me. She was quite tall too, I thought.

'Don't mind granddad, he's very direct,' she said, grinning. She held out a slender hand that had a strong grip. A sign I was not totally unwelcome, I thought.

'I'm Paula – come over here and let me introduce you to everyone,' she said, in a very soft and sonorous voice with the touch of a foreign accent. She wasn't brought up in Leipzig, I noticed.

'We're still shaken about Martha. You know we couldn't bury her until this morning – sad, isn't it,' she said.

I didn't comment – I was feeling most uncomfortable being introduced to all these mourners. I did my best to say hello and mutter some words of condolence. After the introductions were over, a moment of silence passed over the group that was finally broken by Paula, who was being nudged by one of the older women.

'Would you like a cup of tea and some *Biskotchos* or *Halvah?*'

Memories of Anna were awoken. *'Don't object to tea and Halvah, if you ever get the chance of being offered some. That would be a very unfriendly gesture!'* My voice kind of choked. I managed to stammer out,

'Yes, please – thank you very much.'

Paula opened the guest cabinet and took out two cups and saucers and a sugar bowl that I guessed were *Meissner*. She pulled out a drawer in the cabinet, took out a black casket and removed a couple of antique looking silver spoons, which she placed on the saucers. She went into the kitchen to make tea that seemed to take a lifetime. Nobody spoke – they just kept staring. I felt inclined to get up and follow her but the laws of gravity and the stares kept me glued to the chair.

She came back holding a teapot covered by a patchwork tea cosy – placed it on a tea stand, removed the tea cosy, and notwithstanding a touch of professionalism, poured the tea into the cups. I've gotten used to drinking tea without milk in Germany. They forget that Brits have the habit of drinking their tea *with* milk. Under these circumstances, I thought I'd better keep my mouth shut and not ask for milk. I sipped my tea and munched the sesame honey bar with all eyes watching. Only Paula was talking, asking about my journey down, in between sips of tea. Not a word from the others. They remained staring at me. I washed down the rest of the honey bar with a last swig of tea, hoping nothing was left sticking to my front teeth. I waved Paula off, as she was about to pour me another cup.

Granddad piped in,

'The Scottish man will want to talk now, Paula. Take him into the study and tell him all he wants to know,' he said with an undertone of viciousness.

I felt embarrassed – all heat up.

Paula smiled, picked up the crockery and took them into the kitchen. She came back grinning as she noticed they were all still staring at me. She beckoned me to follow her. She led me down a corridor and into a medium sized study. The walls were lined with bookshelves holding many ancient looking books. A large map covered a desk in the corner. A rustic leather armchair was placed behind it. Anyone sitting there could overlook the whole room and anyone coming in. Books were spread and piled up around the desk and on the floor, some of them open. I felt I was about to discover something very important.

Paula waited until I was in the middle of the room, before she shut the door. She turned towards me giggling herself silly for a few seconds. I knew I was the object of her amusement.

'I'm sorry, but you should see yourself. You look like a young schoolboy who's been caught in the act by teacher.'

'Well, in actual fact that's exactly how I feel.'

I relaxed and gave a smile of relief.

'I felt like I was in front of the inquisition,' I added.

Her faced tightened. Her voice turned solemn.

'It wasn't meant to be. You see they're all confused. Aunt Hera was in Auschwitz and grandma and granddad just missed transportation and now Martha's been murdered. But first of all you'll have to be patient, I've a lot to tell you. Granddad insists you stay here tonight. We've made up the guestroom bed for you. What do you say.'

I was overwhelmed.

'I really don't know what to say – it's as though I'm a long lost brother on my first family reunion instead of being an intelligence crime analyst investigating a crime.'

'Just say yes,' she said.

'Yes, of course,' I stammered, 'I'll stay.'

'Allright then, that's settled,' she paused for a moment and looked me in the eyes quizzically.

'You really don't know about us do you?'

'I don't know what you're implying!' I said, not wanting her to know that I knew about a connection between them and Anna. Well, all I knew, there was a connection, but I didn't know what it was.

'This may come as a shock, John. We are Anna's relatives.'

I looked at her, struck dumb for a moment. The whole misery of my wife Anna being killed by a hit and run driver in Schwenningen wakened memories. I pictured it all again – identifying Anna in the morgue, the funeral and the emptiness afterwards. I choked as I attempted to answer. I felt the impedance in my left ear rising. Bloody tinnitus again – it never really leaves me, but now I feel as though I'm in the disco, instead of in the middle of an IRA bomb blast! Looking back, it had just been my bad luck to have aproached Castlereagh RUC Station as a hijacked paper lorry exploded. Paula pointed to the leather covered chairs in front of the desk. We sat down, both moving our chairs to face each other.

'Well, gathering from your reaction you don't seem to know, so I'll start with grandma and granddad.'

She started to talk. I felt like getting up and leaving as I hate hearing the horrifying stories about the Nazi deportation and gassing of the Jews, but I managed to sit there and just listen.

'They managed to escape shortly before the Nazi's started deportation in our street. Martha's granddad, who was one of the youngest Rabbi's in Leipzig, was one of the very few who didn't believe the Nazi's. When he found out their street was next, he managed to leave beforehand through a Christian organization, who helped them get to Schwenningen in the Black Forest, where they stayed hiding for some months in the catacombs of a Protestant church.

A priest in Schwenningen, now amalgamated with Villingen and called Villingen-Schwenningen, which is only 40 Km from the Swiss border, fed them and kept them hidden for months. They were given authentic new identity papers and were eventually led safely over the border to Switzerland. The rest of our families were murdered by the Nazi's.'

I felt very uncomfortable.

'Don't take this as an admonishment,' she said. This is the way we all feel. It's part of our life. You should know that.'

'Why do you say that?' I asked.

'Well, from what Aunt Hera has told us, she knows you were the husband of Anna Zukowski, who's step-father Ephraim Suckenic was a famous Archaeologist. He was very young at the time and was one of those who helped to find and save the remains of the Dead Sea scrolls in 1947. He passed away last year.'

I was thunderstruck and looked obviously anguished.

'You don't know do you? I would have thought Anna had told you.'

'No, she didn't. Anna was very secretive about her family.

All I know is about a half-brother called Ben who's in the Israeli Diplomatic Corps.'

'You mean the Mossad,' she said maliciously, her face contorted into a sneer.

'Well, that's what I'd assumed.'

'Ben is not to be trusted.'

'Why's that.'

'Just take my word for it, he's a real heteronomic.'

'Tell me about Anna, then. How close were you to Anna?'

'I was brought up in Haifa in the German colony near *Kiryat Eliyahu*. Anna's parents got divorced and Ephraim Zuckenic got married to Anna's mother Sarah when Anna was five years old. My mother is Ephraim Suckenic's sister Sara, which makes her Anna's Aunt and Anna my half cousin. My mother, who didn't marry, is still in Haifa. Martha is the daughter of Ephraim and Sarah, making Anna her older stepsister. Martha took on the name Stern later on. I don't know the reason for that, though.

Anna's mother Sarah was an archaeologist too. They were very often away from home at archaeological sites for months at a time, so Anna stayed with us. She was the sister I always wanted to have. We are, eh, were, both the same age.'

'But why didn't she tell me all this and why weren't you all at our wedding?'

'That was granddad – he was against the wedding, you know, you being a Catholic and all that. Anna's mother was working at an important site with Anna's stepfather. They said they were on a time bonus so they couldn't leave the site. Anna was very upset. I talked to her about it. She told me, *either they all come, or they can stay away.*'

'Why didn't you come to the funeral at least?'

'Well, we didn't know. It was only months after when we found out through Ben. By then it was too late.'

I thought – that was odd. Why didn't Ben tell them? I informed him on time.

'Aunt Hera, who is Anna's grandma's sister, grandma and I went to see her grave some months later. You have given her a beautiful resting place, John. I may call you John?'

I felt an overproduction of eye fluid make my eyes water. I sniffed it away.

'Yes, please do... Paula.'

'Did you notice the stones we left on top of the gravestone?'

'Yes, I did. I thought her half-brother Ben had left them.'

'Well, after visiting the grave, we all went to Zurich to see some distant relatives.'

'What happened to Anna's natural father?'

'He went to a Kibbutz north of Tel Aviv where he met a new partner, Alda Goldmann, but they didn't marry. Their son is Ben Goldmann. We haven't seen or heard of Anna's father since.'

'You know John, we believe Anna was killed deliberately.'

'Why do you believe that?'

'Well, just before she was killed, she rang us up – granddad had a long talk with her.'

My senses were up.

'Where did they have the long talk and what did they talk about?'

'In here. You haven't noticed a telephone because granddad puts it away in the desk cupboard. I don't know what they talked about, you'll have to ask granddad.'

'Apropos telephone, I've got to give someone a call. Do you mind showing me my room? We can carry on our conversation later.'

'Yes, of course,' she said, looking at me bewildered. I followed her out of the room and shut the door. She went to walk down the corridor but I grabbed her by the arm. She immediately tried to squirm out of my grasp. I let go and put my finger to my lips.

'I think you've been bugged,' I whispered in her ear.

She pulled her head back and looked at me annoyed. Slowly, though, her face smoothed as she caught the meaning of my words. Her mouth opened. She moved her lips and pointed to the study. I nodded and carried on down the corridor. She followed with a little girl look on her face. I let her pass. She pointed to a room on the right.

'That's the guest room,' she whispered, her voice sounding excited.

We entered the room.

'Your bag's over there,' she pointed to a cupboard, where his overnight bag was lying.

I went over to the bag and pulled out one of my bug-detectors. I motioned her out into the corridor. I followed her out, shut the door and stopped. She stopped too. I whispered in her ear.

'Just a precautionary measure – this is a bug-detector. I just want to be sure about my assumption before we carry on with our conversation.'

She nodded, looking relieved.

'I'll go through the room on my own, but I'll leave the door wide open so you can see what I'm doing.'

We went back to granddad's study. I checked to see the blinds were down and went over to the radio on the sideboard cupboard and switched it on, tuning in to a German folk music channel. I opened the desk cupboard, lifted the telephone onto the desktop and twisted the mouthpiece off, checking the inside. I didn't need the bug detector here. My eyes and experience showed me this was bugged. I waved Paula over, putting my forefinger to my lips to caution her. I pointed to the tiny gadget that I recognised as a type used by the East German *Stasi* during the cold war. Paula shrugged her shoulders. I pointed to my ear and nodded my head to Paula who cottoned on. I carried on my search of the room finding another three bugs. At this point I decided I'd found enough evidence and catching Paula's eye I pointed to the door moving my hand in a shoving movement. I switched the radio off before we left the room making sure the door was shut properly. I took her hand and pulled her gently down the corridor a bit before I stopped, let go of her hand, and addressed her,

'I've done a first check of the room, but the range of my bug detector is limited. Normally I would do a grid search of the room to be absolute certain of finding them all,' I whispered.

'Is the bathroom on the back side of the flat?' I asked.

Paula nodded, a smile had formed and her cheeks were slightly reddened. I motioned her to show me the way.

I went into the bathroom and did a quick sweep with my bug detector.

'It's clean, you can come in,' I urged her, motioning with my hand. I turned the shower on and let the tap run just in case directional microphone beamers from the outside were active. She stood at the door hesitating. I went over to her, pulled her arm gently and shut the door. She was stiff – an awkward situation.

'I'm sorry Paula, but someone's listening in on all conversations in the study, and maybe elsewhere in the flat. If I remove the bugs, then they'll know. That could make things dangerous for us all, as we don't know what their reaction would be and what organisation we're up against. One thing we do know is they might be perpetrators who don't stop at killing people. Speaking in here is just a small precaution. I expect there are more bugs throughout the flat. This is about the only place we can talk at the moment I'm afraid. I would have suggested going for a walk somewhere, but I don't like the look of the district and I haven't got my team with me. Conversations outside can also be eavesdropped by directional microphones, so we can forget that.'

'Yes!' she said, 'I understand. It's not very comfortable though,' giving me a wicked smile.

I smiled back, squeezed her shoulder slightly and moved her gently to the one and only seat in the room. Her smile continued.

'Quite the gentleman, John!'

We both laughed.

'Before we carry on, I'd like to give my HQ a ring for reinforcements. Okay!'

She nodded.

I gave *the Agency* a call on my cell phone.

'Alpha ten eight, zero Juliet Golf Golf, ten nine, over.'

'Zero Juliet Golf Golf, over,' came the reply.

I attached my scrambler dongle and entered the combination code for digital scrambling. I spoke urgently, giving my requirements for a support team and the liaison policeman and rang off. I turned to Paula,

'It's 8 pm now, so my team won't be here before 1 am early morning tomorrow. I think we'd better carry on our chat in here and you fill me in,' I said, adding a warning, 'I would prefer you didn't tell anyone whatsoever about the bugs. Not until the team gets here and the whole flat's been cleared. We have to let whoever is listening think they're undiscovered. My team will arrive in a special ops van so they'll be able to locate the exact position of the eavesdroppers. They'll have a liaison man from the Regional CID with them who'll inform the German anti-terrorist squad. I hope they'll be able to arrest whoever's responsible,' I said, thinking about Anna's and Martha's killer, 'but before we carry on with our conversation, I'll just do a quick check of the flats opposite from the guest room. I'll be back in a few seconds.'

Not waiting for an answer I went to my room to fetch my generation 4 DARK INVADER, multi-purpose pocket-scope, Night Vision Device (NVD), from my bag. Leaving the lights off, I pulled the blinds up just enough to see across the road.

On a quick sweep of the apartments opposite, one of the flats caught my immediate attention. My binoculars picked up a figure at one of the windows wearing NVD goggles. I immediately stepped to the side away from the window. That recce told me – no curtains – blinds up on all other windows except for one that was halfway down. The one in particular had curtains and the window was open, the curtain flapping in the wind. Experience tells me a static surveillance team has a stakeout over there and the Sterns are the targets.

I let the blinds down slowly to the bottom. Keeping the lights off, I moved along the side of the room to the door, opened it quickly and slid out. I went back to the bathroom where Paula was still sitting, shifting her bottom impatiently.

I went over to the wide ledge at the end of the bath, shoved a few bottles and bathroom accessories aside, took a bath towel from a rack and laid it on the tiles to sit on. Better sitting here on this shelf than on the floor below Paula's eye level, I thought. Besides I didn't feel like getting piles by sitting on the cold tiles.

'Okay Paula, I hate to say this, but my check of the flats opposite made out at least one surveillance team.'

Paula looked grave – her face dropped – the cheeks that had been full were now drooping. My mind was doing overtime. Obviously the stakeout has been there for quite some time. That is good news because they obviously haven't yet got what they want. On the other hand they know of my presence and most probably know I'm from *the Agency*. Of course there is the possibility they might not be assassins, maybe a different *bunch* or even official.

'What was it Anna told you?' I asked.

'It's a bit complicated and has to do with a theory of Anna's stepfather. His name was Ephraim Suckenic – an Archaeologist as I already said. The deciphering of the scrolls was eventually taken over by a few so-called illustrious experts. Typical of Jewish scholars, the older they are the more experienced, thus there being no room for the expertise of younger scholars. They were treated like young children. Ephraim used to say *'they were to be seen but not heard – just like the Victorians!'* In other words they were the *dogsbodies*.'

She noticed his raised eyebrow.

'What is it?' she asked.

'You *are* talking about the Dead Sea Scrolls?'

'Of course, what did you think?'

I kept further commentaries to myself, not wanting to get her worked up, so I just shrugged my shoulders, trying to remember what I knew about the most enigmatic documents ever found. The only surviving Jewish manuscript library of the late Second Temple period recording the years between 150 BC and AD 68 – found initially by Bedouins who sold a lot on the black market before archaeologists cottoned on and began excavating the eleven caves at Qumran and a settlement of the Essenes nearby. Most documents officially found have been recorded and translated.

Paula, with a slight look of admonishment on her face for my disturbance, carried on with her story,

'Ephraim managed to stay on the team for some time. The information he gained, and his ideas, were mostly waved aside. He found a lot of writings at the Qumram library reputed to be from some papyrus scrolls found in caves between Masada and Qumram where the Dead Sea Scrolls were also found. The writings however date back to the early first century – 30 AD.'

'That puts a blow to the bible then, eh!' I said with an undertone of sarcasm in my voice.

She looked at me quizzically.

'What do you mean by that?' she asked, pointedly, obviously annoyed by further interruption but made curious by my remark.

'Well, if those writings were reputed to be from the early first century then there must be a lot in it that's been left out in the bible. From my knowledge, the New Testament was based on the Gospels of Mark, Luke, Matthew and John that were originally written between 60-90 AD and they were contradictory too,' I answered.

'I don't quite follow you,' she said.

'Look, how about, if I tell you what I know of the basics and you fill in the rest, or correct me if I'm wrong. Otherwise we're going to be here all night passing the why's and wherefores to and fro.'

My mind needed something to do to stop me thinking too much about Anna and the threat across the street and I wanted to keep this conversation as short as possible.

'Okay, then tell me your version, John,' she sighed.

I nodded and took over,

'Well, Anna had great patience explaining early Christianity to me, so here goes. There has been an upcoming yearning for information by moderate Christians and Jews over the last three or four decades to confess to the 'sins of scripture'. They feel they've been misled. The Essenes were a Jewish orthodox movement that settled on a plateau we now call Qumran near the Dead Sea. The ancient biblical name was Secacah. We know a lot more about the Essenes and the possibility that their way of life influenced Jesus and his followers, and formed the basis for the Christian way of living we know today, at least that now seems more than likely.

Liberal scholars have been questioning the historical accuracy of the New Testament for more than a decade, now that the contents of numerous scrolls have been interpreted and the far-reaching links have been opened to the public. In their view, the Gospels should now be reduced to just a couple of verses. Great doubt remains that the context of the New Testament Gospels, ignoring early scripts and written some time after the incidents happened, are at all accurate. To be banal, in a courtroom the entity of the Gospels would not be allowed as evidence, it would be waved off to hearsay and contradiction. The same can also be said about the Koran. For too long Muslims have been sticking fingers in their ears, chanting *Islam means peace* to drown out the negative noise of their holy book. For instance – the Islamic Jihad or holy war of today is an oxymoron. Allah of Islam, Adonai of Judaism and the Father of Christianity are all the same. It's never holy to take the life of another believer just because he or she has a slightly different understanding of God. Such a war can only be an unholy war. There's an interesting section in the Muslim Koran backing this. It says:

To each among you – we prescribed a law and an open way. If God had so willed, he would have made you a single people, but his plan is to test you in what he has given you – so strive as in a race in all virtues. The goal is to God – it is he that will show you the truth of all matters in which you dispute.

That's from the Koran, Ali translation, *The Table 5:51.*'

Paula smiled, her eagerness to hear more simplicities quite apparent. I carried on,

'The main message God is also telling us, is that he derives more pleasure from kindness to each other than he does from worship,'

I noticed she was enjoying my little speech and felt encouraged to continue,

'The diversity of early Christianity is in the minds of a lot of Christians. Nowadays they have a craving for mystical spirituality and enlightenment. They simply want to know the truth without any frills. Why weren't the early scripts of James and Paul made known earlier like the bible, not to mention the numerous other scripts that were known at the time the bible was written? The answer to that is quite obvious – they didn't come up to someone's expectations. There was obviously great censuring, perhaps even the *swords of Damocles* hanging over the writers? A lot was left out on purpose. That seems to be the general opinion. Some people believe the New Testament, as we know it, is not the message Jesus wanted to give us. They think he must have left us a personal written guide, or message that is being kept from us, or is still hidden somewhere. There was also a significant find in the Egyptian town of *Nag Hammadi* in 1945. A remarkable trove of 46 non-canonical Gospels, biographies of Christ, epistles and apocalypses dated the end of the first century AD, were found and some of them point to the Gospel of Thomas. Due to the findings, more liberal historians came to view early Christianity with names like *Gnosticism, Ebionism* and *Marcionism*, each of them offering a different version of Christ and Christians. The orthodox stem, it seems had only gradually strangled or absorbed the others. The scarcity of lost script texts did not reflect unpopularity in their day so much as a later campaign by the church in our day and age to eliminate what it deemed as misguided teachings. This points towards a tailored New Testament bible also excluding the Gospel of Thomas.'

I stopped my favourite topic and waited for Paula's approval.

'John, you really surprise me. You have made things easier for me to explain, because that's the way Ephraim and many others think. This was what Ephraim was trying to tell his superior scholars at Qumram decades ago. You see, the documents and scrolls found in the Qumram caves was like finding a lost library. The fact remains – it is the only surviving Jewish library of the late *Second Temple* period covering the years 150 BC to 68 AD. Ephraim was very upset about the blindness of Jewish and Christian scholars for disregarding all those references. On the other hand, it's easy to criticise once you know what they mean and where to look. There are so many pointers even from 300 AD onwards that were blatantly ignored in many scripts. It is so surprising how the Christian church has ignored them so willingly or failed to recognise them. In many cases Greek translated copies of the original scrolls were used, which means there are definitely mistakes. Translation errors have been proven in numerous cases. A lot of the answers could be found by simply doing modern digital copies of the documents held in the Vatican and have them checked with the original scrolls. That *would be* progress and enlightenment,'

Paula had taken over that's for sure, I thought!

'Ephraim was fully convinced, Jesus of Nazareth may have left a message for mankind in some form, either written papyrus scripts or maybe even copper plate. He was obsessed by the fact that Jesus may have left a key to the Ark of the Covenant in written form in his testament for mankind. I think Ephraim went over his head. *Any* notes from Jesus would be a salvation. Many of our wars are religious in nature – indeed, the cause of war has always been attributable to very few causes – disputes over territory, natural resources and economic/political systems, capitalism vs. communism, or religion. An Ark find would make a religious re-awakening and peace possibility to all the religious conflicts. Jesus was apparently able to read, according to the scripts, so he must have been able to write. It is so unbelievable nothing is ever mentioned in that direction. Not even a hint or any questioning of this factor. At a young age he was able to discuss with the elders in the temple at Jerusalem – where did he gain all the knowledge? So many scripts have been found that were written by others who followed his preaching and wanderings but nothing so far has been found that Jesus has ever written. One of the writings in Qumram library suggests holy scrolls that were enshrined in a secret place two years after Jesus from Nazareth was crucified. Ephraim reckons the original scrolls of these particular Qumram records didn't come from the Dead Sea Caves but originate from somewhere else. Bits of scrolls from *Cave 7* also make similar indications. They point to an Area in the South Lebanon known as the *Dead Sea Trade Route*,'

'I still don't think that's enough reason to kill Anna? Most of that information is open to the public nowadays.' I commented, at the same time recalling Ben Goldmann, the unknown factor and what he may have to do with it.

'And Martha, don't forget Martha's been murdered too!' cried Paula.

'Yes, but we don't know if it was by the same person or organization,' I countered.

'Yes, but don't forget nothing is known publicly about Ephraim's findings of the secret place described by the writings in the library at Qumram!' she shouted vehemently,

I put my finger to my lips. She lowered her volume.

'John, it's not only that but it is something granddad hasn't told me about.'

'Then it's high time he did,' I said bluntly, adding, 'a lot of people would like to be in possession of any documents supporting the theory. Three come immediately to mind – Jewish religious leaders, the Christian church and the Islamic Mullahs – all in order to destroy the documents. Maybe even other organizations that would benefit from the aftermath if they were published,'

I thought to myself – maybe that something granddad keeps from you is keeping you alive?

'That doesn't leave many out, does it?' she said.

'You have no idea who could be behind the bugs and the people observing this flat?'

'No, John! Granddad will be petrified and I really don't know how I can console him. If we'd known about these bugs and those people then Anna and Martha may still be alive. Oh! My God, and granddad holds you in some way responsible for Anna's death. He thought it had something to do with you being in the Secret Service.'

I swept over the last argument, swallowing slight feelings of guilt and replied,

'Well, technically speaking the bugs were used by the Stasi, so we know it's possibly an organization instead of a nation without their own ordnance facilities. On the other hand, these bugs are easy to obtain now in various stores throughout the BRD. The Mossad have a habit of scattering evidence so they can't really be ruled out either. No, I'm sorry – I guess we can't rule anybody out. Not even colleagues of Anna's father, or any relatives.'

Paula stared anxiously – waiting to hear something that would relieve her from the heavy burden of Anna's death.

'Paula, what we haven't really talked about is Martha and Ian's relationship. I guess I don't have to ask you if the subject was talked about in the flat or on the phone?'

'Martha used the phone in granddad's study most of the time, even when she talked to Ian when her cell phone batteries weren't empty. Granddad used to balk her, as it all went on his bill.'

'Did Martha or Anna ever make notes?'

'I know all Anna's things are in suitcases in the cellar. We'll have to ask him about Martha, though. I assume she did most of her writing on her computer.'

'I know this sounds presumptuous, but is there any chance of having a look through her computer files? There might be something of vital importance. I know it's a bit early, seeing the funeral's just over.'

'I think the computer's in the cellar too,' she answered.

'You'll have to ask granddad to come here for a few minutes. Don't ask him anywhere else in the flat openly until it's been cleared of the bugs. When you talk to him in the living room, turn the radio or television on first and still make it a whisper. Tell him the room is bugged and the only safe place at the moment is the bathroom, which really is only half the truth.'

'Okay John, I'll go and ask him now.'

I remained in the bathroom waiting for granddad's fury.

A few seconds later I heard hurrying feet in the hallway. I went to the door and eased it open a bit to see the cause.

Paula appeared, looking worried.

'John, we've got a problem! Granddad left over ten minutes ago to accompany Hera home.'

That's all we need now, I thought, granddad getting mugged or kidnapped.

'Okay, Paula – does Hera have a telephone?'

'Yes, she has.'

'How long does granddad normally take to get her home?'

'It's strange you know, he's never escorted her home before, not to my knowledge. I would say it takes about ten to fifteen minutes. If they have tea and a chat before he comes back, it could be longer.'

'Okay, then let's give Hera a ring from my cell phone.'

I handed the phone to Paula – we were still in the bathroom. Paula dialled the number and waited – no answer.

'Okay, don't fret Paula. Let's give it another couple of minutes and we'll try again.'

'Look John, something may have happened to them. They might be lying somewhere, hurt. Let's go after them, please.'

'Maybe that's exactly what, whoever is staking this place out want us to do. Let's just wait out another few minutes. If there's no answer I'll call Berlin and get our people to contact the authorities here for safety's sake. I don't want to take the risk of anyone breaking in and hurting your grandma. Oh, bye the way, are the others still here?'

'No, they all left when granddad went with Hera.'

'Do they have the same direction?'

'Only the first block, then they have to take the bus.'

'I'll just get something from my bag – be back in a jiff'.

I went back to the guest room, took out my ankle holster, strapped it on and placed a small semi-automatic in it. I put on my lightweight bullet-proof waistcoat and pulled a long black-necked pullover over it, one that went down to my thighs. On top of that I put on my modified black two-piece commando suit and zipped up the joints – a good cover for the bullet-proof waistcoat and of strong lightweight material that can hold off knife-slashes. I checked my 9mm browning, and being right handed I put my two spare magazines in my bottom left pocket and the silencer in the top left. I went back to the bathroom, ready for the worst. I heard someone speaking when I got back to the bathroom. It was Paula on the phone to someone.

'Okay, thanks very much Aunt Hera!'

She pressed the cell phone button.

'Granddad is on his way back!'

'Okay, let's hurry and make sure he gets home safely.'

We went into the sitting room where grandma was watching telly.

'Grandma, we're going to meet granddad on his way back home from Hera's, so please lock up after us,' I said, looking at her severely until she nodded. I turned to Paula and said,

'Paula, do you mind waiting inside while I check to see if all's clear?'

'No not at all,' she said, sounding slightly irritated.

I only wish I had the team, or at least a partner to keep my back clear, I thought. I put the light out in the hallway and opened the front door. Paula closed it from the inside. She was thoughtful to use the handle, keeping the noise to a minimum. Leaving the lights off, I went over the landing quietly and leaned on the balustrade, at the same time listening for any sounds and sniffing the air intensely. My macrosmatic nose picked up a strong smell of cheap camel leather and garlic up towards the last flight of stairs that led to the loft. I tapped on the Stern's door lightly. It opened and Paula looked out through the crack. I beckoned her out with my hand putting a finger on my lips and pointing upwards towards the stairs leading to the loft with the other hand. I cursed inwardly when grandma shut the door after Paula rather fiercely. I stayed put and held Paula's arm. I waited a few minutes before letting go and moved towards the stairs, at the same time thinking granddad is probably nearly home by now. Initially I'd planned to go out the back door, over the neighbours' plots and onto the street at the end of the block. As time was now critical it was the front door or nothing.

We left the lights off and moved silently down the stairs, stopping on the first floor, where I listened and sniffed the air, thinking the stairs down to the back door could be a problem. I took out my 9mm and silencer and screwed it on without looking at Paula. She would be realizing danger by now and I knew what her face would be telling me. It was too dark to tell anyway. Normally, I can sense the presence of strangers in the dark. This wasn't the case now, so I turned around and tugged Paula's arm. We moved down the last flight of stairs and into the hallway. At the front door I turned to Paula and whispered,

'We'll have to walk very quickly so try and keep close to the cars parked on the side of the road and stay directly behind me.'

I moved out – taking in a faint touch of oriental perfume and the feel of Paula's warm breath on my neck. I jerked my thoughts back to reality – making a note of possible cover the row of parked cars would give if we came under fire from the building opposite.

We had gone about 20 metres when I spotted a figure crossing the road at an angle towards us. I recognised the gait as that of an elderly person, thinking immediately of granddad. He had reached the middle of the road where the street lighting caught his features when a dark figure moved out from a doorway further up on our left. My gun hand was already rising as I saw the dark figure raise a hand bearing a gun. Instinctively I put off two fatal shots and moved quickly towards the figure that fell onto the pavement. I went into a crouch. Remaining half-crouched and keeping an eye on the fallen figure, I traversed my gun arm, looking for any other assailants. I pocketed the gun that had fallen on the pavement picking it up by the barrel. I wasn't going to check him out on my own – too risky! A few seconds had gone by and the guy on the pavement still made no movement. Paula was still standing and looked fairly calm, despite the situation. Granddad stood stock still in the middle of the road. I ran over to him grabbed him by the arm and dragged him behind one of the cars where I had to forcefully push his shoulders down, making him crouch. Paula moved over and crouched next to him.

'Don't go near the guy on the pavement under any circumstances, do you hear,' I said urgently, looking at Paula, 'and keep down, there is probably someone else out there.'

Paula nodded.

I moved away from them looking around the street and up towards the flat opposite. After a couple of minutes when I thought it might be safe to move back to the flat, the door to the Stern's flat burst open and a figure ran onto the pavement and up the street like a rabbit in the opposite direction. Fellow Scots would say I'm very canny – in this case it was instinct. I immediately thought of someone in the attic – the smell of garlic and cheap camel leather on the landing, and grandma. I immediately gave her a ring on my cell phone. After three rings she answered. My senses were so alert that at such times I always think of the worst possible case, so I shouted through the phone,

'Grandma, leave everything and get the hell down here

straight away, it's an emergency. We'll be in the hall downstairs. Do you hear? Get down now. Here's Paula!'

I put my hand over the mouthpiece and spoke to Paula.

'Please tell her the urgency Paula – I think something dreadful is going to happen.'

I hoped to God grandma would do as she's told and handed the phone to Paula.

'Grandma, it's me Paula – he's right, you must leave everything and come down immediately, please – now,' she shouted into the mouthpiece.

Paula must have sensed my urgency because her voice was loaded with overwhelming persuasion. It also told me she trusted my intuition. She handed back the cell phone as we moved towards the entrance. We arrived just inside the hallway as grandma was coming down the last flight of stairs into the entrance hall. We were barely inside the front door, when a terrific explosion upstairs caused our eardrums to close. We were all momentarily deafened. I ran forward to catch grandma who was holding onto the banister shrieking her head off. Paula followed and put her arm around grandma.

'It's okay, granny,' she said, 'it's okay now – nothing's happened to you. Let's go down, you're safe now, *bewakasha!*'

Paula's pleading, got the right reaction, 'cause grandma stopped shouting and moved down the rest of the stairs real fast.

'Are there any other people in the flat opposite yours Paula.'

'No,' she said, as we reached the hall. Granddad was nowhere to be seen.

'Look here's my cell phone, you'd better ring the fire brigade, police and ambulance services, tell them there's been an explosion and a four storey building's on fire. I'll just run up and get everyone else out.'

I gave her my cell phone and dashed up the stairs knocking and ringing at each door. Most people were just standing at their open doors doing nothing whilst smoke was already creeping down the stairs.

'Get the hell out of here, the building's on fire. If you don't get out now you'll be burned or suffocated to death,' I shouted at them.

I reached the third floor landing where an elderly pair was standing at their door.

'Does anyone live there?' I asked bluntly, pointing to the flat opposite.

They nodded.

'How many,' I asked.

'Just one old lady,' answered the man.

'Okay, now get the bloody hell out of here – do you hear!'

Typical of neighbours in tenements, I thought. I didn't wait for their reaction. Probably my kicking open the door opposite caused them to wake up to the danger. It was the flat directly under the Sterns. I heard coughs from a room on the left and went in. The smoke was dense. I saw a slender old lady sitting on the side of a bed. I didn't bother about the other rooms knowing they'd have been hit bad by the bomb as the flat was directly under the Stern's. The old lady was more or less senseless so I lifted her over my shoulder in a fireman's lift and left the flat quickly, shutting the door as best I could with my foot. I reached the third floor occupants who seemed to think they were on a Sunday outing. I overtook them saying,

'For Christ's sake get a move on before the building collapses.'

That message got through – they really picked up memento and stayed directly behind me the rest of the way down. As we climbed down the last steps I saw there was no one in the hallway that was now full of smoke. Firemen appeared through the front door and hurried towards us. I stopped when the first fireman reached us.

'We're probably the last out,' I said.

'I've knocked everyone up. There is definitely no one on the third and fourth floor. You'll have to check the first and second to be sure. This lady is from the third floor flat on the right. It seems the fire broke out after an explosion in the attic above the fourth floor flat on the right.'

'Okay, thanks a lot,' said one of the firemen. The other one was passing the information through his personal radio.

'You okay to carry her out?'

'Yes, thanks – I'll manage fine.'

The firemen tipped their helmets in salute and ran up the stairs with their fire axes at the ready. We carried on down and out onto the street. I saw the other three standing near an ambulance where I was going to bring the old woman anyway. I carried her the last 40 metres and put her onto a stretcher.

A Red Cross doctor asked if I was okay. In between coughs, I said I was, but gladly accepting his offer of oxygen from the tank. I turned to the other three who were standing with blankets around their shoulders and wavered them away from the commotion. The two women were gazing at me in amazement. For them this was unbelievable and what I didn't know at the time – I was covered in soot – black as a chimney sweep.

'Are you okay, grandma, granddad, Paula?' I asked.

Grandma and Paula nodded their heads – granddad just stared. I smiled a big smile at the two ladies. Who cares about grumpy granddad, I thought.

'We're fine now John – it's you we're worried about. Are you okay?'

'Lungs are a bit smoky but nothing to worry about, I can

still breathe normally.' I said in between coughs, smiling in relief that all three were still alive.

'Have you still got my cell phone dear?' I said to Paula – saying oops to myself for calling her dear.

She gave me a shy smile and handed it back. I moved away from the group and rang up my HQ in Berlin, giving the duty officer a briefing but omitting the man I'd shot. I asked him to contact the German special operations department in Leipzig to pass on the details, then went back over to the group.

'Well folks, I have to deal with the official side for a while but before that I'd like to see you in a safer place. I don't know how badly damaged the flat is, but judging by the quickness the flames were put out, it's mainly water damage apart from the destruction caused by the explosion. I'll ask German special ops to put a guard on it until my men come. What about Aunt Hera? Do you think you could stay with her temporarily?'

'That's no problem John, she'll be more than willing to take us in and she's enough room to take you in as well!'

I smiled at the thought of maybe sharing a room with Paula but knowing the night wouldn't be long enough. I looked at my watch.

'My men will be here in a couple of hours so I'll hang around here until they arrive. I reckon I could manage Aunt Hera's for an early breakfast though, if that's okay with you? I'll be bringing a couple of my men with me to look after you for a while if that's allright?'

Grandma piped in.

'Mister Scotsman, you can have as many breakfasts with us as you like for the rest of your life and your men are more than welcome.'

I squeezed her shoulder lightly and said,

'Thanks grandma – I'm afraid I have to help making

arrangements for a funeral on Friday afternoon, so I have to leave Leipzig on the 9.10 am train. I'll try and get back later on though.'

'And you'll be staying with us at Aunt Hera's,' said Paula, with a *no further arguments allowed* look on her face. With such an offer I wasn't going to object anyway.

'Here's the address and phone number,' she added, handing me a slip of paper.

I took the note with Aunt Hera's phone number and address and said,

'Thanks Paula. It would be best if you stay put here for a few minutes while I arrange transport for you. Oh, and another thing – no mention of the gunman please. I'll clear that up when the German special ops team arrives.'

I glanzed at granddad – his looks said he wasn't too pleased about something. I left them and went over to the other two ambulances looking for the man I'd shot. I asked a Red Cross orderly if there were any casualties other than the old woman I'd carried out. There hadn't been any, so I reckon his cronies had picked him up after we'd entered the building.

The fire brigade had two large vehicles with their pneumatic ladders high up, just above the level of the roof and two men in each platform basket were hosing high-powered water into the cavity of the blasted out roof and the flat below. Fortunately the fire hadn't broken out too severely, so the flames were extinguished fairly quickly. Most probably they were pumping in more water just in case some cinders were still glowing.

I went over to a police car and showed them my credentials, which have authorised jurisdiction throughout EU countries. I told them briefly what had happened, leaving out the shooting and mentioning that the German special ops anti-terrorist group were informed through my HQ in Berlin and they should be arriving shortly. I emphasized that the Stern's were the main victims of this attack and extremely traumatized. They agreed to wait until the next day before questioning them and would arrange to get a vehicle to drive them to Aunt Hera's. I knew, if I have anything to do with it they'll not be debriefed at all. I went back to the Stern's.

'Okay folks, your transport will be arriving shortly, so you'd better give Aunt Hera a ring that you're coming,' I said, smiling and handed my cell phone to Paula. Her hand lingered just a moment longer on mine as I passed it over.

Paula gave Hera a ring. It was ages before the call was answered. Paula didn't bother to ask if they could stay, she gave her a brief rundown of the incident and that they would be on their way in a few minutes. She handed back the cell phone. I kept my hand on hers and pulled her slightly away from the others.

'Paula, I think you'd better give me the keys to your cellar – it would be better if my team got there first, don't you think?'

'Yes, of course, John,' she said pulling a set of keys from her jeans pocket. I took them with both hands cuffed over hers, pressing them gently.

One of the policemen I'd spoken to waved us over to a police car that had just arrived. We went over. Granddad and grandma climbed in the back without making any comments. They were obviously just too exhausted and extremely disturbed. Paula jumped into my arms, her legs leaving the ground and her arms clinging to me very tightly. She let go and without another word climbed in after her granddad and grandma. For the first time in years I felt this hardened Scottish heart of mine do overtime, 'cause my pulse had really shot up.

Olaf Ertl – Syria, Wed 17th August 2005

Olaf rang up Hans's digs and talked to Achmed's mother immediately after he got back to the hotel from *Percy's*. He arranged to go there and check out the room Hans had rented out during his studies at Damascus University. Olaf would have preferred a chat with Achmed first, but his mother said he was visiting some relatives in North East Syria, which he thought sarcastically, was very convenient!

The next person he phoned was Achmed's Uncle, Hussein Idris, a retired Syrian Army Brigadier, who quite adamantly declared he knew nothing and no, he wasn't prepared to meet Olaf – not very forthcoming at all. The fear of the Syrian Secret Police obviously keeping him from talking openly or maybe he just didn't want to be involved, worried about his pension being cut, probably. Olaf sensed he knew something and maybe it would be fruitful if he got to meet him clandestinely. He kept him on his list. He centred his thoughts on the meeting Munir had arranged for later on that evening.

A black Russian sedan, with a crude sort of air-conditioning, picked him up at the hotel and took him to an upper class residential area in the outskirts of Damascus. They stopped at a big white colonial style house, surrounded by a well-lit, whitewashed wall, three metres high and topped with barbed wire. CCTV-cameras were mounted at various strategic points. Two security guards stood at the gate with Kalashnikovs at the ready.

He was shown into a lounge the size of a tennis court. The marble stoned floor was beautifully designed, comprising a huge mosaic. The walls were draped with carpets and the purpose of the room was made apparent by a group of low settees and armchairs placed about two-thirds up the room.

Three people in Arab attire were sitting and another two, obviously bodyguards, were standing apart. The servant who'd let him in conducted him to the group. Munir was sitting in the most decorative armchair Olaf had ever seen. More like a throne, he thought. Something he hadn't even seen in some of the kitschy Arab movies. It definitely put Munir in a different light. He started to wonder if he'd contacted the right person.

Munir got up and extended his hand casually. A sign he wasn't supposed to appear too friendly towards this nosy European.

'Welcome to my house, Olaf – I'd like you to meet His Excellency Paarviz Sawwaf, who represents the Education and Culture Ministry and Colonel Rashad Said from the Syrian Secret Service, both of whom are close friends of mine. They are both aware of your identity and the purpose of your visit here.'

No smiles this time he thought as Munir's two illustrious friends shook hands with him briefly. He sat down at the settee after Munir gestured with his arm. He accepted the cup of *chai* that Munir offered him. After the exchange of some polite small talk, during which *chai* was occasionally sipped, Paarviz Sawwaf addressed him in a very slow soft voice, just as soft as the podgy hand he'd given him to shake,

'Herr Ertl,' he said. Not Christian names anymore – nor cordial, thought Olaf.

'First of all we would like to express our full sympathy and understanding. We accept your grief and anxiety. We will help you in your quest to find your nephew and I assure you we will do as much as we can.'

Olaf braced himself on the last words – *as much as we can* –

thinking, he's not going to get much assistance here, or they're not willing to hang their necks out.

'We are obviously very concerned at the Ministry when our foreign students go astray. I am not saying your nephew was abducted and I am not saying he went of his own accord. What is apparent from our findings is that he didn't turn up at the airport for his flight back to Europe. There were turbulences in his class. Apparently they generated from a certain group from your own country and your neighbouring country Holland.'

Colonel Rashad Said took up the cue.

'We do not interfere with the political views or characteristics of foreign students. This has always been the policy of the University of Damascus over the last two thousand years. However, the behaviour of some students has not passed our eyes unnoticed. Our government does not wish to be involved in this matter, which means our hands are tied. Whatever has happened is not under our control.'

Olaf couldn't withhold himself any longer.

'Have you any information at all? Even if it may seem trivial to you it may be of importance to me.'

'Herr Ertl, be patient please and I will tell you what we know. Firstly, Hans Ertl was last seen in the Lebanon, in the coastal town of *Tyre*. He booked into a lower class hotel on Saturday the sixth of August.'

Ah, at last something to go on thought Olaf.

Colonel Said continued speaking,

'As you know the popular Lebanese Premier Rafiq Hariri, who would undoubtedly have been re-elected in the coming election, was killed by a car bomb some weeks ago. Everyone seems to be blaming us, the Syrians, which is utter nonsense. We don't know who was behind the assassination, but it seems now most of the Lebanese are up in arms about our continued presence in the Lebanon. World opinion has also turned against us. We have already moved our forces back to Syria. So you see, we are in a very difficult position to aid you in the Lebanon. We have given the disappearance of your nephew careful consideration and can only think of one further possibility. Last year, a group of students were given permission to visit the restricted southern area of Lebanon near the Israeli border, which is under our protection. Your nephew was with that group. They also stayed at the same hotel where your nephew stayed on the night of the sixth of August. The purpose of the student journey was to show them the poverty and conditions of that area imposed on the remaining people for many decades by the Israelis and to show them the ruins at *Tyre*, particularly the remains of the Christian Cathedral. In the presumption you will probably wish to follow this lead, I have brought some official papers with routes and written permission to pass through the checkpoints. Perhaps you might find a clue in that area. That is all we can do for you I'm afraid. What I must also tell you, is that due to our withdrawal from Lebanon, you may come across some difficulties, as ID and checkpoint passwords may have changed by the time you get there. I'm afraid you will be travelling at your own risk.'

Munir took over.

'Well what do you think my German friend? Will you be tracing your nephew through the student route?'

The whole thing stinks, thought Olaf. Sounds as though they really want him to go. Maybe get him killed and they'll be rid of a nuisance. Olaf gathered his thoughts carefully before he answered. Arabs can be very finicky at the choice of words especially as his Arabic was a bit stale and he didn't want to give away his true feelings about the matter. I'll let them think they've achieved their goal and think he's gullible. It's the only lead he's got anyway,

'My friend, I am very grateful for your help and also the help of your friends here. I thank your friends also for the comforting words and advice. Yes, I think I'll start with *Tyre*, where some answers to Hans's disappearance may be found. I shall take great care and again I am very grateful for any visas or travel permits that will lighten my task at control points.'

'So be it dear friend,' said Munir and lifted his hand towards the servant, the sign for Olaf to get up and go.

After the customary thanks and farewells and the handing over of the travel documents, Olaf was escorted out of the house and taken back to his hotel in the same car.

He rang up his sister Elsa and told her the news. She listened to him for a few minutes before she let out a real burst of indignity and hauled him over the coals for not keeping his calls to the agreed times, something he'd completely forgotten. Once she calmed down she gave him her news,

'John has nothing yet,' she told him, 'I met Robert's mother at the bakers this morning. She said Robert has remembered something that happened last time Hans was home. You know there are a lot of bible groups in this area? Well, Robert thinks it has something to do with one of the groups from Koenigsfeld. Robert thinks he ought not to talk to anyone other than yourself about it.'

Olaf noticed the worry in her voice.

'Look, don't worry about it. I think you ought to get Robert to tell John, though, as I'll be tied up here for a few more days. It may be of importance.'

They kept to their agreement and didn't blether, although he thought Elsa would have liked to.

Lebanon, Thurs 18th August 2005

Early that morning Olaf Ertl had bought a battered old Ford Escort in Damascus at a reasonably low price. The hotel doorman had arranged it for him. Considering it had no air-conditioning, he haggled a bit longer than usual over the price. It was just past 10 am and he was travelling down the Lebanese coast on his way to *Tyre*, on his second day after arriving in the Middle East.

Perspiration gathered on his forehead, trickling over his eyebrows in a constant stream, aggravating his eyes. He should have put a sweatband on, he thought, but there again he might have been mistaken for a *Mujaheddin*. His shirt clung to his chest and his back stuck to the seat. The sand and dust became part of his skin, just like a mudpack in the spa.

The smell in the car was devastating. The previous owner must have spilt some goat's milk or something in the back and just let it dry out.

He arrived in *Tyre* at a primitive hotel at 11 am – the hotel where Hans had apparently stayed. The entrance was up an outside wooden staircase situated in a filthy backyard. He walked up the steps, his duffle bag over his shoulder, each worn-out step yielding as he put his weight down. He kept alert, worried that his foot would break through on the next step. He balanced most of his weight on the previous step, gradually exerting his full weight on the next one, until he thought he wouldn't break through.

He reached the top, thinking *'I'm the king of the castle'*, pushed the mosquito beads aside and entered a shabby lobby. Behind a desk, the top of which looked more like a plank of driftwood, a skinny old Arab with a grubby shirt and half a mouth full of teeth didn't even take the time of day to greet him, just mumbled to see his passport and $20 in advance for the night.

The old bloke scrutinized each page, mouthing endless curses at Americans as he stopped at the pages revealing the stamps of the US Immigration Office. He was angry and mouthed curses at the Jews as well, although he had no stamped entries to Israel in the passport. He flipped through it once more, his face lightening up for a moment as he prolonged his look at the emblem of Germany, the great German eagle, muttering something incoherent. He's seen that before, thought Olaf.

His room had a sea view. He could see some dilapidated concrete block apartments situated on a fairly flat limestone plateau curving out to sea. It was joined to the mainland by a sandy isthmus – a dreadful sight depicting the poverty and uselessness of today's city of *Tyre*. Pondering over this misery, he thought back to his ancient history knowledge of the area.

This was nothing to compare with *Tyre*, the ancient predecessor that lay on a group of islands offshore on reefs and cliffs, built mainly for defensive purposes. However, Alexander the Great took the city after seven months of siege by building a dam from the mainland to the island. Over the periods thereafter, *Assyrians, New Babylonians* and *Persians* came and conquered, putting the citizens to the yoke. In the fourth century, the city of *Tyre* was mainly Christian. An important basilica was constructed during that era, possibly the oldest Christian basilica in history.

In the year 1124 the Crusaders came with a sharpened religion and erected the largest cathedral in the Middle East. Some time later the Templars arrived. It is not known to what purpose.

He moved back into the room, away from this sad sight. Olaf

decided to go out for a recce near the hotel for a restaurant. Maybe he can get something to eat and pick up some titbits of information.

After checking out the layout of the hotel and surroundings, he settled on a seat near the entrance to one of the small bistros on the beachfront. His attention was attracted to a tent store directly adjacent, where a Lebanese was selling all sorts of bric-a-brac.

He ordered a *chai* and something to eat and sat there for a while afterwards contemplating his next moves. After a while, he said hello and made some remarks to the Lebanese merchant about the apparent lack of business.

The merchant was obviously curious and didn't stop babbling – very talkative! He introduced himself as Ali. Olaf thought Ali was just the right person for his purpose and indeed an Arab who seemed pleased to meet a European who was reasonably fluent in Arabic.

From the conversation, he gathered that Ali dealt in import – export. Olaf chatted freely for a while with Ali, who willingly explained the current history of the area. He chatted loosely about the border area, the obstacles and the *Hezballah*, which wasn't really surprising as *Tyre* is only 50 km from the Israeli border. Boasting a bit, it seemed, he gave him some general information willingly. In the *Bekkaa* plane, Ali told him the control powers were constantly changing hands, from the police, the secret service and soldiers of the Lebanese army and para-military, mostly at night but sometimes during the day.

Ali was a wise man – he knew Olaf wanted something else from him.

'If there is anything I can do for you let me know.'

Olaf contemplated a moment before answering.

'Well I was thinking of selling my Syrian registered car and buying a Lebanese one – after what you've just told me about the border area I don't think it would be wise to travel with Syrian number plates.'

Without further ado, the merchant called a youth who was playing football on the beach and told him to look after the store. Ali beckoned Olaf to follow him. They went to the hotel where they picked up his Ford Escort. They drove a few kilometres down the beach road and stopped at a garage.

Leaving him in the Ford, Ali said he had to talk to someone first. He came back a few minutes later with a mechanic, who nodded and smiled briefly, but thankfully didn't offer his dirt-greased hand. They beckoned him to follow them into the garage where the mechanic pointed to a sandy coloured battered Toyota jeep with a hard top. The price difference was bargained, which he thought was within reason but being a European and not used to bartering, he thought he didn't do a bad job getting the price down a bit.

He raised his eyebrows and hesitated, trying to look concerned after the money handover, when he exchanged vehicle papers with the mechanic. The mechanic assured him the papers were in order. Olaf mentioned sightseeing as the purpose for his travels and that he was a German citizen. He also explained that he would be back within a few days and maybe he would resell the jeep for his Syrian registered car again. With this hint he was hoping the papers were really in order. He felt relieved when no response came.

It was 12.30 pm as he drove towards *Rmaich*, the fictitious border on the Lebanese side, where according to the instructions from Munir, he is supposed to be guided over into no-man's land and then on to the Israeli border.

From *Rmaich* he moved on the pre-defined route to *Tibnine* and then on to *Nabtîyé*. From there he went east to *Marjayoûn*, which at this point runs along the Syrian border – *Hezballah land*.

Posters seemed to be on show everywhere – on street light posts and on flagpoles, depicting the martyrs who had sacrificed their lives against the Jewish Satan. Young men and woman, average age of twenty who were led to believe the cause and let themselves be blown up by explosives strapped to their bodies taking as many of the enemy with them as possible. Heroes and hatred were being preached on those posters. The *Bekkaa plane*, known in the past as a major drug-growing area, is the territory of the *Hezballah*.

Israeli combat jets and reconnaissance planes flew over continuously. The streets were empty – thoughts of dust and sand everywhere settled in his mind. The temperature was now 40°C in the shade. He got used to the roadblocks every 2-3 km, carried out by regular army soldiers, para-military and secret service. Some of the regular soldiers were wearing gym shoes and sunglasses. So far Munirs documents seemed to work.

At the next checkpoint, after passing through the previous ones without any trouble, an officer waved aside his Arabic and spoke in English, asking his reason for transit. Olaf replied with a lot of waffle about sightseeing and mainly tourist interest. The officer seemed surprised and genuinely accepted his motives. The officer shook his head and told him no person with a sane mind would want to risk his life just for sightseeing and let him pass through.

South of *Tibnîne* the network of roadblocks got denser. The area was very rocky – scattered villages – hardly any larger towns – more like hamlets. He arrived at the third main checkpoint, where an army officer refused to let him pass through without even looking at his papers, telling him he should drive around the area and not directly through it. He argued in Arabic but the officer was adamant and called his guards over. The sight of the raised sub-machine guns were enough conviction for him to shove into reverse gear and drive back to a point where he could turn the jeep around and drive back the way he'd just come.

Back through the checkpoints to *Tibnîne* and then on to *Nabtiyé,* which meant a 2-hour detour. Most of the guards at the control posts seemed to be standing idle the whole day. In a curve, just before he got to *Bent Jbail*, after driving about an hour along the fictitious border, he ran into another checkpoint. This time there was more armaments and men were holding sub-machine guns at the ready. His trained eye told him they were two strengthened groups of the National Lebanese Infantry. The soldier in charge wouldn't let him pass through. He told him it was a *'no go area'*. Olaf asked him why and got the same answer. Olaf showed his anger and raised his voice, protesting. He told the soldier defiantly he'd already had to make a detour because the officer at the last main check point sent him this way. The soldier seemed unsure and moved towards the camouflaged tents at the side of the road saying he'd check that by radio.

Olaf waited for about 20 minutes in the jeep. Soldiers were loafing around it drinking tea, laughing and making loud remarks most of which he couldn't decipher. He couldn't see if the soldier who went into the shack to check by radio was still there. Olaf raised his voice and called out for the soldier. After three tries Olaf got out of the jeep and made a move towards the shack. He was stopped immediately by the soldiers who told him in local dialect to shut-up and get back in the jeep.

Olaf ignored the warning and raised his voice a bit more, slightly on the verge of a scream. It worked – the soldier came out of the shack and told him he had to go back because he couldn't reach the previous post by radio. At that moment a young officer approached. He said he was from the immigration office. Olaf caught on, reckoning he was secret service. He spoke with the soldier and they disappeared into the tent. After a couple of minutes both of them came out again. The young immigration officer smiled at Olaf whilst the other turned and walked away nonchalantly with a fag dangling out of the corner of his mouth. The young officer, still smiling, told him he could carry on his journey.

Olaf was quite surprised. He got back into the jeep and continued his drive into no-man's land between *Rmaich* and the border.

No-man's land comprised of small hamlets, poverty and dust. The Israeli border was very near now. On the way to an old, abandoned border defence post he came across a lone sentry. Judging by his stripes he was a corporal. Olaf told him he had permission from the officer at the last checkpoint to climb up to the old defence post. The corporal looked very unsure and picked up the radio to have his story verified. Fortunately he couldn't get through, continuous static, probably jammed by the Israelis. Olaf tried to ease the situation by chatting about himself and where he came from. The corporal smiled, still unsure but decided to let him carry on. He parked the jeep at the side of the road and got out. He climbed up to the old defence post, the corporal in tow. From there he could see the border strip.

On both sides the expected fortifications – barbed wire, ditches, detectors, infantry positions and on the Lebanese side from where he was standing, he could see the rocket launchers, machine-gun posts and SAM – air-defence missile systems.

He sat down on a broken concrete slab and opened his duffel bag. The corporal became tense, but relaxed when Olaf pulled out two cans of coke. Warm coke is not really the right drink for quenching one's thirst. The corporal smiled and took the coke offered. Olaf told him to watch out for the spray on opening the can. They were both amused when neither was saved from the huge gas escape followed by coke spray. They sipped what was left of the warm coke in silence. Olaf pulled a couple of damp travel tissues from a small packet he had in his duffle bag. He offered one to the corporal who accepted. They wiped their hands from the stickiness. Olaf pulled out a few more and held some out to the corporal who again accepted. The corporal looked at him and Olaf smiled and wiped his face and neck with his tissues. The corporal followed suit.

Olaf reached inside his bag and pulled out some photographs. He showed them to the corporal, explaining this was his only family, his sister and his nephew. One of the photographs was quite recent and all three were posed.

The corporal took the photograph and let out a cry of recognition,

'I know this man, he was here last year with a group of students from *Damascus*.'

'You're sure he wasn't here recently?'

'How recent?'

'Within the last couple of weeks!'

'No, of course not, I'm in charge of this important post here and I've been here since the beginning of July.'

Olaf felt disappointed, but on second thoughts he really felt relieved.

'Why do you ask?' asked the corporal, suspicion mounting in his voice.

Olaf told him Hans was a student in Damascus and has gone missing. He explained he was trying to re-trace all of his steps.

'That was a strange group your nephew was with,' said the corporal.

'Why do you say that?'

'Well, I'll never forget the bossy woman who was with them. She asked me all sorts of strange questions. I had to call-up my superior officer on the radio for permission to answer her, although their guide, who was from the Syrian Interior Ministry told me I could.'

'What was it she wanted to know?'

'She showed me what looked like the copy of an old map and asked me if I knew where the entrance to the cave on her map was. I told her there were no caves to my knowledge in this area.'

'Anything else?'

'Yes, she said there used to be a two-thousand year old trade route from *Tyre* to the *Dead Sea*, part of which goes past this post. I didn't comment on that, though.'

'And is there one?'

'Yes of course, it's common knowledge here. It's of no interest to the Hammas.'

Olaf took out a Dunhill and handed the pack to the corporal gesturing him to take one too. The corporal took a cigarette out and made to hand the pack back. Olaf shook his head.

'That's okay. You can keep them. You've been very kind and helpful.'

The corporal nodded his thanks and put the pack in his breast pocket. Olaf offered him a light and lit his own cigarette.

After a considerable bit of lung inflation two trails of blue smoke were blown out.

'Could you show me on my map where that cave is. The one she was looking for. I would appreciate it you know?' asked Olaf, taking out his wallet and pulling a one hundred U.S. dollar note out and holding it between his thumb and forefinger.

One look sufficed the corporal. After a furtive glance around, he said,

'Okay,' and grabbed the note.

Olaf pulled out a map from his hip pocket. The corporal looked at it briefly and said,

'The one she was looking for is here,' pointing at the map, 'the third one to the East, about here.'

Olaf nodded and said,

'Thanks,' marked it on his map and looked at the corporal questioningly, asking,

'Would you mind marking the other two for me, just so there's no mix-up?'

The corporal nodded, and taking Olaf's pencil, marked them on the map.

'Thanks,' said Olaf and put the map back in his hip pocket, trying hard not to disclose his excitement.

The corporal contemplated his last pillow of smoke and turning to Olaf, said almost friendly,

'You know something! That woman your nephew was with is a nasty piece of stuff. It's my guess if he's missing, she's got something to do with it.'

Olaf looked at the corporal appreciatively, digesting the news and nodding knowingly.

The corporal got up and pointed down to the track.

'You'd better get going if you want to get back through the

demarcation zone without delays. At night a lot of people get nervous and trigger-happy.'

Olaf shook hands and made off down the hill towards his jeep thinking of his nephew in the hands of crazy people.

He got back to *Tyre*, too late to barter back his Syrian car, so he checked in at the murky hotel of the previous night.

He rang up his sister Elsa and passed on some of the news. He said he'd send a more detailed letter the following day from the city before he left for Damascus after having a tour of the ruins.

'John says he's some startling news, but doesn't think it has anything to do with Hans, as yet.'

'I'll give you a ring as usual tomorrow then. I think I'll visit a few people in Damascus before I give you a call – bye for now!'

Olaf rang off and threw off his clothes. He pulled back the gungy piece of plastic camouflage and stepped onto the tiles – being very careful of avoiding the hole in the middle, which wasn't covered. He tried to refrain from looking at the flurry movement of cockroaches running into the hole. He turned on the water and waited until the brown ooze became slightly clearer. It remained luke-warm. He let the gurgling stream flow over his head and body. He soaped himself and rubbed his body quickly, deciding to water himself down and get out of there rapidly, because the cockroaches were now ascending the walls of the shower corner. He didn't fancy a cockroach shower.

After drying and putting on fresh underwear, he sat at the wobbly desk and wrote his letter. When he was finished, he stuck it in an envelope with the map and addressed it, thinking he'll send it off tomorrow after exchanging vehicles and a quick visit to the cathedral. He chewed a bit of gum whilst getting fully dressed – pulled out the drawer and put it aside. He stuck his gum on the back of the desk behind the drawer opening and pressed the envelope onto the gum and replaced the drawer. Leaving the letter here was just a general precaution should he be filched if he got stopped in the city. Carrying such notes and a map of the border area would make him a potential spy in the eyes of the law. He knew Munir might be able to help him out, but there again he wasn't sure. He left the hotel via some steady iron steps on the beach side of the hotel. He was thinking about what he would order to eat once he found a decent restaurant in the city centre.

He made his way to the side of the hotel where his jeep was parked. He forgot all about his training from BND days – avoiding murky shadows when turning into dark corners of buildings at night. He didn't see the slim dark clad figure that moved out behind him. He felt a breathtaking blow in his back that paralysed him and made him senseless for a few seconds, enough for an assailant to whip a garrotte over his head and apply full pressure. His age and the overwhelming unexpectedness of the attack made him an easy victim. His last thoughts were of Hans – had he ended up the same way?

Tel-Aviv – Mossad HQ, Thursday 18th August 2005

Jacob Stein, head of Mossad *Agent Recruitment & European Operations*, was sitting behind his desk going through various documents, some of which had been handed to him by the three men sitting in front of his desk.

He was angry that Ari Davidson, Director General of the Mossad, had given him this burden.

After a while he looked up from the papers and took his

reading spectacles off, dangling them in his left hand as he studied the men in front of him hoping to God they had nothing to do with the mess he was now confronted with – Elias Rubinstein, head of the *Terrorist Analysis* department, Moshe Schwarz, head of ongoing *Mossad Security Operations* and Isaac Orloff, deputy chief of the *General Security Service* department.

'Gentlemen you've been delegated by Ari Davidson with this precarious selection task privilege. So let's just get on with it and start with the easiest problem first.'

His brow rose in deep concentration, as he perceived each individual before continuing. He carried on watching them as he laid out his words carefully,

'The *Liquidation* department needs a new chief now that David Silverman has gone to meet his victims – good riddance,'

A quick squinted look at the three men – not a waver to be seen on any countenance,

'Ari and I have discussed this at great length. We decided we need an experienced field agent this time, someone with intelligence, integrity and a certain amount of hardness when it comes to making the right decisions. What we don't want anymore is a psychopath who enjoys wanton killing.'

He noted Moshe Schwarz and Isaac Orloff were nodding their heads vigorously.

'I have a personal recommendation from Ari to nominate Ben Goldmann as David Silverman's successor. Any comments on that?'

Three nays and heads shaking like sheep, he thought.

'Okay, then that's settled. The next problem is a subtler one. Elias could you give us a rundown please.'

'Yes, of course Jacob.'

Elias cleared his throat and pushed his chair back a little.

'I took over the analysis department last month as you all know. I immediately got an unpleasant feeling that my predecessor had left some skeletons in the cupboard. During the first week I made an introduction tour that included brief individual interviews on job sites. One of the top analysts came to my immediate attention. He was a total wreck and frightened out of his wits when I spoke to him. He couldn't look me in the eye and his gaze wandered furtively around the room. I persuaded him to come to my office on a pretext. He must have guessed I wanted to discuss things confidentially. Before I even got a word out he put a finger over his lips and cuffed a hand over his ear. I knew immediately he meant my office was bugged, so I wrote an address on a note requesting him to meet me there later on that evening. When he came, he kept on about his boss will set a Mossad *hit team* after him if he talks. I assured him that I was his boss and that no *hit team* would be set on him. He affirmed my question,

'Did he mean his department chief when he talked about his boss?'

Eventually I persuaded him to talk. As you are no doubt aware, Jacob and I have known each other more or less since kindergarten. I was at my wits end wondering with whom I could safely confide the information given by the analyst. He kept on mumbling that it would change the face of the world and be the end of Israel. I decided to tell Jacob. Gentlemen, shortly before 9/11 our analysts decoded a number of messages intercepted from the USA, Europe, Pakistan and from our beloved country Israel, originating from the *NSA,* one of our own *Mossad Field Signal Intelligence Units* and the *Central Mossad Communications Department.* The first two *NSA* and *Mossad Field Signal Intelligence Unit* messages point to the known 9/11 suicide pilots and their cells. The message picked up from the *Mossad Communications Department* shows a link to the other two. The analysis of that third message from within the *Mossad* point to possible indirect involvement by our agents in the preparation for the 9/11 targets.'

Jacob took over,

'Thank you Elias – Gentlemen, I don't have to emphasize that the sheer existence of the *Mossad* depends on speedy sifting. We need to set up a small covert investigation team here in Israel, one in Western Europe and another in the USA. The teams will have to work extremely close together. The aim is to find the key person or group and follow all links involved without arousing the slightest suspicion. No arrests of individuals or removal of technical surveillance devices will be made during the investigation in order not to blow it. I would like to propose one of my own men for the European side of the operation – Kenneth Woodward. I haven't yet spoken to him. He is currently in Haifa on a short vacation from Europe where he is head of the group. Or do you have any other suggestions?'

'Can you guarantee his utter integrity, Jacob?' asked Moshe.

'Indeed I can, but there can never be a hundred per cent certainty when dealing with the *Mossad*, now can there?' answered Jacob, his face contorted into a pained grimace as he looked at all three. The moment of guilt searching over, Elias joined in with a comment,

'I would personally underline Kenneth's trustworthiness. I have known him for nearly twenty-five years, so I think I can vouch for him. He is extremely qualified and I would say Jacob – this is a very wise proposal.'

'Thank you Elias – now, do we have any objections?' asked Jacob, looking at the three defiantly.

Jacob cocked his head slightly and said,

'No, then that's settled. What we need now is a central controller, someone who knows each and every department here in Israel and is familiar with the set-up in Western Europe and the USA. It has to be someone we can ultimately trust without restraint, who also enjoys the respects of the high and low in the *Mossad*. I need your proposals on this one. It doesn't matter if we have more than one to choose from.'

Moshe Schwarz spoke up.

'Jacob, the only person I can think of, who has the highest integrity and the weight for this pernicious task, you have already given the post as head of the *Metsada* department.'

'Not at all Moshe, I think that's an excellent choice. Ari and I also had him in mind. He can do the job from his new department where he is able to choose his resources from people he already knows and can trust from his own personal experience with them in the field. Yes, I think we can all agree on that, or is there anyone else to put forward?'

Jacob smiled at the three individuals, each of them shaking their heads.

'Okay then, that's decided upon.'

He looked down at his notes briefly before he addressed the three men.

'One last thing before we adjourn this meeting – not a breath about this to anyone. No conversations outside this office either per email or telephone. Ben Goldmann will be contacting personnel in your departments without your prior knowledge. You will be informed in due course and will allow them to work under Ben's jurisdiction without any personal discourse. I know you would prefer things to go through your hands first, but under these circumstances where our great nation is endangered and evil beings are at work, it would only jeopardise the operation if we go through the normal hierarchical channels. I will keep you informed as necessary. Gentlemen, I am grateful for your coming and thank you for your help. May God keep a watchful and protective hand over our cause for Israel.'

With that he pressed a button in the middle console – the signal for all three that they were dismissed. The door opened and his secretary appeared to let them out.

Ali, the Merchant, Thursday evening 18th August 2005

Ali was closing down his store when he heard his nephew Mousa shouting for help near the hotel. He was well aware Mousa would only shout like that in an emergency. Ali picked up his sword from a cleavage in the tent siding and flipped the front flaps down closing it temporarily. He ran as fast as he could towards the sound Mousa was making. He was now shouting *murder, murder!*

Ali arrived at the side of the hotel where Mousa was standing. A few other people were also running towards them. He took in the scene immediately. He saw a figure in black throttling the German. A second figure was standing behind the killer.

Ali raised his sword and ran towards the dark clad figures yelling and shouting warlord cries. His nephew and two others followed in his path. The killers decided there were too many so they left off their victim and melted into the night.

Ali reached the German and thought he was dead. His nephew, who'd learned first aid at a Christian convent school, pushed his uncle aside, loosened the wire from around the German's neck and removed it. He immediately massaged the neck and applied mouth-to-mouth resuscitation. In between breath gasps and pressing the Germans lungs and heart, he urged his uncle to get an ambulance and the police.

The ambulance was surprisingly quick, which was very fortunate for the German. The ambulance crew were used to being called out in this part of the world.

Mousa went with the ambulance and Ali retreated back to his tent after he told the police briefly what had happened. He emphasised his worry to the policemen that thieves would steal his goods during his absence, so they let him go. The others had disappeared before the police arrived.

After dismissing Ali, the policemen made their way to the convent hospital.

The German started to regain consciousness as the ambulance men brought him into the hospital. His breathing was just a gurgle and his eyeballs were extremely projected. The doctor gave him an injection that put him out. Due to the expected internal swelling Olaf was intubated and attached to breathing apparatus. A cava catheter for long-term sedation was inserted in his arm. It was usually inserted at the throat, said the doctor to the Carmelite nun, who was assisting, but the German's throat was too swollen.

Mousa waited in the corridor outside the operating room until the doctor came out. The doctor patted Mousa on the shoulder and told him he'd make a good doctor some day – he, Mousa, had no doubt saved the German's life.

The police arrived just as Mousa was about to leave. He told them all he knew, also that the German was staying at the hotel where he'd been ambushed. The doctor and nurse took in everything he said even though they were busy with the German. Mousa knew he was the hero and played out every minute of it. The policeman turned to the doctor and asked when they could talk to the German.

'It looks as though his larynx may be damaged so he won't be able to talk to anyone for some time. My suggestion is you go through police central command in Beirut to contact the German embassy. Get them to contact me personally. Tell them it's a top priority and that arrangements should be made for him to be flown back to Germany where he will undoubtedly have much better chances of survival. I'm afraid there's nothing more I can do for him than keep him sedated and on life-saving apparatus until he can be moved.'

Mousa was disappointed. He felt sorry for the German. Sadly he left the small hospital and made his way across the Cathedral Square. Just as he was turning a corner onto the beach road, he was grabbed and pulled into an alleyway. He couldn't see who it was. The figure in front of him was very tall and slim and draped in black like a Ninja or Tuareq. He couldn't see the one who was holding him. He felt the sharp prick of a knife against the side of his throat. The figure in front spoke with a strong foreign accent. He thought it was a European woman. She asked him in Arabic about the German. Mousa talked his head off, leaving nothing out, hoping that might save his life.

The woman in front, he was sure of that now, told him if he ever spoke to anyone about this she would get to know and then they would not only kill him but his uncle as well. The figure holding him threw him out onto the sandy pavement, like a sack of rice. He landed badly, spraining his ankle. Just as he was picking himself up, the police car came around the corner. He didn't dare look around for his assailants. Ignoring the presence of the police car, he carried on along the pavement towards the beach road. He was hobbling badly.

The police car slowed down and kept parallel beside him. A policeman leaned out the window.

'Hey, Mousa! Want a lift home?'

Mousa shook his head savagely.

'No thanks,' he said with a tremble in his voice.

Mousa continued to hobble towards the beach road. The policeman turned to the other one who was driving,

'He was a lot more talkative at the hospital now, wasn't he?' he said.

'Doesn't want to know us now does he?' replied the driver, adding, 'Looks like someone's got to him, Khaleb.'

'Yeah! Well then, you just drive on. Maybe he'll talk tomorrow, some place else. We don't want him killed just for curiosities' sake, do we? Don't want him to end up like that poor outpost soldier in 'no man's land'. Did you hear about him on the radio broadcast at the station?'

'No!'

'Some corporal got his throat cut, probably fell asleep at his post and some Israeli special forces got him.'

'Bloody Zionists – hey! I had to write that report you forgot yesterday. If you've enough time to listen to the radio while others work then you can write the report on the German and ring up headquarters. I've done my share, that's for sure,' said the driver.

The Agency Team in Leipzig – Wednesday/Thursday 17th/18th August 2005

I took in the surroundings after seeing Paula and her folks off. The street was cordoned off at both ends of the apartment block and the occupants of the flats had been evacuated. Satisfied no suspicious characters were about, I strolled over to the Fire Brigade commandant.

'John Jameson ISIA Berlin,' I said, offering my hand, which is a usual courtesy even with casual acquaintances in Germany.

'Heinrich Weiss,' he returned – a friendly grin on his face.

'Have you looked into a mirror within the last couple of hours?' he asked, still grinning.

It was obvious to me the smoke had left its mark.

'No,' I returned, 'is it that bad?'

'Why don't you go over to the ambulance people, they'll give you a cat's wash and my people will give you a hot drink,' he said, his white teeth showing in an everlasting grin.

'Okay, I'll do it in a minute, but I really came over to ask about the state of the building and if there were any signs of further bombs, booby-traps or similar devices?'

'No signs of any further devices. I have some Explosives Ordnance Disposal experts (EOD), and when they say it's clear you can be fairly certain, but for safety's sake we'll have to wait for the okay from the anti-terrorist lot, who, I must say, are a bit late getting here,' he said – a look of reprimand on his face.

'Bye the way, you did a splendid job getting those people out so quickly. That old woman you saved is now out of danger. The building is not badly damaged. My men had a look at the flat in question and the roof. The latter is partly blown off but mostly only the roof slates are affected. One wooden cross beam and a side beam will have to be replaced otherwise the roof's wooden support structure seems to be stable. The flat is a mess though. One room to the front side directly under the roof where the explosion took place is completely damaged and the room in the flat below as well. The water damage is moderate. The rest of the flats on the explosion side have suffered some water damage. The other side and most of the rooms towards the back of the building on both sides are habitable and we are now pumping water out of the cellars.'

'Thank goodness,' I said,

'In that case I think I'll take your advice and look up the ambulance people before they leave. It's fortunate they don't have anything serious on their hands. Thank you and your men too for your speedy response – it's good to see professionals at work. My team will be arriving shortly. The German special ops anti-terrorist people will be here soon too, I expect – they have a fair way to drive. We'll be working with them together. So it will be all right for us to enter the building to do forensics then?'

'Yes, of course – you have my word on that,' said the commandant,

'It won't fall on top of you,' he added, still amused and grinning again.

I didn't see the funny side but there again firemen are diligent and used to danger, it's part of their job. I expect their attitudes change over the years. It's much easier to laugh things off when they're called out and all goes well. I wasn't so sure about the building being safe – I still had those images of the uneven brickwork and scaffolding.

'What about media people? Have there been any around?' I asked.

'Yes, there were to start with but the police moved them out behind the sealed off area, but that won't stop that lot. They'll probably be out there somewhere recording everything – they're like the paparazzi and terrorist attacks are hot news these days.'

I nodded to the commandant and went over to the ambulance.

After a hot cup of coffee and a hot damp towel wash, I felt ready for the difficult part – reasoning with the Leipzig anti-terrorist special ops people about jurisdiction. What I didn't want was a one-way street. I hoped we could arrange for our forensics to work together, that way, we would be in a position to get to important material that hadn't been damaged. Failing that I would press for one or two of our team to be present as bystanders.

Talk of the devil – a few moments later the German forensics arrived, together with the anti-terrorist special task force. The fire brigade commandant met them so I went over and stood aside waiting for my chance. I didn't have to wait long before the commandant himself brought me into the conversation. Hands were shaken. I introduced myself, showing my credentials and the chief did likewise in perfect English,

'Pleased to meet you Mister Jameson, I'm Detective Chief Superintendent Helmut Holzbein, Eastern Central Command. This is Chief Inspector Holzhaus from Special Operations Leipzig and these are our teams.'

He waved his hand in a half circle at the two groups who were awaiting further orders. We shook hands. I nodded to the others. Some of the SOs were already moving in on the building and one was taking shots of the building and the surrounding people with a video camera. He spoke to his men and gave them their instructions before turning back to me.

'Mister Jameson!'

'John,' I replied.

'Okay, John, call me Helmut – I had a call earlier from Berlin from the LKA, a Marcus Anderson – he's put me in the picture. I agree, I think we would be better exchanging information rather than blocking out, so if you or your team want to be bystanders you're welcome. You understand that for the executive this investigation lies entirely in our jurisdiction?'

'Yes, of course – what do you want to know?'

'How about a résumé, that'll do to start with.'

'Okay,' I said and put him in the picture about the murder of Ian and Martha – the reason for my visit to the Sterns. Knowing the intricacies of the German police hierarchy I told him the local CID ought to be informed, as they were no doubt investigating Martha's murder. I mentioned putting off two shots at the assailant in the street but left out the fact that his gun was still in my pocket, also leaving out the bugs and the stakeout action in the flat opposite. The possibility the man I shot wasn't there anymore I put down to a possible slight injury, knowing full well my shots had been deadly. I made sure he realized the importance of leaving the Sterns out for the moment, mentioning Aunt Hera and the concentration camps. I told him I'd been given the Stern's keys and their permission to get some things out of the cellar that were of great importance to them. I also told him where the Sterns were staying and that I would be going there later with my men to secure their safety. I noticed he was getting fidgety, thinking maybe my information was too much for a starter.

'Em... and,' I started to say, overdoing things on purpose.

'Well, I think that's enough to go on for a start,' he said, impatiently,

'You'd better get some protective clothing from my people, if you want to come in with us now. Let me know the items you take from the cellar – a written list will do.'

I nodded my approval. He turned and disappeared hurriedly into the building. I was glad he'd interrupted. At least I couldn't be blamed for not mentioning the surveillance team from the flat opposite. I don't think I would have told him anyway. It's always good to have information for exchange purposes just in case they withhold information, which is almost certain to be the case. It may also turn out that the stakeout was official in which case we wouldn't be informed anyway, or if so, then too late to be of any use. The same applies to the pistol. Being an old hat at this I always regard it as playing the game. It's always the same, whichever nation or national investigative forces are involved!

Granddad's study was no longer recognisable as such. Both adjacent rooms, the ceiling and parts of the inner walls were disintegrated. The fire and water had done the rest. Nothing I could save in here I thought. Poor granddad, came to my mind immediately, but changed a few seconds later, thinking maybe we could have avoided all this if he'd been straight with Paula and myself to start with, not to mention Anna. The pure thought made me fume. My cell phone rang – the team had arrived. I went into the guest room, retrieved my night bag, went rapidly down the stairs and out onto the street. David Shepard, one of our best forensics came forward. He brought my attention to Marcus Anderson who was speaking to one of the policemen. David called him over.

'Glad to meet you at last Marcus,' I said, shaking his hand.

'Thanks for preparing the locals – it was a great help. They've agreed to let us be bystanders. But, before we start anything let's get into the van and I'll bring you all up to date.'

In the van I gave them a brief rundown but didn't mention the assailant's pistol or the stakeout. I sent David Shepard, Marcus and another man up to the flat. Once they were out of earshot I asked for a forensic bag, deposited the pistol in it and locked it up in a fixed forensics box, retaining the key. I told the three men who were to check out the stakeout flat that it was going to be a quick job in the dark using NVD goggles, as the other team would no doubt make them out immediately if they saw lights. Used to doing stakeouts they should know the places to look. I sent them off to the stakeout flat with the hope of getting some fingerprints, DNA or any other evidence.

I told the rest not to mention the stakeout in front of Marcus and to warn the other two who went up with Marcus to the Stern's flat. I went down to the cellar with the last man, who happened to be the driver. About three centimetres of water swilled about. I unlocked the door and went in. There was a compact computer on a shelf that hadn't seen any water, so I felt slightly relieved, hoping it was Martha's. I checked the suitcases, of which there seemed to be about a dozen. Judging by the weight, only three had contents and were quite heavy – maybe soaked up a bit of water too. Thinking maybe Anna's stuff might be amongst them I decided to take all three and the computer.

We went back upstairs and loaded the stuff into the van. I wrote out a list for the German Chief Helmut Holzbein and sent the driver up to give it to him. I told him, whilst up there, to have a look over at the stakeout flat to see if he could detect any movement from our team, then get over to them to see how they were doing. I decided to stay in the van and lock myself in – a few minutes snooze would do me good.

Aunt Hera's – early Thursday morning 18th August 2005

Yawning, I moved over to the van door, looking about before I opened it. The driver was standing a few metres away smoking a cigarette. Polite guy I thought – didn't want to disturb my sweet dreams, remembering briefly what the dream was about. Maybe one day it'll come true I thought.

'Everything all right?' I asked the driver.

'Yes, sir – they finished the stakeout flat about five minutes ago and are sitting in the other vehicle. The others are still up in the bombed-out flat. There's nothing on at the moment. I had a look over at the stakeout flat and didn't notice anything. The team says there wasn't a crumb to be found. It looks as though they were professionals – even the toilets were *pico bello*. They managed to check the toilet and the rooms at the back for fingerprints using more light, but didn't have enough light for fingerprints at the surveillance rooms up front, or rather – didn't want to blow their presence.

'That doesn't make our job easier, does it,' I said, thinking more or less out loud.

'No it doesn't,' he replied politely.

But there again it told me something. Whoever was behind the stakeout was a major suspect for the bombing. You can't clean a stakeout that quick – they must have been in the picture. Perhaps they were just one of many who'd been listening in.

'Okay, I'll pop upstairs to the others, I think they've been there long enough. Lock yourself in – there're too many unknown stratonics out here,'

He looked at me incomprehensively.

'Stratonics – means pertaining to armies, unknown armies or just the enemy, all right?'

'Oh, em... yeah!' he returned – still not convinced. Maybe it's too early in the morning, I thought.

I went upstairs looking for Marcus Anderson thinking he'd be the one the Germans would be talking to. I found him in what was left of granddad's study. He saw me – moved out to join me in the hallway and gave me a rundown,

'Place was really wired out you know. The telephone was nearly intact. A nasty *Stasi* bug planted in it. As for the explosive device – they found part of the timer and bits of the fuse. Judging by the spray direction, the explosive device was directed to hit the study. There appears to be a 90 % certainty that Czech Semtex was used. Chief Holzbein says he's happy with a written report from your side and says, whatever you were looking for in the flats opposite he'd like to know about it,' he added, grinning from head to toe.

I grinned back – knocking my respects up a few notches for the chief and his team.

'Okay, I think we know enough, unless they can tell us who made the bomb?' I said, looking at Marcus questioningly.

'That would be the day, wouldn't it,' he replied, smiling, 'but who knows, maybe a small slip-up like a fingerprint, register number of bomb parts or DNA – sometimes we're lucky,'

'I expect you've exchanged addresses and telephone numbers?' I asked.

'Of course, we exchanged cards,' he said naturally.

'Yes, we used to do that too in the old days, when not everybody could afford them,' I replied laconically.

Marcus didn't reply, I guess he wasn't sure what I meant. I wasn't really sure myself about my snobistic remark.

'Well, then, I guess we can call it a night, or rather a day here. Could you get the men down to the vans, Marcus, I'd like a quick word before some of you move back to Berlin,'

'Yes, of course,' he said.

I turned away and made my way downstairs thinking now we'd been caught out it wasn't appropriate for personal goodbyes to Chief Holzbein. I waited across the street until the team was complete and asked for three volunteers for protection purposes at Aunt Hera's. I told them they'd be working on shift, sleeping in normal beds and eating normal food. I left out the kosher bit 'cause not everybody knows what kosher means. Judging by the ignorance of the younger generation nowadays they would probably think it was some sort of vegetarian food.

I gathered all the evidence we had and asked the team going back to Berlin to make a brief consolidated report and have it put in my in-tray when they get back to Berlin. I said my goodbyes to the other part of the team thanking them for their good work and joking about night vision, knowing full well it was my blunder.

We were four – the driver, two other volunteers and myself as we made our way to Aunt Hera's, several blocks away, hoping it wasn't too early. When we got there I cursed myself, thinking I should've done a recce first. I'd assumed it was a flat just like the Stern's. I ought to have cottoned on when Paula said they could put us all up. It was a huge *art nouveau* villa fenced in by a low wall and high railings. Surrounding the villa was an ancient park with huge trees and metre high shrubbery – a nightmare to secure.

I saw lights on in the villa as I pressed the outside bell at the gate. At the sound of electro-static I identified myself before the voice at the intercom had time to ask our business. The electronics at the gate buzzed and the gate opened automatically. At least something reasonably modern here I thought.

We were met in the hall by a man dressed like a butler, ex-boxer type, armigerous judging by the bulge in his jacket.

'Good morning Mr Jameson, welcome, we've been awaiting your arrival. I'm Heinz the butler, please come in,' he said pleasantly.

'Good morning,' he repeated to the others, bowing slightly as they walked in one by one behind me.

He closed the door behind us.

'This way please, Miss Paula gave instructions to serve you breakfast when you arrive and you are not to disagree,' he said, placing a polite smile on his lips, without creasing his cheeks –

a professional butler and bodyguard – all in one – a real servant.

We carried our bags in, including the suitcases and computer from the Stern's cellar. I wasn't taking any chances until I'd cleared things with the Sterns.

We sat down at the huge kitchen table that was laid out for kings. Hot coffee and tea, milk and cereals, müsli, oven warmed rolls, various types of bread, jams, sliced cold meats and cheese. I guess if I'd asked for porridge, Heinz would have obliged.

I slipped out my cell phone from my hip holster and gave Marcus a call, explaining the situation here and urging him to make an immediate official request for extra police patrols or a stationary wagon or two at Aunt Hera's villa until we get things sorted out.

Heinz stood patiently at the side, noticing when the coffee was nearly finished and replacing it with a new pot. Other than myself, nobody seemed interested in tea, but at least I had milk this time. Once the men had more or less finished their breakfast I spoke to them.

'We are here purely to give the residents an increased feeling of security. Our presence will be required until we get a private company to take over or get the Sterns and Aunt Hera moved to a safer place. I have to get back to Berlin later on this morning. I'll be going by train leaving the three of you here to look after things. I don't have to tell you what to do – just work it out between you. I want you to be on full alert – with all senses and that means no smoking outside. When you're outside, be wearing your lightweight bulletproof waistcoats with your arms at the ready, safety catches off and silencers fitted. We don't want to raise the curiosity of the neighbours with loud shots, do we? There maybe professionals out there ready to kill you and we're also at a slight disadvantage regarding the terrain. I'd like a brief report in writing on any information you picked up from the German teams in the Stern's flat and from the stakeout flat, and I mean brief. Leave them on the table – I'll take them with me on my way back to Berlin. Do it now – I'll do the first outside shift. By the time my shift's over the house occupants will be getting up.'

I turned to the driver,

'You don't have to make a report so I'll need you at computer control, okay?'

'No problem,' he said. He went over to their gear and started setting up the computer and loading the object image security control program. On second thoughts I asked him,

'Do you have a mirror system installed?'

'Yes, we have,' he answered,

'I think it would be wise if we made a physical copy of the disk from the compact computer we saved from the cellar. It would mean changing your system configuration a bit because I want you to dismantle the copied disk – I'll be taking it with me to Berlin. Is that possible?'

'No problem, but we don't need to use the mirrored disk. We always have an external drive for data back-ups. We can use that and have the copy done in a jiff,'

'Great,' I said, 'can you arrange to do it then? Oh, and don't make a logical back-up, I need a physical copy, okay?'

'Sure,' he said, shrugging his shoulders as if I'd just insulted his integrity.

I put on my NVD goggles and waited until the program was running and the various personnel, location and environment parameters had been entered. He gave the thumbs-up and spoke into the microphone. I checked the earphones giving him the OK through the mini-mike. All systems working I made my way outside into the dark through the back door. I could see the lights of dawn approaching from the horizon. First things first I thought, as I made my way quietly around the vicinity of the house, nightmare scenarios going through my mind as the proximity of the shrubbery and trees loomed menacingly, my night vision trying to pierce their density – the sheer impossibility of securing this establishment. They'll have to be moved elsewhere and pretty soon. Granddad is the key here. He knows something, maybe had something he doesn't possess anymore. A security risk maybe, if he passes on his secrets. Maybe they got what they want, or am I on the wrong track?

Leipzig – Hera's Villa, Granddad and Paula, Thursday morning, August 18th, 07^{30} hrs.

I finished my outside shift and took over indoor computer control. I committed a major sin – I dozed off – the bleeps from the laptop loudspeaker and the moving blips on the monitor had the tendency to strengthen my urge to sleep. I was dreaming again – using the auxiliary motor to get the yacht out of *Aeroskobing* harbour, both hands on the wheel and Paula leaning on me with her hand on my shoulder. Her hand was shaking me and I didn't know why – there was no danger now as we were just outside the natural harbour enroute to *Fâborg* and no other boats in sight.

'John, John, hello..'

I woke up to find Paula smiling at me her hand still on my shoulder. That part wasn't a dream I thought, maybe given some time.

'Sorry, I must have dozed off. Hello, Paula!'

Inwardly, I cursed myself for breaking the rules – you don't ever sleep on duty. That would have been a serious 252 in my early days with the Junior Leaders.

'No wonder you're tired, it's been an exhausting time for you these last few days, I don't know how you manage it,' she said.

Her motherly look caused me to forget my sin for the moment.

'We're having breakfast in the morning room, do you want to join us?'

'Em, no thanks, I'll just have another coffee here and join you when you've finished. Then we'll do some straight talking. Anna's granddad has to talk, he's brought enough death and destruction to all of us – it's showdown time now. The sooner he talks, the chances are those who already know anyway, may lay off you.'

'It's going to be difficult, he's a very stubborn man, John. He told me once he had to swear an oath not to reveal what he saw and what he was told.'

'Maybe you can soften him up a bit – try and spell out the urgency. Others seem to know anyway because he's probably blabbed out most of it into the hidden microphones that were in his study and elsewhere in the flat. Once that point gets to him there's no reason why he shouldn't talk to us about it.'

'Yes, John, that sounds sensible. Maybe that'll do the trick. It's most difficult with old people when they've a spleen about oaths and loyalty even though half the world may know about it – anyway I'll try and prepare him. See you in about twenty minutes, John.'

'Okay, Paula.'

Paula picked me up from the kitchen and led the way to the music room – granddad was alone.

'Mr Scotsman,' he started.

I interrupted,

'Look, I don't know why you decided to address me this way, but now I know part of the story you could call me John or if you prefer you can call me Mr Jameson. It was Paula and I intervening that saved your life and that of your wife, so the least I can expect is a bit of cordiality.'

Granddad's face changed to purple, his eyes and features contorted – spelling hatred. He stood up from the chair to his full height trying to straighten his bent back. It was all written for anyone to see – he was the one who judges and punishes. In that moment of remonstration his whole life's arrogance came to light.

'You stupid person, why did you come into our lives? You took Anna from us. I was being polite, I should have called you *monsieur le crétin!*'

I couldn't believe what I was hearing. I stood up and turned to Paula who was white in the face, probably thinking this is not Anna's granddad as she thought she knew him.

'Paula, I'm sorry, but under these circumstances we'll be leaving this house immediately. I've asked for extra police patrols so we'll stay outside the villa until they take over. This guy needs to see a doctor or be locked-up before he gets the rest of you killed! I've arranged for the police to give you a chance to recover, but under these circumstances I think they should take granddad into custody and give him a grilling. If I'm not mistaken he knows what's going on here.'

I turned and left the room, the sounds of granddad's shouting and screaming ringing in my ears. I wonder if he really was the person he gave himself to be. Very strange behaviour for a

Rabbi I thought. I think he did that on purpose – like a rat in a corner, his only other choice would have been the truth or another cooked up story – attack seemed to have been his best means of defence!

I went into the kitchen and told the man at the monitor to pack up and tell the others we were leaving immediately. I looked around for the compact computer, it was nowhere to be seen. Granddad came immediately into mind or even Heinz the Butler. Maybe one of my guys had put the computer in the van. Granddad didn't know that we'd made a backup copy of the hard disk. Thank goodness I'd put Anna's suitcases into the van and locked it up early this morning just after my first shift and long before granddad or Heinz were up.

I went out to the van and sure enough the suitcases were still there but no sign of the compact computer. I had a sudden thought about granddad, the way he'd acted reminded me of someone from the past, an old case, or maybe I was being canny again. I know I've seen that behaviour before! On second thoughts maybe I'm just being careful, seeing and hearing things normal people wouldn't. After all, I do have some experience and a lot of training, or am I looking for excuses again? I opened the technical surveillance box and took out two mini cameras that I stuffed into my pocket and went back into the house. Seeing no one about I went into the toilet between the dining room and the study and placed a mini camera to cover anyone having a stand-up pee – regardless of the official consequences should it be blown. I did the same across the hall in the toilet next to the music room. I wanted confirmation of granddad's circumcision – I had a hunch he wasn't even a Jew. I checked the kitchen to see if we hadn't forgotten anything and made my way out to the van.

I came out of the kitchen hallway leading to the outside door when Paula crossed my path from a side door blocking my way out.

'You can't just leave like this, John. I'm so sorry about granddad but that's the way he is sometimes.'

'Paula, your granddad is probably to blame for getting Anna and Martha killed, you do realize that don't you? I think you should leave with us – he's a dangerous man to have around. All he cares about is his own vanity and well-being. He doesn't care a sod about anybody else, he's proven that.'

'I'm sorry John, but he is Anna's granddad.'

'I'm beginning to have my doubts about that Paula. No Rabbi in his right mind behaves the way he does.'

'You're upset John, I understand that, we'll figure a way of getting at the truth.'

'Quite honestly, Paula, I acknowledge your kindness and forgiveness but this goes too far for me. Look, here's my private address in Berlin. It's a small two-roomed flat. If at any time you're in trouble or want to talk about things then you know where to find me. I've written the number of the ISIA on the back. I'm really fond of you Paula, so please don't hesitate to come, or just call me even if you're not in trouble, promise?'

'Thanks John, I promise.'

'Okay Paula, we'll be across the road until the police arrive.'

Paula fell into my arms. I felt her chest heaving – she was trying to keep her sobs back. I pressed her all the harder and let go. She looked up at my face, tears were strolling down her cheeks.

'I'm not as strong as many people believe, John. You seem to be part of my life now even though we've known each other only for such a short time. Thank you for all you've done for us, I know it all came from your heart even though you try to fool people that you're a tough guy.'

I smiled at that bit of truth and pulled her back in my arms. I kissed both eyelids and her tears, brushing her mouth with my lips, suddenly realizing the last time I'd done that – Anna had been upset because no one was coming to her wedding. I pressed my lips lightly on Paula's. She responded by opening her lips slightly in a pout, letting our lips join in unity. We lingered – the tips of our tongues touched like small electric jolts. We pulled apart, both accepting our new bond and realizing this wasn't the right moment.

I left her in the hallway and carried on out to the van. The others were already seated. We pulled out of the drive through the open gates and parked opposite. I got the monitor out and checked to see if the mini-cameras were functioning – explaining to the others what had happened and wanting to know something important about granddad's *what's-it*. They all laughed until I finished explaining.

I reckoned that being older – granddad would more likely want to pee after breakfast, especially after the row with Paula and me. All of ten minutes went by before we got what we wanted. I pressed the freeze function with a good close-up and saved it in a file called *granddadswhatsit*. If granddad's a Rabbi, I thought, then I'm the Pope.

'Looks like granddad's a phoney folks – I want two of you to go back into the house and retrieve the mini cameras from the toilets. Pretend you both need to go to the toilet urgently – they'll let you in. While you're at it, put enough fingerprint forensics gear in your pockets to get prints from the inside door handles and toilet lids. Don't bother about the handles or doors on the hall side. We don't want granddad thinking his guise is blown. Maybe we can find out who this jerk is and anyone else who's fingerprints we find – and make sure you remove the fingerprint dust after you!'

My thoughts were revolving. Maybe I knocked off the wrong guy on the street. No.., he obviously belonged to the lot who blew up the flat. They wouldn't have cared who was in it, or would they? Nagging thoughts about the Sterns crossed my mind.

Berlin – Ian's oration Thursday morning, August 18th

We arrived back in Berlin at 11.³⁰ am. I dozed for most of the journey. Just before reaching the outskirts of Berlin I gave Jack Orlowski a call, his secretary Susan Hanson answered,

'Hi, Susan, John Jameson.'

'Oh, hi, John.'

'I'll be in the office in about half an hour. When's my session with Jack this afternoon?'

'Your appointment's at 2 pm – Jack says he wants a word with you if you call.'

'Tell him my batteries are low – bye Susan.'

She must think I'm in an ugly mood – well I haven't really had much sleep this week. Jack will probably take insult as usual. He'll be thinking I'm trying to avoid him – how right he is – I also hate orations!

We arrived at *the Agency* and took the suitcases, hard disk and other forensic material down to our property lock-up in the basement and had them registered with strict access and withdrawal privileges only to my person. I won't take any chances of anything being changed or removed without having had time to go through it myself. To be on the safe side, I had the hard disk put in a metal box, which I then locked, and pocketed the key. I had registered seals put on all items.

Back in my office I found a number of emails that received my immediate attention. The one I judged most important was from Chris Fenton. Among other things I'd asked him to have Ian Ferguson interviewed at the Intelligence Centre at Chicksands, which I recall as a sprawling army complex, more akin to a US military base than a modern British Army Intelligence Centre. The previous location at Ashford, Kent, had been much more suitable for such an institution – lesser Army interference. The search for Ian Ferguson had been complicated due to security barriers. Why on earth he was doing language training in a place like Damascus is very strange, because Army Intelligence personnel usually do their Arabic studies at other British universities in the UK. Chris didn't get any further on that line though.

Email from Chris Fenton:

Dear John.

Ian Ferguson had some valuable information. Apparently Hans and Ian were in the Kasbah in Damascus together with Elias, the youngest of the three Jews from the Arab class a week before it ended. They were sitting in an alcove, unseen from the rest of the locality, when they heard voices discussing an abduction and execution from the adjoining alcove. They recognised two of the voices as Helga Schulz and the Dutchman Henrich van Gelders from their Arab class. Two others joined them shortly after. Neither of the three could recognise the new voices. Ian describes them as Arabs with a difficult accent. They couldn't decipher the jargon.

Elias disclosed to Hans and Ian that he was engaged to a Palestinian woman from Nablus and was going to visit her on his way home from Damascus. Elias was worried about re-routing – he hadn't yet informed his father about his engagement. Hans said not to worry, he'd accompany him and inform his mother about a later flight home from Tel Aviv. Hans also said he'd see if he could get help from some Syrian friends. Whoever those were he didn't say. Ian was asked if they had any inclination about the abduction and execution. He said Schulz and van Gelders were always talking radically and he didn't see any personal indications at the time. I know what you are asking yourself! No, Ian doesn't remember Elias's Surname. That's it, end of the story – the lads are itching to go over. looks like it's going to be pretty soon, eh? See you on Friday!

Regards Chris

Well, I thought, that's a bit more to add. Now we've got: Damascus -> Tyre -> Nablus.

Where are the two of them now?

I went down to the canteen on the ground floor, thinking early birds get the best pickings, but most of all to avoid the queue. I was starving and could have eaten a horse. I knew I needed my wits about me later, so I thought I'd have to make do with a mixed salad and yoghurt. I was glad I'd made a few notes in preparation for my meeting with Jack. No queue, but luck wasn't with me – someone touched my elbow – I recognised the,

'Eh, hem,' that followed.

I turned to see Jack Orlowski behind me.

'Oh, hi, Jack, hungry too are you,' I said, nonchalantly, turning my attention back to the cook who was waiting for my order. I'd changed my mind instantaneously about the mixed salad when I saw smoked haddock on the menu for today.

'I'll have the smoked haddock with French fries and salad please.'

'Sauce?'

'No, thanks,' I said, thinking – ugh!

I moved along the counter – got myself a beaker of yoghurt and a bottle of mineral water and reached the cashier in a jiffy. Jack was still pondering and the look on the cook's face told its story. I saw the men I was with in Leipzig and one spare seat left at their table, which I made a dive for. I wasn't going to let my food get cold by sitting at another table where Jack would definitely have joined me and held me in conversation for the next half hour. I was just scraping the bottom of my yoghurt beaker, when the same hand pulled at my elbow again. I didn't have to look back to see who it was. This time I thought I'd catch him out. I half pushed my chair back, careful not to catch him in the shins and stood up – turned around, smiling.

'Well, that was good food for a change, eh lads.'

They all knew Jack the mandroid and murmured their agreement.

'Well Jack, now my stomach has had it's first treat this week I think we could start Ian's oration right now, that is if it's convenient? I've gone to some trouble and made some notes that will help us. What do you say,' I said to Jack, beaming over my face – knowing he'd cancel any other appointments because he couldn't write the oration on his own and wouldn't get help elsewhere either.

'Eh, yes, that's a splendid idea, John. Upstairs in ten minutes?'

'Sure, Jack – make it twenty minutes though – okay?'

'Oh, all right then, twenty minutes,'

That's enough time to get interrupts organised should Jack keep me too long, and time for a shower and a change of clothing.

I went back upstairs and got some clean underwear, socks and shirts from my locker. I took out the necessary and made my way to the showers.

Jack was surprised at the meticulous notes I'd made. I knew all along I wouldn't get away from this pestilent task so I wrote out the whole funeral agenda myself – I owed it to Ian. For the oration I used words I knew Ian would've appreciated.

Jack had a few objections – mostly where he'd to rearrange details already organised. All in all we were finished in half an hour.

'See you tomorrow at 2 pm, Jack,' I said ardently, shoving my chair back abruptly.

Jack just nodded, obviously succumbed to acceptance. Susan Hanson was astonished to see an exultant John Jameson stride out of Jack's office after such a short session – after all, she'd cancelled all other appointments up to 4 pm.

I went into my office to make more phone calls – finish reports and then home and early to bed. I needed to catch up on lost sleep and I'd three suitcases and a hard disk to look through early tomorrow.

Olaf's Rescue – late Thursday evening 18th August 2005

Elsa was awakened from her doze in front of the telly by the ringing of her telephone. She pressed the mute button on the remote, got up from the sofa and stood for a moment listening – where had she last put the darn thing? The ringing was fairly loud, giving her the best clue – the kitchen. She walked bare-footed into the kitchen, picked it up from the table and pressed the telephone button.

'Elsa Ertl speaking.'

'German Foreign Office here, Jochen von Harburg is my name. Sorry to disturb you at this late hour. Are you Ms Ertl the wife of Olaf Ertl?'

'No, certainly not – I'm his sister, he's not married – why what's wrong, has anything happened to him?' she asked – a dark cloak of dread folding over her.

'I'm sorry to inform you that your brother was attacked and is in a critical condition. He is in the Lebanon in a Christian hospital at Tyre. We have a request from the Lebanese authorities for him to be flown by *Medivac* back to Germany. We need to know if you are prepared to carry the transportation costs, and if so, to which hospital he should be taken?'

Elsa couldn't get any words out – her mind was racing between Hans her son and Olaf her brother.

'Ms Ertl – hallo, are you still there?'

'I'm so sorry, this comes as a big shock – you see my son is missing and my brother went to find him,' she spoke the words out between sobs and nose sniffling – the tears were flowing now.

'I understand Ms Ertl, but at the moment it is vital for your brother's health should complications arise, that he is brought back over here to a German hospital. His chances of surviving in the Lebanon are not so good.'

'Yes, of course I'll pay any costs involved,' she answered defiantly and added, 'if it is at all possible, please arrange for him to be flown to the University Hospital at *Freiburg im Breisgau*, in Baden-Württemberg.'

'Okay, Ms Ertl – we'll inform the authorities in Beirut and the *Medivac* organization in Germany to go through with his evacuation. You'll be contacted either by us, or *Medivac* during the course of tomorrow. With a bit of luck we should have him back in Germany by tomorrow late afternoon or evening – at the latest Saturday.'

'Thank you very much Mister von Harburg, thank you so much,' she said the sobs coming faster now.

'Goodnight Ms Ertl.'

She couldn't get anything else over her lips to answer the kind official – her sobbing had increased so much she just pressed the telephone button to end further embarrassment. Clutching it, she went back to the living room, threw herself on the sofa and let herself go – thinking she'll have to call John.

Elsa phones – late Thursday night, August 18th

I was sitting at the stern, the rudder in my right hand, looking up into the mainsail that was filled and stretched out beautifully. I had just set the main sail down a few reefs, removed the rope holding the rudder and tacked to starboard windward coarse. The sun was shining and a force five South Westerly was blowing. I jumped at the sound of bells ringing and lost control as a huge wave caught the yacht off balance. I was thrown overboard listening to the purring of my cell phone near my ear, drawn down into the depths of the ocean gulping down salty water.

I woke up in the bedroom of my second home in Berlin, disappointed and cursing. Grabbing the phone from the bedside table I pressed the button.

'Yes,' I said angrily – thinking the ringing of the phone disturbed the best part of my dream.

'John, it's me, Elsa.'

'Oh, Elsa – what's up – what's happened?' I said, looking at the alarm clock – 11^{30} pm.

'The foreign office rang up a few hours ago. Olaf's been attacked in the Lebanon. He's in a critical condition but they'll be flying him home tomorrow or Saturday by *Medivac*. They're taking him to the University Hospital at Freiburg.'

'Did they give you any more details of his whereabouts in the Lebanon?' I asked.

'Yes, they said he was in a Christian hospital in *Tyre* in the Lebanon. Oh, John – if something bad has happened to Olaf then what has happened to Hans? I'm at my wits end worrying.'

I thought – just what I needed!

'Look, Elsa – there's nothing we can do now until we get Olaf back home safely into a German hospital. Take a few valerian drops or a stronger tranquillizer, you must try and get some sleep. I'm in the middle of an investigation at the moment so I'll have to ring off. Don't worry, we'll get this sorted out. Once I've got this end tied-up and Ian's funeral is over tomorrow, I'll be going with a team to Damascus to find Hans. I'm sorry I can't talk to you any longer now, but I promise to ring you up tomorrow – okay, Elsa?'

'I'm sorry, John – I know your hands are full. I'm glad to have you as a friend. I'll take your advice and make myself a herb tea to settle me down. I hope I can give you some better news when you ring up tomorrow. Bye then, John.'

'Bye, Elsa,' I said softly, pressing the off button not embarrassed at all for my little white lie. I dropped the cell phone onto the bedside table and went back to sleep looking for my yacht.

Berlin – Ian's Funeral – Friday, 19th August

First thing after waking up I gave Elsa a call, 'John, I'm so glad you rang, Olaf is on his way with *Medivac*, he should be in the ENT Department of the University Hospital Freiburg by 3 pm. I was just going to give you a call as I'm about to leave for Freiburg shortly.'

'Well, that's good news, Elsa. Did they mention how he was?'

'Yes, in fact they said he's in a favourable condition. I take it that means he's over the worst, doesn't it?'

'Of course, Elsa, that's really good news. We've made some progress here too, look I tell you what – I can't promise, but I'll try and get a flight to Basel and hire a car to take me to Freiburg tomorrow. I'll give you a call in the morning or you can call me, you have my cell phone number.'

'Okay, John, maybe I'll see you at the hospital in Freiburg then?' asked Elsa, with a longing sound in her voice that made my loins tingle.

'See you tomorrow, Elsa, if all goes well.'

'Bye, John.'

I pressed the telephone button and wondered what I was doing to myself. Paula and Elsa, wasn't that overdoing things a bit!

That's typical of Ian to make his last journey on earth on a day like this. Why couldn't it have been a normal Scottish funeral with lots of rain giving the extra sad touch? The weather's too perfect, a blue nearly unclouded sky with a slight breeze going, not really enough to disturb the hairdos of the meticulously clad mourners in the funeral procession, preceded by the Pipe Major playing *'Scots wha hae'* followed by two drummers and the pall-bearers and Ian's old colleagues and friends in dark suits.

I'd just arrived as the church service was over. I was waiting at the freshly dug grave, watching the procession on its way from the church. The guard of honour from the 1st Battalion Scots Guards was behind me ready for the last salute. We were fortunate to get them, as they'd just returned to Munster a couple of months earlier after a heavy tour of duty in Iraq. I did a sweep of the cemetery and spotted our observation team – their conspicuousness bugged me a bit. An arrangement I thought necessary. Jack had tried to talk me out of it. I asked him if his training at Langley had ever covered such events. At that he gave in.

My attention was immediately drawn to a figure in a long black outfit walking behind the pallbearers, a position normally reserved for relatives. She was wearing a black shawl, which the wind blew out occasionally from her cheeks. Her face seemed somewhat familiar. Next to her was Jack Orlowski and behind them a priest and four church servers.

Now where had I seen that face before – I was sure Ian had no relatives? I watched her as the procession gained proximity, turning a sharp serpentine bend going slightly away and then coming directly back towards us – quite a young woman. I wonder who she is? Her looks, despite efforts to appear associated in remorse, couldn't quite conceal a taint of mockery, almost as though she was showing off her presence. Like – you didn't want to know me before and yet I'm the only bloody relative you've got. These thoughts brought me to the conclusion she might possibly be an illegitimate daughter or a relative who'd been denied nearness to Ian whilst he was alive.

You really could have picked a lousier day Ian. I haven't had this suit on for months. This morning, I was distressed to find my funeral attire all creased up in a pile with some other trousers at the bottom of the cupboard and smothered with long white hairs from my neighbours' Persian cat. No, this really is not the type of weather for a funeral. The sky should have been overcast – deep grey, with gusty winds bearing biting raindrops onto my nose and cheeks. My heavy dark trench coat collar, covering most of my face, held in place by one of my hands, taught across the knuckles by the strain, turning a slightly mottled blue through the cold – my eyes trying to adjust to the funeral scene in the clamminess of the cemetery atmosphere of a late autumn day. Yes, that would have been more fitting than on this hot summer's day, at least it probably would have been so if the funeral was taking place in Scotland.

It's not just the thought of people looking closer at my hasty ironing making me feel like this. Of course it could be my Scottish heredity making me feel a *wee* bit melancholic, or maybe it's just because I'm bloody angry it had to be Ian. Somehow or other, I've always managed to avoid personal involvement at funerals of my own relatives or colleagues like Ian. I even remember the times playing *Last Post* and *Reveille* at some military funerals when I was a young boy soldier of the Junior Leader's Regiment at Dover. It didn't disturb me then. Maybe though, it was the tough ordeal I went through, being forced to become a man at the age of fifteen. It's always different each time, apart from the nasty, empty and nagging feeling in my stomach that will soon turn to cold-blooded reasoning – I always get when the good guys get killed. A cold rage takes over – giving way eventually to the rules of the game – there's no place or time for remorse in this business. Ian trusted his superiors though and always obeyed orders, never ever suspecting betrayal – where the hell is Martin Cole?

I stood near the hole that was very discreetly bordered by green synthetic turf, dispelling any chances of getting my shoes dirty.

Jack Orlowski paid tribute with an oration to be proud of. Even his southern drawl seemed fitting. He'd have made a good undertaker! He finished off with a verse I'd given him, although I can't even remember who wrote the words,

'..Now is weighed down by ago and sight is overloaded, the smell of the earth burdened by memory'.

The drummers took over with rolls as the coffin was lowered into the grave followed by the guard of honour who fired their last salute. The priest gave Ian his blessing followed by rolls from the drummers – the Pipe Major taking up 'Going home' by Anton Dvořák. I thought that was more appropriate than 'Amazing Grace', which is nearly always played.

One after the other, the procession of mourners shoved a small spade into a black iron cauldron filled with earth and threw it onto the coffin that was now lying in its last resting place.

As the queue dwindled and I got closer, I managed a closer look at Ian's so-called last relative, the young lady in black. I registered eyes that seemed to be gleaming. Maybe I'm seeing things I thought – then came my turn. From watching others offering condolences I noticed she was oblivious to words, so I just shook her hand and gave her a short nod. She returned my weak effort with eyes that seemed to be spelling out hatred.

I sincerely hoped Jack Orlowski would fill me in who the hell she is. As far as I knew Ian had never married, although I knew he'd had a number of longer lasting relationships. I was annoyed at Jack for being secretive.

For me the funeral was over, I don't believe in a binge afterwards – it gets my gall when I see so-called friends and relatives filling their bellies with good food and drinking themselves to oblivion, talking and laughing about the deceased – as the drinks go down faster some of the talk getting sometimes contemptuous.

I went over to Chris Fenton and the others – we had serious business to talk about. I suggested we meet at the ISIA at 5 pm, where I'd arranged with Jack to use the conference room. I went home to change back into casuals and have a quick nap and think things over – I was exhausted.

Freiburg – Olaf in the University Hospital

I joined Chris Fenton and the others in the Agency conference room, which is bug-checked daily, but not before picking up the back-up disk, suitcases and forensic material from property lock-up and stowing them in my car.

I suggested we have a drink on Ian at a more convenient time and made known the change of plan – we'd be using other premises. I didn't mention the reason to them, but I had a hunch *the Agency* was the last place we should be. On previous instructions I had Chris Fenton hire two vehicles that were now parked in the visitors' car park. Before we left, I gave each of the drivers a sketch describing the route to the next location and asked Chris to accompany me in my car. On the way, I gave him a rundown and the reason for my decision not to trust the

ISIA premises – one of my canny moments or just being careful. It really goes much deeper than that. As a youngster I was often accused, in a nice sort of way, by relatives of being clairvoyant, which often ended up in my reading tea leaves from their cups. What I do know is, when I get this feeling on the job, I'm nearly always right – well, so far I've never been wrong! It's kept me alive! Chris has always respected my far-sightedness! There was too much uncertainty and a general security problem as the disappearance of Martin Cole could not yet be explained. We discussed the possibility of Martin having someone in the *bunch* as an informer. Chris ruled that out – he said Martin never had any closer friends in the *bunch* other than myself. As there was so much at stake, I decided to trust the *bunch* and told Chris we were going to be using an old factory I'd bought for next to nothing shortly after I joined the ISIA in Berlin. I explained it wasn't all that big and I was really using it as a workshop for my new hobby – building a boat.

I'd managed to get hold of the original plans of the building complex with the purpose of rebuilding parts of the old factory maintenance building and came across a bunker system under the main workshop that had been closed off by a brick wall. Over the last couple of years, in between building my boat, I'd also built in a secure area with a hidden passage to the bunker system that I'd turned into special working and resting facilities. They would undoubtedly please him and I'd fitted out the five double bunk beds with new mattresses and bedclothes. Working on the boat in the open workshop was an ideal cover for any small amount of men.

I gave the *bunch* a run through the premises. An eyelift or two was confirmation that some at least were impressed. I explained to the men that the search for Hans was a private enterprise. Initially, only travelling expenses and boarding would be reimbursed for services rendered. The loyalty of the *bunch*, without payment for services in such matters, goes without saying. What we were going to do, was to combine Ian's murder investigation with Martha's, thus inadvertently retaining official status. In which case we could expect a reimbursement. I hadn't yet mentioned Martin Cole other than to Chris Fenton – I was holding that back until we got more information. I brought them all up-to-date with events, mentioning that I'd be working between them and the ISIA.

Our first priority was to investigate the back-up disk, which I gave to one of our analyst specialists, whom I knew could find any hidden byte on the disk, or bit, come to that. The suitcases that were really personal to me, having mostly belonged to Anna, I handed over to Chris Fenton together with the gun and the fingerprints from granddad's toilets. I knew he would categorise each suitcase item meticulously and go through the contents looking for the needle in a haystack. I'd decided it would block my thinking if I devoted too much time to them.

The rest of the team would be checking through massive worldwide archives trying to find any fingerprint matches. I showed them the complexity of the workshop and my computer satellite set-up that had direct links to major computer networks of some of the worlds most secretly guarded organizations. I also had a link to the ISIA computer system. I'd learned how to do some hacking without getting caught, which comes in very useful at times.

Leaving them with enough to analyse and investigate I made my way to the airport to catch a flight to Basel. With a bit of luck I could be with Elsa in Freiburg by 10 pm.

The University Hospital complex at Freiburg in the Hugstetter Strasse, is a typical German University conglomeration of new and old buildings, fifteen minutes walk from the city centre or from the railway station. The various faculties have been added over the last century according to technological and scientific advancement and the necessity for specialisation. Under modern financial aspects the complex could be described as uneconomic and disorganised, but because such establishments carry out research they are subsidized.

Olaf was in the ENT building in a special care sick room on life support equipment. Elsa was asleep in an armchair, so I pulled a wooden stool from under the bed and sat down quietly.

I studied Olaf's injury. A haematoma ring and a cut went around his neck like a tight-fitted necklace. I thought the swelling didn't look too bad, but there again I'm not an expert, maybe it's internal. I shifted my stool a bit nearer making a scraping noise on the floor that woke up Elsa.

She stretched her arms and smiled – a fawn awakening to a new morning's rise.

'John,' she said, with such warmth I automatically put more feeling to a return smile than usual.

'Hi, Elsa,' I replied quietly, swivelling my stool around towards her but remaining seated, not quite knowing how to react to the situation.

Elsa slid from the armchair, brushed the creases from her skirt and tiptoed over on her bare feet. I didn't get a chance of standing up to greet her – she just came between my tree trunks that were suddenly cemented to the floor and put her arms around me holding my head to her bosom, saying,

'John... John, I'm so glad you're here.'

She let go – pulled my head up with both hands and gave me a kiss on the lips with such tenderness that I was immediately worried about my loin reactions being noticeable to the general public should anyone come into the sick room. I stood up slowly and Elsa melted onto my body. That was it I thought – she ought to be feeling my reactions by now. Elsa smiled, put her arms around me and laid her head on my chest, pressing her body closer to mine – letting me feel her soft protrusions.

That really did it, I thought, as she let a hand go down my spine and pull my back closer to her. I let both of my hands close in on her soft buttocks. I could feel the softness and the warmth of her skin through the thin cotton skirt. I murmured into her ear,

'Elsa,' putting feeling and longing into that one word,

'Oh, John,' she said, her head looking up again and her lips finding mine again.

We lingered on a long kiss, tongues exploring and my loins exploding until we were interrupted,

'Ah, hem,' said a voice from the other side of the bed near the door.

We broke up our embrace like two juveniles caught playing doctor and patient. Elsa moved immediately in front of me to conceal my embarrassment.

'Would you mind leaving the room for a few minutes,' said one of the four people in blue, with a slight glean of amusement in her eyes.

'Yes, of course,' said Elsa, taking my hand and pulling me on her other side away from the doctors and nurses. She pushed me past them and I exited quickly. Elsa turned back to fetch her shoes. We waited outside in the corridor looking in through the glass window. Elsa broke the silence,

'This afternoon the doctor said Olaf may be taken from the life support machine this evening if the swelling continues to go down. He said the breathing pressure is receding enormously, which is a good sign,'

'It looks as though they're doing that now,' I said, before a nurse came over and closed the curtains.

Elsa moved back into my arms, holding me tight and moving her lower body ever so slightly, feeling the revolution in my loins. I cursed inwardly for wearing boxer shorts – they have too much leeway.

'When do you have to go back, John?' she asked, softly.

'My flight leaves Basel at 3.20 pm tomorrow afternoon. I hired a car so I'll have to be leaving Freiburg about noon.'

'I booked a room for you at my hotel just in case you came,' she said, turning her head up and looking at me expectantly.

'Thanks, Elsa – that'll give us more time together,' I said.

She smiled back knowingly.

The curtains were pulled back and we could see into the sick room again. Olaf had been taken off the breathing equipment. A nurse remained at Olaf's bedside and the others came out. I moved behind Elsa.

'Ms Ertl, your brother is out of danger now and breathing normally,' said the doctor.

'Thank God,' said Elsa.

'With a bit of luck you may be able to see some response when you speak to him later. I suggest you take a couple of hours break,' said the doctor, with a slight twinkle in his eyes.

'Yes, all right,' said Elsa, blushing slightly, 'Thank you doctor – I'll just get my belongings and take your advice. I'll be back later on.'

The doctor nodded and the entourage of doctor and nurses carried on down the corridor to the next room. Elsa turned to look at me. I perceived a mischievous look in her eyes telling me she was glad having to be told to take a break and knowing what she would be doing during it. She went back into the sick room to get her things and leave, but not before she went over to Olaf and watched over him for a few minutes. We left the ENT department by the back door and walked down the staff car park leading to the main road.

'Let's get you booked into the hotel first John, then we can have some eats in the restaurant, if it's still open – the food's OK.'

We crossed over the main thoroughfare to the hotel. What I didn't know was she'd booked me into her double room.

Freiburg – Olaf awakens – Friday, 19th August

If I hadn't known Elsa had given birth twenty years ago I would have sworn she was a virgin. She's probably never slept with a man since Hans' father made her pregnant. I stroked and kissed her whole body and the barely perceivable scar where she'd had her caesarean birth. Maybe it was the situation we were in – the attack on Olaf, the anxieties attached and Elsa's feelings that Hans was alive and the fixed idea I was going to save him. We were both hungry for the love we then shared in the hotel room. It was of an intensity I hadn't experienced for some time. I decided not to spoil the moment and not to inform Elsa of the latest news we'd obtained about Hans from Ian Ferguson. I'll do that later.

Afterwards we went downstairs to the restaurant and had something to eat – it was late so we only got snacks. We sat there for nearly an hour, both acting like two teenagers, giggling and laughing at stupid things.

The moment of truth arrived later at Olaf's sick bed. We were both anticipative, would he be awake – would he be able to hear us – when could he talk to us – when would he be fully recovered?

Olaf's eyes were open when we stood over him at both sides of his bed. I asked the nurse if the bed could be raised a bit so Olaf could see us and not just the ceiling. Olaf was dazed but we noticed recognition in his eyes as we leaned over near his head. Elsa grabbed the arm that wasn't on a drip and caressed it saying,

'Dear Olaf, you're safe now – you're back in Germany – in Freiburg. We'll soon have you home.'

Elsa didn't bother about the teardrops running down her cheeks and dropping on the bedclothes. Her brother was safe that was all that mattered – for the moment.

Olaf opened his mouth to speak but the nurse leaned over and put a finger over his lips saying,

'Don't try to talk Mr Ertl – it's too early – you'll only make things worse. Here's a block of paper and a ball point pen if you want to communicate,'

Olaf closed his eyes and continued to breath normally – he was off again. We sat at his bedside, waiting and talking in whispers. I broke the news to Elsa about Hans, doing my utmost to give it a positive touch and explained our plans for finding him. I informed her I'd probably be leaving for the Middle East on Sunday, depending on the arrangements that had to be made. She enclosed my right forearm with her hands, pressing it like a tourniquet, her nails biting into my flesh as I passed on the news. Her eyes were watery again but fixed on mine piercingly, trying to discern if truth or lie, or maybe because I'd held the news back so long.

Olaf woke up again. This time his gaze was more direct. He moved his hand towards the writing block and let it fall back again. I picked it up and put the ballpoint pen between his thumb and forefinger. His first attempt was a scribble. He was obviously not able to write words. His second attempt was more like children's pictures until I cottoned on. He was explaining himself in pictures. I couldn't make head or tail of what he was trying to tell us. Anyway, he was off again for another twenty minutes. When he woke up again, he was still holding the ballpoint pen. I told him to write one picture at a time and I would ask him questions in between where he should nod or shake his head. With a lot of questioning I got the picture and explained it back to him in coherent words. Olaf smiled his acknowledgment and was away again, this time he seemed to go into a deeper sleep.

Elsa and I made our way back to the hotel long after midnight holding hands and stopping now and again to engage in in-depth kissing. That night, or should I say morning, Elsa was extremely active – more like, she couldn't get enough, so I didn't get much sleep. I guess she was catching up on lost years, having just woken up, or maybe enjoying life to the full again.

Had I at last found a new partner, I thought, or was it just the situation that made us both react like this? I think it was the latter.

Damascus – Hans and Elias – Early August – before class break-up

Before Achmed left for his Aunt's in the north, Hans expressed his thoughts of perhaps going to Nablus with one of the Jews from class – probably hitchhiking.

'You must be mad, you a European and him a Jew – hitchhiking!' said Achmed, laughing cynically, 'You may as well pin tags on yourselves because your chances of getting picked up by the wrong people are a 100 to 1!'

'Yes, but we can't find a car hire company, that will give us a car for the journey to Nablus.'

'Look, Hans, I have an Idea. I'll ask my uncle Hussein, maybe he'll know.'

'Oh, would you, that would be great – thanks Achmed.'

'But why do you want to accompany a Jew to Nablus?'

'Oh – well I think I can tell you, Achmed. Elias is engaged to a Palestinian girl there. His relatives and the other two Jewish classmates don't know about it. He also doesn't want to go back with the other two Jews in his class who are flying back to Tel Aviv, and I thought I'd just accompany him and also because I'm just interested in the Middle East and the Palestinian-Jewish conflict. I'd like to see what it's like.'

'Well, I admire your noble gesture but I think you're putting yourself at great risk. You should just go back home and watch television – it's on there daily.'

Despite his apprehension, Achmed spoke to his uncle Hussein who agreed to make arrangements for them.

Start of Journey to Nablus – Saturday morning, 6th August

Elias was waiting outside for him when he arrived at uncle Hussein's in a taxi, as was a big army lorry loaded with various sized wooden crates.

Uncle Hussein was talking earnestly with Elias as Hans stepped out of the taxi. He went over and joined them.

'Hello, Hans – your transport's been arranged but it only goes as far as *Tyre*, which is on your way. I've just been telling your friend that the rest of the journey is along the main coast road into Israel. You should have no difficulties getting a further lift from there to the Israeli border, which is about another 50 kilometres. From there on it's a bit of a zigzag course to Nablus. Omar the driver is ready to go now, so you'd both better get up front with him and don't forget to give him some money before you leave.'

'Thanks a lot, uncle Hussein, how much do you think we should give him?'

'Ask him, then halve it and barter a bit – you should know the score by now Hans,' he said with a twinkle in his eye.

'Okay, uncle Hussein – thanks for everything and give my regards to Achmed when he gets back from the North.'

'I will, Hans and God be with you.'

With that, uncle Hussein went back to his front door where he stopped and turned around to watch the departure process.

Hans and Elias went to the front of the truck and greeted Omar the driver, who was smoking a cigarette. He returned their greeting in a friendly manner as though he was glad to have some company on his journey, or was it the extra cash he was expecting?

Uncle Hussein waved them farewell and fled into his house as bellows of hideous oily smoke emitted from the truck's exhaust.

The drive was murderous. It was hot and sticky in the cabin that had no air-conditioning. The seats were extremely uncomfortable – some of the springs were poking through the horsehair upholstery and just being held down by the worn leather. Omar talked nearly all the way to Beirut, his first stop. He didn't have much else to do, as their cruising speed was only 80 kmph.

Fortunately uncle Hussein had given Omar a document with official permission allowing them to accompany the driver with the military cargo – otherwise they would have been arrested along with the driver. Being an ex Brigadier of the Syrian Army, he no doubt still has some good contacts.

They went over the border at the major crossing point, between Syria and the Lebanon, without any problems with customs or immigration. They had a long hold-up at a control point, and detours due to road works on the main road and were looking forward to a glimpse of the rebuilt Arab city.

They arrived on the outskirts of Beirut to be confronted with the full weekend bustle of people shopping and going about their business.

'I'm afraid I'll have to drop you off at the next corner. There's a restaurant there so you're better off inside than waiting on the street. I have to deliver some cargo and pick up some stuff for *Tyre*, so I'll be back for you in about an hour. Don't go wandering about – it's not advisable – you two looking like Westerners and with all that luggage.'

'Not the luggage as well?' Hans asked.

'I'm afraid so – I'd have difficulties explaining where it came from, so it's best you take it with you.'

Hans and Elias both looked walleyed at that bit of information.

'Don't worry, I promise I'll be back. Hussein, the Brigadier, would have my guts if I left you here, now jump out I'm late as it is.'

The restaurant looked clean and Western-like and had air-conditioning. The waiter gave them a welcoming smile and a short wave of his hand as they entered, then carried on singing and jiggling his body to the music on the radio behind the counter that was playing modern Arabian pop music.

Hans and Elias sat down at a table overlooking the road outside. There were a number of cars and lorries parked there and quite a few people in the restaurant – probably because it was well situated on the main road from Damascus to Beirut. The friendly young waiter came over to their table, stopped his singing and took their order. By now they were able to do it in fluent Arabic. He went away from their table singing his way towards the kitchen having picked up the tune again.

Omar arrived at 12 o-clock noon, just as they were standing outside and contemplating how to carry on their journey without him.

'Sorry gentlemen, there was some trouble at the depot entrance. A car bomb blew up killing five innocent people and injuring many just before I arrived, so I had to wait until they got another side entrance open, which was only wide enough for one way traffic.'

Hours later, *Tyre* and the sandy isthmus appeared in view. They'd already decided to stay the night at the hotel they'd once frequented whilst travelling the southern part of the Lebanon with the Arabic class.

Nothing had changed thought Hans, as he went into the filthy room. He had a cat's wash at the wash hand basin hating the thought of cockroach attacks, especially from one's the size of matchboxes that fell onto his head last time he had a shower. He was disappointed to find the telephone communications down, so he couldn't give his mother a ring. Instead, he sat down at the writing table and wrote her a letter, explaining the reason for his delay in coming home. He knew she would forgive him, because she'd been to Israel in her youth and was a very understanding person. Next morning Hans gave the letter to the old man at the hotel desk and five US dollars requesting him to arrange stamps and postage *par Avion*.

Nablus – Tuesday, 9th August

Hans stood with Elias in the courtyard of the *Abdel Hadi Palace* that stunk of urine and dampness. 'You must be mistaken Elias, your fiancée Elena can't be living in this hovel?'

'She doesn't live here – she stays here from time to time to look after her great aunt. We agreed to meet here because they don't care about courting rules,' said Elias, annoyed Hans had pointed out the poverty.

A little girl with a dirt-smeared face and skirt shuffled barefoot across the courtyard, her big brown innocent eyes eying the arrival of these two strange looking young men.

Elias explained the history hoping to compensate the current miserable state of the building complex. The palace had been built for one of the richest families in Nablus over 250 years ago. Now, the run down palace was home to many poor families.

Some women were leaning out of one of the windows overlooking the pitted grey stone Ottoman arched courtyard.

Elias moved to an opening leading to a spiral stone staircase. They walked up the worn steps past an evil reeking squatting-toilet and along the first floor corridor, stopping at a huge, beautifully carved cedar door. Unfortunately the paint was peeling and long cracks were showing in the woodwork. Elias knocked on the door, opened it and walked in, Hans at his tail.

The smell of old age – geriatric wards – urine and decay lay in the air. An ancient woman, who looked like an unravelled Egyptian mummy, was sitting at the window in a rocking chair and next to her was one of the most beautiful woman Hans had ever seen. The radiance of her smile as she looked over her shoulder to see who was coming in and recognising Elias held a powerful meaning – Hans thought it had more secretiveness than the famous Mona Lisa. An English song came to his mind – *'Love was in the air'*.

'I understand now, why you wanted to come to Nablus,' whispered Hans, as Elias closed the door behind him.

Elias smiled and went over to his loved one. He took her hand – kissed the back of it fondly and brushed her cheek with his lips. He moved his hand over the head of the old woman who raised it and smiled in recognition.

'So, you have indeed come, young man! Elena said you would but I had my doubts,' said the *"vieille femme"*.

'This is my friend Hans,' he said to the two women, turning to Hans,

'Elena, *et notre dame – Yasmin.*'

'Pleased to meet you, madame Yasmin, Elena.'

The old woman laughed – Hans thought he'd just seen one of those skeleton heads from the fun fair ghost train gagging.

'I can see what you're thinking young man – yes, I would have been dead long ago if it hadn't been for the loving care of Elena that has kept me alive. As I said last time Elias came – I always wanted to meet the young man she would one day fall in love with. Now, I can go in peace to the *Royaume des morts*,' the old woman said, chuckling.

Elena stood up and shook the hand Hans held out.

'Welcome to Nablus Hans, and thank you for accompanying Elias, it is a dangerous journey!'

'Well, it took longer than we thought,' said Elias, apologizing.

'You're here, that's all that matters,' said Elena putting her arm around Elias' waist, 'Let's sit down and have some *chai* and a bite to eat, you must be hungry,' added Elena pointing to a niche of cushions surrounding a small round table barely above the floor that stood on a beautifully designed Gebbah rug. The old woman nodded her head and closed her eyes – time for a nap she was telling us, or just you three leave me I'll be all right.

'Tell me Elias,' asked Hans, when Elena had gone into a small alcove to make the tea, 'where are we sleeping tonight?'

Elias laughed.

'You didn't think we were staying here did you?'

'Well, in actual fact I'm not quite sure what to think after all we've been through the last two and a half days getting here from *Tyre*. If you'd said we were sleeping in the courtyard I guess I'd have believed you.'

Elias looked concerned.

'No, Hans – tonight we'll be staying at Elena's cousin's place. She works as a dancer in a night club not far from here.'

Hans' face took on a look of dismay that turned to amazement, the – you can't be serious look. Elias burst into fits of laughter, causing Elena to pop her head around the corner from the alcove. Her inquisitive look – what's the joke about, caused Elias to laugh even more, making them all join in. Hans had never seen Elias at such ease before. He realized Elias was having him on – Elena explained. Her cousin had a spare room she herself uses normally that they could have during their stay in Nablus. She would remain here with her great aunt who will be pleased of the company.

Later on – as dusk approached – Elena suggested they should make a move because nights are dangerous in Nablus, as in many parts of the Palestinian autonomy area. They locked their luggage in a cupboard at madame Yasmin's, stuffing what they needed for the night in their pockets and followed Elena out into the fading daylight.

They would have remained in that stinking rat hole for a week if they'd known what they were about to encounter.

Hans had only brief reminisces of what happened when they arrived at the cousin's flat. He was a bit behind because he stopped at the front of the nightclub to look at the lighted display of dancers displayed in a window casing. He heard shouts and a scream from the side entrance around the corner that made him move forward stealthily, awake to possible danger. He halted at the corner and saw Elias and Elena being trussed up by a group of dark clad figures. He turned on his heels as he heard a shout – one of the figures had spotted him. Hans ran for his life and immediately got swallowed up in the Kasbah. He looked back to see two figures still behind him. One of the figures threw something at him just as he turned to look back. The look back probably saved his life. He felt a stinging blow as something pierced his left shoulder. He staggered a few paces but managed to maintain his memento. A large crowd ahead drew his attention – hoping they wouldn't stop him and turn him over to his assailants. He was lucky – the crowd, realizing his predicament, opened up a passage for him that they closed immediately behind him. Hans risked a glance back and saw the dark clad figures trying in vain to push their way through the thickened wall of people. That was his chance – if he only knew where the *Abdel Hadi Palace* was in this maze? His shoulder bleeding, he stumbled through the dark passages of the Kasbah for what seemed to be an eternity. He was beginning to feel the effects of blood loss when he suddenly recognised his surroundings. He found the old palace and managed to climb and crawl up the steps, nearly fainting as his hand touched the sill leading to the squatting-toilet. He dragged himself along the first floor corridor stopping at the huge oriental carved cedar door – his only thought of haven –

meagre and filthy as it was. He banged at the door with his fist, reached up to the door lever using his last reserves and just managed to pull down the handle. His weight caused the door to burst open. He landed in the room and dragged himself over to the niche onto a pile of cushions where they'd been sitting so happily together just a few hours ago and passed out.

Nablus – Hans's ordeal

Hans woke up to a bedlam of noise – he was already very weak and hallucinating. He wanted the screaming and shouting to stop and felt great pain as someone shouted at him, pulled him up into sitting position, sprinkled water over his head and dabbed his face with a wet towel. Only then did he realize he was the one who'd been causing the noise.

He opened his eyes only to see colours – darkness – waving shadows – a state of *dantesque* – a skull and a God in white gabbling to him in a Berber language he couldn't understand. A snake was pushing his mouth open and scraping the back of his throat with its fangs. The snake spat its poison down his throat and he became tired, letting go – feeling himself being drawn down into deep dark chasms.

'I think he'll sleep now, madame Yasmin. I don't think there's been any damage to his vital organs. He is a very lucky young man – another centimetre and his heart would have been pierced. Arab knives are used for almost everything and are usually filthy – I just hope the wound doesn't fester. We'll have to wait and see. I'll take him with me and put him up in the spare sick bed in my surgery next to my home. I'll have to inform the Palestinian authorities, you know that, but I'll do as you bid and wait until he's recovered so we may learn what has happened to your niece and her friend.'

Tel-Aviv – Mossad, Friday 19th August 2005

David Silverman's team was gathered around Judith's desk discussing who was going to be the new boss, when Ben Goldmann, the newly designated head of the Mossad *Liquidation* department, walked into the office.

The talking stopped abruptly – everyone gazed in horror at his appearance. All but Judith, who, immediately realizing the obvious indication, smiled politely and said,

'Good morning Mr Goldmann.'

He returned her greeting with a smile and a warm greeting,

'Good morning Judith, good morning everybody.'

Muffled answers came in return and looks of bewilderment were showing on most of the faces.

'I know what you're all thinking! Yes, I'm your new chief and I assure you the deeds of the Ben Goldmann you've heard about are mostly hearsay and were spread deliberately. I'm sure, once you get to know me, you'll realize I'm not even a grain of the monster David Silverman was. Please carry on with your work if you have any to do and during the course of the day I'll call you into my office for a chat. I think I'll start with you Judith – come into the office with me now, please – thank you.'

Judith looked at her colleague Sarah who was sitting behind the desk opposite with that unbelievable look on her face again. Judith stood up, gave Sarah a weak smile and followed Ben Goldmann into his new office. Ben waited for her to move in before he closed the door behind her.

He motioned her to take a seat, which she did – feeling most uncomfortable – thinking her time's up in this department. No boss would tolerate staff members that weren't loyal.

He sat on the corner of the desk and looked at her gravely.

'Miss Judith Salomon, for the first time in my life I'm at a loss for words. You see I was brought up to always obey my superiors, which at times in the past I have deeply regretted. I must say though, you are the first Mossad agent I've ever come across who's been so directly disobedient,'

Here it comes she thought,

'From the information I now possess, I do appreciate the purity of your motives. I owe you my life. You've not been in the Mossad very long and yet you have such human foresight to have recognised the wrong in David Silverman's doings. His wanton killing methods have been a thorn in our side. No one has ever dared to oppose him. I would like you to know he died of natural causes. I had nothing to do with it. It was his own conscience that caused his heart attack. Two of my men accompanied me and followed him into the toilet at his favourite restaurant shortly after you looked me up and gave me the news about the Kidon team he was going to set on me. It was the sight of us that gave him the shock. We waited to make sure no one would interfere with God's will and got a stranger to inform the restaurant staff. I'll be quite honest with you – I'd like you to be my right hand Judith, but only under one condition, that you waver judgement over any misdemeanours in my decision-making. I would prefer to have a team about me that can think independently, show initiative and is able to lead their chief should he be on the wrong track. What do you say?'

Judith didn't know what to say – she stared for what seemed like ages at the huge safe in the corner. Without thinking she spoke spontaneously,

'You'll have to get that safe opened in the corner – none of us have the combination. I guess there are a lot of ugly secrets in there,' she burst out, 'I don't like the bit about being an agent and your right hand, though. I just want to be one of the staff and not be treated above the others, that's all,' she said, sniffling her nose, knowing she was above herself at that moment, but not caring.

A fatherly smile appeared on Ben Goldmann's face. He recognised Judith's qualities immediately.

'Of course, Judith – I didn't intend you to be my lieutenant in the field – I've got others to do that. I need someone I can trust in the office, and as I said to start with, I regard you all as a team, as equals – okay?'

A smile of relief appeared on her face.

'Yes, of course – teamwork – that's the environment we were trained to work in.'

She felt she'd said enough for a start and didn't want to go any deeper for the moment, but she was excited and it showed on her face. The initial dread of getting the sack was gone.

'If there's anything you need you just have to press the red button, that's the one Mr Silverman uses, em.. used. It buzzes at my desk. Oh, and there was a message for you that started all this – it should be in your in-tray,' she said, her face turning crimson.

Ben Goldmann realized she wanted to be dismissed.

'Okay Judith, and thanks again for saving my life and I mean it.'

Judith's face was burning. She nodded her head, turned about and left the room making sure she closed the door. She made her way to her desk and sat down knowing everyone was looking at her to see if they could interpret anything from her looks or actions.

Berlin – Paula talks – Saturday, 20*th* August 2005

I arrived back in Berlin at 8.30 pm and gave Chris Fenton a call from the airport.

'Hi, Chris – how's it going?'

'John, we're still going through the stuff we found in the cases and on the disk. The documents hidden in the lining of one of the cases are ancient. Looks like they'll have to be analysed first – some may need decrypting. We also found what looks like a copy of an ancient map in a side pocket, and papers with a lot of hieroglyphics between the lining and the leather casing of another suitcase. There's also a lot of archaeological stuff on the disk too that's been deleted logically but is still physically on the disk and is being re-located to the FAT and analysed. There are also some personal letters, John – between Anna and a Jan Hellstern. Looks like she was a Mossad *Sayanim,* what we call a sleeper. Jan Hellstern accompanied her through part of her training in Tel-Aviv – I'm sorry John.'

I didn't answer – a dozen or so sledgehammers were hitting my brain.

Chris continued,

'I think we'll need another couple of days to get this lot sorted out. We haven't got a match to the fingerprints yet, but we've still got a few databases to go through. John...! Hello, are you still with us?'

'Sorry Chris – that was something I had coming to me wasn't it,' Chris didn't answer.

'I guess you won't be needing me today, so I'll call it a day and try and catch up on lost sleep. Olaf is on the mend now. We'll see what we can do about his nephew Hans tomorrow. Good luck Chris.'

'Don't go on the binge John, that won't do you any good at all – sleep on it. See you in the morning, oh and bye the way – we like your little hideout – the lads were saying we'll have our reunion here in future.'

'Yeah, well we'll have to see about that, won't we. Anyway – thanks Chris.'

Weekends were normally a private matter and although I should have gone to *the Agency* or reported in by phone, I had only one thought in mind – back to my second home and sleep!

I got out of the lift to find myself confronted by my next-door neighbour – the one with the Persian cat.

'Ah, John, glad I saw you getting out of the taxi – you, em... have a visitor – a young lady, well not really young but tall and very attractive. She said you were expecting her. She showed me your card and your work number, which you haven't even given to me so I let her in to your flat with your spare key. I hope I didn't do the wrong thing?'

'No, of course not Ms Holzmann – you did perfectly well letting her in. Did she say she was from Leipzig?'

'Yes, she said you'd know who she was if she mentioned Leipzig, should I have to ring you up to verify. I didn't because she made such a nice appearance and is so sophisticated and you haven't got much to steal anyway,' she said chuckling.

'Yes, well, thanks very much Ms Holzmann,' I said, knowing she was inquisitive and all the other neighbours would like to be in on any news regarding Mr John Jameson.

I put my key in the lock, opened the door quietly and moved

into the hallway, shutting the door gently behind me. Just to be on the safe side – I withdrew my semi-automatic from my shoulder holster, put my bag down gently on the hall carpet and walked forwards, traversing my gun hand towards the likely spots. There was no one in the bathroom, kitchen or living room. That just left the balcony or the bedroom. I tiptoed into the living room and noticed the balcony door was locked so I moved towards the bedroom. The door was ajar – an opened suitcase on the floor. Judging by the slowness of the chest movements someone in my bed was fast asleep. I shoved my gun back into its holster and moved over to the bedside. Paula was in the land of nod.

Moving out of the bedroom as quiet as a mouse, shutting the door soundlessly behind me, I made my way to the kitchen and put the kettle on to make myself a cup of tea. A wee drop of the hard stuff would have been preferable, but under the circumstances I needed full control of my senses.

I went into the bathroom and had a shower – trying to wash away the weight from my shoulders. I have a habit of doing that – sometimes it helps. At least I always feel better afterwards.

I got some crackers from my bread bin and found some Gouda cheese in the fridge that hadn't gone mouldy. I cut a wrinkled apple into four pieces and ate them with the skin and seeds between bites of cheese and crackers and an occasional sip of evening herb tea.

My bed was big enough for two but what about the complications – oh.., shit! Forget it – just play it by ear and shut these other penetrating thoughts out – it's over – Anna's dead and whatever game she was playing got her killed. Maybe Paula was in on it? Maybe granddad was behind it all? I got myself a blanket from the hall cupboard and lay down on the living room sofa. I was asleep within seconds of my head hitting the cushion.

It was 1 am when I got up to go to the loo. I wandered into the hallway and nearly collided with Paula who was on her way back. We both startled and grabbed each other automatically. It was the unexpected encounter that did it. It wasn't too dark in the hallway as the Berlin street lights never go out and a slight sliver of light showed through the kitchen blinds into the hallway. It wasn't the sight of Paula in a negligé, it was the memory of our farewell that all came back to both of us at the same time. We hugged each other, but I avoided kissing her on the mouth, having forgotten to brush my teeth after the cheese crackers.

'Give me a minute Paula – I need to go to the toilet.'

'Yes, of course, John,' she said.

I brushed her forehead and her right ear lobe with my lips and let her go, moving past her into the bathroom.

I made it as quick as I could – washed the sleep from my face, cleaned my teeth, had a good gurgle as well and made my way back into the hallway. She wasn't there anymore. I went into the living room and saw her standing just inside the door to the bedroom unsure of further actions. I went towards her, still a bit nervous until I was about a metre away from her. She rushed forward and into my arms with such vividness and yet with an impact so soft – expectations of love and wanting. I let myself go – I knew I wanted her and she felt the same. It was frantic to start with and awkward standing up because we were still half-clothed, yet feeling each other as though we had nothing on. The situation changed as Paula pulled my t-shirt over my head and caressed my chest and we kissed and our hands carried on exploring. Paula pulled her negligé over her head to reveal a beautifully curved body. She was just a few centimetres shorter than me. That made us pretty equal when it came to kissing. The kisses intensified. She pushed my boxer shorts down with her hand – having difficulties with the overhang. Paula manoeuvred me over to the bed where she gently nudged my shoulders down, making me sit on the end. She moved in between my legs, still standing – letting my lips touch her nipples that were raised and stiff. She pushed me gently onto the bed and got on top – her knees nearly under my armpits and my legs over the end of the bed – my feet on the floor now acting as stabilizers. She moved herself down slowly, just touching me slightly and making me want her all the more. It was a long night – a night with someone I felt I knew. There were no holds – it was completely natural, with so much love and tenderness. She was my goddess, but it was two way – I gave and she gave back and we both knew what we wanted and even laughed whilst enjoying our love. We caressed and kissed and the moments of joy passed from one bliss to the next – not getting enough of each other, wanting more and more and not stopping at one act but holding many – unfolding unknown depths until our strength receded and we fell asleep entangled in love – or maybe it was exhaustion!

I awoke to the sound of someone singing a beautiful song in Aramaic.

..a beautiful bird visited an old lady who fed it tit-bits from her hand daily. The bird sang the old lady a song of thanks that made her happy and contented. One day the bird appeared and found no food but still sung its song for the old lady to hear. After a while it flew away to come back each day to sing the old lady her song...

I went into the kitchen and put my arms around Paula who was standing in her negligé making coffee. She wriggled around and laughed as I tickled her tummy. We kissed and caressed and made love again in the kitchen – in the living room and back into the bedroom. Afterwards she half turned to me smiling,

'Would you like some breakfast, John?'

Somehow or other that was the signal or it was the mischievous way she said it. I turned her over fully and kissed her softly on her lips. My kisses followed up onto her eyelids, moving behind her throat to catch her ear-lobe with my tongue and caress it, biting it gently before I moved downwards exploring again and making love to a woman I knew was holding secrets I wished to know, yet sharing her body and her love without restraint. I wish I had more time in this world to unfold completely without having responsibilities – just let myself go – this was the nearest I had ever got. Alas, the realities of life catch up on us just when we want to forget their existence. My bedside phone rang. That meant *the Agency* was trying to contact me. I made a face and picked up the phone from the bedside table,

'Yes,' I said.

'Mr Jameson – Ms Pelz, duty officer here – we've had an official call from the office of a Ben Goldman. Jack Orlowski was in this morning to check the log and says you should ring him back – it could be important.'

'Okay, thanks Ms Pelz, I'll ring him up later, bye.'

I put the phone down without waiting for a reply – I seem to be getting used to doing that since I got to know Jack Orlowski. I let my head fall back on the pillow.

Ben Goldman – Anna's half-brother. Both Ben and Kenneth Woodward came back to mind. I'd obtained both their direct numbers from Jan, and I'd already tried to contact Ben through official channels a couple of days ago, that's probably why he's been trying to ring me. I'd nearly forgotten. Determination took hold as I rolled over to face Paula who was watching me with half-opened eyes that were pleading me just to lie down again and go back to sleep. I kissed her on her nose tip and said,

'Sorry dear, I've some business to attend to – I'll be back in about a half hour or so. Just carry on sleeping – I'll do a bit of shopping and we'll have breakfast together in about an hour's time,' thinking – but only if I can find some shops that are open.

Her eyes were closed again – she murmured,

'Mm..,' and was back in the land of nod.

I left the flat after doing a weapons check. I crossed the road, my legs wobbly, and went down the block and into the local park. I sat down on a concrete ledge overlooking the park and a water fountain just ten metres away – my favourite spot for outdoor phone calling, and rang the first number – a cell phone number.

'Yes,' a voice said.

'John Jameson, I would like to speak to Kenneth Woodward.'

'I'm Kenneth Woodward – what can I do for you?'

'This is a very delicate situation but under the circumstances I have no other choice but to tell you on the phone. First of all – are you *the* Kenneth Woodward that was in a Kibbutz about 20 years ago where you got to know a German girl called Elsa Ertl?'

'Good grief, yes – Elsa! I remember Elsa well – she didn't answer my letters when she went back to Germany and I wrote quite a few!'

John had to clear the frog in his throat – he felt as though he was betraying Elsa in some way, or maybe it was jealousy.

'Well, Elsa bore your child – his name is Hans.'

'Good God – but why didn't she tell me – we could have got married.'

'You'll have to ask Elsa that. Look, may I ask you a personal question?'

'If it's not too personal, after all I don't even know you.'

'Look, I work for the ISIA in Berlin and I know you work for the Israeli government with an organization we won't talk about on the phone. Is there any chance we can meet – it looks as though Hans has been abducted in Damascus where he was learning Arabic,'

A moment's silence at the other end, 'Hello, are you still there?' I asked.

'Mr Jameson – I'm in Berlin at the moment, I've just got back from Israel and I think we should meet within the next few hours. What I have to tell you is beyond your imagination.'

'What about the *Gedächniskirche* at 4 pm this afternoon – I can't manage it earlier, I'm afraid,' I said.

'Yes, all right – I'll be there. How do I recognise you?'

'I'll be standing at the entrance wearing a khaki bush jacket, grey shirt and washed out jeans. I'm dark haired and one metre ninety tall, and how do I recognise you?'

'That doesn't matter does it, as long as I know how to identify you. I'll see you at 4 pm.'

Kenneth Woodward had ended the conversation on his terms.

My next call was to Ben Goldman – another cell phone number.

'Yes, Goldman speaking.'

'Ah, Ben – it's been a long time hasn't it. John Jameson here.'

'Yes, John – you've been trying to contact me I believe. What can I do for you?'

'Ben, I think it's time we met – I've discovered a number of things about Anna and the Sterns and need your advice and help. I believe it's of great importance.'

'Look John, I'm up to my eyes with work at the moment, give me a ring in a few days time and we'll arrange a meeting. That's all I can offer you at the moment.'

Well, that didn't sound like the Ben Goldman I used to know – such politeness and so accommodating.

'That would be great Ben. I guess you won't be coming over to Europe?'

'No chance John, not in the next few weeks or so.'

'Okay! It looks as though it'll have to be Tel Aviv or nothing, eh?'

'That's it, John.'

'Okay, I'll give you a buzz in a few days or so, see you Ben.'

'Yes, goodbye John.'

God, so forthcoming – this definitely isn't the Ben Goldman I used to know. Ah, well – maybe I'll just have to fly over and meet him. Maybe Chris's findings might mean an official visit anyway, who knows. Apropos Chris, maybe I should give him a tinkle too,

'Hi, Chris – how are things developing?'

'Morning John, looks like we got a hit on granddad. According to our WWII criminal database he was a German of Ukrainian descent. As a 20-year-old lieutenant of the SS Special Commando Group C, he was one of the officers in charge of the murdering of 33771 Jews at Babij Jar on the 29/30 September 1941 near Kiev. His name is Heinrich

Bolkow. In 1943 he was transferred to the German Parachute Regiment under Otto Skorzeny, who grounded ODESSA. I don't have to tell you the rest – that's your speciality. He was probably given a new identity at the end of the war – one of those 18,000 SS officers who managed to escape justice – until now.

The other one with the gun is, or was, 29 year old Manfred Metzler, who has a criminal record for rape, extortion and manslaughter and is a member of the Nazi group NSPD. He comes from Passau in Bavaria and ran, or runs, the South German Viking Youth Organization there, where they had or still have a training camp.

We're still sifting through the disk and the suitcase contents and keep on coming up with a lot of ancient stuff from the Middle East. I reckon you'll be needing an archaeologist or two to sort this lot out John.'

'Thanks Chris – sounds promising – I wonder what on earth an ex-Nazi is doing pretending to be a Rabbi – that's the best one I've heard yet.'

'Yeah, it's got us baffled, you can bet on that.'

'Okay, Chris – I've got a visitor at the moment. Maybe she can shed some light on the matter. I'll also be meeting Kenneth Woodward, one of our Israeli government friends at 4 pm at the *Gedächniskirche*. Maybe you could spare a couple of the lads to watch my back. But please ask them to remain invisible until they see me moving away from the Church, unless I'm not perceivably going of my own accord. If that's the case then they'll know what to do.'

'Okay, John – all is said and done. When are you coming back to the premises?'

'I'm not sure I can promise, but I'll try and get over sometime later on tonight, latest tomorrow. Oh, and bye the way –

I spoke to Ben Goldman – he was very forthcoming and will see me in Tel Aviv sometime within the next few days.'

'You *are* meeting very dangerous people John – take care.'

'Will do, bye Chris.'

I pressed my off-button and made my way back to the flat. I bought some fresh rolls and bread and other groceries at a small Turkish store that was fortunately open – it was time to fill up my fridge again, which was more or less empty.

I smelt fresh coffee from the hallway and talcum powder and perfume as I passed the bathroom on my way to the kitchen, where Paula was standing barefoot in an armless white cotton pinafore dress with a deep cut at the front that showed the distinct cleavage of her breasts. The light olive tan of her skin and shoulder length brown hair made a beautiful contrast to the colour of the dress. Her smile was radiant – she loved me that was for sure – it was her blue eyes telling me this and from my experience eyes tell their own story. I placed my plastic shopping bags gently on the floor and went into her arms. We held our heads so we were looking each other in the eyes, our noses just touching and our lips pouting, just tipping the skin and sending waves of excitement through our bodies. Our eyes were searching and finding what we were looking for, only as true lovers can do. Paula broke the silence,

'Lets have breakfast John, I'm starving and I have a lot to tell you,' she said, grinning all over her face and then frowning.

I nodded and let go.

We had breakfast in near silence both enjoying the sight and company of the other, but dreading the moment when we had to talk. Paula started – I felt myself at a slight advantage.

'John, there are some things I found out mostly from Aunt Hera, about the Sterns of Leipzig. For one, Anna's granddad is not a Rabbi. He isn't even a Jew. When you left us we had lots of rows. Granddad hit me when I grabbed him after he shoved aunt Hera, which made her fall. Aunt Hera pulled out a revolver and threatened to kill him if he didn't leave her house immediately. He went over to hit her and she gave him a warning shot that grazed his ear. I think he was shocked – he covered his ear, which was bleeding badly, with a towel and ordered Heinz the butler to pack his things. They were gone in an hour. From what grandma and Hera told me afterwards it looks as though he has kept them in a threatening situation since the war. He is a very powerful man says aunt Hera.'

'But what really happened to Anna's mother and her real grandfather, and why have they all kept mum and covered for him all this time?' I asked.

'It's a bit strange after so many years to find out people are not what they make out to be. Now I know why there were no photographs of Anna's granddad in Haifa or why we were never allowed to take pictures of him. He never ever wanted to visit Israel either. Anna's mother was with grandma all the time and was lucky granddad didn't have her sent to Auschwitz too. After the war grandma had Anna's mother, Sarah, sent to our relatives in Haifa. Aunt Hera says granddad was a powerful man in the SS and still is – has something to do with a world wide Nazi organization. Grandma says he talks in his sleep about taking Adolf's place to rule the world.'

'It sounds like I know the type you're describing.'

'What I told you on Wednesday evening seems to be only partly true now. Apparently Anna's real granddad was transported to Auschwitz together with aunt Hera. Grandma was a very beautiful woman,'

I thought – probably not as beautiful as you Paula.

'and granddad kept her from being transported by making

her his mistress and moving her to a small village in the Swabian Alps. He kept her as his *maîtresse* – always under the threat of having her husband and aunt Hera killed.'

'I expect Anna's real granddad was killed at Auschwitz?'

'Yes, aunt Hera says he was sorted out on arrival to the group that went straight to the gas chambers. Aunt Hera was put in a Siemens labour group.'

'Surely grandma was able to leave him after the war was over?'

'I asked that too, but granddad had her paralysed with fear and kept her under the threat of having aunt Hera killed, which he is quite capable of doing.'

'I think we ought to get them both moved to a safe place.'

'Aunt Hera has already done that. They are both in Zurich now with some distant relatives. They should be safe there.'

'Paula, come here will you.'

I stood up and took her in my arms – so many pieces of the puzzle were now in place. I held her for a moment before loosening from the embrace and picking up her hands gently. I looked into her eyes hoping mine showed enough compassion.

'Things will turn out all right Paula, you'll see. We'll get him in the end if the Mossad or others don't get him first. But let's sit down again, I found out something you ought to know.'

Paula sat down obediently. Still holding one of her hands I told her about Heinrich Bolkow and his murderous life. Paula broke down upon hearing about the killings at Babij Jar,

'I've seen the documentary films where the officers use their revolvers. Oh, John – that monster.'

I nursed her in my arms and on my lap until her sobbing subsided. I didn't have the heart to tell her he was probably behind the blowing up of the flat in Leipzig, possibly to kill Paula and myself in the process. He was the one that had suggested we use his study. The guy I shot was probably moving out to protect him or greet him. No doubt his standing on the landing on my arrival at the flat wasn't meant to be a special greeting – he'd probably been up in the loft checking to see the explosives were set correctly and that his crony knew his instructions. I didn't tell her about Anna, her role as a Mossad *Sayanim* – that she was probably after him and he was most likely responsible for her death. When I thought of Anna my eyes got watery and I let the drops run down my cheeks – my mind was back in the past, the image of her in the morgue and then back to the present – the heinous face of Heinrich Bolkow greeting me as Mr Scotsman.

Paula must have felt the drops. She turned her head and looked up, sadness and despair had taken over. I bent down and kissed her softly on her eyelids, her nose and her lips.

'Paula, we know now, that's the important thing. I'll do all I can to stop this madman and bring him to justice and if that fails I'll kill him with my bare hands.'

'No, John – if anyone has that right then it is mine. He has robbed Anna of her grandfather and is most likely the cause of Anna's and Martha's death, not to mention the great grief he has caused Anna's grandmother and Aunt Hera.'

'What are your plans Paula – you know you can stay here as long as you like – or would anyone have any objections – us not being married?' I asked spontaneously – letting a wicked grin envelope on my face.

Paula smiled knowing I wasn't being serious.

'I'm not that prudent and none of my relatives in Haifa are either. Don't worry about the unmarried bit because my mother was never married. If it's all right with you I'll stay with you for a few days, then maybe I'll have to go home to pass on the news. I want to tell them personally.'

'That's great Paula – I'm glad you're staying. I have to pop out now and then to *the Agency* and elsewhere. It looks like I'll have to go to Tel Aviv within the next few days, so maybe we can fly over together.'

'That's wonderful news, oh, John – I'm so happy.'

Paula threw herself into my arms and that was it for the next two hours – I think I'm in love and I sincerely hoped she was too. I don't give much for the *I love you darling* and she answers *I love you too* or vice versa, so I've never ever said it up until now. I just hope to God she has no ulterior motives!

Monastery outside Rome

In a monastery on the outskirts of Rome, Henry Bush was enjoying the lust of flagellation ministered by two members of the Opus Dei – nuns in black leather bodices, laced nylon stockings, black, knee-length leather boots and nun caps. The whiplashes hit him on his bare bottom as he scuttled whimpering on all fours, obeying the loud domino voice of the prioress. He is certainly looking forward to his turn of flagellating the prioress and the other nun, and relieving his well risen piece of manhood in their unworthy orifices, after tying one on the table and the other on the cartwheel and whipping them afterwards for making him horny.

He is utterly dismayed when his cell phone rings. Blasting himself for not turning the darn thing off, he gets up and walks over to a chair where the nuns had neatly deposited his clothes after chastising him like a child whilst undressing him. He fetches the cell phone from his jacket pocket and presses the phone button,

'Yes, what is it,' he shouts into the microphone piece.

'Hello, am I speaking to Monsignor Henry Bush?'

'Yes, who is this?' replied Henry Bush, annoyed, yet inquisitive.

'Names don't matter, not on the phone. I've been given your number from my diocese Bishop. We are both members of the same organisation you are apparently in charge of – so he says.'

'Allright, what can I do for you,' answers Henry Bush, now all ears.

'I understand you're interested in a certain testament buried somewhere in, or just outside Palestine?'

'Yes indeed – what do you know about it?' asked Henry Bush, now very excited – using the back of his hand to wipe the saliva that was slivering down his chin.

'I've been instructed to inform you that I'm with a team of analysts working on documents and a map that may have something to do with what you're looking for. I'm in Berlin at the moment and it looks as though the group I'm with will be going to Palestine soon to look for some lost student. The information about the testament is a pure coincidence. At our last meeting the Bishop mentioned the search you are undertaking and I just thought my information might be of help. We are still in the evaluation process, though.'

'Well, certainly,' answered Henry Bush, 'any further information would be a tremendous help. Look, when you've got something definite, give me a call, day or night.'

'Of course, Monsignor – I'll let you know as soon as we get a direct location pointer. Good night, Monsignor,' said the anonymous voice.

'Good night to you too and God be with you,' answered Henry Bush.

Berlin – Gedächniskirche – Kenneth Woodward, Sunday, 21st August 2005

I was in position at 3.55 pm, not bothering to look around for my support team. Expecting someone tall and dark skinned, I was really surprised when an average sized blond hair, blue-eyed Kenneth Woodward stood in front of me grinning, obviously amused at my startled expression.

'John Jameson, I presume,' he said, with a pleasant voice, 'Expecting an oriental type were you,' he chuckled.

I held out my hand to shake his and said,

'Glad to meet you Mr Woodward – no, as a matter of fact, I was so surprised because you look like the grown up image of Elsa's son Hans.'

At that he turned pale. Maybe I was going too fast breaking news like that or maybe I wanted to be on equal terms. I added,

'Sorry, I forgot. It must still be quite a shock to you.'

'You can say that again, but there are some things that are difficult to believe. Do you believe in destiny, Mr Jameson?'

'John, call me John – yes as a matter of fact I do. We Scots are very superstitious.'

'Ken, please call me Ken. Tell me Mr, I mean John, how does a person in your position get to meet someone like Elsa Ertl?'

Well blow me down I thought, the guy's jealous.

'Okay, Ken, I think I should start at the beginning, but let's sit down over there on that bench, it'll take a few minutes.'

I hoped my backup would realize the ten metres to the park bench wasn't a kidnap.

'Well, I was in the security forces during the cold war when I came across Olaf, who was in the BND, on a clandestine job in Leipzig. It became a long lasting friendship and I visited

Olaf and his sister Elsa in the Black Forest with my wife Anna who was a Jewess. She was murdered on our last visit together in a town near Olaf's place just over two years ago.'

Ken nodded knowingly. Most probably he's informed himself about my background, including the circumstances of Anna's death.

'Elsa has never married you know, and from what Olaf tells me she's never had any male friendships since Hans was born.'

That bit of information seemed to smooth the worry marks from Ken's face.

'Elsa has only spoken once about the Kibbutz and that was just a few days ago when she talked to Olaf and myself about Hans. She spoke about Hans' father as if she was still in love with him.'

Why I said that I don't know. Maybe because I had the feeling he was looking for something like that.

'Tell me about Hans, John,' he said, colour gaining in his pallid features.

'Hans is studying law and has a thing about the Middle East and the Arabic language. He knows his mother was in Israel in a Kibbutz but doesn't know who his father is. He's never pushed Elsa to tell him. My guess is he's put two and two together and that's the reason for his big interest in Israel and the Middle East.'

I told him when Hans went missing – about Olaf's misfortune whilst looking for him – that Hans had last been seen in *Tyre* and that it may have had something to do with some Right Wing German and Dutch members in his Arabic class in Damascus.

'I spoke to Ben Goldmann who you probably know. He was my deceased wife's half-brother. He's agreed to see me in Tel Aviv within the next few days. From there I shall pursue the search for Hans that Olaf started a few days ago before he was nearly murdered.'

Ken's face was as white as a sheet when I finished.

'Thank you John for being so open,' he said, his voice now much milder, 'I don't know how to say this – it's so difficult – you see, I was married to a Jewish girl that my parents had arranged shortly after Elsa left the Kibbutz. I was still in love with Elsa though. My new wife Ria died of cancer a few months after the birth of our son Elias, who's probably about half a year younger than Hans. I've never remarried. My sister has more or less brought Elias up.'

'Good God, did you say Elias? Is this the information you said was beyond my imagination?' I asked,

'Yes, and now I know both my sons have found each other and don't know they are brothers, but sadly to say, Elias is missing too.'

'Well, I was just about to tell you. From the information I have gained from other members of their class, Elias is in love with a Palestinian girl from Nablus. In actual fact he talks of her as his fiancée. Elias, Hans and a Brit, Ian Ferguson, were often together and Elias confided this information with them. What we also know is Elias wasn't going to fly back to Tel Aviv with the other two Jews from the Arabic class, but going to find an overland means of transport to Nablus and stay there a while with his fiancée before continuing his journey to Tel Aviv. Ian Ferguson says Hans had spontaneously offered to accompany Elias as he was very interested in the Israeli-Palestinian conflict. As I've already mentioned, Hans was last seen at a particular Hotel in *Tyre* where Olaf took up his search, and also where he was nearly murdered.'

'My God – it's so good to know they get on so well together,' said Ken, ignoring my mention of Olaf and adding, 'I'll be leaving for Israel tomorrow evening. A meeting with Ben Goldmann is planned within the next couple of days. I'm now in a great predicament because I have to come back to Europe immediately afterwards. What I can do is to prepare Ben Goldmann and ask him to give you all the support you require. Maybe I should go and see Elsa and tell her about Elias?'

'Under the circumstances I think that would be a good idea. She could do with some support. I'll give you her cell phone number and address. She's probably in Freiburg at Olaf's sick bed,' I said, a stone hitting me in the stomach with the realization if they hit it off again – they might end up in the same bed I'd left a couple of days ago. Ah, well that's life I thought.

'John, I can't remember when I've last spoken to someone so openly as I have done today. I thank you for being so informative, which isn't usually the case in our line of work,' he said – now speaking like a Mossad agent.

'Look Ken, I've more or less been an uncle to Hans or at least that's how he's regarded my person and both Olaf and Elsa asked me to help and I'll be damned if I don't fulfil my promise.'

'Well, you can count on my help and I assure you, also the resources of a powerful organization.'

'Thanks Ken, here's my cell phone number. If you have anything for me then you can get me on that number or through the ISIA Berlin.'

'Okay, John – you have my number, and thanks again,' he said.

On the spur of the moment, I decided to ask him a last question,

'Tell me, Ken, do you happen to have a brother called Robert?'

He looked at me queerly and answered,

'No, why do you ask?'

'Oh, just curiosity. I knew two Jewish brothers called Kenneth and Robert Woodward in Dundee, Scotland when I was a lad.'

Ken shrugged his shoulders as though he was saying – well it wasn't me.

We shook hands heartily, like two old buddies. He turned and left. I stood there for a few minutes until he was out of sight before I made a move. I thought of ringing Elsa, but decided against it. Let her be the one to decide when he rings her up to make a date.

Alistair Gravestone – John Jameson's Hideout – Berlin – Sunday, 21ˢᵗ August 2005

After the meeting with Kenneth Woodward, I went across the city to my factory hideout to see how my *bunch* was doing.

Chris was sitting at my long planning table upon which various maps and documents were lying. Two others were sitting behind laptops – on their tables were masses of printouts. I couldn't see the others. Chris is fifty-five now, I thought – balding and getting greyer at the temples.

'Hi, Chris – how's it going?'

'John – a bit of a muddle at the moment – a lot of Greek and too much Aramaic and Hebrew, I'm afraid. To top it off, we've come across some ancient Egyptian hieroglyphics as well, so you'll need more professional help for that area. I know someone from the British Museum in London who might be able to help out in all three areas, that is if he isn't off at some dig or other.'

'What about notes or documentation?'

'Yes, well we've managed to decipher some of the deleted files that we've re-located to the FAT. They were cryptographic files – ciphered with a fairly ancient code that was easy enough to break. They are notes from an archaeologist called Ephraim Zuckenic. Does that tell you anything?'

'Indeed it does Chris, let me put you in the picture.'

I gave Chris a rundown on the Dead Sea Caves and Paula's interpretation of Ephraim Zuckenic's findings.

'Blimey, John – that's a bit thick ain't it?'

'Yes, it does sound preposterous, but these are facts and I think it would be a good opportunity to go after this if it's authentic, as we're going over there anyway. I think it would be a good idea to bring in an independent archaeologist too. Someone who isn't as fixed in his ideology as Ephraim Zuckenic seemed to be.'

'Shall I get him on the team then John?'

'Who?'

'Jack the Ripper,' said Chris grinning, 'Alistair Gravestone, from the British Museum, of course.'

'Ah, yes,' I said – my mind was wavering around Paula.

'Name seems to be suited to the profession doesn't it?' said Chris.

I didn't react on his comment – my thoughts were already in Israel.

'I guess we'll have to ask him, because we're not up to this lot are we? Tell him there's nothing more than fame and expenses in this if we succeed in unravelling the mystery.'

Chris nodded.

'Bye the way – where are the others?'

'I gave them the evening off John, they've earned it I think.'

'Yes, of course, how stupid of me – you're darn right – glad you're looking after them Chris, thanks.'

I paused and looked at him gravely.

'Chris, the way things are moving at the moment it would be wise to keep a couple of the lads here with Alistair Gravestone whilst he goes through these documents – for safety's sake, don't you think? Maybe we should make copies and put them in a safe place before he arrives, after all I don't even know him.'

'Agreed John, I'll get the copying organised tonight. That leaves us with ten we can take with us – not very many though?'

'This does sound a bit weird Chris, but I think we might be able to get some support from the Mossad if I've read the signs correctly.'

'Blimey, John – you're not serious are you?'

'We might be in a position over there where we'll be glad of their help. No, I think my judgment here is sane enough, Chris – don't worry.'

'Ah, well – in for a penny..,'

I interrupted, 'I'll be in again during the course of tomorrow, Chris. I have to spend some time at *the Agency* working out my strategy for financial support and writing reports and see what else has been going on.'

'Til tomorrow then, John.'

'Aye, Chris – see ye!'

I nodded to the other two, who had half turned in their seats at my mention of help from the Mossad and were now grinning. I looked around sadly at my hideout, which wasn't my secret anymore and made my way back to my Berlin flat and most of all to Paula.

Nablus – Hans recovers – Monday afternoon 22nd August

Hans awakens from his coma.
'Ah, our patient has at last come back to the land of the living! Good afternoon young man, I am doctor Saad Haddad. You are very lucky indeed, another centimetre and you would be meeting Saint Peter at the holy gates instead of us,' he turned to the woman, dressed in a bright turquoise coloured nurses uniform, who was standing just behind him,' and this is Maria, the nurse who's been taking care of you.'

Hans looked at the nurse and was immediately struck by her beauty.

'Where am I?' he managed to croak out, 'What's happened?'

'You're in my sick bay. Madame Yasmin sent for me twelve days ago. You fell over her threshold with a knife stuck in your back. Since then you've been in delirium with a traumatic fever. The knife must have been contaminated or extremely filthy.'

'Oh my God – Elias and Elena – I was lagging behind and saw them being attacked. I managed to escape through the Kasbah. *Mensch, Elias und Elena!*' He added walefully in German – now fully aware of his situation.

'It wasn't your fault – just take it easy. As I understand from madame Yasmin your name is Hans. We were not sure of your surname and I didn't want you getting into the hands of the wrong people, so we kept you here. Your injury and infection wasn't that serious, so we decided to wait until you recovered. We didn't think it would take so long though.'

'You've been talking in your fever about black Ninjas and people being beheaded,' said Maria, 'who were you talking about?'

'*Oh, mein Gott – oh, mein Gott!*' Hans replied in German.

'What is it?' asked Maria, who had now taken seat at his bedside. She placed his free hand in hers and held it gently.

Hans felt his heart pump furiously as his thoughts went back to that terrible moment when Elias and Elena were snatched and he had to flee for his life. The presence of Maria holding his hand now, reassured him he was safe – he had managed to escape. Hans looked up at the doctor who was injecting something into his drip. His brow furrowed – a big worried question written on his face. Doctor Saad responded,

'I'm just giving you something to help you relax,' said doctor Saad, 'your pulse is too quick. You've lost a lot of blood you know. It won't put you to sleep I assure you.'

Hans relaxed – he noticed he'd been pressing Maria's hand too hard. She gave him a convincing smile. Just like Elena, he thought. Hans told them the important parts, especially his suspicion about the German girl Frieda Schulz and the Dutchman Henrich van Gelders and overhearing them talking about kidnapping and beheading someone. Hans noticed tears form in Maria's eyes that she quickly sniffed away.

'I think it's time we informed the authorities – especially your Embassy,' said doctor Saad, not saying what else he thought – things looked extremely bad for Elias and Elena.

'Please, don't go through the Embassy. If you have a phone, please phone my mother in Germany, she must be very worried,' said Hans pleadingly. He gave them the number.

'Yes, allright young man, I'll give her a ring – no problem – she must be worried stiff. That will make things easier for us too, if we can leave out the official channels,' said the doctor, apologetically.

Hans looked deeply into Maria's eyes searching for further likenesses to Elena. She smiled again – this time somewhat weaker but still that Mona Lisa smile! He asked her spontaneously,

'Tell me, Maria – are you by any chance related to Elena?'

'Yes, Hans, she's my sister – that's why I've sat here all this time, hoping for your recovery and..,'

Hans interrupted her.

'Look Maria, don't worry – as soon as I'm on my feet I'll get help from some pretty powerful people – we'll find them – you'll see!'

Hans closed his eyes, his hand still holding on tight to Maria's. He felt himself drawn down into a deep blackness.

The doctor checked his blood pressure and nodded in reassurance to Maria.

'His breathing and blood pressure are back to normal – his pulse is still fast, though. Look now, the lines in his face are smoothing.'

Maria nodded but anxiety for Elena still gripped her.

Freiburg University Hospital – Monday afternoon 22nd August

Elsa's cell phone rang. She'd been dreading this call. After all these years, Ken had the audacity to ring her up last night and tell her he was coming down to Freiburg to see her. No apologies, no regrets, and no words of love or longing – just like an order – I'm coming, be there!

'Hello Elsa, Ken here! I'm in the ENT entrance hall – just arrived! Shall I come up, or would you like to come down so we can talk first. I know it's difficult after such a long time,' said Kenneth Woodward.

'Hello Ken, I'll be down in a jiff,' she answered briefly and rang off.

Olaf watched her closely from his sickbed, a slight frown on his face.

'I know Olaf, but he's Hans' father after all,' she said.

She patted the back of his hand and without further ado, left the sick room.

Olaf shook his head, as he watched her leave. He'd seen that determined look in her eye.

Elsa spied Ken first and stopped behind a pillar to watch him for a moment. He was pacing to and fro in the entrance hall. The splitting image of Hans she thought, as memories of long ago came flooding back, causing her stomach to cramp-up. She had no recollection why she hadn't answered his letters though. Maybe it was the different culture and the restraints of the Jewish religion she felt at the time. Even now, looking at Ken in full manhood, she realized her heart wasn't throbbing anymore. That gave her reassurance she'd made the right decision two decades ago – remembering – Ken had been too dominating. She brushed the creases from her skirt, put on her best smile and went forward to meet him.

Two hours later they came back to the entrance hall side-by-side, after a long walk – two grown-ups – ex-loved-ones. She – no longer a young girl, infatuated and influenced by Ken and the Kibbutz.

Ken was feeling miserable – he couldn't understand Elsa's arguments and her strange attitude.

She'd let him do most of the talking. Maybe he'd got persuasion mixed up with passion. At least she reckoned he wasn't the Ken Woodward she knew anymore. She was willing to remain good friends though.

He'd decided not to give-up that easily!

Just as they reached the middle of the hall, Elsa's cell phone rang.

'Hello! – Yes, this *is* Elsa Ertl speaking,' she said, flushing at the same time whilst watching Ken's face for reactions.

The voice at the other end spoke,

'Hello Ms Ertl, this is doctor Saad Haddad. I'm speaking on behalf of your son Hans from Nablus, in the Palestinian autonomy area,' he said in English.

'Oh, my God, Ken! It's about Hans,' she cried.

Ken moved over near the phone. Elsa held it so he could hear what was being said.

Berlin – early Monday evening 22nd August

I'd just finished my report on Leipzig at *the Agency* when the phone rang.

'Hello John, Elsa here – good news – Hans has been found. He's in *Nablus* in a Christian sick bay. He was knifed in the back but is now recovering. Apparently he had a horrible experience. I'm going over with Ken tomorrow morning to Tel Aviv. He's arranging Hans' movement to a hospital there,' she said, her voice sounding relieved.

'Well, that's great news Elsa – I'm really pleased for you.'

'Bye the way, you are a wicked person you know, taking advantage of me like that. You could at least have informed me beforehand about Ken,' she said, with a hearty, yet somewhat, mischievous undertone.

'Sorry Elsa, under the circumstances I thought it best for you to decide without my influence, after all he is Hans' father.'

'Yes, he is, but I finished with him more than 20 years ago

and I'm definitely not going through all that again. He's much too possessive.'

'I'm sorry Elsa, I got a different impression when you used to talk about him in Buchenberg.'

'Maybe I did give you that impression, but I was talking about my teens and my first love,' she replied.

'You know something! When I spoke to Ken I got the feeling that guy's still in love with you. That's why I gave him your number. I never mentioned us, in actual fact I told him you've never been out with anyone other than him,' I said, hoping she wasn't going to be too mad at me.

'Is that the way you get out of your female encounters? Pass them on to somebody else?' she declared, a slight hurt sound in her voice.

'God no, Elsa – he *is* Hans' father and I got the impression he was still infatuated with you when I gave him the news about Hans. Has he told you about Elias, Hans' half brother?' I asked, hoping to avert the line of conversation.

'Yes, isn't that wonderful – they're both such pals and don't know they're related,' she replied.

'How is Olaf, bye the way?'

'He's mending, but he still can't talk. The doctor says it's too early to say if his vocal chords are damaged. His psycho has definitely taken a bashing,' she answered.

'He also asked, if you were going to *Tyre*, maybe you could check behind the back of the drawer at the desk, in the room he stayed at, to see if his notes are still there.'

I groaned inwardly at the thought, but said,

'I'll be going over to Tel Aviv Wednesday morning, Elsa. I'm having a meeting with Ben Goldmann. First things first – we'll have to find Elias and Elena now Hans is safe. After that I guess I'll be in the area for a while. It looks like we'll be going into the Lebanon. Most probably we'll start at *Tyre*. Maybe we can get in touch in Tel Aviv?' I asked.

'Yes, of course, John! No doubt you'll be looking Hans up in hospital – I'll be there,' she replied, with certainty and a touch of longing, lingering in her voice.

'Great, Elsa! I'll see you then. Have a good journey. Bye for now.'

'Bye, John.'

My thoughts were causing an overproduction of testosterone, but wisdom prevailed. Counting the odds – it wouldn't be a good idea to carry on with Elsa in Israel, not with Ken Woodward and his Mossad lot to deal with. They'll be all eyes and ears in Tel Aviv and besides, I'm with Paula now, or at least until I know for certain she's not conning me.

Falluja, Iraq, Monday evening, 22nd August 2005

The half-derelict old farm complex in the North East outskirts of *Fallujah* was in a neighbourhood extremely unhealthy for non-Muslims. An old couple had settled there after the ousting of Saddam Hussein. At mid-day they were approached by a *Wahhabi* Sheik who considered it an ideal meeting place for that evening. To avoid suspicion, the gathering took place over several hours. They arrived in small groups of two or three, others singly. The men were dressed in white robes – each one distinguished by a long beard. They greeted each other very solemnly as they turned up. Approaching dusk, groups of Arab Sheiks then gathered inside the inner courtyard to discuss the *Jihad* they and their followers were waging against the occupation forces and newly elected government. Although the new government had taken up office and is still bickering about the constitution, the group continues to kill US and British Forces, and those from other allied Nations, people from help organisations and civilian contractors – all helping to protect and support the Iraqi rebuilding process. Most of them were *Iraqi's*. Their main belief was the orthodox *Wahhabi,* a line of the *Islam* that had suffered severe repression under the reign of Saddam Hussein – a very strict belief not allowing pictures on the wall or any audio or visual means of communication like television or radio – these are forbidden. Not much different to the *Taliban* in *Afghanistan.*

A tall, stately man with a long beard turning grey moved out from a group of *Saudi's* at the back of the room and spoke to the gathering in Arabic,

'This is a war of liberation for *Muslims* of all *Muslim* nations. It is for the *Islam*. There is no room for negotiation with this enemy. We have nothing in common with these Western infidels. They are greedy and spread filth and poison to all peaceful and abiding *Islamic* citizens. We will fight them and their kind until they all leave even if it seems an unending task, it takes a lifetime or becomes a world war.'

He'd just finished speaking when a roar cut out further conversation. A missile bound for a nearby US Marine base soared over from about 50 yards or so East of the farmhouse.

The Sheik cursed inwardly – for the crowd, he uttered different words, *'Allahu akbar.' (God is great)*

The Saudi turned back towards his own group. He nodded to two of his henchmen, former Saddam Hussein secret police officers, who not long ago had been boozing and whoring. Now, they wouldn't even dare smoke a cigarette. The two of them left the courtyard with two others from the group – ex-Republican Guard officers. They came back a few minutes later with a group of six, clad in black, their faces masked in black scarfs like the Tuareq, dragging a young Caucasian man and a Palestinian woman who seemed incapable of walking.

The Sheiks were all eyes and ears as the stately Saudi moved towards the Caucasian who had been forced to kneel in the middle of the courtyard. The Palestinian woman was thrown on the stone courtyard and forcedly turned to lie on her stomach. Both had their hands tied behind their backs. Judging by the torn, bloody clothes and swollen faces, they'd been badly mishandled.

'This, my friends is the decadent enemy. She is a *Muslim* and chooses to fornicate with this feculent imbecile. Speak, woman! What have you to say?'

Spitting out spots of blood, she spluttered out with great difficulty and barely understandable,

'I'm not a Muslim. We are engaged. He's a good man...'

'Enough woman,' said another voice. A man they call *Abu Mousab al-Zarqawi – the Butcher*, moved next to the tall Saudi.

A lanky figure, one of those clad in black, shouted in broken Arabic with an envenomed undertone,

'If she's still got her clitoris, let me remove it.'

Judging by her voice, she appeared to be a female, probably European. A murmur of disapproval went through the crowd, but no one in his right mind would have countered that vicious statement, especially as it came from one of those clad in black and acting under the authority of the *Butcher*.

The group of black clad figures converged on the woman prisoner, who tried to scream, but only whimpering noises could be heard. She was scared to death and her mouth was damaged.

The other prisoner, a non-practising Jew, was fairly fluent

in Arabic and also understood what was about to happen. He couldn't contain himself any longer.

'Leave my fiancée alone,' he shouted in Arabic.

'If you want to take it out on somebody then take it out on me.'

'Shut your filthy mouth you Jewish bastard!' said the woman in English.

Could be German thought the young Jew! How did she know he was a Jew? He thought he'd heard that voice somewhere. His eardrum seemed damaged – maybe he was wrong.

She bent over and pulled the woman prisoner over onto her back. She turned to the Jew and grabbed his hair. She pulled his head back roughly and said in English,

'You're gonna be next you Zionist mother fucking Jew boy. I'm gonna get your balls and stick 'em up her bloody cunt after my lot here have fucked her stupid. An' I mean a bloody cunt! Before you start to go, you bastard, my boss *Abu Mousab* here is gonna see if his sword is sharper than it was last time. It took five heaves to get the last one off. But don't you worry we're gonna send your Mom some nice pictures of her headless Jew boy.'

She was so worked-up – she didn't notice that a tiny strand of blond hair had worked its way out from under the black mask. Judging by her accent he felt pretty sure now she was German. He could see the colour of her eyes – a poisonous green – recognition started to dawn at the back of his mind.

'You fucking German whore, you're mad!' shouted the young Jew in German.

'Someone shut him up!' she screamed in broken Arabic as she let go of his hair, letting his head fall onto the stone courtyard.

One of the men in black moved towards him, raised the butt of his rifle and thumped him in the back with it.

The whams, followed by the whining of approaching retaliatory artillery shells from the US base stopped all movement for a few seconds. Apprehension caught the gathering, giving way to anticipation – hoping they weren't the target.

He was just regaining consciousness when the first shell struck the derelict farmhouse area. As the group scattered, he instinctively rolled over on top of his fiancée who was lying on her back. Explosions all around. One shell after another came over, some hitting the outside walls, others blasting the outhouses to smithereens. The half-roof caved in. Rafters and ceiling fell on top of them. The woman tormentor and most of the men in black had disappeared after the first hit, the rest were knocked over by the rafters and falling debris. His fiancée had gone faint just before the first shell hit. The Jew decided to play possum for a while. He listened carefully to the pandemonium around him. It seemed it was everyone for himself. He lifted his head up to watch some of the shadows stealing off into the night. After a while it got quieter. He heard a few groans occasionally and decided to try wriggling out from under the guard who'd half-fallen on top of them and wasn't breathing anymore. It was fairly difficult because a rafter pinned down the guard. Eventually, he managed to disentangle himself.

It was dark outside. Now that the rest of the roof was gone he could see the stars. He turned around and moved his hands so he could grasp the captor's knife he'd seen previously hanging from the guard's belt. It was difficult manoeuvring it out of the sheath. He only managed to move it halfway before it got stuck, so he decided to try and cut the ropes tied to his hands from this position. He felt the sharp pain and the stickiness of his own blood as he missed the ropes. The knife was very sharp, which compensated a bit because it meant quicker work, but he'd still have to take care. Ignoring the burning pain from the cuts he soon managed to slice his way through the ropes. Careful not to dislodge further debris, he lifted some from the guard, then from Elena. He bundled his remaining strength and managed to pull her from under the guard and into an area with less debris. Using the guard's knife that he'd now removed from the sheath, he cut her wrists free, pulled her arms around and massaged them. She started regaining consciousness. He spoke urgently into her ear to be very quiet. He told her they were going to get out of there now. He looked around to confirm his own words – debris and bodies everywhere and no sign of their dementors – at least, none living. Fortunately neither of them had serious injuries, so they picked their way as quietly as they could through the debris, stopping and listening, until they got outside the house. An old Arab was lying in the courtyard, apparently dead. Thinking he might need the tunic later as a white flag, he pulled the white tunic from the Arab's shoulder sending him rolling a few metres. They climbed over a couple of walls until they reached open land. He tried keeping in the direction the shells had come from. Judging the time element between the whams and contact, it couldn't be too far away. It must be a US base, he kept telling himself. He was now worried how the security posts at the base would react when they saw the white flag – whether they would give them the benefit of the doubt that they were friends, or some greenhorn would react trigger happy in the dark – or even at daytime come to think of it. Much like his fellow Israelis at the West Bank, some of them not really caring much who or what they hit.

Falluja – Monday evening, 22nd August 2005

Henri Walker was pissed off. That green-eyed monster Frieda gave him the creeps. He was beginning to long for *'big tits'* Gertrud.

He'd also noticed for some time now, that Helga had been using him. Once he'd passed all the tests at the camp, she let him have sex with her, but always bound by certain conditions he had to fulfil first.

Dauntless of risk, he was surprised at first, of the cold calculated relentless feeling that overcame him during pursuit of the ordered assassinations. But as time passed, his memory began to relive his first ordered killing – the Jewess in Leipzig. He was surprised and distressed about the mists of compassion that have engulfed him since. He's realized too late he's just been a tool to them.

Frieda orders him about like a dogsbody. Even sex with her was no better than a wank-off. Going for that German guy in *Tyre* was sick. Frieda, he has long since realized, is a psychopath. That gave him much thought as to how he would describe himself. Their wanton killing distressed him. That's all Frieda ever thinks about – torture and kill. Just forget this lot he'd decided and go find Gertrud. He knew he couldn't just leave. They'd kill him wherever he went. He'd have to make it look as though he'd had an accident or something and been killed in the process.

Once the shells started hitting the farmhouse he knew instinctively, that this was his moment for departure. He took shelter in an archway just outside the farm perimeter and watched the shadowy figures scattering in all directions. The barrage continued for five minutes, then stopped abruptly. He studied the ruins and the surrounding outhouses with his night glasses for another twenty minutes. During that time he saw two figures making their way stealthily from the courtyard where they stooped over a dead body, pulled off its white tunic and made off in the direction the shells came from. After a while he felt satisfied. There was no further movement. Avoiding the outhouses and parts of the building that were still burning, he made his way to the jeep they'd come in. A heavy wooden beam lay across the bonnet and front screen. But the rear was undamaged. He lifted the tarpaulin back, pulled out two twenty-litre petrol canisters from the back of the jeep and made his way to the central courtyard.

A huge pile of rafters, bricks, corrugated iron and dead people lay in the courtyard. He searched the bodies for money, some of which he took. He was careful enough to leave some notes in the burses. One old man was groaning – masonry and rafters lay across him from the chest downwards. He put him out of his misery by crushing his head with an iron rod lying nearby. He found what he'd been looking for – a big guy about his size. He saw fairly light hair poking out of what was left of his head. It had been smashed to pulp by a rafter. He pulled off the rafter and swapped clothing, shoes and weapons with him. He gathered some more planks and rafters that he could move, and placed them on and around the big guy and others lying near. He poured some petrol over the bodies and rafters, leaving enough left in the canisters for a blow-up afterwards. He lit a rag soaked in petrol and tossed it into the centre of the courtyard, hoping everything would burn enough to make identification of the bodies impossible. In Iraq they don't bother much anyway.

He went back to the jeep – poured some petrol over the front and back and placed the canisters back in their original mounting supports. He lit the jeep and went around the outside of the courtyard to an archway on the other side. He waited there for fifteen minutes, searching the area with his night glasses for any movement. He knew though, no one would dare to come back so soon. Everyone knows the Americans usually send out patrols afterwards to their hit areas. Deciding he'd waited long enough, he went into the courtyard to check. Satisfied, he chucked three grenades into the courtyard, went around it to the jeep and threw a hand grenade into what was left of the back. He took cover behind a wall and waited for the shrapnel to stop cutting the night air before he went on his way. His knowledge of Arabic was very basic, but he knew how to travel unseen. If it came to the worse and Frieda's lot caught him, then he could always fake memory loss due to shell shock. He was hardened to any torture methods so he reckoned his chances were good, besides, he knew the Nazi-Arab killing game, his adversaries and their organizations and most important – in a soft moment, Helga had informed him of the organization's future plans. Gertrud and revenge were now put foremost in his thoughts – longing for the day he'd have green-eyed Frieda and Helga at his mercy. Helga will pay, oh yes. She'll be his biggest pleasure. Maybe he'll wait for that until he finds big tits Gertrud. She'll enjoy it too, he was sure, especially if he told her how Helga had used him.

Tel Aviv – late Monday night 22nd August

One of the first things Ben Goldmann got organised when he took over the department was a duty telephone roster. The general census of opinion was, it's better being on duty at home than in the office. Tonight, it was Judith's turn and her telephone was ringing.

'Yes, Judith Salomon speaking, can I help you?'

'Command Signal Headquarters here – we have a priority one message for Ben Goldmann, can you take it?'

'Yes, let me press the fax receiving button – ok, you can send it now,' she said and placed the telephone back on the cradle to wait for the fax.

Once it was through, she read it and decided it was urgent enough to ring her boss, but first of all she had to verify the missing persons referred to in the fax. She logged herself into the main Mossad program and went to missing persons. Bingo, both had been reported missing. She noted down the other person who was linked, a Hans Ertl who'd apparently been found, then rang her boss up.

'Yes,' he answered.

'Judith Salomon here, I have a priority one fax from a US Marine Base in Falluja – apparently they know you. It's addressed to you personally. Shall I read it through?'

'Yes, go ahead Judith,' he answered, I'm all ear.

'Okay, the message reads as follows:
From: Camp Mercury, 82nd Airborne Division, US Army, Falluja 2315 hrs, Monday, August 22 – 2005

To: Ben Goldmann, Mossad HQ, Tel Aviv

Dear Ben.
One of our patrols picked up two persons trying to enter one of our bases waving a white flag – one male and one female. Male person describes himself as Elias Woodward, Jewish, from Tel Aviv. Says his father works for the Mossad. Says, he and his fiancée were abducted in Nablus two weeks ago. Female person describes herself as Elena Fadl, a Christian from Nablus. Both persons have been badly beaten and show severe torture marks.

Both claim they were about to be beheaded, when an artillery barrage from one of our bases apparently put a stop to it and they managed to escape. Please send us verification and details for repatriation.

Regards
Alistair Fitzpatrick (Major)
82nd Airborne Division, US Army, Falluja

'I've checked missing persons and can verify on both. A third person linked to them has already been found, a Hans Ertl from Germany. What's the procedure now, sir?'

'Good, Judith, that's all for the moment. I'll manage the rest. Just scan the fax in to a *Metsada* department priority action-working directory tomorrow. I'll make the arrangements for repatriation back to Israel. Goodnight and thanks for the quick reaction.'

Judith felt her face heating up again. Why does that always happen when her boss praises her actions?

Berlin – early Tuesday morning 23rd August

My cell phone rang – it was on the opposite bedside table. Paula was nicely cradled in my arm – I felt it such a shame to disturb her. I let it ring three times before I gently pulled my arm from under her, got out of bed and walked around to her side to pick it up.

'Yes,' I said quietly, as I walked out the bedroom, not wanting her disturbed any more.

'Hello John, Ben Goldmann here, sorry about the early hour.'

'No, not at all Ben,' I said, knowing it must be important.

'Well, some good and bad news – the good news is Elias Woodward and his fiancée have both been found. I understand from our records, he is linked to Hans Ertl from Germany, the person you were looking for who has also been found in the meantime. The bad news – Elias Woodward and his fiancée have both been badly beaten and tortured. I've made arrangements to have them moved expediently to Tel Aviv to the same hospital where Hans Ertl will be arriving shortly. They'll get there sometime later this morning. Kenneth Woodward's cell phone seems to be switched off so I've e-mailed him. I would prefer to have told him personally. Maybe you know his whereabouts, I believe you met up with him on Sunday?'

I knew the reason why his cell phone was off-line – he was having a rendezvous with Elsa and didn't want to be disturbed.

'Thanks, Ben – that really is good news. Hans was another reason I wanted to meet you tomorrow to ask for your help. As to your question! Yes, I do know where he is and if you don't mind, I'd like to have the pleasure of telling him the news. Wounds can heal. The main thing is they are all safe.'

'Okay, John – as far as I'm concerned you may pass on the news and give him my regards. I'll be seeing him later on this afternoon in Tel Aviv anyway. See you tomorrow then.'

He rang off. Things were moving fast and luck was on our side, it seems. Now a call to Elsa and Kenneth – I wouldn't miss this for anything.

Berlin – 7.15 am Tuesday 23rd August

I left the bathroom, freshened up after a long awakening session under the shower and wandered into the kitchen with the intention of making breakfast. I was contemplating on a real British breakfast – nice cuppa, cereals, eggs, bacon and toast and a.., just as the bedroom phone rang – at this time of the morning that probably meant ISIA business. I guess the ringing has wakened up Paula by now.

Paula's head popped up from under the covers as I went into the bedroom to get the phone. Her sleepy complexion seemed to say – is it always this busy in the morning.

I sat on the edge of the bed and Paula moved over to give me more room. I gently brushed a wave of hair from her forehead and gave her a peck on the cheek, before picking up the phone. Paula's head disappeared back under the covers.

'Yes,' I said.

'June Hayward, John – you'd better come into the office immediately – looks like Martin's been found in London and Jack's going crazy.'

'What do you mean – been found?' I asked.

'We had a call from New Scotland Yard. A body was found last night in a weir north of Ash Island on the Thames near Hampton Court Palace. It was fished out by the river police and taken to the morgue. It seems the body's been in the water for just over a week. Martin's identity tag was found sewn in the lining of his trousers and Jack wants you to go over to identify him.'

My immediate thoughts were – Martin hadn't betrayed us. I felt ashamed that I ever took to that way of thinking. Jack was to blame for that – the sod.

'Okay, thanks June – just tell him I'll be in as soon as I can. Okay?'

'Allright John, I'll tell him you'll be in as fast as you can,' she said, her tone sarcastic, yet tinted with a slight touch of amusement – knowing I never ever run when Jack shouts.

I put the phone back on the hook thinking – shit, what do I do now?

I turned my head towards Paula who had reappeared from under the bedclothes. No further words were necessary – my face expression sufficed.

'Bad news, John?' asked Paula.

'Yes, I'm afraid so. I'll have to identify a body in London. It may be one of our guys, so it could mean putting off our trip together.'

'Oh, no John! Did you know him well?'

'Yes, I guess so – we've known each other and worked together for decades. Martin Cole – one of those sort of friends I trusted. He's been missing since Ian Stewart was shot in the Old Opera Hotel last Monday, the same day Martha was murdered in Leipzig. There was even a suggestion Martin had something to do with Ian's death. I must admit though, I was beginning to think so too.'

I hesitated for a moment, gathering my brain digits until I thought I had the answer.

'Look Paula it'll be a bit boring staying here on your own so why don't you accompany me to London. I'll get our flight to Tel Aviv re-arranged to fly from London instead of Berlin. Fortunately, we have a security agreement with the Israeli government, so we can skip some of the normal air-traffic security procedures. What do you say?'

'What a splendid idea John, I'd love to come with you. I

won't get in your way. Maybe I can visit the Tate Gallery whilst you have the sad task of identifying your friend.'

I waved out the last bit from my thoughts, not wanting to get sentimental, and replied,

'Well that's settled then, I'll just ring up and get the flights rearranged for tomorrow and new flights booked for London this afternoon. I'll have to make some other calls too, so you'll have to excuse me for a few minutes. I'll organise our breakfast, then we can talk about our further plans.'

'Okay, John – I'll go to the bathroom and get ready.'

I went into the living room and made the necessary phone calls, the last one to Chris.

'Morning Chris, sorry again about the early hour,' I said.

'Mornin' John – no apologies necessary, you know that mate,' he said.

'Bad news, Chris – seems Martin's been found. A body was found at a weir near Hampton Court Palace with his nametag sewn in the lining of his trouser. It has been in the water for just over a week, which makes his death a day or two earlier than Ian's, only different locations. I'll be going over this afternoon to carry out the identification process. Furthermore, our search for Hans Ertl appears to be over. I'll send you an email with all the details. Now the pressure's off finding Hans, we can concentrate on finding Ian and Martin's killers and follow up on granddad – I mean Heinrich Bolkow, and of course go through the archaeological stuff. We now have three countries to cover. What about the archaeologist? Did you manage to find one?'

'Yes, John, Alistair Gravestone – he's arriving this afternoon. He nearly went off his rocker on the phone when I mentioned Zuckenic, the Ark of the Covenant and Jesus. I thought he was on the brink of saying he'd pay for the pleasure.'

'That's great Chris – we can certainly use someone who's personally interested.'

'Look John, you just go on to Tel Aviv on your own. Maybe you can do some digging for information at you know where. But watch your back. I wouldn't trust that lot with a farthing. Oh, and I think under the circumstances I'll send some of the lads home – we won't be needing all of them just yet. What about 24 hours notice will that be sufficient?'

'I'm not so sure, Chris – you know the score better than I do. If things get hot we may need them immediately, so you'd better put them on immediate standby. I don't want to use any of the ISIA guys, even though some of them seem to be ok. But before you send them back over you'd better give them their money dues, I know a couple of them are always living on the brink.'

'Okay, John – we'll keep in daily touch then, shall we?'

'Of course Chris – I don't think I'll stay over there longer than necessary. Cheerio, for now.'

'Bye, John.'

I thought Chris was being very rational suggesting I go on to Tel Aviv without him and the *bunch*. Alas, I won't have enough time for the long breakfast and cuddle with Paula, I'd had in mind – it's going to be a continental breakfast, as the schedule will be tight today. My next task, before I report in to Jack, is to search Martin's flat for DNA evidence or any medical documents I can find. I detested the thought of reporting in, which was totally unnecessary. I know my job. Jack still thinks too much Langley-like, or maybe I just didn't feel like meeting the prick and listening to his stupid comments I knew were forthcoming. But I had to go – and besides I needed Martin's personal file from the ISIA and details of my contact at the yard.

London – Tuesday afternoon, 23rd August 2005

We passed through Heathrow customs at 2.35 pm. Paula was good company during the flight. I guess I was very much in deep thought to start with. Jack's remonstrations rang in my ears – blaming other people to cover his bad conscience for having openly declared that Martin had been involved in Ian's death – typical of some manager types in positions they shouldn't be holding. The way he tore me off a strip for withholding information I didn't even know I possessed was preposterous. I'm beginning to think I'm with the wrong lot or he thinks he's still in Langley. I've been suspicious of his attitude right from the start. It has something to do with loyalties. Most of the personnel in the ISIA have been recruited from previous intelligence organisations, mainly from NATO countries. A certain amount of loyalty to their home countries is understandable but the rules are, ISIA members receive full support from the top. The problem here, is, that Jack is not respected and obviously has an inferiority complex. I guess he's jealous of anyone receiving more respect than he gets himself. He knows people laugh at him behind his back. To me, he's a liability – like a lot of Americans who take on more than they can chew – thinking of Dick Cheney and George double-u-what's-it. If I'm not careful, one of these days, Jack will end up provoking me enough to make me do something I'd regret.

Paula was very excited about the Tate Gallery so I couldn't withhold asking why. The explanation that followed expelled my suspicions. As an antique restaurateur she deals mostly with the restoration of biblical items – books, buildings, paintings, crosses etc. She adores going to the Tate Gallery and similar places whenever she gets the opportunity. I must confess, my first thoughts, when she mentioned going to the Tate, were, she was going to meet some conspirator or spy, because that's usually where they often meet.

We took a taxi and had an agreeable and most certainly, instructive journey. Paula knew more about London than myself. Unfortunately I let this piece of information slip out, by naming a building wrongly, so she took the opportunity of pointing out the various buildings and places and their historical background. I saw the taxi driver glancing back a few times in his rear mirror – grinning all over his face, but didn't have the heart to stop her.

I gave her my other cell phone and told her I'd pick her up at 5 pm. I dropped her off at the Tate.

The taxi driver seemed to change his attitude when I mentioned our next stop – New Scotland Yard – I think I noticed a little more respect, or maybe he was wondering if he should charge less than was shown on the meter, which seemed to be doing overtime. I had an appointment at 3.30 pm and we just made it in time.

I was picked up by a staff officer and taken to the Deputy Director of forensics, who introduced herself as Joan Miles.

'Mister Jameson, pleased to meet you, thank you for coming.'

I hate meeting female forensics in leading positions – they have a tendency to over indulge their own importance. I realized instantly we were not going to get along too well, so I decided to take the lead.

'Thanks for meeting me personally Ms Miles. I have a tight schedule. Before I leave for the forensic laboratory and the coroner's office I need to see AC Cross, so could we cut out the niceties and get straight to the facts.'

'Yes, of course Mister Jameson, then you won't be requiring

any refreshments?' she asked – her eyebrows raised in admonishment.

'No thanks, I had enough on the plane.' I replied, bluntly.

'Allright then, the facts – Chief Inspector Pat Hughes and his team were called to a weir at Ash Island where a body was found by anglers at 3.16 pm yesterday. As the body was still in the water, it became a matter for the Metropolitan Police Marine Support Unit, which is, bye the way, the oldest police force in the country. He reported the finding to Chief Inspector Jack Daley of the Operational Command Unit, OCU, who arranged for specialist support from the Marine Support Unit. The MSU unit at the River Police Station, Wapping sent out a team on a semi-displacement patrol boat, supported by a Zodiac inflatable dinghy, to retrieve the body. It was then transported by boat to the Marine Police HQ morgue at Wapping wharf.'

For a moment, but only just for a moment, the thought occurred, should I ask her to get to the point – common sense held me back.

'The body is a male Caucasian and fully dressed – that is to say, underclothes, shirt, jacket, trousers, socks and shoes. According to initial forensics done on body retrieval, the apparent cause of death seems to be two gunshots, one to the back of the head and one to the nape of the neck. The body had been in the water for just over a week. There were no personal documents or any items whatsoever found in the jacket or trousers, which of course warranted a closer look at tags and labels for identification purposes. That's when we came across an identity tag of a Martin Cole, British, Roman Catholic, O-Pos blood group, member of ISIA Berlin sewn into his trouser lining.'

I thought – typical of Martin – always meticulous right to the point of no return.

'You do realize, we require DNA samples, medical or dental documents and photographs?' she said, sharply.

'It's all in this bag, Ms Miles. I have instructions to deliver it to the forensic laboratory,' I replied, thinking – she doesn't miss a thing. However, her reporting is a bit overdone – supporting my theory about people in charge. I would tend to describe her as a very career conscious woman.

'Allright then, my staff officer will take you to AC Cross and wait for you. Don't be too long, we have tight schedules too, you know.'

'Yes, I know – it's the same the world over in our business,' I said, adding,

'Two questions before I go?'

'Yes?' she replied, that little word cutting the air like a whip – her features changing to annoyance at my direct impertinence.

'I'm not used to dealing with bodies that've been in the water for long, so is there a chance I'll recognise him, I mean – facially and what was the calibre?'

'The calibre is 9 mm and his face has been bashed about a bit. It's bloated, discoloured and flaky in parts, so it may not be possible for facial identification. Maybe you are aware of some other distinguishing marks not otherwise recorded?' she answered blatantly, looking at me coldly.

I got the shivers – thank goodness I'm not in the homicide department where they have to deal with the likes of these! I guess I'll get better information from the coroner's report than trying to ram her butt for more.

'Okay, then,' I said, 'thanks for the information,' and extended my hand to shake goodbye.

'No, problem at all Mister Jameson,' she replied, her iris's staring stab wounds through to the back of my head.

She reluctantly offered a thin, cold, mushy piece of flesh for me to shake, after I'd been holding my hand out at arm's length for at least three seconds. I turned without further ado and left the room without looking back. I felt those eyes hitting the back of my spine like pine needles followed by icicles as I walked out. I tried to discern the feeling I experienced shaking that hand. It suddenly dawned on me – it was like holding a piece of cold wet clay – ugh!

The staff officer was waiting patiently in the outer office and smirked when she saw me exit after such a short time. No doubt she'd contemplated on that. We went up the stairs, avoiding the lifts. I know too many at the yard and didn't want to be held up.

AC Cross was his usual jovial self – his facial expression impervious, or he was trying to avoid the subject of my discomfort – my encounter with the Deputy Director of forensics.

'John, good to see you again, glad you could spare a few minutes.'

'Charles, well, that was a close counter, I must say. Glad I'm not in homicide.' I said, chuckling.

Charles Cross, smiled briefly, his facial expression changing rapidly back to *straight face Charly* as he's usually known by.

'She's absolutely number one in her profession John. When she's had a few, she's a good bang, so don't be too fretful about your first encounter. Anyway, sorry to hear about Martin, we've had some good times together haven't we.'

'Aye, we have that Charles,' I said reminiscently, dismissing the thought of Charles seducing or being seduced by that piece of cold hake. We both nodded our heads in agreement, thinking briefly about good times past. Charles broke the moment's silence.

'John, I hear you've been meeting some dangerous people of late?'

'You can say that again, Charles. I had my back covered though. I'm not the loner Martin was and never will be, or at least I try to bear that in mind and I do have some good friends who remind me now and again,' I said, showing my teeth in one of my big grins.

Charles ignored my comment – he obviously had something on his mind.

'Listen John, I can't talk in here and I know you've got female company. A nice girl – had her checked out – she's quite clean you know.'

'Bloody hell, Charles, what's going on? What's the score having a guy like me on surveillance and checking out my company?'

'That's what I wanted to talk to you about, but not in here. Do you think you could manage twenty minutes or so this evening at your place. I know your study's soundproof and you check it out daily – when you're at home.'

I studied Charles' face intensively before I replied.

'Can you make it early Charles, I want to take Paula out to dinner and, well I really didn't want to be disturbed afterwards.'

Obviously Charles was too worried about getting the chance of a meeting at all to worry about the time as he replied,

'What about 7 pm? Is that okay? I won't stay long you know.'

'Yes, that's okay, Charles – see you at my place then.'

I nodded to Charles and moved back to the outer office and into the corridor where the staff officer was waiting to take me to the forensic laboratory and then on to the morgue to see if I could identify Martin's body.

London – Tuesday, late afternoon 23rd August

Despite my attempts at small talk, Joan Miles' staff officer, Jill Bennett, was not bent on conversation during our journey to the forensic laboratory to deposit Martin's DNA samples. Probably been given orders from her *icy* superior not to chatter. Ballistics weren't complete either, so I couldn't follow up on that line. The ballistics expert couldn't exclude the fact it may have been fired from a 9mm Browning, a weapon used by the regular Army and some British government and civilian organizations, but still had to be verified.

We left the forensic laboratory and made for the morgue. When we got there, Jill – her hands on the steering wheel, her head pointed towards the front windscreen and chin uplift, declared her part as done for the day.

I got out of the staff car, leaving the door half open, and bent down to say goodbye. She pulled the door to, nearly crushing my hand in the process and just drove off, leaving me standing at the curb without even having had a chance to thank her. I couldn't withstand the thought – probably a man-hater, maybe lesbian, or she's just been around her boss too long.

After a five-minute wait in the entrance cubbyhole, I mean cubby hall, one of the coroner's assistants appeared and led me through to a corridor leading past the main autopsy theatre. I had a glimpse inside and was caught by the stench of opened stomachs and bowels as the automatic doors opened to give entrance to a new arrival lying on a trolley, being steered in by an assistant. Only the feet were visible, poking out over the end of the trolley that was much too short, or the corpse was oversize. One team was already at work and some individuals were hanging around the next shining metal table, probably students – waiting to pounce on the new arrival to test out their knowledge of anatomy with their scalpels and newly sharpened knives.

I spotted a gutter on the left that was pulled out of its anchoring – some dark gunge spilled out onto the tiled floor. Probably blocked by congealed blood or other human remains, I thought. We waited until the trolley was inside the autopsy theatre. I was just about to follow it in when the assistant grabbed my arm, shook his head and pointed up the corridor.

A few metres further, at the end of the corridor, was a separate room adorned like a funeral parlour – an identification room. I was thankful Martin was given this little piece of dignity.

The silhouette of a body could be seen, lying on a table and covered by a white cloth draped over the edges. We went in. The assistant moved to the head of the table, placed his hands on the ends of the cloth hanging over the table and glanced at me for confirmation to remove it. I nodded my head in affirmation.

I was hit in the gut by the state of Martin's face and his naked body – only a vague resemblance of the Martin I used to know. I stated this fact for the report and asked the assistant to turn the body onto its right side. I then checked the left shoulder blade for Martin's *Warrior of the Skies* tattoo, a reflection of his pride as a young lad when he passed his initial training and completed his jumps. Having recognised the tattoo, I made a remark to that effect and reminisced, thinking back to days gone by. I remembered the many talks I'd had with Martin when he'd had a few too many. He usually ended up groused at the branding caused by Bloody Sunday and Margaret Thatcher's ministers presenting the Para's in Northern Ireland as front-line troops and the IRA propaganda declaring them as brutes and killer Battalions. There was also the stigma that ran in the regular Army that the Parachute Regiment drew its recruits from the lower intelligence levels, which was utterly untrue. When grades of one to five were given, the Parachute Regiment would only take applicants down to grade three. They had to be intelligent and extremely fit and strong. No mention of the heroics of the Parachute Regiment in WWII and the Falkland War, to mention just a few places where they saved a lot of lives and lost many of their own in the process. Martin did a long spell with the SAS, that's where we met up. I was already a member of the intelligence services and persuaded him to join me if ever he thought of leaving the SAS. Alas, he remained very much a loner like most who stay with the SAS too long.

I added my signature to the coroner's identification report and made a handwritten note at the top requesting a copy of the coroner's end report be sent to me to the ISIA in Berlin.

I gave Paula a ring and didn't bother to leave a message in her mailbox when asked to. Probably had to deposit her cell phone for security reasons. I walked the four blocks to the Tate Gallery to pick her up, hoping she remembered to look at her watch occasionally. I was late myself anyway and didn't have to wait long before Paula rushed out, flung herself into my arms and kissed me all over the face like a cat-mother. She was all flushed-up and in between her pecks, a staccato of apologies were intermixed with a detailed excursion to sixteenth century paintings and the techniques used.

We took a taxi to my apartment block – Paula went on about her thrilled experience and described the works of some great masters. I thought – wait 'til she sees my library – I'll probably have to give her a tranquillizer to calm her down.

We arrived at my apartment block. Before going up, I gave the first floor flat a buzz. Clive Allthorpe, a 70 year-old ex-barrister, opened the door. I like to think of him as my *concierge*, because he looks after my flat, sends on my mail and winds up the clocks. He has my key and is allowed to use my library that is full of ancient books, seafarer's maps and atlases. An admirable hobby I'm very proud and thankful to possess – passed on to me by five previous Jameson generations, all of them enthusiastic collectors. I'd made arrangements for our baggage to be delivered to Clive's apartment. Clive suffers from rheumatism and arthritis, so just in case he hadn't been able to take the mail and bags up to my apartment, I thought I'd check him out first.

'Well, hello John, I was expecting you to knock at the door when your bags arrived this afternoon. Here they are,' he said, as he moved to the side of the door.

'I emptied your letter box this morning and took the mail up.'

'Thanks Clive, I'm only on a night stop. I'll be off again tomorrow,' I said, as I moved inside and picked up the bags lying behind the door. I moved back out into the main entrance hall holding the bags and turned to face him,

'As usual I'm in a hurry Clive, so maybe I'll have time for a chat next time.'

'That's allright, John. I know you're a very busy man,' he said, after following me out. He caught a glance of Paula, whom I'd sent forward to wait at the lift. A cordial smile appeared on his face. He nodded to Paula, which she returned with a courteous nod and a dazzling smile. He half whispered out of the corner of his mouth,

'Knew you were going to have female company when I saw that ladies bag! Just wanted to see what she's like!'

I ignored his last comment and moved towards Paula, dismissing any further comments,

'Thanks again, Clive,' I concluded, without looking back, as I walked towards the woman I'm falling in love with the more I'm in her company. I hope she won't spend too much of her time in the library, but at least it'll keep her occupied when Charles comes shortly.

Paula was overwhelmed with my apartment. It's mostly furnished in antiques, each room combined to suit the particular epoch. Anna had insisted the kitchen and bathroom be modernised and thought some drastic changes in the bedroom were necessary. I must say, I'm proud of the result – it's really a beautiful combination of antique and modern, if it wasn't for the nagging feeling of possible betrayal, now descended that has started to destroy her image in my memory.

'John, it's so beautiful and the library is magnificent – but the slight oriental touch can't have been your choice,' she commented, her quizzical gaze requiring a full explanation.

I choked a bit on answering,

'Anna made all the changes. It's really her touch you'll notice in most of the rooms,' I replied, my voice much dryer than usual.

'Oh, John! I'm so sorry. How stupid of me not to think of her.'

I felt miserable and distraught. I couldn't withhold the destructive feeling that overcame me,

'I haven't told you the worst, Paula – Anna was a Mossad *Sayanim,* a sleeper – a covert agent in hiding, waiting to be called. I only found out a few days ago when we went through Martha and Anna's belongings – those we recovered from the cellar.'

Paula's face reddened, her eyes widened and her mouth

opened. For a split second she was speechless. She caught herself, and said,

'Oh my God, John – why didn't you tell me? What dreadful thoughts must be going through your mind? Anna and now me, not to forget Martha's involvement – all Jewish and all related,' she said, her voice quivering.

She came over and stood directly in front of me. She took my hands in hers and said,

'John, speak to me – tell me if you have bad thoughts about me, now you know about Anna. Please tell me?'

I looked into her eyes, thinking she couldn't possibly be acting.

'Dearest Paula, I've never been so happy, yet so miserable in my life. Deep down I feel the love you return. Of course I'm upset. It's all too agonising and I haven't really had the time to think about it because life's become dangerous and destruction is perilously close. Sometimes we're not sure who our friends or enemies might be. One thing I do know – the more I get to know you, the more I love you and I've never ever in my life uttered those words, not even to Anna and ..'

I saw the tears running down her cheeks as I spoke about love. She gave me no chance of carrying on my little speech. She pulled my head down and her lips touched mine forcefully. She grabbed the hair at the back of my neck, kept my head forward gently, but firmly, so that our eyes were centred and closer and said,

'John, I've never lied to you and never will. I've always lived a safe and secure life. My mother and my relatives gave me so much love and a good education. Apart from my National Service I've had nothing to do with any government agency. I know how to carry a gun and I'm a fairly good shot, although I've never shot at anything other than targets on the firing range. I enjoy my work as a restaurateur immensely, it's something I've always wanted to do and the people around me encouraged me to go for something I like doing. I've never looked down on any other profession. I was taught to accept people as they are and not by their origin, religion or way of life. My attitude towards life changed when I was in my teens. You see, I had thyroid cancer. It was discovered at a very early stage, so the chemotherapy and radiation-treatment was successful. I was told I'd never be able to bear any children because the treatment made me sterile. Try and find a Jew, or an Arab come to that, who would marry a woman they knew would remain childless.'

I listened to her words carefully, realizing how open to the world she was. Such openness in my world was naive, but in her world it was sanity, peacefulness and purity of mind. I hope I never get her thinking my way of life, that's something I'll make sure, never happens. She seems to have recovered from the wounds of sterility. But something tells me that such wounds, especially for a woman, go much deeper than a man could ever imagine. I accepted her explanation without asking any questions. I know when to stay quiet.

We kissed and cuddled and would have ended up in the bedroom if the doorbell hadn't rung. Paula made her way discreetly to the library we'd previously agreed upon.

I switched on my CCTV screen and checked it was Charles before I pressed the button to open the outer door.

I led *straight face Charly* – AC Charles Cross – into my study.

'Something to drink Charles?'

'No thanks John, I'll keep this fairly short and to the point. I know that's the way you like it and I've another meeting at MI5 later on – very serious business. Tell me, what were the results of your visit to forensics and the morgue?'

I gave him a rundown and my own particular comments concerning Martin's death.

'I disagree, John! You see, I have information that points to someone in MI6. We have positive identification.'

'Wait a minute, Charles. You're not by any chance suggesting someone from Tom Atkins' department, a certain Joshua Grossman?'

'I think you'd better tell me where you got that piece of information, John?'

'Well, in the early hours of Tuesday, the day after Ian was taken out, I was asked to an all night session at MI6 to bring them up-to-date on the Muslim-Nazi links. You were there too. That's when I found out about Ian. Jack Orlowski, the European CEO at ISIA had apparently given the okay for the session, even though I'd just started my annual holiday. He also told MI6 about Ian's assassination. Well, when I was finished I needed to make a few calls, so they let me use their conference room near Tom's office. That's where I came across Joshua Grossman, Tom's personal assistant. Strange character if you ask me. His manner is too suspicious for a trained MI6 agent and I got the impression there was someone in Tom's office I wasn't supposed to encounter. The whole scenario stunk, that's what my trained mind registered. I've nothing to support my theory, but I was fairly certain something dubious was going on and either Tom or Joshua or both parties were involved.'

'I see,' said Charles, 'it was your intuition again, was it John – your trained mind? Well, I can put your mind at rest, it isn't Tom, I assure you. As for Joshua, we've had him in our sights for some weeks now, and all we need is to catch him in the act. But let me ask you a question first. What ever in this world *are you* doing palling-up with the two most important Mossad chiefs, Ben Goldmann and Kenneth Woodward. Do you have any idea of their positions, John?'

'Well, in actual fact I don't but I'll be meeting Ben Goldmann tomorrow in Tel Aviv and I guess I'll most probably be seeing Kenneth Woodward too.'

I could see Charles was upset. He didn't stop fidgeting, obviously something was troubling him.

'Okay, out with it Charles – what the hell's going on, that I don't know about?'

'Jesus, Joseph and Mary, our government is at wits end worrying about the infiltration of Mossad agents sabotaging our intelligence networks and one of our best ex MI6 agents is having *tête-à-tête's* with their most ingenuous bosses. That's what's up, John. You're on your way to become *persona non grata*. Ben Goldmann is now in charge of the assassination department and has been given a major role in a Mossad wide clean up. We don't yet know what it's about. Kenneth Woodward is the European head of the Mossad.'

'Bloody hell, Charles – that really sounds as though you've been misinformed! Has Jack Orlowski been speaking to you by any chance?' I asked.

'Well, as a matter of fact Jack *has* been expressing his anxiety about your actions lately.'

'Funny, Charles, that's exactly where I think your wrong information is coming from. Let me put you in the picture.'

'Em, John! Do you mind if I tape this?'

'No, I don't mind, but only if it stays at MI5.'

'Okay, John, you have my word.'

I gave Charles a rundown on Hans and Elias – the involvement of German Nazi organizations working with Muslim terrorist organizations – my own personal views that ex-Stasi cadres are also involved and where the Mossad came in. The whole misery of finding out my deceased wife Anna was a *Sayanim*. Ben Goldmann's connection to Anna – his being her half-brother and Kenneth Woodward being the father Hans knew nothing about. I left out the bit about the *Ark of the Covenant*, thinking that might push him over the edge and knowing others would become too interested. I told him about granddad being Heinrich Bolkow and his involvement. That he was probably running a highly sophisticated worldwide Nazi network, aimed at taking over the world. The latter not yet having been verified, but all pointers showing in that direction. When I was finished, Charles just said,

'Blimey, John, if I didn't know you, I'd say bullshit. Would you do me a big favour. I know it's asking a lot. Would you give me a written report sometime in the near future, just to put the record straight.'

'Well, I've given Jack a preliminary report. I guess I'll use that and fill in more of the facts I've just told you.'

'That'll be great, John!'

'Listen Charles, I know this must sound daft to you but I think I may be able to put more light on this once I've picked a few brains in Tel Aviv tomorrow.'

'For Christ's sake be careful, John!'

'I will, don't worry about that, Charles. There's much more to this than meets the eye I assure you.'

'Well, I'm glad I spoke to you personally. I can put our lot's minds at rest. Some of them were doing summersaults trying to convince others you'd changed sides, so it looks as though you have a few enemies you don't know about, or wouldn't even dream of. Watch your back, John and do me a favour, will you?'

'Aye, Charles?'

'Let your friends know what's going on in future will you, and don't be too scarce with the information.'

'You know me Charles, I've always been careful who to trust and how much information I pass on.'

'Okay, John, I'll have to rush now.'

Charles stood up – I saw him to the door.

Charles settled the goodbyes – he just nodded on his way out, adding,

'Do be careful, John.'

I nodded to his back and closed the door after him. Now I do need a wee drop of the hard stuff. I decided I'd had enough for today and just wanted to relax and enjoy Paula's company, so after visiting the bar, I wandered into the library with two glasses of Oban's best malt in my hands. Paula was sitting in one of my oversized armchairs, near the artificial fire burning in the hearth, a huge middle ages atlas on her lap. She looked up when I entered,

'John, oh, John, it's so exciting in here. I could spend weeks and months and even years in here and still not manage to take in all the information. Most of your books and atlases are in good condition but some of them need professional restoration, you know,' she said, a distant look on her face, as though she was already working out how she would accomplish it.

'I know, dear. But for now, let's call it a day shall we? How about a toast to all my ancestors who made this library full of history be possible?'

'To all your ancestors, John – may they know these treasures are in good hands,' she said, and laughed – taking the glass I offered and swallowing it down in one go. I expected her to splutter and cough up, but obviously she's used to drinking that way. I nipped mine and said,

'What do you say to us getting some eats delivered and having a grand dinner on our own?'

'Oh, yes, John, what a splendid idea. I know the English

food's atrocious, but you can't go wrong with Chinese take-aways!'

I laughed, taking her hint of what not to order, knowing she was right anyway. I went into the hall to fetch the menu of our local Chinese restaurant from the hallstand. It's just around the corner and I'm very much in the habit of using their deliveries when I'm at home.

I raided my wine cellar and picked out two bottles of '91 Italian Massetto red wine we enjoyed with the meal that was not only delicious but more than enough in quantity as usual.

In vino veritas – Paula was back in her teens and we were both laughing so much at her imitations of various famous characters, we ended up in stitches. After two espressos each, Paula left the dining room. I thought she was going to the bathroom. A minute later I heard her tuning in my violin at the piano in my study, so I went in to join her.

When she was satisfied, she started playing some fast Yiddish music. I tried accompanying her on the piano but couldn't keep up, so I listened to her solo. It was so fascinating to watch and listen to her playing. She was in a world of her own and happy, that was for sure, because the smile and the eyes that looked on me were so readable. I guessed she was working up to some sort of climax and the pressure in my trousers was my own bet on what it was.

North of Falluja – Tuesday morning 23rd August

They were waiting at a meeting point North of Falluja. 'Where's that fucking sod Henri,' she shouted in English to no one in particular, as the congregation of terrorists were all gathered at the agreed meeting point

North-North-East of the shelled-out farm complex. They were incomplete and had already waited more than two hours after the agreed time.

'Anyone seen him?'

No one answered her stupid question.

'Abdul, give Abu Mousab's adjutant a call on his cell phone and ask him if he could spare someone to recce our last meeting place and see what's happened to that idiot Henri. Maybe he's lying there injured. If he is, tell the adjutant to put him out of his misery.'

Abdul, their Shi'ite guide did as she said. He punched some numbers into his cell phone and garbled off in an Arabic dialect she wouldn't understand. Abdul was sick of this European woman ordering him around. If he had his way, he'd use his sword and cut her head off. But she has the blessing of their greatest leader, Bin Laden and his supporters in Saudi Arabia and Iran, where they were supposed to have crossed the border an hour ago on their way to Damascus.

After a while his cell phone rang. He nodded and grimaced at the confirmation he received. The man she was asking after was the only one in that group worth a Drachma and now the adjutant says he's dead. He looked at the woman, his eyes forming slits, his face converging to hardness – like Bedouin tribesmen in a sandstorm and said,

'He's dead,' making the motion of cutting his throat, 'head crushed by wooden beam.'

She didn't react at first. Disbelief was foremost in her thoughts – she couldn't believe their best killing machine was now dead. It took a while to register with her. She then shrugged her shoulders in acceptance and shouted,

'Then let's get a fucking move on,' shoving Abdul lightly for him to show the way.

More ugly thoughts gathered in Abdul's mind as he jumped into the foremost jeep to lead the way over the Iranian border to a secret camp where they would spend the rest of the day and night.

Nazi HQ – Switzerland – Tuesday afternoon 23rd August

Heinrich Bolkow, better known as granddad, was standing on the porch of an outlook post, 1750 metres high up in the mountain range of Toggenburg, Switzerland, roughly 40 km from lake Constance. Any hikers passing by, who may have wandered off the official hiking routes, would put it down as one of the many typical weekend Swiss chalets to be found in the area.

His mean eyes took in the panoramic view North East to Lake Constance and Germany, his beloved fatherland. It was a beautiful day and the Mount Saentis massive, due East, restored his thoughts of greatness that had taken a bad turn in Leipzig last Thursday.

He touched his ear that was still sore – utmost humiliation. Curse that Scotsman – his riddance was long overdue. He'll now need a special hit team, that's for sure, and include that woman Paula too. The German woman from the special services department revived in his evil memory – Frieda Schulz.

He turned to his personal assistant, a lanky, grey-blue-eyed, dark haired, 1.80 metres tall, extremely reliable German in his late fifties. He studied the Saxon features for a moment that were as always, unreadable – recalling some of the difficult personal missions he'd sent him on and remembering the overwhelming results.

Gustav Bormann eyed his Fuehrer with the obedience of a German shepherd, without a change in his expression.

'Gustav, I want you to carry out a very delicate mission. I've not informed our organization about the balls-up in Leipzig. I regard the incident as a most unfortunate coincidence that a top British agent happened to be present. Find out where that agent Jameson and Paula Zuckenic are, and get Frieda Schulz and her team onto them to finish the job those fools from Passau buggered-up. I don't want them messing around in Palestine looking for the Holy Grail – that's our business.'

'Yes, my Fuehrer – do you want me to look them up personally, or shall I just organize it from here?'

'Certainly not Gustav, you know we recently caught the Swiss authorities nosing around in our computer network, so we won't be doing any such organizing from here. Ever since our organization bought this atomic bunker system through our comrade Kamal Kassas of the Swiss Bank International in the nineties, they've been keeping a watchful eye on all our activities, so we must still play things low until *zero-day*. Then they will no longer be in a position to annoy us.'

'Yes, my Fuehrer, I'll get comrade Ralf Neukirch to assist you whilst I'm away, if it's agreeable with you?'

'Yes, he'll do. But before you go, I want you to get that lorry of x-ray equipment checked and set-up in the barn-house position together with the other ingredients. This time, nothing is to go wrong, and I want the farm complex secured round the clock, do you hear?'

'Yes, my Fuehrer, I'll have it done before I leave. Is there anything else?'

'Yes, don't come back here if you fail,' he sneered, turning back to the landscape and searching the horizon for his fatherland.

Gustav Bormann was used to such outbursts. He was also a man never to be underestimated – he always took precautions to protect his back. In this business, he knew if he did fail, then he'd make sure someone else would take the blame.

Heinrich Bolkow waited some minutes before he went back into the chalet. He called out for his valet Heinz to follow him.

He went through to the back and opened the door of a closet. On the opposite side was a hinged clothes hook he flipped over to the right. The panelling slid aside to reveal a huge metal sheet with an opening in the middle. He climbed through the opening to the atomic bunker system in the heart of the mountain. He waited until Heinz was through before he pulled the metal door to and let the heavy lever fall back in place. This was something he preferred doing himself – part of the checks he carries out daily. He retreated another two metres into the bunker and pulled down another lever attached to a metal casing holding an array of 1.50 metre long cylinders. A hissing followed and a second thick metal sheet slid out to double seal the entrance. There was no means of opening it from the outside and it was airtight. The opening and closing mechanisms were based on a simple self-contained hydraulic system. When they bought the atomic bunker complex, the first thing he had done, was to change all systems to run autarkic. Should the electricity generators still run by the Swiss authorities ever fail, which they will do on *zero day,* he chuckled – they would be prepared – he had his own generators.

Ben Goldmann – Mossad Headquarters, Tel Aviv North – Wednesday, 24th August

The Airbus sliced through a slight morning haze. The ground came up close, very fast. The wheels skidded a couple of times on touchdown followed by a rush of air, thrusting against the breaking mechanisms and drowning out all conversations.

The flight from Heathrow to Ben Gurion airport at Lod, just 25 km East of Tel Aviv, is always an exciting experience. Well, from the point of view of a security analyst. Otherwise, it can be said, nothing is taken for granted and any passenger on board is a potential terrorist, unless of course he's in possession of the necessary papers to exonerate him, or her, from the nuisance of multiple controls and questioning, or has been put on the VIP list.

I don't usually travel first class, but this time they were the only seats available at such short notice. When we boarded the plane, Paula was at first confused and shook her head, pointing to the tail, towards the tourist class, whispering something that sounded like,

'These seats aren't for us.'

I answered her quietly,

'Sorry dear, they were the only seats available,' giving her my biggest smile of conciliation.

Paula frowned, and took her window seat without further comment. After we were settled in, it wasn't long before she turned her head towards me and declared,

'Why on earth didn't you tell me?'

'I guess I wanted to, but then I thought I'd make it a surprise,' I answered.

'Well, it certainly is,' she said, a smile in the form of two small, playful dimples appearing on her cheeks, 'I thought we were just going to be treated specially, like, you'd used your connections, or something in that line when we boarded with the first class. Anyway, just in case you've more surprises up your sleeve, what are *our* plans, or should I say – *your* plans – when we get there?' she asked, impishly.

'Well, I thought you were not in too much of a hurry to get back to Haifa, so I booked us in to the Carlton for the night,' I answered – taking advantage of the situation by moving my head towards hers and touching her lips with mine, just poking the tip of my tongue out to touch the crack in her lips.

Paula blushed, but kept her eyes looking steadily into mine. I saw that mischievous look appearing just before she laid her hand on the inside of my right thigh, high enough up to cause the blood rush down into the vicinity of my loins – I was saved by a stewardess who interrupted our little game,

'Excuse me sir, madam!'

Well, I thought I was, until she asked,

'May I see if your safety belts are fastened correctly?'

She bent down to pick up a leaflet lying in the gangway near my seat. As she straightened up, she put a hand on my head-rest to help her balance. I felt a soft nipple through my shirt, as it lightly pressed into my left shoulder. If she's wearing a Bra it must be very thin, was my first impression, as I wondered what perfume she was wearing or was it the deodorant under her armpits?

'Thank you,' she said as our arms went up to show we were correctly fastened in. My loins were burning. The stewardess smiled and moved on to check the next row. My embarrassment was complete. I glanced down at my loins, relieved to see everything was in order – no boxer shorts and no leeway trousers on today, thank goodness, just a bit over-tight. Paula laughed when she saw where I was looking.

On arrival, we were both ushered into a separate room at passport control and asked to hand over our baggage tags. A uniformed security guard escorted us out a separate exit to an awaiting black sedan, with a blue police siren on top.

'Compliments of the Israeli government,' he said, as we stopped at the car.

'Your luggage will be forwarded to the hotel.'

Without further ado he saluted, turned, and went back the way we'd just come.

The driver held the door open for us, so we took our delegated seats in the rear of the sedan.

Paula whispered in my ear as the driver closed the door.

'How does he know where we're staying?'

'I had to give an address on a special security form,' I answered.

The driver took his seat behind the steering wheel and turned his head slightly to address us,

'I have instructions to drop Ms Zuckenic at the Carlton, then drive you to your appointment Mr Jameson and wait for you, then back to the Carlton. That's all. No further questions please, thank you.'

With that, he started the car.

The highway from Ben Gurion airport to Tel Aviv got crowded as we reached the outskirts of the city. The driver switched on his blue police siren. He turned off audio though, thank goodness. Checkpoints were no problem. He kept the lights flashing all the way to the hotel Carlton, a noble four-star hotel with access to the marina. I asked the driver to wait and escorted Paula into the hotel. I went through all the formalities at reception, asked for the two cell phones I'd had ordered via Internet at ATS Telecom Systems, including two copies of the invoice with the phone numbers. I checked the back of one, noted the number and checked it against the invoice, putting my name against it on both invoices. I gave the other cell phone and invoice to Paula, also a big hug and a long kiss. She clung on to me as though we were departing forever. I told her I'd be back in the evening for dinner. I know all the dangers and felt she was experiencing similar feelings of awaiting perils. I told her not to worry.

The drive North of Tel Aviv to Mossad Headquarters was nerve-racking. We were in the middle of rush hour and the driver wove the car in and out of the spaces, changing the lanes continuously and turning his siren on and off all the way, with audio on full blast.

At Mossad Headquarters, the security formalities were not unfamiliar. The only difference was the quiet effectiveness, bordering on diffidence with which the officials carried out their duties. Used to dangerous situations, they were obviously always on the alert, not easily fooled, just staying cool.

I was ushered in by a secretary who was blushing as red as a beetroot. Ben Goldmann stood up and came around his desk to greet me,

'Nice to see you again John,' he said.

Blimey, I thought – what's happened to the taciturn, grumpy Ben I used to know – being so polite? Ben's words were nearly drowned out by the whistle of the train to Haifa approaching a level crossing a few hundred metres away.

I took his heavy grip in my right hand, returning the pressure and was about to repeat his words when the whistle blew again. What a welcoming break – we couldn't help laughing – the ice was broken. Anyway, as such occasions require, I returned the friendly greeting,

'Good to see you too, Ben – it's been a long time.'

'A hell of a lot has happened since,' he replied.

'Some of it not so good, but I hear you're well established now,' I added.

Ben waved his hand to the corner opposite the door, where some chairs were placed around a conference table. He ignored my last comment.

'What about some coffee John, or would you prefer tea?'

'Well, I'd rather have a cold drink, if you don't mind. Plain soda water if you've got any, as long as it's cool, but anything similar will do.'

Ben moved to the door, opened it a crack and called out a name. He came back to the conference table. The door opened and the same red-faced secretary appeared.

'Ah, this is my personal secretary Judith Salomon. Close the door please, Judith.'

She closed the door and waited patiently.

'Thank you,' he said.

'If you ever try to contact me John, and I'm not available, then ask for Judith Salomon. She has my complete confidence and full authority to act in my absence.'

Judith's face was really burning. I nodded my head in appreciation, putting on a smile of acceptance.

'Could you arrange some plain cold soda water for Mr Jameson or something similar?' he asked her, smiling.

I thought I was seeing and hearing things. I have a completely new person here I noted. Maybe I'll have to change my mind about Ben – anyway, at least it's détente for the time being.

Judith nodded, turned about and left the room. Well, she sure seems to be infatuated by her boss, I thought. Has Ben noticed or is he just ignoring the fact?

'Okay John, let's get down to business shall we?'

I nodded.

'Ken Woodward had some very interesting things to tell me. What can I do to help you?' he asked.

My first thoughts were about Anna, my murdered wife, who had also been Ben's half-sister.

'Tell me Ben, were you aware of Anna's status as a Mossad Agent?'

'I wondered when you'd ask me that question,' he answered, 'I didn't contemplate on it being the first one though. But I forget, you've always been a direct person, John,'

I waited without commenting – thinking – this is Ben's softening-up waffle.

'I didn't know, at first,' he replied, 'It was the Cold War days – you should remember what it was like,' he said, apologetically,

I kept my gaze and features stony.

'Well, you were after a Right-Wing organization, a follow-up organization using the Nazi network ODESSA, at the time, and Anna was recruited through Jan Hellstern's group, long before you both met. She was to keep an eye on her so-called granddad, Heinrich Bolkow, whom we suspected was one of the leaders. The KGB, CIA, MI6 and BND weren't the only ones after the organization, but apart from ours, no other organization ever suspected Bolkow's involvement. We had information pointing to Stasi links, so we decided that, as a so-called relative, Anna was the best possible choice. Anyway, I do want to emphasize, Anna wanted to drop out after you both got married. Anna was well aware you were MI6, even though you were outwardly an overt Military Attaché, and that's the reason she gave us for wanting out. She said she didn't want to betray you. I suspect in some way Bolkow cottoned on, or he became suspicious of her when she married you, an MI6 agent, especially if he found out the field of interest you were investigating,'

Ben raised both hands to form fists. He rested them for a moment on his chin, the thumbs supporting underneath. He looked at me intensively for a moment before he let them sink to the edge of the table. They remained fists.

'John, what I'm about to tell you is normally against Mossad rules, but I have been given the necessary authority to inform you,'

I twisted in my seat, uncomfortable thoughts going through my mind. Are they passing the buck onto me? I caught the seriousness of his expression, registered his fists, and thought, he couldn't be giving this information of his own accord, he's more or less just said that, so I remained all ears.

'You know the old saying – once a member of Mossad you die as a Mossad member. That's not so nowadays, or rather, we are making sure such things never ever occur again. We have had some bad leaders in our organization in the past and are currently in a re-organizing process. I can't tell you more, other than to say we were definitely not responsible for Anna's death.'

His, 'yes,' to the secretary's knock at the door saved further embarrassment.

The cool drink was welcome, despite the air conditioning. After the secretary left, I thought it was a good cue for taking up on Ben's words,

'Thanks for sticking up for Anna, Ben. It has torn me apart

ever since I found out. I discovered a lot about her so-called granddad, so let's give him his correct nametag, shall we? Heinrich Bolkow, a murderous fucking Nazi criminal. I'd like to hang him up by his balls on the nearest tree. I'd appreciate it, if you'd fill in some of the gaps I seem to have on him?'

'Well, there are a lot of people on the revenge list, who've suffered a lot more, John. Anyway, I guess you're entitled to the whole story, so I'll tell you what I think you don't seem to know,'

I felt my expression harden – my teeth were grinding, as I pictured getting my hands on that evil creature – the person who may have murdered, or had Anna murdered.

'Anyway, it's something I myself felt hard to believe at first. Bolkow's organization has infiltrated many intelligence organizations and political parties in the East and West, including Russia and China. They have an economic and para-military set-up far greater than you could imagine. Even Goebbels would envy the propaganda organization created by Stasi cadres that have infiltrated numerous religious-, teaching- and esoteric institutions worldwide. The para-military part is of a cell-type structure, making it almost impossible to infiltrate. Their main goal is to cause havoc. Where can you create the most havoc? Amongst religions and educational systems! They've been sowing the seeds of hatred over the last five decades. Their main objective is against the West, and especially Israel. Their aim, is to rid the world of Jews and take over world control – when, is the big question.'

'Bloody hell, Ben! That's a nightmare even Hollywood couldn't produce. Worse than Hitler, the plague, aids, and anything else I can imagine.'

'Yes, John – it's the biggest Maximum Credible Accident (MCA), you can think of. To describe it as an accident is out of place, I know, but it's the only description for an all-out catastrophe that fits. Apropos, MCA – we have information that lead us to believe they are in possession of HEU and are capable of setting off a small number of atomic bombs in the region of 5 Kt. Furthermore, there have been numerous thefts of x-ray equipment in Holland and Germany, originally designated as aid for poorer European countries. With the help of chemicals and fertilizers, they've got a nasty dirty bomb, or bombs, therefore a forthcoming atomic fall-out catastrophe could occur – where, we don't know. Our guess is the dirty bomb, or bombs will go off in Europe and the 5 Kt bombs will be mounted on some rocket heads aimed at targets in the Middle East.'

'Knowing the expertise and capabilities of the Mossad, I guess you have a member list of the organization of some sort?' I asked, hoping for some possible hints or even a handout.

Ben smiled, knowingly,

'It's a bit early for a complete list John, but my superiors have agreed *you* should be supplied with a few names, especially as you've always been a good friend of Israel. They know you'll use this knowledge wisely and of course it'll benefit us all. We don't have a big choice in the Western world. It's almost impossible to decide who to trust, sometimes even in our own ranks.'

'Before you tell me Ben, let me put some names forward that I think I can trust and others I don't.'

'I don't want to test your integrity John, but if you insist – of course!'

'Okay! First of all those I think I can trust – Paula Zuckenic, Chris Fenton, Charles Cross and Dave Haddock, both Scotland Yard, and Martin Cole, deceased. I guess you've been watching my steps in Berlin so you know the guys in my *bunch*, can I trust them too?'

'Well, your intuition hasn't let you down – they all pass the test as far as we know. You are very fortunate to have hit it off with Paula, John. I know you are a ladies man, so my advice to you is – forget the other ladies on your list and concentrate on Paula, she's really worth it.'

I took that in and drew a deep breath, knowing he's right about Paula. Thank God the people I've trusted got a positive Mossad vetting. I don't know what I'd have done if any of them got a negative. I took a deep breath,

'Okay, now the ones I'm not sure about: Tom Atkins from Special Ops – MI6, his deputy Joshua Grossman, my boss at ISIA Berlin – Jack Orlowski, Olaf Ertl and his sister Elsa, John Scarlotti – Director of MI6,'

I paused for a moment, thinking hard,

'Oh, and a newcomer to my group – Alistair Gravestone from the British Museum in London.'

Ben laughed at the last name,

'Why on earth did you put Professor Gravestone on your list, John?'

'Just to be on the safe side, he's just joined us for his expertise. I'll tell you about it in a minute.'

'Mm,' murmured Ben.

He knows Alistair Gravestone, then, I thought. Probably been here on a lot of archaeological expeditions.

Ben continued,

'Well, we're not sure about Tom Atkins. It seems, he spends too much time in gay bars in London. He's a security risk at least. Jack Orlowski and John Scarlotti belong to a multi national intelligence group that played a big part in manipulating Bin Laden's terrorist organization to target twin towers on 9/11, in order to march into Afghanistan and Iraq. Joshua Grossman was one of ours, but he's certainly not any more. You could consider him a renegade within the Mossad, one of a group we're after and not to be trusted. Why do you ask about the Ertls, John?'

'I don't know. Maybe it's something from Olaf's BND days in Leipzig. I got the feeling then, he was hiding something from me.'

'I see. So you've been friends all these years, yet still with a touch of doubt?'

'Yeah, just like you and me Ben, although I must say the stories that go around about the sadist Ben Goldmann are quite gory you know.'

'So that's why some people shun my presence. I always wondered,' he said, laughingly and waved it off by adding,

'All part of my guise, you know. Don't believe all you hear.'

I couldn't laugh with him because I wasn't sure if I could believe him. Ben continued,

'Olaf Ertl was caught trying to smuggle a girl out of East Germany. They gave him the choice of becoming a Double Agent or they'd have put the girl in prison. Ertl agreed and was allowed to return to the West. He didn't keep to the agreement and told his superiors, who decided to use him as a DDA. It didn't last more than three months because there was a mole in the BND. The girl disappeared and died later in Bautzen prison.'

'Tell me Ben, was he a DA when we were working together?'
'I'm afraid so, John.'
'So they knew all about me too, then?'

'I presume so, but you'd better ask him yourself. Maybe he didn't denounce you. If he had, I'm sure you'd have been hauled in by the Stasi, but there again you were a covert agent protected by your official embassy status.'

'What about Elsa, his sister?'

'Pure innocence John, although we had a question mark running for some time, mainly because of Kenneth joining the Mossad.'

'How come?'

'Well, Kenneth Woodward named her under the foreign persons he'd met when he joined the Mossad. We had her checked and found out about her son in the process. We thought it wise not to inform him. The consequences would've put a stop to his career. I told him about our knowledge this morning. He was quite livid, I can tell you.'

'I would be too, bloody right I would,' I said, indignantly, thinking – that's just the way it is in intelligence organizations, no matter what country you serve.

Talking about Olaf, I told Ben about his escapade and near death in *Tyre*. Ben took it in without comment. Maybe he knows already, I thought. Instead he asked,

'What I want to know is, John, what are you going to do with the information I've just given you?'

I thought for a few seconds before I spoke,

'First of all it strengthens all my options and decision-making. Secondly, it hasn't gone unnoticed to Charles Cross that Joshua is in some way hot. Now that it seems you've dropped him, decision-making will be easier for Charles. I've always had my doubts about Jack, too, which is a reassurance, so I'll have to watch my back even more now. I haven't decided about John Scarlotti. He's right at the top and a very important person. He can pull a lot of strings and make things very uncomfortable indeed. I'll have to consider my *modus operandi* very carefully now. This information is worth all the gold in the world, Ben. I'll never forget, and that's why I've something important for you to know. It's something the Jews have been searching for – a real treasure. We came across some ancient documents in Leipzig we think may have belonged to Anna or Martha. Maybe they even belonged to Bolkow.'

'You surely don't mean the Holy Grail, John?'

'As a matter of fact, I do, well it seems to be something in that direction!'

Ben laughed. It was so hearty I couldn't help but join him. Maybe it was my timing, or the simplicity of my statement. Our laughter continued for ages until the door opened and the secretary poked her head in. She was no longer red-faced and smiled a smile of reassurance – maybe she just wanted to check if her boss was really laughing.

The door closed quietly – my signal to inform Ben in detail about our findings from Leipzig and the reason for bringing in Professor Alistair Gravestone, although I suspect he'd already deduced that. During our further conversation he hinted Gravestone was a possible MI6 agent, but had no further information on him.

An hour later Ben's words of warning were still ringing in my ears. He thought the decision to continue my annual holiday and spend it in Israel, looking for the treasure, was very wise. He wasn't happy when I mentioned starting our investigation in *Tyre* and suggested we use mainly trusted locals able to supply safe locations. I told him I couldn't use official sources, so asked him if he'd any suggestions. Caught out, he grudgingly agreed to supply me with two safe houses in *Tyre*, but I was only to use the guys in my *bunch* who were fluent in Arabic and dark enough to pass as Arabs, providing they dressed appropriately and that went for me too. He also pointed out that Bolkow's organization was after the same thing too, which made the chance of finding it very slim. He warned me not to start a guerrilla war in Hezballah territory.

I informed him of my actions for the next few days in Israel.

He offered his support any time, day or night. It's a strange feeling being offered so much information and help from a foreign intelligence agency, especially from the Mossad. Newcomers to the business could never manoeuvre themselves into such a position unless they became Double Agents and that's what bugged me a little. Maybe others might tend to think that way too about me, or maybe Ben has a purpose behind it. Fortunately, I had the advantage of knowing Ben personally – the half-brother of my murdered wife Anna. Maybe it's just pure chance he happens to be an important leader in the Mossad and there's Kenneth Woodward too – pure chance again. I tried to console myself with these thoughts.

Ben told me to contact him to talk about any armaments, satellite communication equipment, or border permits for the area if and when it was required. I felt like a tourist when he mentioned possible guides for the Hezballah country. For a moment I was benumbed by the expertise with which he seemed to grasp the situation and requirements needed. Then I realized that for him, this was normal in his daily Israeli environment. Do I believe the information Ben has relayed to me – as he purports, with the authority of his seniors, whoever they might be – or is there something else behind this? What's the big question behind Joshua Grossman, what has happened that the Mossad has dropped him and may be in the process of getting rid of him. Who else was involved? Is Gravestone acting under the traitor Scarlotti or black-eyed Joshua? As in many past cases, I guess I'll have to rely on my intuition and that is telling me Ben has only given me part of the jigsaw puzzle or maybe he's shown me the entrance to the maze and I've got to figure out how to get to the centre.

I left with the assurance of help from a powerful organization at hand, should I require their services – a good feeling, but as always with a certain feeling of restraint that goes with the profession. My thoughts clouded, thinking about Olaf's secret – poor guy. I don't think he sold me out to the Stasi – I would've noticed, or our lot would've informed me, as we'd enough insiders of our own in the Stasi organization. Maybe I'll ask him to join the team – possibly help him get his mind back on track.

I was struck by Paula's imposing appearance in our hotel room when I arrived back from Mossad headquarters. She was wearing a light beige sustainable-chiffon river-top supported by thin straps exposing her bare shoulders. The river-top front just covered her magnificent breasts and belly button – the cleavage of her breasts showing discreetly through the thin material at the top. A manus skirt, a touch lighter, highlighted her slender figure. She greeted me shyly, swirled around and asked me if I liked it. Ben's words hadn't gone unnoticed. I took her in my arms feeling a lump rise in my throat as I told her how much I liked everything about her and at the end added,

'Darling, you'd make the front page of *Vogue,* you're so beautiful.'

As I said that, thoughts of loss nagged in my mind. I was worried about Paula's safety, about losing her just like Anna. I pictured all sorts of scenarios too horrible to talk about. Paula's eyes were watching me – noticing every change of muscle either relaxed or tightened up.

'John, tell me – what are your plans for tomorrow. I suspect they won't be including me, judging by the face you're making.'

I tried to relax a bit and countered.

'Well, I've got some sick visits to do tomorrow morning at the Sourasky Medical Centre. It's something I'm not very good at. I may be having a meeting at lunchtime, so I reckon I should be free after 3 pm. If not, I'll give you a ring on your cell phone. We'll stay another night at the Carlton if it gets too late, otherwise we'll take a taxi and move on to your place in Haifa – if that's okay with you?'

'That's splendid, John. That'll give me enough time to revisit the Tel-Aviv Museum. They have a new gallery of nineteenth and twentieth century paintings I'd like to study. I'll also have to arrange for some groceries to fill up my fridge and larder.'

I admired her openness and enthusiasm. I wished I could accompany her, but under the circumstances I knew I wouldn't be able to concentrate on paintings, not until Heinrich Bolkow and his organization were brought to justice, or liquidated.

'Listen, Paula – we've some serious talking to do, but not in here. Give me 20 minutes to get ready, then we'll take a walk down the marina before dinner and I'll fill you in, okay.'

She nodded. I made a bee-dive for the bathroom.

We walked up and down the marina twice, arm in arm. I told her the news on Heinrich Bolkow, his organization, their plans and his possible craving for vengeance. She took in my warning about being more careful in the future, but didn't say anything until I was finished – I left out the bit about the Holy Grail. She stopped and turned to face me. She looked me straight in the eyes with a seriousness I hadn't seen before and said,

'John, ever since you turned up in Leipzig, I've felt safe in your company. I understand the risks. Don't forget I'm an Israeli and live with the feeling of danger daily. So I'm going to be armed when we get to my place in Haifa,' she said, boldly – shrugging her shoulders and giving me a reassuring smile.

I couldn't help but grab her by the shoulders and kiss her

eyes, lips and ears, seemingly all at once. It was the simplicity of her statement – she is prepared. I felt so proud of her bearing.

We had dinner on the terrace restaurant overlooking the marina – an appealing ambience to finish off an eventful day in the company of a beautiful person. Paula remained charismatic – her bewitching touch was still predominant but I got the feeling a wee bit of apprehension had crept in.

Tel Aviv – Sourasky Medical Centre – Thursday, 25th August

After a light breakfast, I took a taxi to the Sourasky Medical Centre, a huge complex spread over an area of 150,000 sq metres to the North of Tel Aviv. It comprises three hospitals – the Ichilov General hospital together with the Ida Sourasky rehabilitation centre – the Lis Maternity hospital – and the Dana Children's hospital. My destination was the Ichilov General hospital.

On the way, the taxi driver made me well acquainted with the dangerous country I was now travelling in. In recent years the medical centre had treated victims of terror attacks in Tel Aviv – among them – the attacks on *bus line 5*, *bus line 20* and *bus line 51*, the *Dizengoff Centre*, the *Apropos Café*, the *central bus station*, and the infamous attack on the *Dolphinarium disco*.

I made a note, not to use the bus and to avoid cafés during my stay. Another thought occurred – maybe he was just telling me all this, so I'd stick to using taxis in future.

The taxi driver carried on waffling, stressing the importance of the hospital complex that has a national and international patient *clientèle*. I nearly fell asleep.

I checked in at the main hospital reception and found the ward where Hans and Elias were convalescing. I was told to check in with the ward sister, as access is only permitted for those registered on the visitor's list. It was now 10 am, so I guess Elsa or Ken, or both would already be there. I hoped either Ben or Ken had added my name to the list. At the ward sister's office I was told to wait. A security guard appeared and checked my credentials against a list. Satisfied, he told me to follow him.

We arrived at the door of a sickroom where an armed guard was sitting at a desk. He checked my passport, added my name to his list, glanced at his wristwatch and noted the time. I felt a slight assurance the lads had a certain amount of protection. Satisfied, the guard nodded his head and pressed a button. The outer door to the secure sickroom opened. I went into a further corridor. I knocked at the door ahead, pulled the door handle down, pushed the door open gently and walked in.

I recognised Hans despite his pale, thin face. He didn't look too bad, though. The other lad was in a worse state. His head, chest and hands were bandaged and from what I could see of his face, it was badly bruised and swollen.

Both lads were on drips. A plastic catheter bag was hanging at Elias' bedside.

Elsa was sitting between the two beds. No sign of Ken.

'John, oh John, thank goodness you've managed to come.' she said, tears rolling down her cheeks.

I went over and took her briefly in my arms just as she was standing up. She tried very hard not to make too much out of the embracement, probably remembering what happened on our last one in Freiburg, or maybe because of the lads – it was still a very tight situation.

Elsa let go. I went over to Hans who had the window bed

and took his left hand in both of my big paws. He nodded and smiled weakly.

'Glad you're safe Hans,' I said.

Hans murmured something indiscernible. I took it to be a welcoming greeting because my tinnitis was playing a high-pitched concert in both ears – always a reminder what a bomb blast and years of stress can do to your ears. I glanced over at Elias, who seemed to be asleep.

Elsa interrupted by tugging my left arm. She moved her head signalling me to follow her. I let go of Hans' hand, patted it gently and followed Elsa out onto the balcony.

'They haven't done much talking yet, John. The doctor's having a specialist from the rehabilitation centre sent over. For the time being, they've been given tranquillizers. He says it's the shock from the terrifying experience they've had and it's too soon for heavy talking. They're used to such cases here. The doctor also thinks Hans is better off here than in Germany. Hans did tell the Arab doctor what happened, but since then he's gone into a deep depression. The doctor says it'll be a few days before they're ready to talk. Elias' kidneys have been bruised badly and some ribs are broken. Elias' fiancée, Elena, is in the adjoining room,' Elsa pointed through the window to a door just beyond Elias' bed, 'they had to operate on her, you know. Her cheekbone and nose are broken and she's lost some teeth too. Both Elias and Elena have torture marks and cuts and bruises all over their bodies. It's dreadful, John! Some of Elias' fingernails have been torn off. Elena's sister Maria is a nurse and took care of Hans you know. She sleeps in the bed next to her sister in the adjoining room and comes in now and again to see to Hans and Elias. It looks as though Hans is very fond of her. When I'm not here she sits at his bedside and holds his hand.'

I nodded, thinking it was typical of a mother to take more notice of such things and asked,

'Where's Ken?'

'He was in early this morning to say goodbye to the boys. Unfortunately he had to go back to Berlin this morning. He's very frustrated you know and anguished. I promised to stay here for a while and look after the boys. Ken's sister Golda Goldsmith is coming this afternoon. Ken says she took the place of Elias' mother who died shortly after childbirth.'

'Yes, I know. Ken told me when we first met on Sunday. How is the situation now? Do they know they're brothers yet?' I asked.

'No they don't. Ken wanted to tell Hans this morning but the doctor forbid it. He says it'd be too much at the moment. They will be told in due course, once they get over the initial shock of their bad experiences. I'm not sure about Han's reaction to Ken, though. It worries me a lot. You know he's a pacifist and hates what the Jews have been doing to the Palestinians and I know Ken is a government official.'

'What a terrible situation for you Elsa,' I said. She fell into my arms letting her body melt into mine for a brief moment, before she abruptly pushed herself away. Her voice was quiet but serious when she spoke,

'John, it's best not to in front of the boys. Hans may be looking through the bay window. He's never seen me in the arms of another man and I don't want to worsen his condition,' she said, and added, 'I hope you understand?'

'Of course, Elsa, I understand completely. I thought for a moment it was because of Ken?'

She smiled weakly,

'I told you already, John – Ken and I were teenage lovers. I'm a grown-up woman now and it's over as far as I'm concerned. Ken doesn't seem to have given up, though. I dislike the way he reacted when I told him there was no place for him at my side. He was furious and tried very hard to dissuade me.'

'Well, maybe it'll just take time for him to accept it,' I said.

'You know, John, at first, I thought it was terrific, Hans having a half-brother, but now I'm not so sure.'

'I can imagine how you feel, Elsa.'

Elsa looked at me intensively – there was obviously something else on her mind.

'What is it Elsa? Come on, out with it,' I said, softly, putting reassurance into my voice.

'John, where is all this going to end? I'm so fed up with the secrecy. All the years with Olaf, and now I've got Ken on my back and I may lose Hans to the Middle East. Oh, John,' she cried out.

She pulled me out of sight of the window and pushed me against the outside wall. I could feel her body through the thin dress and my situation was becoming difficult.

'Halt mich fest, John,' she said, so I held her tight. I caressed her hair and cheek and my hand stroked her back gently. She sobbed for some minutes but stopped when my hand – not thinking – stroked her bottom a couple of times. She looked up – a weak smile appeared. She pushed herself away from me gently and said, 'Not here, John. Let's go to my room shall we?'

I frowned.

'What is it, John?' she asked.

I decided to put her in the picture. I bent down and whispered in her ear.

'I'm going to whisper this into your ear – a very quiet whisper. Just press my hand if it's too quiet and I'll repeat, okay, and don't forget to whisper back! Elsa, I'm sorry I have to tell you this, but I think it's time you knew about Ken. Whatever your reaction, I want you to promise me you will never ever let on to him that you know – promise?'

'Yes, John, I promise,' she whispered back reluctantly.

'Okay, well here goes.'

Elsa nodded – I bent down and started whispering in her ear,

'Ken is head of the Mossad in Europe – a very important man in their organization. I would bet you a million he's got a team covering you, mainly for safety reasons. Every move you make here, whatever you do and whatever company you're in – he'll get to know, so I don't think it would be wise if we were seen too close together. I think he's a very jealous person and jealousy is an unpredictable element when you're dealing with such a powerful person.'

Elsa held my head down and whispered in my ear,

'Oh, my God, John! I presumed he was an agent or something, but I never thought he had such an important position – it's that bad is it?' she asked.

I whispered back,

'Yes dear, I'm afraid it is. Now you've rebuked him he's probably in a very nasty mood.'

Elsa's features changed into a grimace. She maintained her whispering,

'I was looking forward so much to having you stay a few nights with me, John. Now, the thought of being here on my own is depressing, but I do understand the situation, John. What a terrible shame.'

A second later, her face brightened up a bit.

'We'll just have to wait until this is over then, won't we?' She said, full of anticipation forgetting to whisper.

I nodded my head in agreement, not knowing when this would be over, or when or where that occasion would ever occur.

'Listen, Elsa – I've some business to do in the North, before I fly back on Friday evening. I think you'll be allright here. Keep in touch. Here's my Israeli cell phone number. You can ring me up any time, day or night whilst I'm over here and keep me informed. I'll be moving on now. Other than hanging around and waiting, which is not one of my virtues, there's not much else to do,' I said, pulling her close, so she could feel the bulge in my loins.

Elsa made a face.

'John, Jameson!' she whispered, chuckling, 'you are wicked – you've just told me to be careful. What *are* you trying to do? You've got me so heated up I would let you have me here and now – on this balcony – if my son wasn't in a sick bed next door.'

She finished her whispering by biting me gently in my ear-lobe.

I accepted – grinned and backed off.

'Bye the way Elsa – how is Olaf?'

'He should be back home by now, John. I spoke to him last night. They were going to release him from hospital this morning. He's also able to speak a little. Not very clearly but I can just about decipher what he's trying to say. If you speak to him on the phone, you may have to get him to repeat his sentences.'

'That's good news, Elsa. I'll be coming back over here soon. It's not for general knowledge, so keep it to yourself. Maybe I'll get Olaf to accompany me.'

'Do you think that's a good idea after all he's been through?'

'Well, it's sort of a treasure hunt and his language expertise would be a help. It would also get his ego back to normal, don't you think?'

'Well, I don't know what to think. I don't like the idea of us all being in the Middle East after what's happened to Olaf, Hans, Elias and Elena.'

'Look, I'm taking some of my most trusted men with us and they're all very highly trained, so we shall be prepared.'

I didn't mention the Mossad helping us in the background.

'Don't ask for my approval, John. I'd say no, because I'm beginning to detest everything to do with the Middle East.'

'I don't blame you for thinking that way Elsa. Once Hans recuperates though, things will look a lot brighter. Now, let's not get down in the dumps, eh! He's safe, that's the main thing.'

'Yes, he's safe, for the time being, but I hope he doesn't get too involved with that girl, he may not want to come back home to finish his studies,' she said, her voice full of gloom.

I tried to cheer her up.

'Hans, is a bright lad. He knows, without a good education and a degree, his chances on the global market are thin.'

The more we talked, the more Elsa was getting depressed. I hated leaving her now, but I knew it was time to go. She's just talking, trying to keep me here just a little bit longer, I guess. Under the circumstances, I don't blame her. I took both her hands and spoke to her in a soft voice,

'I'll be going now, Elsa. Don't fret, everything will turn out allright.'

I hugged her briefly, kissed her softly on the mouth and cheek and turned away without looking back. I left her on the balcony, went back into the sickroom, waved at Hans and Elias, who seemed to be asleep anyway and made a quick retreat. The guard seemed surprised to see me leave so hastily.

It was lunchtime now, well, for an early lunch, really. The thought of meeting Paula right now was discarded. I wouldn't be able to contact her anyway, as she'd probably had to deposit her cell phone upon entering the museum. I decided to have a light meal in the hospital restaurant and take a slow walk into town. Looking at my town map, I noticed the Tel Aviv museum was about halfway.

Haifa – Paula's residence – Thursday evening, 25th August

Daylight was gradually fading as we arrived at a building in the Western Carmel area of Haifa on the slopes of Mount Carmel after just over an hour's drive from Tel Aviv. At first sight I thought the building should have a sign displaying:

> No Admittance
> Government Property

I paid the taxi driver off, giving him a generous tip and was surprised when he offered to carry our luggage in. I guess my tip was too extravagant, or Israeli taxi drivers are just polite.

The path to Paula's place went down the back of the building from the North to the South East end. Paula unlocked the door and pushed it wide open.

I stopped the driver from entering the building – perhaps my tone was a bit too sharp.

'Just leave the bags on the porch, that'll be fine,' I said.

He literally dropped the bags outside. He was obviously upset – muttered something I couldn't decipher and walked back up the drive, shaking his head a couple of times until he turned the corner on his way back to his taxi. Maybe I got things wrong and he was just a nice guy or he has Anglophobia and has just been reminded of it.

'Sorry mate', I muttered to myself, 'just being security minded, as usual'.

'Just leave the luggage in the hall, John. Be quick – I must show you something,' she said – her face glowing with excitement. Did I catch that little telltale gleam in her eyes? Maybe she'll drag me into the bedroom was my immediate thought. I moved our luggage into the hallway and shut the front door. Paula grabbed my hand and dragged me through her quarters to the terrace. I just managed a brief glimpse of the flat. It seemed to be extremely large for a one-person household, or maybe her mother lives here too? I hoped not. It was a very noble residence indeed – comparable with my flat in London in quality, yet more modern – hard to decipher the character or period – quite a mixture. The high ceiling gave it a monumental touch. It had one thing my flat would rarely have a call for – air-conditioning. I wondered if some of the paintings we passed in the hall and living room were copies or originals – some did seem familiar.

Paula pulled me out onto the terrace. I stopped to take in a breathtaking panoramic view over the city – right down to the harbour and over the water to the horizon that seemed to be drawn up, very close – possibly due to the unique sunset.

The fading blue of the sky was blended with streaks of cumuli, some very dark, others emulsified in red and orange casting a convex dome over the whole scenery. It was like looking at a three dimensional picture from the edge of an enormous glass cheese dish cover – out of this world!

She put her arm around my waist and asked,

'Do you like it, John?'

'I'm lost for words, Paula – it's fantastic!'

We stood leaning against each other for a while, taking in this peculiar scene. After a while Paula gave some explanations,

'As you can see we are in a beautiful area surrounded by parks and various types of gardens, with many exotic trees and shrubbery. It's really a sanctuary you know. From here you can see the Zoo to the right – some Museums and the garden paradise of *Gan Ha'em.*'

She went on explaining more scenes, and places. Some of it went out the other ear – too many Hebrew names to cope with. I was mainly watching the colours of the sky run together that were gradually fading and the sky becoming darker and darker. The view down the mountain towards the city and harbour and out to sea was certainly a sight to behold, no doubt about that. I was flabbergasted too with the exotic surroundings now becoming vague shadows, some illuminated by the city lights.

All of a sudden I felt dog-tired and couldn't stifle the yawn that no doubt cracked-up my features, spelling out the stress of the last hours, if not days or even weeks. It didn't go unnoticed.

'No wonder you're tired after all you've been through,' said Paula.

'I know just the right thing that'll do wonders,' she added.

My first thought was way off base. I couldn't sense any kind of invitation on her features – just a nice, plain smile! She took firm hold of my hand and led me into her bathroom. It was an immense room, tiled up to the starting point of a dome-shaped ceiling painted in an *art nouveau* sky. Four imitation marbled half-pillars filled the corners making the room seem like an open-air bathroom. The marble stone bath and floor gave it an ancient Roman touch. Beautiful mosaic murals, mostly landscape scenery, decorated parts of the walls – fitting in contrast to the tiles. I thought I detected Peloponnesian figures in the foreground. One in particular seemed familiar – like the work of an ancient master depicting *Penelope* – wife constant during her husband's long absence. Did this have a hidden meaning? No doubt it was designed and either carried out, or directed by Paula. Apart from the obligatory toilette and bidet, the bath itself was huge. Its exterior was diamond-shaped and half-centred in the room opposite a huge mirror hanging above an oversized wash-hand basin. The bath was half let into the floor and judging by the jet-nozzles at the bottom and sides it also functioned as a Jacuzzi.

I watched her as she went over to the bath. She bent down low to turn the tap on. A strong flow of water shot out, drawing my mind away from the voluptuous shape of her bottom.

'By the time you've undressed, John, the bath will be full.'

I started undressing and laid my clothes on the plush seat of an *art modern* chair of the late sixties that had an exceptionally high back. A white dressing gown hung over the top. She went over to the sink and chose a packet from a marble stone shelf running from both sides of the sink and ending just short of the pillars. She turned around and looking directly at me, said,

'Don't mind me, John, I'm just going to put some effervescent tablets in the water,'

A slight grin forced a dimple to appear on her left cheek. She looked at the packet as she moved over to the bath saying,

'They contain various oils – valerian, rosewood and sandalwood and will no doubt help to rejuvenate your body and mind.'

Looking up from the packet – this time her expression contained no hidden messages, she said,

'Try the Jacuzzi jets – they work wonders. When you're finished you can put on my dressing gown and join me on the terrace.'

She bent down and let two tablets glide to the bottom of the bath. She straightened up, smiled at me fondly and left the bathroom, leaving me a little disappointed – standing like a half-undressed teenage schoolboy at the end of the boy's queue, waiting for the doctor to check my breathing, grab my balls and ask me to cough.

I turned the tap off and let my body glide into the bubbly, greenish water, my body weight taken over by the water, just relaxing and mind resting.

I seemed to have dropped off for a few minutes. The sound of a shower running in an adjacent room must have brought me back. As Paula had suggested, I tried out the Jacuzzi jets for a few minutes – totally refreshing. I felt like a new person ready for a ten-kilometre run. A few minutes later the door of the adjoining room opened and Paula appeared, wrapped in a large bath towel. Our meeting place on the terrace had apparently been changed. The jet stream of the Jacuzzi made my bath water foam-up. The warm water and Paula's appearance made my manhood rise bigger and harder than ever before. Must be the heat moving all my blood downwards, – like a dose of *Viagra*, although I've never had to use it and hope I never have to! Maybe it was Paula's secret weapon – the effervescent tablets. She walked over to the bath, letting her towel drop just before she moved around to the head-end. My neck became half-stiff from watching her movements. She gave me a side kiss and moved my head gently back to the front. Her hands ran lightly over my shoulders and breast, her nipples brushing and breasts pressing occasionally on my achaetous scalp to slide down slowly over my ears. She pressed her fingers softly into the back of my neck, massaging it professionally. After a while I was burning with desire. I envisaged my heat causing the water to bubble even more – like a volcano. She walked graciously to the foot-end of the bath, climbed in and sat on the edge, her long legs in the water and wide apart. She placed her feet on either side of my legs, forcing mine slightly inwards. Thank goodness it was a big bath. I caught a glimpse of the glistening inner lips of her vagina that slightly opened at the movement.

Paula held her gaze fixed on my eyes whilst she glided into the foaming water. Hers were now ablaze. With her weight resting on her knees, she used her arms to pull herself along the sides of the bath towards me, and my *phallus* that was peeking above the foam, showed Paula the way. With an upward movement she positioned herself onto my manhood, finding immediate contact. She let herself down slowly. Oh, brother – this really was my answer to the ten-kilometer run.

The bath turned out to be extremely exhausting. Paula climbed out and pulled on my right arm for me to get out too. We ended up on the tiled floor – allright for a quickie but not for what we had in mind. After giggling and laughing at our clumsy efforts – we kept slipping on the tiled floor – Paula picked-up her towel to dry herself.

'Let me do it,' I said.

I took it from her with the intention of drying her. She pulled it back when I started to kiss her breasts. Grabbing a towel from the rack and throwing it at me, she said, humorously,

'We'll break a leg or something in here, John. Let's dry ourselves and move to the bedroom.'

Her eyes and unspoken words were also saying, I want you, but for more than just a *quickie* – I couldn't have agreed more.

It was dark when we moved out onto the terrace where we had a light meal – overlooking the city lights and listening to the far distant sound of traffic and the very occasional blast of a ship's horn. I decided against alcohol. We'd a lot to discuss and I had to fly back to London tomorrow night. I'd made up my mind and was about to tell Paula about the hunt for whatever ancient relic was hidden. Paula's elucidation regarding her profession put a different light on the matter too. She, or perhaps even her connections could prove useful. I left out the bit about possible Mossad support. She waited until I was finished before she commented.

'I think you'd better wait until Professor Gravestone has finished his evaluation before you make any major decisions, John. But what you've told me supports a lot of theories that are general knowledge and have been the reason for many a hunt in the past. Only the correct coordinates have been missing so far. Many archaeologists, historians and Rabbis think the Arc of the Covenant is still hidden somewhere, if that's the object you're looking for?'

I nodded slightly and said,

'More or less.'

'Look John, I haven't told you too much about my person. I didn't want to appear to be boasting or anything, but you see I take up an honorary Professorship at the University here in Haifa in January next year, just after the winter vacation.'

I felt my eyebrows go up at this revelation.

'My restoration work requires a wide knowledge of history too. Perhaps I may be of help to you. I'm an expert in Hebrew, which is my native language, also in Arabic, Aramaic and I've a general understanding of Egyptian hieroglyphics. I've also spent many a vacation helping out my mother at archaeological digs here in Israel and also in Egypt, Syria and the Lebanon. The latter was during the Israeli occupation. As I understand from what your friend Olaf has told you, there seems to be a connection with a cave or caves in the Hezballah region of the Lebanon between Rmaich and the Israeli border?'

I nodded again. Paula continued,

'There appears to be a connection somehow with the cathedral at *Tyre*. As I remember, the basilica was the oldest Christian church built in the fourth century. I think it was in 326 AD, at a time when most of the inhabitants of *Tyre* were Christians. As you've just said – the corporal that talked to your friend Olaf, told him about a woman who mentioned a 2000 year old trade route from *Tyre* to the *Dead Sea* and asked about a particular cave showing him a position on what looked like the copy of an ancient map. He also told your friend, that he gave a negative answer to the persistent woman, saying he knew of no caves in that position, which he seemingly reverted afterwards to your friend. Taking all this into consideration, it seems if you think granddad's – I'm sorry – that monster's organization is after the same goal, then it's going to be a very dangerous treasure hunt indeed, especially as most of it will take place in the Lebanon in an area that's highly guarded. Have you had any thoughts as to how much that monster knows and how you are going to carry out such an undertaking?'

Paula's last comment hit dead centre.

'That, dearest Paula is the most disturbing part of the whole venture. I hope he only knows, or has just recently gained part of the information we have from the computer he took at Aunt Hera's. Fortunately we made a copy of the hard disk beforehand that he doesn't know about. Most of the other information was hidden in the lining of two old suitcases. The whole lot was in the cellar, as you know, so if Bolkow knew about it he would definitely have removed it before he had the bomb explode in the attic, when he tried to have us killed. Another thing, if he knew about the existence of the information on the computer, he would never have left it in the cellar in the first place. He would've had it transported to his headquarters long ago, wherever that might be. The documents in the lining of Anna's suitcase were ancient. One in particular is very interesting and was found apparently by Ephraim Zuckenic in cave seven at *Qumran*. There is also some correspondence with a Professor in Italy about another piece of parchment supposedly originating from *Qumran* that was bought by the Italian on the black market.'

Paula butted in,

'That's very interesting, John. There seems to be a connection here somehow with the cathedral ruins at *Tyre,* and with *Qumran*, in ancient biblical days known as *Secacah*. They were main towns on the biblical trade route that travellers passed through between Rmaich and the Israeli border in the area you are interested in.'

'That sounds promising, Paula, maybe we'll have to pay a visit to the Basilica ruins. Anyway, from what that corporal told Olaf, the German woman from Hans' class seems to have the copy of an old map. Bolkow and that German woman could belong to the same organization too. If that's not the case, then we have two opposition parties to deal with. Bearing in mind the anti-Semitism in the targeting of Elias, and Bolkow's hatred of the Jews, I think though, we really only have one opposition organization to deal with. Of course, there may be others. Don't rule out possible religious organizations if they've gotten wind of this,'

Paula nodded her head. Her hand supported her chin. She was obviously in deep thought. I carried on explaining,

'I've never yet quite understood why he let the explosion in Leipzig take place at all. Maybe whatever's been planned is now in progress and he was just getting rid of the evidence of his presence and getting rid of us two as well – killing two birds with one stone,'

Paula remained silent – still doing some deep thinking, I guess.

'My reasoning says, if and when we do have to operate in the South Lebanon, then we have to be absolutely sure of the whereabouts of what we're looking for and we'll have to try and make it a quick in- and out job.'

A reaction from Paula – she smiled – probably glad I'd listened to her words of wisdom, and thinking I was following her advice. She took the stage,

'If you do have to go there, I may be of help to you, John. You see, I know the region well. I helped some university friends at some digs there during the Israeli occupation. We stayed at one of the Shebaa Farms on the South East side of the Alsheikh Mountain that belong to Israel, although the Lebanese maintain it's theirs. The Shebaa Jews are acquainted with many secret paths that bypass the Lebanese control points. The Hezballah in the area are not regular soldiers and tend to be careless, even accept bribes.'

'Sounds very promising indeed, Paula – I'd feel honoured to have you with us. You are a mine of information, you know. Maybe we could set up our camp at the Shebaa Farms?'

Paula smiled, pleased her suggestions were being taken into consideration and she was now a member of the party.

Paula cleared her throat – her face reddened,

'John, there's something you ought to know. Years ago, I was more than friendly with Professor Gravestone on a dig. That is, until I found out he was still married, although he'd told me the contrary. He was the first man in my life, John. The friendship only lasted a week and ever since I've never been with another man – not until you came into my life.'

I saw the pain lines form in her face as she recalled the episode with Gravestone and talking about it still seemed to cause her grief. I realized also she was a one-man woman.

'Looks like we'll have to find someone else to replace him – can't have him hanging around and causing you embarrassment. Maybe we could find someone from here?'

I looked at Paula searching for some sign of betrayal. Was she just telling me this so I would make such a suggestion, or was it the truth. I was wrong again.

'No, John, he's the best you can get for this job. Our paths have crossed since. For him, it's as though it never happened, so please don't take it out on him or make him think I told you – promise?'

'It'll be hard, I do promise, but only if he leaves you alone.'

Paula sighed and spoke a bit sharper,

'John, I've just told you he's harmless – okay!'

I shrugged my shoulders and answered,

'Oh, allright, I'll take this private mentioning out of my personal logbook. Let's just forget you ever told me, Paula.' I said. At the same time I was thinking – Gravestone, I'm gonna watch your every movement, then realizing as it went through my mind – bloody hell, I'm jealous.

I leaned over and took her in my arms. We sat there for a while listening to the night sounds and the city noises gradually decreasing. My yawning intensified in numbers. Paula got up, touched my arm and said,

'John, let's go to bed,' adding sheepishly, 'and this time to sleep, agreed?'

The four-poster bed was huge. Mosquito netting covered the openings and deep purple satin curtains hung from each post – tied up by golden twisted flax, tasselled at the ends. The mattress was extremely comfortable. My last thoughts as my head hit the pillow were: *Somehow the flat and some of the contents don't seem to fit to the Paula I thought I knew, especially the bed. I made a note to ask her.*

Next morning I asked her quite innocently at breakfast about her taste. She laughed so hard I had to join her. Between fits of laughter she asked,

'You didn't think this was my flat, John?'

I didn't get a chance to answer her question – probably my facial expression – the laughter continued. After a while it subdued. She smiled and was just taking a sip of coffee when I spoke,

'The bed..'

I didn't get a chance to finish – she spluttered, spitting some coffee out but didn't seem to care – she was off – laughing in fits. In between laughs – Paula tried to get some words out – her statement came out staccato,

'It belongs to my mother – I'm sorry you got the wrong impression, John. I'm definitely not so complicated as she is, you know.'

Once it was out the laughing and giggling ceased. A question mark obviously still hung on my face. Paula carried on with her explanation. This time more slowly,

'My mother inherited the building years ago, it used to be a factory, well part of it became a museum as well. Most of it she's let out to some of the university faculties. She also has some workshops of her own she lets me use. I only stay here when she's on a long dig, far enough away. My flat is in town above one of the shops in a busy shopping street called the *Rehov Yafo*. To answer the obvious question – why didn't I ask you to stay there? The answer is – I've let it out temporarily to two female students, who prefer not to live in the sterile atmosphere of the university students home. If I need it, they've agreed to leave at short notice. Anyway I like the peacefulness up here and I've got my *atelier* next door,' she said, smiling – hoping she'd answered any questions that had formed in my head.

There was one she hadn't answered that I popped,

'Do you always sleep in the four poster?'

She laughed, heartedly,

'Certainly not – it's much too big. Mother has four guest rooms. I've more or less taken over one of them.'

A big question started to form, but I thought it wasn't the right time to put it. Perhaps my *bunch* could use one of the working rooms when we come over! I guess I'll have to wait a while before I drop the question. But priorities first – I've got to get back to the UK and inform Charles Cross of the immense dangers ahead, especially the betrayers in our midst.

'You'll have to be leaving soon, John. I'll ring up for a taxi shortly. Do you want me to come with you to Tel Aviv?'

'I hope you're not upset dear if I go on my own. I dread farewells at stations and airports and besides, if all goes well I'll be back with my *bunch* and Professor Gravestone sometime next week,' I answered, adding, 'once I can get suitable accommodation arranged in this area.'

Paula took up my cue,

'My mother won't be back until late November, John. You could use some of the working rooms if you like – they're quite large. I'd have to get some beds organised and a telephone installed. There are ablutions and showers and of course, air-conditioning. I'll get the janitor to see about hot water and anything else that might be needed,' she said, almost apologetically.

'Fantastic, Paula – you sure it won't be putting you out too much?'

'Let's leave out the soft talk, John. Of course it's allright. You know you and your men are more than welcome,' and added,

'Let's look at it as our first strategic camp.'

'Well that is really a terrific start – it takes a lot off my mind,' I answered, 'and I like the bit about *our first strategic camp.*'

Paula blushed,

'I'm looking forward so much to working with you and your *bunch*, John.'

She emphasised *bunch,* too – great!

'Don't forget, Paula, whatever we find belongs to you and your country. Some of the information was Anna's and Martha's, so it should stay in the family.'

Realizing my implication we both got up from our chairs and fell into each other's arms. I told her to forget calling the taxi for a while – I kind of liked her mother's four-poster.

Tel Aviv – John Jameson, just before flight back to UK – Friday evening, 26th August

I gave Elsa a buzz from Ben Gurion airport. She was still in a negative mood, even though her news about Hans and Elias seemed positive. I got a fairly detailed rundown.

'Both lads are now recovering fast, John. The girl is still very weak. She speaks to me quite a lot, you know. Ken told me before he left, he was going to send in his men to interview them when they get better. Well, they were here this morning and have been able to obtain a clear picture of the events leading up to the kidnapping of Elias and Elena and the attempted murder of Hans. It's now clear a German woman called Frieda Schulz was the leader of the terrorist group involved. Can you believe it, she was a member of Hans' class in Damascus. Elena says there was definitely another German man in the group who mostly spoke German, sometimes in broken English and badly pronounced Arabic. She says he was very polite. He kept the others from harming her. He nearly killed an Arab who tried to rape her. Frieda Schulz told him off in front of everyone and raved at him in English saying she, Elena, was going to be beheaded anyway. Elena breaks down quite a lot, you know. I've told Hans he has the same father as Elias, John. He's very angry with me. I think it has cooled his relationship with Elias too. Maybe he needs more time. How are things your end?'

'Well I got things arranged and if all goes well I'll be back over sometime next week.'

'That's not so good, putting yourself in danger again. I told Hans he should come back with me to Germany – he's not going to get better here, that's for sure.'

'What was his reaction, Elsa?'

'He's still sore, but I know my son – he'll come with me, I'm sure of it.'

'Well let's hope you're right, Elsa.'

Looks like Elsa's pissed off, I thought.

'Bye the way Elsa, how's Olaf?'

'Oh, Olaf – well Olaf's back home now and he keeps on at me about *Tyre*. Give him my love when you ring him up. He's still expecting your call,' she said, venomously.

'Sorry Elsa, I haven't been able to manage it. I'll ring him up as soon as I can. I'll give you a ring in Germany next week then, maybe you'll be home by then.'

'I bloody well hope so, John.'

'Well, bye for now, Elsa.'

'Bye, John – I miss you. Take care!'

My heart did a double beat – somehow I missed Elsa too, but I'm sane enough to acknowledge the danger. My next call was to Charles Cross – his private number. It was very brief. He's going to pick me up at Heathrow with an escort.

John – back to London, Friday night, 26th August

Charles Cross was waiting next to the passport control vestibule. He came forward and led me through to a separate room. He remained standing, looks of anticipation and anxiety creased his features.

'Not in here Charles,' I said, 'We'll have to go elsewhere. Not my place either, any suggestions?'

'I've already made arrangements – that bad is it? Anyway, let's get your luggage first, eh!'

I grabbed my bags from the luggage conveyor after standing around for another fifteen minutes eyeing my fellow passengers suspiciously. Charles waited discreetly near a couple of security guards. We walked out to a separate security area and got into his car.

'How many back-up teams have you got arranged Charles?'

'Three, John – I knew when you rang, it must be bloody important.'

'Have you got a tech-ops van with you, possibly with jamming equipment aboard?'

Charles grinned,

'Thought you'd ask. Yes, we've got our latest high tech special tech-ops van just up the road, so don't bloody fret.'

'You know as well as I do, Charles, the people we're up against will be prepared and will try to break up the team.

They probably believe I now possess information that might endanger their game, if they know where I've been. Oh, and don't let your men use the official radio communications network.'

'For Christ's sake, John! Don't tell me how to do my job. I'm not a bloody rookie you know. We've a prearranged code for using the cell phone and also for the location I've chosen.'

'Okay, Charles, then I don't have to remind you it's only small talk on the journey. No mention about my last whereabouts or contacts,' I said, without further ado.

'Bloody hell, John – it must be hot stuff. I've never seen you like this before.'

'Let's concentrate on the task ahead, Charles. You don't happen to have any extra armoury for me, by any chance?' I asked, dryly.

Charles spoke to the driver,

'Give him something to keep him quiet will you Graham, but make sure the safety catch is on,' he said, dryly.

A tedious task lay ahead, we both knew that, but it was too important to have us eavesdropped either from his car or from any other location. We drove in silence. Obviously my penetrating nagging had served its purpose.

Twenty minutes later we arrived at what he called a suitable location – his sister's place at Hounslow West. When we got there, I noticed the tech-ops van and other obvious vehicles. They were the only ones in the street that were occupied – how conspicuous – it's always the bloody same. I got out of the car on the driver's right side. On an impulse I bent down to pull up my socks. I heard a *ping..* and felt the air movement of a high-velocity round pass just above my head from left to right,

'Down, down, down!' I shouted, adding, 'sniper,' as loud as I could.

Charles threw himself in the gutter the instant I shouted. He must have felt the air rush of the bullet too. The sniper must be using a high velocity rifle with a silencer and a telescopic night vision lens, I thought. I didn't hear the shot.

Graham, the driver, wasn't crouching low enough. The next bullet made its way through the left hand door window, out the window on the driver's side and hit him just above the left ear. Three other bullets followed at my end, missing their mark, thank God. The assailant was shooting blind through the car.

I remained crouched as small as I could get behind the right rear wheel, hoping Charles's team would be on the move. In my crouched position I made signs with my hand to his men, pointing in the direction where I thought the bullets originated. The minutes seemed to fly until the all clear was given. They came to the car and gave us cover as we hurried over to his sister's house. Charles called out a special ops murder squad from New Scotland Yard to cover the shooting and oredered his men to remain at their posts and keep an extra eye on the special ops van too, until the murder squad arrived. He made it quite clear we were not to be disturbed in the house.

We weren't involved in any of the crime scene activity – he was obviously keeping my name out of this.

It was quiet in Helen's house – it hadn't always been. Helen was a policewoman before she got married and had children. They now had their own families and were spread about the globe. Helen's husband died of cancer a few years back. Helen placed a large tray with teapot, big mugs etc., and a pile of sandwiches on a side table. With a, 'Dig in and help yourselves,' she left the room closing the door quietly.

Charles and two of his men were present as I passed on the information given to me by Ben Goldmann. The scene was recorded on video camera by one of the men. When I finished reporting all I'd learned about traitors and moles, Charles asked a question,

'What was your impression about the information, John?'

'Coming from the Mossad – absolutely one hundred percent. The information concerning Joshua Grossman, who was, or is one of their agents, shows something deeper has happened, is happening or is about to happen in the Mossad set-up. My bet is, it has something to do with 9/11. Ben Goldmann gave me to understand they have their situation under control and as far as they're concerned Joshua Grossman is *persona non grata*. If we don't get rid of him they will. They don't want him to appear in any court though, that's the impression I got. The other information concerning John Scarlotti is very alarming. I'm afraid it's all in your hands now Charles. What Ben Goldmann did give me was a bank safe where you'll find enough evidence to support all accusations against Scarlotti. How you get at the information is your business. Here's the address,'

Charles accepted the slip of paper and said,

'I am accepting evidence given to me by John Jameson. The information written on this slip of paper is as follows:

UBS Bank, Zuerich, Schweiz

Konto-Nummer 78936-JS-5861

Erkennungs-Code: Alex-7891

Thank you John. Is there anything else you can add?'

'Well, Jack Orlowski should be no problem. I was wary of him anyway and have taken some steps that in the end will cause him to hang himself. Tom Atkins is a liability – once Scarlotti is taken care of he ought to be moved to a less sensitive area. I think you should have a *parlez* with Kenneth Woodward who is responsible for the Mossad in Europe. As I understand, they are willing to cooperate with us especially regarding the danger from possible dirty bombs or direct nuclear attacks. Here's his number in Berlin, should you want to contact him. Oh, yes, and for the record – I shall be taking the holiday I started when I was called out by Tom Atkins to give that briefing on Nazi-Terrorist links, and since I seem to be on someone's hit list I'd like to avoid naming my destination.'

I leaned forward and grabbed a sandwich from the table, not listening to Charles repeating Ken's telephone number to the video camera. As far as I was concerned, I was finished – I'd done my share. The sandwiches were in quarters so I shoved the whole quarter into my mouth in one go.

Charles gave an order. The video camera was switched off. That was the signal for the others. They dived on the sandwiches too. I played mother and poured out the tea. After two cups of tea and six sandwich quarters, I grabbed Charles by the arm and nudged him over to a corner,

'Charles, looks like I'm a target now – is there any chance of a safe house for the night? I'll make a few calls myself and have arrangements taken for a private backup from Heathrow from tomorrow onwards. I'll be catching a flight to Berlin tomorrow morning and just off the record Charles – here's my cell phone number in Israel. I'll be moving on to Tel Aviv on Sunday.'

'Thanks, John – I'm really sorry things've turned out so badly. I'll have to be going soon. I need to get emergency plans activated. Look, we've got enough men positioned here, so I think you're just as safe here than moving to a safe house that would take some organising and under the circumstances just possibly what the people we're up against are hoping you'll do. Helen has plenty of room now the boys have left.'

'Aye, okay, Charles – that'll be fine.'

Charles left with his men shortly after our conversion. I

gave Chris Fenton a ring and told him briefly to call out the cavalry to meet me at Heathrow tomorrow morning. Just as I was about to ring off I suddenly remembered Gravestone. I added, we'd not be taking Gravestone with us to Israel – I'd tell the guy personally when I get there tomorrow. I also put the dreaded question,

'Will you be available for the next four weeks, Chris?'

'Well, I'm glad you're not taking me for granted John. It's a blessing we've got Internet, ain't it! Otherwise you wouldn't 'ave me at all,' he replied in his strong cockney accent and gave a chuckle, 'I've got me missus doing my end in London, John – she hardly has to communicate, cause she's good. That answer your question?'

I ignored commenting and said,

'See you tomorrow, Chris.'

Helen and I remained in the living room chatting about old times, trying to play down the situation. She was still the beautiful lass Charles introduced me to years ago and she'd kept her slim figure. Her eyes were glowing and I knew that seductive look too well. She was obviously flirting with me. I think Charles had a personal motive for putting me up in her house. She's a very lonely woman now, but I don't think a one-night-stand would look good in Charles' book if he got to know about it. I wouldn't take advantage of the situation, period, and Paula was waiting in Haifa. Besides, there was also a van outside with high tech equipment. They would hear every breath from this house and they'd be watching the thermal images too. I could imagine their amusement, watching two blotches fornicating and laughing at the particular heat images of the different body parts.

Damascus – arrival of Gustav Bormann, Friday evening, 26ᵗʰ August

Frieda Schulz waited in a car outside Damascus airport whilst two of her Arab cronies picked up Gustav Bormann from the arrivals area. She watched over their movements until they got into the awaiting black Mercedes.

The Mercedes pulled out into the main traffic lane. Her driver waited until another car was behind it before he followed both cars at a discreet distance – fairly difficult in the city of Damascus.

She'd have met Bormann herself, but well known as she was to the Syrian Secret Service, she wanted to avoid drawing too much attention to him being seen in her company. That would possibly endanger her life, because Bormann likes to travel incognito. He also has a peculiar habit of using many guises, so woebetide anyone who caused it to get blown.

The message she received to pick up Gustav Bormann, head of their special services organization – liquidation department – meant they were in for some difficult targeting. Bormann was a perfectionist who stayed in the background. If she made a balls-up he would personally deal with the target and then her. That meant an unpleasant and painful death. Bormann's a sadist, who tortures long, always trying out new and painful experiments – worse than anything she'd ever tried on her victims. If it were a balls-up, it also meant she'd have to take care of Bormann first then disappear. She'd enough Euros and gold stashed in Switzerland and with Helga's help they'd start afresh in Argentina or Venezuela. They'd plenty of friends there. She was nervous and had started biting her nails again.

The cars drove into an unknown location. Obviously Bormann's place, she thought. Some Arabs, who were awaiting their arrival, closed the gates of the compound as soon as their car entered. They pulled in next to the Mercedes and got out. Bormann nodded to one of the Arabs cradling a Kalaschnikov who motioned them into the house – no greetings – an extremely bad sign, she thought. God, I hope he's not going to kill me now for the balls-up in Falluja. Maybe he doesn't know about it, she thought hopefully. Anyway it wasn't her fault. If those bloody Arabs hadn't sent off a rocket into the US base, they wouldn't have retaliated.

She followed them into a room. Her men were refused entry and ordered back to the courtyard. She started to shake inwardly.

'Tag, Herr Bormann,' she forced herself to say loosely in German, as she entered the room and saw him waiting with some Arabs.

Bormann ignored her greeting. He waved her over to a table where two chairs were placed on either side. The rest of the room was bare apart from a grotty bed in the corner.

'Sit down Frieda,' he ordered.

She sat down. Her thoughts went back to their last encounter. Bormann had ordered her to have sex with him. It was the worst sado-masochistic escapade she'd ever experienced. She still had the scars to remind her.

Bormann walked over to the table and made the motions of sitting down, half smiling. Halfway down he wavered in midair, his gloved hand rushed out and smashed across the side of her head with such force it knocked her off the chair.

Her nose was bleeding and the welt forming around her eye caused it to water.

'You stupid woman, who do you think you are?'

He went around to her side and grabbed her by the hair. He pulled her head back and shouted at her. Drops of spittle spattered into her eyes,

'You bloody bitch. Your private escapades endanger our cause,' His tone suddenly changing to the quiet sadistic purr she remembered so well, 'you are very fortunate, though. The Fuehrer has explicitly asked for you to remove two most dangerous persons. Otherwise I would now be taking the greatest pleasure of dissecting you alive for going after the son of one of our closest Mossad friends, you stupid bitch.'

He turned to the others in the room and said,

'Get out, all of you.'

They left the room hurriedly.

'Now dear Frieda, you are going to show me how lucky you are to be alive and how much you appreciate your friend Gustav Bormann being the cause for your well being. I think you know the rules. I've had a tiring day and now I expect some special leisure before I give you your new instructions.'

Frieda knew what was coming. This sadistic bum-fucker is going to leave some more scars. This time, though, she knew once she'd carried out her new orders from the Fuehrer, she was definitely going to kill this bastard – maybe tie him up and cut him up in pieces slowly, making sure he kept awake, giving him back what he's done to me and others.

London – Heathrow, John Jameson, Saturday morning, 27th August

The night at Helen's was short. It was past three before I got to sleep. I was extremely tired yet my mind was still abuzz with countless unanswered questions. I had the tendency of working out some problems during sleep, so I made a half-hearted attempt at persuading my subliminal system not to overdo it before my head hit the pillow. I drank too much black tea before going to bed – a bad British habit, probably what kept me awake. That added an extra trip to the loo to contend with as well. I was glad I didn't collide with Helen on the way – she could have mistaken my hard-on for a gun. It wasn't the first attempt on my life, but this time I was a little paranoid because I suspected some of my old colleagues at MI6 might be involved. It was fairly obvious those on Ben's list would go to any lengths to eradicate any dangers and I was number one on their list. The thing that annoyed me most was, that establishment staff were being misused – unaware their orders were coming from traitors. I dosed mostly, my mind not even in a subconscious state – going through many scenarios until it was time to get up.

Charles Cross sent an escort to pick me up at Helen's place and take me to Heathrow. I was thankful for that. Now the information's out I may still be on somebody's list but perhaps not so much of a priority any more. We drove directly into one of the airport's special security areas. Charles and a number of armed special ops men escorted me to a secure VIP lounge.

I gave Charles the names of my *bunch* that were due to fly with me. He assured me he would arrange for them to be escorted into the same lounge when they checked-in. I said cheerio to Charles and wished him luck, hoping next time we met we could have a real binge together without the fear of someone slitting our throats or burning holes in our heads.

On parting, Charles said,

'It is vital we keep in constant contact!'

Berlin – the Agency and Chris Fenton – Saturday morning, 27th August

I was very glad indeed when the *bunch* was congregated in the secure VIP lounge at Heathrow – all accounted for. I gave them a short briefing regarding the attack on my person at Hounslow, leaving out Graham, stating we were now on red alert. Further information would be given when we reached appropriate premises. They all knew what that meant. I motioned for two ex SAS men to come over to the corner window where I was now standing.

John Wilson and Jack Ripple, the latter better known as Jack the Ripper – both single – a good two-man team I trusted.

'John, Jack – I need you both to cover my back from now on until I give you the word to back-off, okay?'

'Sure Jock,' said JW, without a change in expression.

'It'll be a pleasure, Jock,' said Jack the Ripper, grinning all over his face, knowing what the consequences for me would be. I couldn't go for a pee now without company! We'd agreed on nicknames years ago – it helps to differentiate when there are too many identical Christian names. Besides it helps to confuse outsiders in certain tricky situations. I accepted Jock, which is the general name for a Scotsman anyway. Only Chris calls me John.

'When we get to Berlin, you'll be accompanying me to *the*

Agency. The others will be going to the hideout. Okay? I'm going to have a nap now until the flight's called up.'

They nodded. I made my way to an alcove and a very comfortable looking sofa. As I dosed off, I reminded myself to give them the latest on Martin Cole. I hadn't a clue when the funeral would be, or if I would be attending. Maybe I'll have to send a couple of the lads to represent the *bunch*.

It was two pm by the time we arrived at *the Agency*. I didn't expect to encounter Jack Orlowski, so I was very surprised when he came forward to meet me at the secure gates on my floor. The security guard at the ground floor entrance, a new guy I noticed, had probably given him a tip.

'You're not bringing these men in here John, I forbid it,' he said.

'How come you knew I'd be coming this afternoon, Jack. I haven't told anyone here,' I said, wondering how he was going to squeeze out of that.

'I, eh, heard the news about the attack in London and made a few phone calls,' he replied, obviously realizing I might ask him whom he'd phoned. I didn't need to – I knew already from Ben Goldmann he was a traitor.

'Jack, I think you'd better decide where your loyalties lie. Perhaps the next ISIA board meeting will discuss that question. I think you've gone a bit too far, trying to make me *persona non grata* in my own country. I know you don't like my working style, expecting reports on every move I make. You seem to have all the time in the world to be able to bombast some of your employees with more than ten emails a day. You know something, that's a sign of weakness, shows you can't communicate eye-to-eye with your employees. That's why most of them ignore you, or don't bother to look you up for advice.

Well Jack, I'm now going to take the four weeks holiday you interrupted. Oh, and you seem to forget too, I still have a lot of influential friends in the UK. Now get out of my way, I have some official business to do.'

'Not in here, anymore, John,' he said, smirking, 'You no longer have access privileges, I've suspended you from duty.'

'Ah, you have, have you,' I said, 'Well then, I want it in writing, if you please and have it sent to my London address by registered mail.'

With that I turned about, leaving a white-faced Jack standing behind the bars of the secure area. Funny I thought – he looks good behind bars! I left the building, hoping I'd provoked that Yankee twit enough. I could have laid it on a bit thicker, but he just wasn't worth it. Fortunately, I'd transferred enough Euros from *the Agency* expense account to cover our venture in Israel immediately after Charles had informed me Jack had been stirring things up against me. Experience had warned me something like this would happen. The years of training and working in the intelligence field has indeed impregnated my system – a useful basis for survival. Always be prepared for eventualities! I had already laid a trap for Jack. My revenge is nearing. What he didn't know – all interactive information within his so-called secure stand-alone system was being transferred to a third location outside. I'd done that before Ian was killed and Martin was declared missing. I'd never put any trust in Jack, right from the beginning. I could enter his system from the outside any time, using a special super-user code I'd embedded in his kernel. I re-programmed and re-generated his operating system before hearing him brag about his changes shortly after Ian's murder. Jack has always underestimated me. My adrenaline level was up, that was for sure and I certainly didn't want to know what my blood pressure was at the moment, probably 200-120. My aim in provoking Jack was, he'd get over-nervous and make contact with his cronies via *the Agency* system, either by telephone or Internet. The latter was my best bet. I had a double computer mirrored system in a concealed room in a safe house sensitive to every interactive movement Jack made in his computer system and logged every *bit* of information. The room in the safe house was also soundproof. No one knew about it, not even Chris. The system was running twenty-four hours a day. Both operating systems were Unix based and had been quite expensive. Jack hasn't even a clue they exist even though they were bought from the Berlin *Agency* account. The next person on my list was Gravestone.

We made our way to my hideout in silence. I could see Jack the Ripper and JW were itching for an explanation. They knew by now they wouldn't be getting one today. Gravestone wasn't there when I arrived,

'Hi, Chris! Where's Gravestone?' I asked.

''Ows about a what's up mate, allright mate or somefink,' replied Chris, seemingly annoyed.

'Sorry Chris, let me put you in the picture. I'm worried about our project getting into the wrong hands. You see, we'll be working from a place in Haifa I've already arranged and the lady who owns the place had an affair with Gravestone. He apparently lied about his marital status. I'm going to have to leave him here and get some professional help in Israel.'

'Bloody hell, John – that's a bit rough ain't it. I mean, ee's only been ´ere a few days and ee's been workin' ´ees ´ead off, blimey,' said Chris, in his East End slang – his pronunciation deranged – obviously upset.

'Look, Chris, I know you arranged to have him help us and it's a bit late in the day to send him home, but believe me the whole thing's too important to have personal problems upset the whole thing. If you like, I'll tell him,' I said.

'Bloody right you're gonna tell 'im,' he said.

I was a bit disturbed at Chris's reaction.

'Tell me, Chris is there something I should know about Gravestone that you're holding back?'

Chris's face turned cherry-red. He didn't say anything.

'Let's talk about it shall we, Chris,' I said softly, trying to take the wind out of his sails.

'You know the score, Chris – no secrets – so out with it now and no more beating about the bush.'

'Sorry John, I wasn't sure but I think I've seen him in the company of the new MI6 lot, more than a couple of times. I asked him straight-out. He denied it, so I thought it wasn't worth mentioning. I thought maybe I was wrong,' he said.

This time Chris's pronunciation was nearly Queen's English. He's got over whatever's been biting him, I thought.

'You weren't wrong Chris, and that's the main reason I don't want him with us. So let's assess the damage he may have caused us. What does he know, and has he taken any of our stuff into his possession?'

'Not that I know of, John – there's always been someone with him. I put everything not in direct use into your safe and made copies. I had one of the lads put them in the safe at your safe house. It looks like I can't really tell you what he hasn't looked at.'

'Hmm,' I murmured.

'I'm sorry, John. Seems he was very keen. I should have known, even as a professor he was too inquisitive, now I come to think about it.'

'Did he make any separate notes?' Chris.

'I'm afraid he did, John. He used a thick notebook now and

again. Now I come to think about it, his note taking was extremely acquisitive yesterday, more than on previous days. He went through everything very quickly looking for something in particular. He cursed now and again too.'

'Was he in today, Chris?'

'Nope! Said he had some private business to attend to in Berlin.'

'I have a feeling he may not be coming back here at all, Chris. If he does, then I'm going to get a couple of the lads to grab that notebook, discreetly of course. Now, where is the bastard staying, Chris?'

'He said he rented a house near *Zehlendorf*. Here's the telephone number he left.'

I made a note of the number. Thank goodness it wasn't a cell phone. Our chances of locating him with a cell phone with my reduced resources were low. It's going to be difficult enough getting the telephone address especially on the weekend. I didn't have *Agency* status anymore, so I couldn't go through normal police channels. I did have one contact at German Telecomm in Berlin I think may be of use. I gave her a ring on her private number – it was worth a try.

Whilst we waited for her return call I asked Chris when he'd last done a security sweep for bugs and other eavesdropping devices.

'Yesterday, John,' he answered, then swore,

'Jesus, Joseph and Mary!'

He didn't say any more – we remained silent, hoping Gravestone hadn't left any bugs behind. I went over to the shelf where our bug-detector lay. I looked at it without picking it up, searching for any telltale tampering. My mind registered the object in question – my brain was looking for an image to compare it with. My intuition was moving my thoughts even further – Ulster – Belfast – Leipzig – booby traps and high explosives. Without touching it, I looked at it from all angles. I saw a flat piece of material – sort of cardboard looking, about 15 centimetres long and a centimetre thick that seemed to be stuck on the bottom. I didn't have to look any further. I walked over casually to Jack the Ripper and JW and whispered in their ears,

'We have a bomb scare, possibly booby traps. Get the *bunch* out of here and make sure they have their safety catches off when they go outside. Do it quietly and tell them not to touch or take anything that's lying about they didn't bring with them this morning, even if it belongs to them. Tell them to just leave and get them to check the cars before they get in and drive off a safe distance.'

They nodded and went into the other room.

I looked at Chris, pointed to the bug-detector and made a sign of cutting my throat. Chris looked dumbstruck. My only hope was there were no cameras watching us right now, especially if there were explosives attached to detonators that could be set off by a remote control signal. Christ, what a situation. I did a quick visual around the room – no deal – I couldn't detect any hidden cameras. I thought hard – no, I didn't think Gravestone or whoever laid the devices would be stupid enough to use cameras. He, or they, knew they were dealing with experts with trained eyes for such objects. It could only be a minimum amount of bugs – I hoped. I motioned Chris with my thumb to leave too. He shook his head defiantly and motioned me over. I went over. He whispered into my ear,

'John, you bloody twerp, I'm the best bomb disposal expert you'll ever get and you're thinking of sending me out?'

'Sorry Chris, I was just thinking of your wife and grandchildren. It certainly would take a lot off my mind if you helped me deactivate any devices we find.'

'Me help you! You twit – you mean you help me! Now let's get on with this before I start shouting.'

We found three booby-trapped devices. All were items normally in daily use. It was pure luck nobody'd thought of using them today even though it's Saturday. Fortunately we didn't find any hidden bugs or mini-cameras. It was slow progress de-activating and defusing the booby traps. One of the devices was in a small plywood tea chest, so we weren't sure if it had an anti-handling mercury tilt switch under it. Move it a couple of millimetres and it would blow up.

'Remember those *'Castlerobins'*, John?' asked Chris.

'Aye, Chris – Belfast, eh.'

'Are we up against the bloody IRA, John. Does Gravestone use some of those maniacs, do you think? Got borin' for 'em, eh – nothing more to blow up in Ulster, eh!'

Chris was obviously letting off air. It was a wearying task – we were technically at an advantage but still had to dismantle all of the devices to check their insides for double or triple activators and detonators. There was enough Semtex inside or attached to each device to blow my hideout to smithereens. All in all – it took us four hours.

'Not bad going, eh, Chris,' I said, trying to cheer him up.

'You're a dangerous man to have around, John,' he replied, 'One of these days you're gonna get me killed.'

'Not if I can help it, Chris,' I said.

'That's just the point, John,' he replied, and sighed.

I sent Chris outside to give the all clear just as my cell phone rang. It was my special friend from the German Telecom, with good news. The lads toddled back in.

'Okay, lads – we've got Gravestone's address. Before we go

after him, just a few bits of information. I was given some very powerful information about traitors that I was fortunately able to pass on to the right people in the UK. I told you already, someone made an attempt to take me out. Well, just before they tried to blow my head off with a high powered rifle, Graham Baxter from special ops got a bullet in the head.'

An angered rumble went through the group – I continued,

'We're going on to Israel tomorrow on a treasure hunt. What we're after we don't exactly know, but it's something to do with Jesus and it was buried just under 2000 years ago. It has to do with the Sterns, that's the family of my murdered wife. It's based on the information we retrieved from the cellar of the bombed out flat in Leipzig. We can't trust anybody in MI6. I have a major contact with one of the British security organizations. Currently there is a major clear-up operation underway in the UK. When we're in the Middle East we have the support of the Israeli Government should we require it. We seem to be up against a number of dangerous organizations that have the same goal and they don't care who they kill in the process. We may have to go into the South Lebanon. If so, it'll be a quick in- and out operation. I've managed to secure enough financial support for the operation to last for about four weeks. When we're finished, even though we may not find the object we're looking for, we should be able to obtain substantial reimbursement. I think I possess the means of securing the necessary information that will force them to pay handsomely.'

I paused. The men were eagerly waiting for more,

'It could be dangerous, so if anyone wants out now, I fully understand and there will be no hard feelings either from me or the rest of the *bunch*.'

I looked around. Some were grinning – others remained stone-faced.

'Thanks for your loyalty lads. Another thing I haven't spoken about is Martin Cole. He was murdered a day or two before Ian Stewart and most probably, and I'm not certain about this, someone in MI6 had their finger on the trigger. We don't know the funeral date because other dangerous characters in the system are pulling the strings. Maybe a couple of volunteers can go if it's within the next four weeks. We'll have to be very careful who goes. Whoever we're up against may use the opportunity and take them out too. Preferably, we should get someone from the UK to represent us. When it's over we'll all go and hold a separate service. By then we should know who the traitors and killers are. I hope maybe they're all either liquidated or behind bars.'

I looked at the *bunch* – counting Chris and myself we were twelve – a lot of men to be responsible for – nobody spoke – not one question. They were professionals and knew they wouldn't get any more specifics.

'Allright then, let's go after Gravestone with three teams and don't forget he's an MI6 agent and will have a lot of friends here in Berlin and maybe he's the one that's just tried to blow us all up.'

We arrived in a suburban area. Plenty of trees and shrubbery and a few detached houses with moderately sized gardens. We placed a car at each end of the street. Jack the Ripper drove ours slowly until we reached the house. JW and I checked each side with my NVD goggles.

Jack the Ripper kept the car engine running whilst I directed a microphone beamer at Gravestone's house. I gave Gravestone's cell phone a ring. JW and Jack the Ripper were both in cell phone contact. I gave the thumbs-up. That meant I could hear Gravestone's cell phone ringing in the house.

Nobody answered it. I let it ring until the call was diverted to his mailbox.

'Okay, he's not answering, so judging by what he left at the hideout we could have a serious booby-trap problem here too,'

Jack the Ripper passed the status on to the other teams.

'The other answer is, he's in there, either incapacitated or dead. Personally, I'd lay my bets on booby-traps. Okay, let's do a thorough thermal imaging NVD sweep.'

Jack checked the house slowly using his thermal imaging infrared camera that was also connected to our small monitor. He did a number of sweeps.

'Nope, Jock – nothing that's alive.'

'I agree! Okay,' I said, 'pass it on to the others.'

Jack the Ripper conveyed the info to the other two vehicles. At one point he handed me his cell phone,

'It's Chris, Jock.'

'Yes Chris?'

'I have a suggestion to make.'

'Go ahead, Chris.'

'We're a bit exposed here. Maybe some of the neighbours have already noticed our presence. We'll have to be quick. Let's have two men cover the house – one just behind the garage and the other at the back of the house. I'll go in through the garage side door. It shouldn't cause a problem. What do you think?'

'I'm thinking of your wife and grandchildren, Chris.'

'Cut out the crap, John. I take it you mean yes?'

'Okay, Chris, but be bloody careful and don't forget, the hideout was our environment and Gravestone didn't have the time or means to lay sophisticated booby-traps, or eavesdropping devices, if he was the culprit. This is his territory and I've a feeling he may have a nasty surprise in store for anyone who tries to break-in.'

Another thought occurred – ridiculous really.

'Why don't you just check to see if there's a key in the flower basket next to the door, or under the mat?'

'I'm not a greenhorn, John – I've told you before.'

'I know, Chris. Do what you have to do,' I said, hoping he really knew what he was doing. There was no time for x-ray, endo-scope or more sophisticated equipment to check for booby-traps – we weren't on an official break-in. It was a question of guessing what type of surprise lay in store and that meant it could be anywhere and nasty.

Chris was right this time. He got in without the place blowing about his ears.

Gravestone was lying behind his desk, a hole in his forehead. He was cold – he'd been dead for many hours. There was no one else in the house.

I sent in another three men to help with the search. Chris and the other two men grabbed any notes they could find. Most of them were from Gravestone's desk, including a heavy address book one of the men found under a wooden potato crate in the cellar – a place not everyone would think of looking. Hopefully it contained some useful information. The biggest find was what looked like an old cash registry book Chris had flipped through automatically whilst checking the books in Gravestone's library. The first few pages were full of inventory figures. The rest was a diary of events, including research notes, comments and conclusions. The latest entry was Friday the 26th August 2005. We didn't find anything that would have given me more grey hairs, if I had any. There was no sign in the house or garage of Gravestone being an explosives freak. Now I have a big problem at hand. Was it one of the *bunch* or Bolkow's lot? If it was one of my lads from the *bunch* then we have an even bigger problem but at least we can narrow it down.

The soft break-in and search took all of thirty minutes during which my intestines were cramped up more than usual. We'd been extremely lucky. I was relieved when we were all under way again without having aroused the neighbours – obviously an area where people don't bother much.

I rang up Paula from the hideout.

'Hi, Paula, we're arriving in Tel Aviv tomorrow evening.'

'John, darling, that's terrific. When are you coming to Haifa?'

'We'll be staying the night at a hotel in Tel Aviv. I've got some things to arrange, but it'll only take the better part of Monday morning. If all goes well we should be moving on to Haifa in the late afternoon.'

'Splendid, John – I've managed to get another six beds, but I'm sure you're more than that. How many are you?'

'Counting me, we're twelve, but I'd like to have two of the men in your mum's part, if it's all right with you?'

'I don't mind, John. As long as they don't bump into our bedroom,' she said and laughed, then her voice changed.

'We will be together, John?'

'Of course darling, it's just a precautionary measure. Once we get the bits and pieces and the hieroglyphics sorted out, things could get hot and I want a couple of guys in our part of the building, just to be on the safe side.'

'That doesn't sound too good, John. Has anything been happening?'

'Well, I'm afraid Gravestone might have gone to the opposition. He was very busy studying everything we had the last few days according to Chris, who's my right hand. Do you happen to know of any Israeli professionals? They don't need a doctorate or professorship you know, as long as they, he or she's good,' I asked, hoping Paula knew somebody.

'You didn't fire Gravestone, did you, John?' she queried, reproachfully.

'Of course not Paula, I give you my word. He's just done a bunk.'

'A what?'

'He's just a thief who's buggered off.'

'Hmm,' she said, the undertone showing she still wasn't convinced or not pleased at my choice of words.

'Well, as a matter of fact I was already considering asking if you needed extra help. I know Steve Rothman, who's got a master's degree in computer science. He's on a project at the university here in Haifa that I can't mention on the phone, but it's to do with the same thing you're looking for. Then I also have a friend who's more my mother's age. She lives just down the road and she's a biblical archaeologist, her name's Carla Rubinstein. That's all I'm afraid.'

'Sounds very promising, Paula – would you ask them, or do you want to wait for me to do it?'

'I know enough to be able to persuade them to join the team, if that's what you're implying, John,' she said, wickedly.

'Go ahead and ask them, Paula, you're certainly more the expert than I am. But don't forget to tell them it could become highly dangerous.'

'I know, John. I'll make a point of stressing that.'

'Another thing, Paula – expenses. I don't want you spending your money on this. I'll bring you enough to cover all our expenses for the expedition, allright.'

'John, what's the matter, you sound worried?'

'It's allright, Paula – just the strain, lack of sleep and I'm a bit tired of flying.'

'I think you're hiding something from me, John Jameson.'

'Look, Paula – it's too delicate to explain on the phone but I'll tell you when we get to Haifa, okay.'

'Of course, John, please give me a ring when you leave Tel Aviv, okay?'

'I will do dear and you take care too, won't you. Please carry that thing we talked about with you at all times.'

'I will.'

'Take care,' I said and pressed the off button.

My anxiety for Paula's safety has increased and she's noticed it. Or it's vice-versa.

My next call was to Ben Goldmann. He wasn't in, so I asked for Judith, his beetroot secretary. She remembered me well. I told her it was extremely important I see Mr Goldmann on Monday morning the 29th August. She made a note and told me to be there at 10 am. I asked her if she could make arrangements with the Israeli air security department for my men and I to be accepted for the flight on short notice without security confirmation and also for a small sealed suitcase to be exempted from security checks for a flight from Berlin to Tel Aviv tomorrow. She asked me to send a fax as soon as possible with the flight details and personal data. She gave me the fax number. I gave her my hideout fax number asking her to send confirmation and the flight security code number for the Israeli airport security. I wasn't taking any chances. Who knows what Jack may have been up to? It was vital we got on the flight at such short notice without security protocols. We certainly didn't want to have the documents, maps and hard disks messed about with and funny questions asked by the uninitiated. That would take weeks.

I went looking for Chris and found him on the ground floor near my boat. He was in a corner looking at some leftovers in a big metal box. I moved up behind him.

'Found anything interesting Chris?' I asked.

'Bloody hell, John, don't creep up like that, me nerves are shaky enough as it is.'

'I'll bet they are. Listen, Chris – Gravestone wasn't the booby-trap maker.'

'I know, John. I've just been going through things up here looking for evidence. Nothing so far.'

'Who was with you Chris, and did you leave the building unmanned at any time?'

'There was always at least one man here John, even when we went for eats, or for a break. Let me think, apart from myself there was JB, Dick, Bob and Mike.'

'Okay, Chris, we'll leave it at that for the moment, maybe the person left to guard the building did leave it, or he had a long nap. Decrypting makes you bloody tired, I know. It could have been Bolkow's lot. We just don't know. We'll have to keep a special eye on those four just to be on the safe side. Let's not voice our suspicions too soon either. Oh, and I think we ought to double check anything they decrypt.'

Chris nodded and looked at me intensively. I think he was looking for signs of mistrust. I kept his gaze for a few seconds, as though we were engaged in mind reading before I smiled and patted him on the arm to reassure him. Getting Chris upset was the last thing I wanted at the moment.

Back to Tel Aviv – Sunday afternoon, 28th August

We had some slight trouble with German security personnel at Berlin Tegel airport. They wanted our special suitcase opened. I presented our authorisation from the Israeli Government and told them, if they wished they could ring up the Israeli ambassador in Berlin and have the authorisation checked with the number written on the fax. The woman in charge was unsure and signalled her supervisor to come over. I explained once more and added there were two important hard disks and government papers in the small suitcase. The supervisor had obviously dealt with similar situations. He let us through. Guarded by the *bunch,* the small suitcase found its way onto the plane to Tel Aviv as hand luggage. At the other end we got through the security checks without problems – we were now in Ben Goldmann's territory.

We spent the night at a hotel near the Mossad headquarters. Chris gave me a list of essentials. I put it in my pocket. In the evening I made a lot of phone calls.

Tel Aviv – Monday morning, 29th August

Ben Goldmann's secretary wasn't blushing today. A beautiful smile and a hearty greeting really made my day. Maybe me getting her boss laughing the other day helped. I can imagine Ben not laughing very often, besides the girl's in love with him and anything that cheers Ben up helps to loosen him up, giving her better chances.

'Good morning, Mr Jameson – everything go allright?'

'Perfect, thanks to you Miss Salomon.'

This time a slight blush did appear. I thought she was a very attractive young lady indeed. I must give Ben a nudge.

'You can go straight in – Mr Goldmann is informed.'

'Thank you,' I said, and knocked on the door lightly before I went in.

'Good morning, Ben.'

Ben got up but stayed at his desk. He extended his hand and said,

'Morning, John – you're back earlier than expected.'

We shook hands. He motioned me to take a seat at the chair near his desk.

'Things are moving rapidly, Ben. Getting a bit too hot in London. Someone tried to put me out for good just before I was about to pass on your information. A guy from special ops took a bullet in the head. Oh, and someone was also interested in blowing us all up.'

Ben sat motionless, apparently waiting for more explanations,

'Maybe you've got a mole in your department who's been passing the word around that I visited you and received vital information. I certainly didn't talk to anyone about it.'

He leaned forward over his desk and countered,

'But you did call Charles Cross on the phone to meet you at Heathrow with an escort. That really is enough for a mole to smell a rat.'

I knew his agents were noting my movements, so I didn't comment on his source.

'Hmm, that's true, but I still think the other possibility can't be ruled out.'

Ben nodded his head and said,

'I agree John, and you can be assured we are continuously looking for moles at our end. Apart from your narrow escape, what is it that is of vital importance?'

'Okay, what I tell you is only for your ears,' I said, knowing he would most probably inform his superiors.

'Of course, John.'

I thought, liar – and gave him a rundown on recent happenings and especially Gravestone's death.

'That is grave news. Looks like someone's pouring salt in your wound, John.'

'Well, it's a setback but what I'm worried about is the possibility of attacks on our team, now that whoever put out Gravestone got what they were after. Maybe they were the ones who tried to blow us up. I'm particularly concerned for the safety of Paula and my men. Paula is armed, but we're not. Is it possible to obtain preliminary gun licences and the necessary armoury for my men and myself for the next four weeks or so? I also thought, perhaps you could supply us with some sort of identification papers or warrant, or some form of authorisation? Just in case there's a gun battle.'

'No problem, John – I already suggested last time you were here I'd give you all you needed. Look, I'll give you a blank permission form to obtain what you need from our armoury. I'll have a couple of my men escort you as it's a bit outside of town.'

'That's perfect, Ben.'

'Take anything you need, whether it's grenades, explosives, RPG's or high tech rocket launchers, but don't overdo it. You'll find we look after our friends,' he said, and laughed.

'We're not going to start a war, Ben, so I'll be prudent in my choice.'

'Take my advice, John and take what I've just indicated. Where you're going you'll need it. We also have the latest in computer satellite communication equipment I advise you to consider taking.'

'Ben, you seem to have had a hell of a lot of experience, why don't you join us.'

'I'd like to, John, but my place is here at the moment. What else brings you here?'

I told him about Charles Cross possibly getting in contact with Kenneth Woodward. I left out Jack and my suspension. He needn't know I'm without official support. I also left out the fact that someone from the *bunch* may have laid the booby traps. After all, Ben had said they were all kosher. I thought I'd better mention what we were going to do with anything we find,

'I told Paula whatever we find belongs to the people of Israel. I think it's their prerogative to decide what should happen to it.'

Ben butted in,

'You really are under the presumption you'll find something in particular, John. I must say, I admire your optimism.'

I ignored his sarcasm – sounded too much like the old Ben I used to know. I carried on,

'You see, I've always thought the teachings of Christianity may be based on hearsay and anything we find, might just prove a lot that's been written in the New Testament is hearsay. So I think it would be wiser if a commission of Rabbis or something similar, decide on its fate. I don't have to tell you what would happen in the Christian world if the New Testament was reduced to a couple of pages, the rest being a tale like *Gulliver's Travels*. It would be disastrous for theologians and many others too. The shear existence of the Vatican would be put in question. That is, if we find what I think we're after. The other major problem is, I believe we're up against a Nazi organization desperately interested in finding the same thing. If they get their hands on it, chaos and anarchy will follow, exactly their breeding ground if my theory is proven.'

'I know, John – that's why I suggested you have a rethink about your weaponry. I also think you are being too presumptuous. Our theologians, archaeologists and other experts have been searching for the same thing for centuries. Why do you think, John Jameson, you're the one who's going to find it. You don't even know what *it* is.'

'Ah, but we have documents and information pointing in that direction, Ben. I also wanted to ask you who I should contact on a local scale if we get into trouble. For instance, if we get attacked in Israeli territory and have to use our weapons and someone gets killed. What do I do about it, who do I contact?'

'I see, John. Well, that's really fairly simple. You ring up the local police in normal community areas or the military if you're in the militarised zone. If you have problems refer them to Judith Salomon or myself. I really am in a hurry John, so you'll have to excuse me now. Come back to the office this afternoon at 2 pm. I'll instruct Judith – she'll have all your papers ready for you. She already has a list of your men. You can then go to the armoury with an escort and choose whatever you like. What I'll also give you is an up-to-date Israeli army ordnance map of the border area and a list of numbers to contact should you have to move into the marked areas. We don't want you being shot at by Israeli troops now, do we.'

Ben was obviously enjoying himself. I had to grin. I was now going to give him something to think about.

'That's great, Ben – exactly what we need.'

I leaned forward,

'Tell me Ben, how much experience have you had with woman?'

Ben grinned back and answered,

'Certainly not nearly as much as you, John – why do you ask?'

'Well it certainly hasn't gone unnoticed that Judith Salomon is infatuated with you. The girl is in love with you, it's as simple as that.'

Ben's face turned red. Blimey, I thought, he's embarrassed.

'Touché, John – as a matter of fact I have noticed and it would be very difficult for me indeed in my position if I let it go any further.'

'It's a bloody shame though, for both of you,' I said, meaning it.

A thought occurred – maybe when this is over I'll invite them both over to my London flat – individual invitations of course. They'll be surprised when I'm not there to meet them. I'll leave instructions where to find the key. I enjoyed the thought of playing cupid.

'When you return this afternoon, I won't be here I'm afraid. Judith will look after you,' he said.

This time I caught a movement around his eyes that told me the guy was jealous of Judith looking after me.

I left the building with a funny feeling, as though I was a member of the Mossad and I'd just picked up my credentials and orders. I was pleased with the outcome. At least they're looking after us. I don't have any funny feelings in my stomach about that, which is a good sign.

I returned at two with Chris, Jack the Ripper and JW. All three were abashed at going into the Mossad Headquarters building – the lion's den. Perhaps I was taking things too lightly? Maybe I should be awed or slightly ashamed as well. Well, I just can't remember if any establishment or organization has ever awed me. Maybe impressed is the right word for it. In the building I told them to wait in the entrance hall. I went up to Ben's office and picked up the papers and maps Ben had promised. They were all in a big fat envelope with the exception of the armaments authorisation. It was hefted on the envelope and was indeed a blank permission with a note in Hebrew instructing the armourer to enter all armaments, ammunition and explosives and any other items we chose. Judith said the escort would be waiting outside in the forecourt. It was like Christmas day when I picked up the others, telling them where we were going and what we were going to get. Chris looked at me weirdly. I could guess what he was thinking. John must be a Mossad agent to get a blank permission like this. I left him with his thoughts.

Following our escort vehicle was pretty dangerous as they drove like madmen. It took us twenty minutes to get there and an hour and a half to choose the right equipment. A team of experts guided us expertly as we explained our situation. They were the ones who really picked out the best weapons for us. The only exceptions were the small arms and computer satellite communication equipment. Chris chose the latter from a number of possible configurations. He also added a number of electronic gadgets to the list. The explosives and ammunition we required were put on a separate list.

'You'll have to go over to the bunker in the other compound to get those items,' said one of the armourers, 'we've informed them already, so they ought to be ready for loading by the time you get there.'

We started loading our Land Cruiser, separating the protective vests, small arms and holsters. When we were finished loading, the armourer drove off in his jeep to the next bunker to get the explosives and ammunition. We followed in our Land Cruiser.

A huge, twenty-centimetre thick panzer-steel door slid open. We followed the armourer in. He pressed a button on the remote control he was holding and the door slid to behind us with a deafening clang. We walked down a wide corridor and came out into a small station where we boarded a couple of open carriages.

The armourer sat in the front carriage and pressed a few buttons. Off we went down a long spiral tunnel. After a couple of minutes it stopped. We got out, slightly wobbly. The armourer was grinning. He pointed over to a ramp where two men were standing next to a wire cage on wheels,

'That's yours,' he said, 'We'd better check the contents then against this list.'

He walked over, with us in his wake. He went through the lot with the two men until every item on the list was accounted for. I overlooked the process. When they were finished the armourer said,

'Okay, let's get this carriage over to the lift there,' pointing somewhere behind us.

We moved the wire cage very carefully. I wasn't too happy with the way things were stacked after they'd gone through checking them off.

The armourer pointed to me and said,

'Okay, you go up with the lift. See you upstairs.'

I got in the transport lift with the wire cage and pressed the upward button. It ascended very slowly. They were all waiting for me by the time it reached ground level. We rolled the wire cage out to our vehicle and loaded the rest of our order into the back. Once finished, and under the eyes of the armourer, we put on our lightweight bulletproof vests and picked out our guns and holsters from the pile we'd sorted out previously. We strapped on the holsters and tested them. Thank goodness they were well worn in and not brand new. Once we were all satisfied we loaded the guns.

The armourer grinned, nodded his approval and pressed his remote control – the panzer-steel door began to close.

Feeling not so naked now, we left. We followed our escort back into Tel Aviv and made our goodbyes by flashing our headlights and pressing the horn before we pulled off the main road into a side street on our way back to the hotel to pick up the others.

I gave Paula a call at 5.45 pm, to tell her we were on our way.

Ben Goldmann – Tel Aviv early Monday morning, 29th August

Ben Goldmann picked up his telephone.
'Shalom, Ben – Jacob here.'
'Shalom, Jacob, how's your surveillance of Goldilocks going?' asked Ben.
'We've been watching Goldilocks since she arrived. The only interesting bit was when your friend turned up. They had a very close conversation on the balcony. Goldilocks is on heat. It nearly ended in a sex session on the balcony. Do you want to hear it, Ben?'
'No, not particularly – I know John likes the ladies. Did he give any indication of not wanting to have sex with her?'
'Yes, he did. Sounds like the guy's turning his back on her.'
'That's all I wanted to know Jacob. Destroy the conversation and log entry. You have my permission. If needs be you can quote me on the log entry black-out, okay!'
'No sooner said than done, Ben.'

'Bye the way Jacob, send the Goldilocks report to me personally. I'm also interested in the debriefing report from the boys and the Nablus woman.'

'Okay, Ben – I'll have both sent to you this afternoon. What about central records regarding the debriefings?'

'That's okay. You can enter those details on-line directly. I'll see to any entries on Goldilocks.'

Ben was thinking, good that his best friend Jacob is leading Elsa's observation. It would have been devastating if Ken got his hands on the conversation. John would be a dead duck and he couldn't do anything about it. At least he was trying his best to protect him, that's the most he can do *post mortem* for his half-sister Anna.

Haifa – Monday evening, 29th August

We entered Haifa at 7.15 pm after a reasonable drive. Rush hour traffic, roadblocks and thirty-six degrees in the shade, delayed us a bit. We were certainly glad of the air-conditioning in our Land Cruisers.

On my last call, Paula had asked me to give her a buzz as soon as we arrived at the outskirts of Haifa. She wanted to be ready to greet her visitors personally when they arrived. I guess she's that sort of person – likes to be in the picture. I hope it's not going to be a Honolulu welcome, though.

I gave a few blasts on the horn on arriving at her place or rather, her mother's. The main entrance door opened and out came Paula accompanied by three others. I supposed two of them were the experts she'd mentioned. The other one was a young girl, probably a student. Paula came over and threw herself into my arms.

I hugged her for ages and felt soppy for a moment. I let go and gave her a peck. She wouldn't let it go at that and seemed to have forgotten the rest of the *bunch*, who by now had disembarked and were unloading the Land Cruisers.

She gave me mother kisses and stopped when I put my arms around her and lifted her around so she could look over my shoulder and see the congregation. She let go – embarrassed. Her face was reddening. I took over,

'Paula, I'd like you to meet the best *bunch* in the world.'

They were all smiling or grinning. So much sunshine could melt tons of ice. Paula went over to them and gave each and every one in the *bunch* a big hug and spoke a few words of welcome. I think they were very touched. So was I at the hearty welcome. Paula turned to her group and introduced us to them globally,

'This is Steve Rothman,' she pointed to a young dark bearded man in his late twenties, 'and this is Carla Rubinstein,' she put her arm under Carla's and turned to us smiling.

'Both of these nice people are going to be helping us with our research.'

She moved to the young lady,

'And last not least, this is Jessica, a student.'

Once Jessica had been introduced, voices started murmuring in appreciation. A few lads in the *bunch* had obviously been over keen – just been waiting to hear the young lady's details.

Paula showed the way, leading us into some rooms at the main entry side of the building, directly next to the car park. There were four rooms in all, a big kitchen with a long massive wooden table and thick wooden benches on either side. A range of landscape paintings hung on some of the walls. The table was laid and some pots and pans were simmering on the stove. A big roast showed through the glass oven door – my nostrils were registering something delicious – getting my gastric juices going. Three vases holding flowers with a variety of colours decorated the middle of the long table. A huge fridge stood apart at the end of the kitchen. Stacked on each side were crates of mineral water and soft drinks. Only two crates of beer though, I noticed. Paula was being careful, that's good. On second thoughts, I wondered what was cooling in the big fridge. The walls were painted in discreet pastel colours. The window blinds were halfway down and expensive looking curtains gave the windows a nice finishing touch. Four comfortable looking beds, a table and four chairs were in each room. The only other elements were metal lockers – leftovers from factory days. At least they had a bit of colour – someone had made an attempt to paint out the ugliness. The rooms were cool despite the heat of the day, thanks to the air-conditioning. The ablutions had enough toilets and showers to accommodate twenty people.

I left the main *bunch* to sort themselves out and proceeded with the others through a hallway to Paula's mum's part. I was the last one in. I nabbed Paula inside the door.

'Thanks Paula, the accommodation is ideal. Judging by their faces, the lads are very happy. They weren't expecting such luxuries.'

'Go on, John. You're teasing aren't you?'

'Honestly, darling, the rooms are perfect.'

'I'm so pleased, John. I got the caretaker from the university to send over the beds, tables and chairs. He also helped out with the sheets and blankets, so I didn't really have much to do.'

I thought this was the best moment to introduce my bodyguards.

'Bye the way Paula, this is Jack and this is JW.'

I thought I'd best leave out the *Ripper* bit.

Both nodded and smiled at Paula, but didn't make any motion of handshaking or the likes – obviously not wanting to go through the hugging process again.

Paula smiled, nodding too,

'I'm so glad you're staying with us. I'll feel a lot safer now with two more to keep an eye open. It's sad to say, but we are always on the alert in this country.'

They nodded again, a sober expression on their faces showing their sympathy and understanding.

'Let me show you your rooms,' she said, her tone brightening up.

She hooked her arm under Jack's, whose taint is normally dark – now mixed with a reddish colour, making him look like a native American. Paula pulled him gently into momentum towards the end of the hallway.

'Here they are. The bathroom is between the rooms. I hope you'll be comfortable enough. We'll be eating in the main kitchen in thirty minutes, okay,' she added, as she walked back down the corridor on her way towards me. She grabbed me by the arm and pulled me quickly around the corner. I was now facing the door to her mum's bedroom and Paula was leaning against it.

'John, oh, John! I'm so worried now – all those weapons and ammunition cases, not to mention those other boxes with explosives. What in the world is going on?' She asked, worriedly.

'It's a precautionary measure, darling – Bolkow's lot and maybe others are on the prowl. I thought I'd be able to keep it to myself for a few more days, but it looks like I'll have to put you in the picture about what's been happening.'

Her complexion changed from pallid to white.

'Paula, we went looking for Gravestone when he didn't turn up on Saturday. Chris says he'd been working intensively the days before making notes in a diary on everything we had, so we got worried.'

I thought that little lie might protect his image a bit. No use blowing his real identity and telling her about the booby-traps either. That would get her worried sick. Anyway, I've only got Ben's word he's a suspected MI6 agent.

'We went to his house and found him dead. He'd been shot in the head. His diary was gone too. I suspect Bolkow may have his hand in it, but we're not sure.'

'Oh, my God, John.'

'Yes, it's bad, I know. We did a fairly thorough search and found a book containing comments and conclusions from the notes he'd made in his diary, so we could still be a step ahead of whoever killed him and stole his diary.'

She was about to say something. I held my hand up to stop her,

'Paula, officially we know nothing about it, because we didn't inform the police. It would've held us up too long and minimised our small advantage. We also didn't want any publicity. That would've been a certainty, I'm sure.'

She was about to interrupt again, but I stopped her by carrying on,

'What I'm about to tell you now, is only for your ears, okay?'

She nodded.

'You know Anna had a half-brother, Paula?'

'Yes, I know.'

'Well he has an important position in the Mossad, pretty high up and is helping us as far as he can.'

Her pallid colour receded. Her expression showed pure amazement at my revelation.

'I wondered how you were able to get your hands on that equipment. That's what I wanted to ask you. Thought you'd broken into an Israeli armoury or something,' she said. A quick smile and then sadness overcame her.

'Poor Gravestone,' she added.

I felt like telling her Gravestone's real profession, but after all he was dead, so the statement wasn't incorrect.

'Yes, I agree. Bye the way, when can your expert friends start?'

'Well, as soon as I knew you were coming tonight, I told them we'd be starting tomorrow at eight-o-clock.'

'Great – the sooner we start the better!'

Her hand moved behind her back pushing down the door handle. She kicked the door open and answered, 'Yes, indeed,' pulling me towards the big four-poster bed. I just managed to kick the door shut on the way in. 'we've got twenty minutes, John,' she whispered in my ear and began nibbling my earlobe. Her hand began fiddling with my belt, so I said,

'Let's undress ourselves,' I said, 'it'll be quicker,' realizing we didn't have enough time for undressing each other bit by bit. I started and Paula followed my actions furiously – trying to beat me.

The dinner was perfect. A young cook I hadn't seen on my way in did the carving and dishing out. She was small and slightly rotund but had a very charming smile – most of the time. She introduced herself – her name was Judith. Jessica and Judith served, helped by a couple of the lads who were all around Jessica. I asked Paula if Jessica was one of the girls from her flat – she was.

Two others from the *bunch* joined the clearing and washing up operation, all centred on Jessica and Judith. It was over in a jiffy. Judith seemed to be enjoying herself immensely, she obviously wasn't used to men helping out in the kitchen, as British men generally do. Paula suggested to everyone we go around to her side of the house where we could sit on the terrace and watch the sunset. I told the lads to take it in turns if they wanted to come and see the scenery. It was no more than one beer each – we needed to be on guard. I didn't need to tell them about organising the night watch – they were professionals.

Paula and I and some of the others studied the sunset. The sky wasn't as spectacular as last time.

A deafening explosion from the town centre disturbed the peacefulness. We watched as a huge bilge of orange and white clouds of smoke bulged up and to the sides like a pancake, followed by grey and dark plummets shooting up into the night sky. Within minutes the whole area around the explosion was covered in a coloured blanket of flames, smoke and death. The horror of terrorist attacks against Israel became apparent. To the guys in my *bunch* it was their cue for being here, what they'd been trained to expect and to fight against.

We overlooked the scene for a while until some of the smoke had receded. Paula and Jessica were looking through binoculars and talking excitedly. I went over.

'What is it, Paula?'

'Oh, my God, John – we're not sure but it looks like the bomb went off in the *Rehof Jafo*. That's where my flat is. I hope Janet – the American student who lives in the flat with Jessica is allright. She was due home about the time the bomb went off.'

The mention of Paula's official address and the time element set off alarm signals.

'What does your flat mate look like Jessica?'

'She's quite tall, about the same size as Paula and also has the same...'

She didn't finish her sentence – Paula butted in,

'Oh, my God, John! You don't think it was meant for me do you?' she asked, her voice quivering.

'We can't rule it out, Paula.'

'I'm going to ring her up,' said Jessica, pulling out her cell phone. Her hand was shaking.

After a few minutes she said,

'That's strange – she usually has her cell phone on. All I get is the mail box.'

'Okay,' said Paula, 'let's call the police and find out.'

Nobody commented. Paula dialled and we all waited hopefully for good news. Paula explained the situation, where she lived and if there was any chance of getting to her flat above the shop. I listened in as best I could and got the message I was expecting. Paula's flat no longer existed. The shop and flat including the ones on either side were completely destroyed. Anyone in there would be hard to find. So far eleven bodies had been recovered. *Rehof Jafo* was a popular shopping area and many had been sitting in a café near the scene.

Paula sat there holding her cell phone white as a ghost, staring into nowhere. I took it from her gently and spoke into the mouthpiece, *'toda',* and pressed the off button. The Israeli police had still been on the phone.

Jessica was crying her heart out. Carla laid a motherly arm around her and moved her into the house away from the horror scenario that would still be there in the morning and for many days to come. I tried doing the same, but Paula wouldn't budge. She let me hold her hand though. It was the biggest shock in her life, bigger than Leipzig.

We sat there in silence for about an hour. It was like looking at the television replays of twin-towers on 9/11, watching the planes hit the buildings, over and over again.

Carla came out holding a tray with three mugs on it. She scolded Paula until she finally accepted a mug. She handed me one too. Judging by the taste it was some sort of herb tea, probably to sooth the nerves. I thought I smelt a touch of valerian. The three of us sat there for a while in silence sipping our tea. Halfway through her tea Paula said one sentence only. It was very clear, very precise,

'I'm going to kill that bastard, Bolkow.'

She had gathered all the spiritual hatred of the world during her silence and had proclaimed it with those words clearly. I knew she would be capable of doing it. I recognised the symptoms – knew them only too well. It was time I did some straight talking.

'Paula, I think we should make the worst possible presumption. The bombing was meant for you. It has the same pattern as in Leipzig, only this time the charge seems to have been much bigger. They may now think they've got you, so I think we should use that to your advantage and let them believe it.'

Paula looked at me as from a distance.

'So much killing, John,' she said, 'those horrible German Nazi's. Will it ever end?'

'Paula, I'm not going to let anything happen to you. What I'm trying to say is, it's clear Bolkow's lot will go after both of us whether we're after the Holy Grail or not and the best thing to do is to stall them as much as we can until we have them in our sights. I'm going to ring up Tel Aviv and make sure your name is mentioned as a possible victim.'

Paula's face was full of anguish, but she nodded, understanding the situation.

'What about Jessica? She knows,' said Carla.

'We'll have to talk to her in the morning, once she's calmed down. If she doesn't go along we can't do anything about it. But that would mean the bastards would intensify their search in Haifa and would eventually find us. Don't forget we are dealing with a powerful group that have a worldwide organization. They know we're here somewhere and they had your official address, Paula. Where do you think they got that?'

'Why, of course, from that heinous devil, Bolkow. He can only be the one wanting us killed,' said Paula, now overcoming her shock, 'and he knows my mother's address too, so they will definitely find us.'

I didn't comment on Bolkow being the only one, others entered into the equation too. It was her last remark that got me worried.

'I'll just go inside and make a call.'

It was past midnight. Neither Ben nor Judith answered on the number Ben had given me – it was the duty officer. She promised to pass on the message in the morning. I hoped it wouldn't be too late. We needed help to secure the area around Paula's mum's place. It's obvious Bolkow's lot would check it out, even if Paula's name is mentioned under the dead. It was me they were after too.

Henri Walker – Munich, Monday afternoon, 29th August

Henri Walker stood on the *Bayer Straße* with his back to the main entrance of Munich's *Hauptbahnhof*. His appearance did in no way resemble the brainwashed youth of a few months back. He was an alert male and an experienced survivor. His senses were aroused by the noise of trams, cars and the general bustle of a multi-cultural metropolis. He gazed thoughtfully towards *Karl Platz*, his brain registering and remembering. Back home at last and I'm still alive, he thought. No stenches. No bloody Arabs shouting around and no flies and no fucking Frieda ordering him about like her slave. You could eat off the streets and pavements here – they are so clean, he thought.

The journey had been murderous and he'd had to kill a few cumbersome people on the way, but it was worth it. He's a free man now and he's got some big plans for some people.

He still remembered big tits Gertrud's address and telephone number. She'd made him learn it off by heart before he left House Abax in Bad Duerrheim. Hopefully she still lives there.

His hand paused before he lifted the receiver. What was his excuse for not contacting her earlier? He hadn't any, other than he'd been in Passau for some time and a bit longer in the Middle East. He dialled the number and waited, listening – a click and then a voice,

'Ja, Schwarz.'

'Hello.., Gertrud? It's me Henri Walker,' he said, pausing between words, hoping it wasn't her mother. I'm speaking like a zombie, he thought.

'Henri?' followed by a sharp intake of breath,

'Not that Henri from Bad Duerrheim?' She asked, surprised.

'Yeah, it's me, Gertrud.'

'Where are you Henri and why have you taken so long in calling?' She asked – reproach emphasising every second word.

Oh, Christ, he thought, she really is mad at me.

'I'm in Munich, Gertrud and I've been abroad. It's a long story. I've always been thinking of you though, Gertrud,' he said, lamely.

'Oh, Henri, I've been so hurt. I thought you'd forgotten me. Look, why don't you come to my place. I live in a flat in Ottobrunn.'

Now that sounds like my Gertrud, he thought.

'I'll take a taxi, Gertrud.'

'That'll be expensive.'

'I've got enough. I'll see you at your place then, allright?'

'Oh, Henri – of course.'

'See you then,' said Henri, not waiting for a reply. Soppy conversations were not his thing.

Henri couldn't believe what he saw when Gertrud opened the door.

'Hello, Henri,' she said shyly and stood aside to let him in.

Henri was flabbergasted. This wasn't the dumpling he knew from Bad-Duerrheim.

'Gertrud, you look beautiful,' he stammered out, his mouth left open in astonishment.

Gertrud smiled. She was pleased Henri had noticed. She'd been slimming and doing physical training over the last three months. She was proud of the results and to hear it from Henri, who's not usually open to compliments, pleased her even more.

'Now come on in, Henri,' she said, pulling on his arm.

She closed the door and turned Henri round to face her.

'Now, who's beautiful, Henri Walker? You're a right good-looker yourself, you know, and such big muscles.'

She put both hands around his biceps that filled out the short-sleeved shirt to ripping point, and still couldn't get her fingers and thumbs to meet. Gertrud smiled and slid into Henri's arms.

It was late evening when they left the bedroom and moved into the small living room combined with the kitchen. Henri was certain. That was the best sex he'd had since last time with Gertrud.

'You know something, Henri,' she said, after the third time she'd come, 'having sex with you is something special. You know why?'

'No,' answered Henri.

'We're both damaged goods, you know, and that binds us.'

Henri didn't answer. He knew she was right.

After supper, Henri told Gertrud everything that had happened to him, leaving out some of the more wantonnless killings.

'Oh, Henri, what a wicked woman Helga turned out to be. I always thought she was too nice to be true. How could she do such a thing? She trained you to be her private killer, you realize that, don't you?'

'Yes, Gertrud, but it took a long time to sink in. To start with they made me think I was the greatest recruit they'd ever had. Well, in actual fact I think I was, so I carried on doing what they told me to do without thinking about it. They said it was for the cause. I know what that is. They are going to take over the world and to start with, they're going to set off a dirty bomb in Passau to cause chaos. After that they're going to set off atomic bombs in Israel and Iran to make the world think Iran attacked Israel and Israel retaliated.'

'But we must stop them, Henri. We can't allow them to do that.'

'I know, Gertrud, but their organization is everywhere now. In police networks, the military, politics, banking systems, religious systems, universities, schools. Every key position you can think of – they've got someone there, waiting for what they call *zero day*, which is going to be soon according to Helga's sister Frieda and I think Passau is the key.'

'But who are they, Henri?'

'They are Nazis, Gertrud. Nothing but stinking evil Nazis and their boss sits in an Atomic bunker in Switzerland. Calls himself the Fuehrer.'

'But why doesn't the German government just make Nazis illegal?'

''Cause the juristic system in Germany has never been cleansed from them since the last war and they're the ones that decide,' he said, bitterly.

Henri knew it was a lost battle in Germany. At heart, he knew most German males have a deeply imbedded hatred of foreigners – passed on by generations of their forefathers and the Nazi's, and even current politicians have always used foreigners as *Feindbilder*. It's so imbedded in German's brains – it's become a natural hatred.

'Come here, Henri,' she said, opening her arms out, like she would to a child.

Henri moved into Gertrud's arms. They both forgot about their troubles for a few more hours.

Search for the code key – Haifa Tuesday morning, 30ᵗʰ August

I was up at five. Paula was already in the shower. I went to the toilet first – then joined her. She smiled wickedly, moved over to let me in and hugged me real tight.

'I'm on kitchen duty John, perhaps you'd like to help me?'

'Only if that means you've got a little bit of time to spare with me beforehand,' I said, lecherously.

The gleam in her eyes and her wide smile was the affirmative I expected, mine she'd noticed by the stiffness of my protrusion, the minute I stepped in to join her. My head shrink in London from MI6 days used to say,

"Sex is the best method to relieve stress and for erasing extreme experiences from memory."

I agree with him. Paula seemed to have put the happenings of last night aside, for the moment. Israelis have a very strong survival instinct. No wonder, after what Jews the world over have gone through, last century and all the thousands of years before that.

The first lot were already in the kitchen at six. I noticed they were all armed. Even Paula had a revolver in her holster that was strung from a waist belt. They were all wearing lightweight bulletproof vests. No one had argued when I requested it last night, even though it was very hot outside. The bomb attack was a big enough reminder that the enemy was at large.

There were so many helping hands that mine weren't needed. I sat down next to Chris, the perfect supervisor for our next task – getting the team organised and directed at finding the codes for whatever is hidden. Maybe I'm looking at this a little bit too simplistically. On the other hand I tend to sort out possibilities and think out of the box more than others. In the majority of cases I've been lucky.'

'How many lads do you need for the analysis Chris?'

'Four, John – those who helped me in the hideout – John Barnes, Dick Knight, Bob Turnkey and Mike Jones. They're the best analysts and programmers in the *bunch*. John Barnes is a religious freak. Knows the bible backwards and I'm not talking about the New Testament.'

'That sounds good, Chris. Will you get them all in the workroom at eight o-clock then. Steve and Carla will be joining us. We'll go through what we've got and see what they have to say and don't forget what we said in Berlin about the four.'

'Okay, John – how's Paula taking last night's bombing?'

'She's put it aside like a sane person. I wouldn't like to be Bolkow if she ever comes across him again. She'll blow his head to smithereens.'

'You're bloody lucky, John. You've got a real princess you know!'

'Aye, Chris – she's all of that and more,' I replied.

'What I'm worried about is, Bolkow's lot will be after you now, especially as they're likely to have this address. It's only a matter of time before they strike, so we'll need to be prepared. That might upset our research,' said Chris, 'oh, and before I forget John, remember we found an address book in the cellar under a potato crate?'

'Yes'

'Well, for a starter I had Dick Knight check out one of the underlined names – Monsignor Henry Bush an American and head of the *Opus Dei*. This guy sits in the Vatican and he's responsible for restoration and the Secret Vaults. Now isn't that something?'

'So we've got the Vatican Secret Service, the *Opus Dei* to

contend with too – I guess that's what you're telling me Chris?'

'You can bet your sister's arse on that John. I'm having the other names checked out too. It wouldn't surprise me if we came up with an *Opus Dei* membership list.'

'Christ, this changes things a lot doesn't it. Well done, Chris. I guess we'll have to inform the others about this new threat.'

Chris nodded, stood up and left the kitchen.

I went back to Paula's mum's big room, brushed my teeth and made a call to Elsa I'd been putting off.

'Hi, Elsa,'

'John, oh John, I'm so happy to hear your voice. Things are very boring at the moment.'

I caught that little hint in her voice, but let it pass without commenting.

'How are the lads and Elena doing, Elsa?'

'Oh, they're much better now. I've booked a flight back home for Hans and myself for Thursday.'

'Well, that's good news, Elsa. I bet you'll be glad to get home after this terrible ordeal?'

'As a matter of fact, yes and no – it'll be just as boring alone in Buchenberg as here.'

'Well, Elsa, don't forget that this whole thing may have changed your whole perspective.'

'It certainly has, John. In more ways than you could ever think of.'

'I know what you mean, Elsa,' I said, realising the conversation was going in the wrong direction.

'I hope you do, John,' she said, a slight reprimand in her voice.

Maybe she's got the message, or at least has thought about

the consequences with Kenneth hovering in the background. I thought I'd better give her some assurance,

'When this is finished, Elsa – I promise I'll come and see you, okay.'

'I'm looking forward to that, John. Hans will be going back to his studies you know, so I'll be on my own.'

I couldn't get a bigger hint than that.

'Okay, Elsa – look after yourself and give Hans my love. Bye,' I said, hoping I didn't sound too hasty, but I had to cut the call.

'*Aufwiedersehen*, John,' she said – meaning it.

I joined the others at eight-o-clock in the workroom. With Chris, his four men and myself, there was Paula and her two experts – nine, all told.

'Ladies and Gentlemen – I'm afraid, after last night's bombing, you should be made aware of whom we may be up against. I repeat, maybe. We are dealing with extremely dangerous organizations. I've split our adversaries into three main groups:

-The first group we shall call ODESSA: This group seems the nastiest and is headed by a Nazi called Bolkow. It has a worldwide network and is supported by Al Qaeda. They may have got what we have and a map to go with it.

-The second group seems to be a mixture of persons from various Intelligence agencies – we don't know who's behind it and some of them may be linked to ODESSA. We'll call this group EUCLID.

-The third group is the Vatican Secret Service, *Opus Dei*; we'll call it EPISCOPE.

There may be others, perhaps privateers, other religious fanatics or even Islamic radicals. We don't know and don't have any evidence of anyone else as yet. You could put the religious fanatics in the third group EPISCOPE. What we do know is, some groups of the *Opus Dei* are extreme. It is estimated that members go to great lengths to prove their obedience to God and the protection of the Ten Commandments. *Opus Dei* has huge clout too in international politics. This has reached dangerous levels, although the Catholic Church plays it down and denies emphatically any allegations of a Vatican Secret Service. I thought lying was supposed to be a sin!'

I explained the political situation, and went into more detail about the groups involved and how we came about the information. I emphasised that my wife Anna and also Ian's girlfriend Martha, both Jewish, were murdered in the process. I mentioned Bolkow and his heinous past and how for so many years he had guised as a Rabbi – also, the bomb attack on Paula and myself in Leipzig, where I was investigating Martha's death. I included the link between *the Agency* and Martha. In fact I didn't leave out much, only the information regarding the traitors Ben Goldman had given me. I questioned whether Bolkow knew about Anna or Martha's valuable possessions. He certainly didn't know about the papers that were hidden in the lining of the suitcases. Chris could voucher for that. The lining had been undisturbed and the papers untouched since they were hidden there. I mentioned the kidnapping of Hans, Elias and Elena and their near execution – the involvement of the Neo-Nazi Frieda and Al-Qaeda – the search and near murder of Olaf, who by pure chance got to know where a particular cave was, that ODESSA were, or are still looking for in the South Lebanon. I left out Olaf's knowledge about three caves – he is our possible plus factor. I gave an account leading up to Gravestone's death, mentioning we didn't inform the police and the information was to be kept secret. No one outside of our little group is to be informed.

'If you have any questions, I suggest you collect them and we'll go through them at our daily morning meetings. Is eight-o-clock OK?'

Nods and positive echoes all round – a good start.

'Okay, then. I'll pass you on to Chris who'll discuss the technical details.'

I made for a seat next to Paula and sat down. Paula smiled and took my hand in hers. She laid it on her lap and held it tight. Chris stood up and went over to a flip chart.

'Thank you, John. What I've done is to make a list of what we've got and on a separate chart the conclusions we think Gravestone made from them. What we have to do first though, is to verify if the information written in the conclusion is by Gravestone's own hand. Is there a handwriting expert amongst us?'

Paula spoke up,

'Well, my expertise is demanded sometimes for checking signatures of master paintings, maybe I can help out.'

'Brilliant, Paula,' said Chris, 'you're just what we need,' he said and gave her the most charming smile I've ever seen on his face. He paused, looking serious, 'Well, considering the conclusion is not a fake, we have a small advantage over the three other groups, unless of course we've got a mole in our midst.'

A murmur went through the group.

'Yes, a mole – why do you think I said that? Well just in case anyone here thinks of lifting their importance be telling someone outside our group then forget it. No-one, I repeat no-one is to be told, do I make myself clear.'

It was so quiet, a mouse would have been heard, should it have scuttled across the room. Yes, it seems everyone understood.

'Okay, now here's what we've got,...'

Chris went on to explain the charts, the technical side and what he expected. When he finished, Clara spoke up,

'I think it's time for Steve Rothman to tell you how important he may be. I think you will be astonished.'

Everyone looked at Steve in expectancy. He stood up and went to the front,

'Hmm,' he said followed by a pause of at least twenty seconds. People were beginning to fidget – embarrassed for him. Then he started, 'have you heard of the Arc Code,' he asked, humbly.

I had, so I mumbled, 'Yes.'

Another 'Yes,' came from John Barnes, better known as JB. I wasn't the only one.

'I am pleased. I hadn't expected anyone here to know about it at all. Well, let me explain for the others,' He took a sip of cold coffee, 'The Ark Code or let's call it the Torah code hypothesis makes it possible, using Equidistant Letter Sequencing – called ELS for short – to examine the Old Testament, the Torah, and to gain information that has led some experts to believe the Old Testament was not written by an earthly being. Over the last two decades extensive research has been carried out with the most unbelievable results. During this period the Old Testament in its original form has been entered into computer text in ASCII form. Many a database, programs and enormous amounts of algorithms have been written and tested with search criteria using different parameters. The results are astonishing. Where technology was slow in the past, modern high-grade computers produce results that are beyond a doubt astonishing. I am currently working on such a research project at the University.'

JB spoke up,

'If, what we've already found out can be correlated, then maybe we can find further information by using the coordinates of the cave. I've read Barry Steven Roffman's book on the Arc Code and he describes such search possibilities.'

'Well that may be true, but there are still some hurdles to overcome. It all depends on the question. For instance, let's say we're looking for the Arc of the Covenant. Because Jeremiah hid the Arc of the Covenant, you can't just ask, *find the Arc, search from Jeremiah*. Giving the chapter alone doesn't suffice, you need more parameters. What we should be concentrating on is finding any hidden texts or pointers, anagrams or anything that looks like a code from the information and documents we have. You see, looking for something you know about that has already happened is easy. You just enter a name and a couple of parameters you know are historically correct and with ELS you get a complete and accurate historic answer that verifies your information because you already know about it. This leads us to believe the Arc Code is correct because we can verify it. But looking for something you think you know depends on accurate parameters to support the search. That's where you go wrong, because you don't really know if your parameters are correct, which means you may get many wrong answers. I think to start with, we'll try out a number of possibilities using the coordinates, together with sorted clues as a starting point and that brings me to Carla. Anything you've got, I'd like Carla to have a look at beforehand. She's the absolute expert on biblical archaeology. Before we use it, or if we use it at all as an ELS Torah search, depends on her pre-assessment. She is also very good at picking out original text and coded text or texts that may be anagrams. She knows her Torah inside out.'

'I think you'll find Dick Knight and Bob Turnkey a great help, they are analyst specialists and decrypting was their daily bread,' said Chris, adding, 'and I think you should put John Barnes with Carla. He knows the Torah like the back of his hand.'

'That's great Chris, which of...'

Dick and Bob raised their hands to answer the question Steve was about to ask.

Carla spoke up,

'John Barnes and I have already had a lengthy discussion on the Torah, I'd be glad to have him at my side,' she said, smiling.

I thought it was time I spoke up,

'Well, things look very promising indeed – the only unfortunate thing is, we have a very strict time limit, so our search should be coordinated. I'd like to have Chris take over that responsible task. I think we should limit our searching until we've correlated and deciphered everything we have. The first thing will be for Paula to check the authenticity of Gravestone's findings and to get Olaf over here to show us where that cave is.'

A few faces showed signs of discernment, so I added,

'On the map to start with,' grinned, and carried on, 'Let's keep our daily brainwork to a maximum of ten hours. No more, otherwise we'll have a few mental breakdowns and that's not meant as a joke. That's a fact. If anyone doing decrypting needs a break, he or she should take it. Okay folks, any questions?'

I looked at everyone. All I saw were willing faces.

'Well that's a good sign, everybody keen to get going and crack those codes, eh? Just a little reminder – no contact with the outside world without permission, okay! Well then, good luck everybody,' I said, and gave my best smile.

Paula came forward and gave me a big kiss and a hug before she let go and went to see Chris.

I realized it was high time to get Olaf on board. I gave him a ring.

'Ja,' he answered.

'Hallo Olaf, John here.'

'Ja, John! Well you've taken your time, haven't you. I've asked Elsa dozens of times..'

I cut him off – knew what was coming.

'Look Olaf, things have been happening so quickly I just haven't had the time. I've been spending much of my time travelling too. I'm sorry but it just wasn't possible,' I said and added,

'Anyway how are you now *alter Knabe?* Your speech sounds as though it's back to normal.'

'Oh, I'm all right now. Nothing's damaged. The doctor says I can carry on pulling out trees until I'm eighty at least,' he said, giving a hearty laugh.

'Well, in that case, how do you feel about joining my *bunch* and me out here in Haifa. I could do with someone with your knowledge and experience. You'll be here at your own risk though, you know,' I said, wondering if I was really doing him a favour at all.

'You're not trying to butter me up, John? I mean you really need me?'

'Well, to be honest with you Olaf, I think I owe you the opportunity of helping us. We've already had skirmishes with the people who we think attacked you. So it looks like we'll be having more. Maybe we'll get those bastards, but let me warn you – real bullets have been flying with fatal results.'

'That does sound like you need me. Give me your address and telephone number and I'll be over there as soon as I can. I think I'll manage to get a priority flight seeing as Hans is still in an Israeli hospital.'

'I'll take care of that Olaf. You'll get your flight, don't worry. I'll give you a call and let you know your flight details. I'll get a couple of the lads to pick you up from Ben Gurion. How does that sound?'

'That's perfect, John. Like old days, eh!'

I caught the falter in his voice as he said that – still a touch of guilt. I'll certainly get that off his mind when he gets here.

'Okay, Olaf. Mind how you go. Bye for now.'

'See you, John.'

I thought, if I mentioned we really needed the coordinates of the cave that would hurt his feelings. Hope I did the right thing there. Ah, well, let's call Ben and then Charles and bring them up-to-date.

Collating information – Wednesday morning, 31st August

I joined Chris in the information process control room, 'Good morning Chris, how are we progressing on *Tyre*?'

'Mornin', John – well I don't think we've much of a lead here any more. I've some general information referring to Christianity and the mention of it in the New Testament. Also about *Tyre* being the Seat of the Maronite Bishop of *Tyre* and the Holy land, who was also the primate of all Bishops during the Byzantine period. The reference to the *Church of the Crusaders* at *Tyre* about an inscription may prove to be a red herring, because only the lower foundations and a few re-erected granite columns have remained intact. Bye the way, *Tyre* is also called *key*. That's a coincidence, if you ask me, 'cause we're looking for a key.'

'Much too much of a coincidence, Chris,' I replied and added,

'What other archaeological attractions does *Tyre* have, apart from the hippodrome, arches and aqueduct where we might find the inscription mentioned?'

'Well, there's a large necropolis where hundreds of sand stone and marble sarcophagi of the Roman and Byzantine periods were discovered in 1962. Necropolis is a pagan word and means *city of the dead*. Christians preferred to call it a *coemeterium* where the modern word cemetery originates from, meaning, *place of sleeping people*. The only written clues we have from Martha's notes where she refers to *Tyre*, which she seemingly derives from original hieroglyphics and Greek scripts that were in her possession, are:

Bird, Church, Constantine the Great and a *sleeping Methuselah*, but she doesn't say what it means.'

I thought for a moment and was overcome with inspiration.

'That's it, Chris – what goes with church?' I asked, excitedly and paused briefly, not waiting for an answer before I carried on, 'A cemetery! Maybe we should concentrate our search on a Byzantine sarcophagus with the oldest inhabitant, or inhabitants – probably a marble sarcophagus. Remember, Methuselah reached a very old age and a sarcophagus for this sleeping one, meaning dead one, would have to last a long, long time, because a sand-stone sarcophagus with any sculptured or chiselled references wouldn't survive the withering caused by the fierce environment.'

'Bloody hell, John – that's ingenuous. You ought to be on the deciphering team, with such talent,' he said grinning.

I waved him off as another thought had just occurred,

'Another thing's just gone through my mind, when we go looking on the site. Why is *Tyre* referred to as *Key*?'

'I can see you know the answer to that too,' Chris said, grinning.

'Well, let's look at it from a *bird's* perspective because geographically on the map, or from the sky, the sillouette of *Tyre* does look like part of a key.'

'Yes, I can see that, but what are you getting at?' he asked.

'Well, let's try looking at the inscription of our Byzantine sarcophagus with the oldest inhabitant, or inhabitants in the necropolis from above – meaning – let's look at the top, from above, for any inscriptions or any other clues, maybe even sculptured ones,' I replied.

'Blimey, John, you should've been an archaeologist – that's brilliant.'

'Pure theoretical, Chris – we'll have to go there and find out won't we?'

I took Ben Goldmann up on his promise and arranged for two men to go to a Mossad safe house in *Tyre* tomorrow and use it as a base. They were to visit the hotel and fetch Olaf's notes and then on to the necropolis. I had a hunch there must be a pointer of some importance at our sarcophagus otherwise Martha wouldn't have made a note of it.

Olaf Arrives at Ben Gurion – Wednesday afternoon, 31ˢᵗ August

Olaf Ertl was treated as a normal passenger throughout disembarkation, passport and security controls. He waited at baggage arrival and overcame his boredom by studying the passengers from other flights who were waiting at adjoining conveyer belts.

One passenger in particular caught his interest. Being an ex BND agent, his memory was triggered immediately and recognition dawned – Gustav Bormann his ex Stasi *Führungsoffizier*. The bastard who made him turn into a DA and the same shit who got his fiancée put in Bautzen prison where she was murdered.

He made for a phone booth and rang up John. He would have to tell him now, whatever the outcome. He spoke to John, trying to keep his voice steady. It was very difficult because he was nervous about Bormann and also about his past.

'I know, Olaf. I've known for some time. I've noticed occasionally it must still be bothering you. Look let's forget it. I understand the situation you were in.'

'I'm so sorry, John. I've always wanted to tell you but I thought it would end our friendship. What you must know, John – I never said a word about you.'

'I guessed that, Olaf. But, tell me – what the hell is an ex Stasi officer doing in Tel Aviv?'

'Bormann is a sadist, John. He's also a Hitler fan. If I'm not surprised he may belong to the organization we're after.'

'Okay, Olaf – I'll give my men a call. They should be waiting outside for you. I'll also give the authorities a call to have him tailed. If you think he could still recognise you, try and avoid direct contact. I'll ring off now, Olaf – you know the procedure.

Oh, and don't you get my men to follow Bormann under any circumstances, okay!'

'Okay, John – see you soon, bye.'

I gave Ben a call and passed on the details and description of Bormann's arrival in Israel. Ben was the one who'd told me about Olaf's days as a DA in the first place, so he probably still has a file on Bormann. Ben wasn't at all pleased about the likes of Bormann being in the motherland of Jews. He rang up the homeland security department and requested major surveillance support – the whole works. If Nazi's were in Israel then they were going to be watched very, very carefully.

Necropolis – Tyre – Wednesday afternoon, 31st August

Colin Hughes and Derek Montgomery, ex Royal Marine Commandos, moved stealthily to the back steps of the hotel where Olaf had nearly met his maker. They were fairly dark skinned and dressed as Arabs.

The door at the top was ajar. They could see that from the beach.

'Maybe they're letting the flies out,' whispered Colin.

'Or someone's waiting for us,' replied Derek.

They both knew the score. Colin went up and Derek stayed at the bottom of the metal steps until Colin gave the thumbs-up. Derek moved up the steps. Colin went in and made his way slowly to the opposite side of the narrow hallway. He gave the OK sign for Derek who was covering him from the entrance.

They moved along the hall in turns, covering each other, until they reached the reception. An old man was dosing behind the counter. His head rested on the desk in front of him. Colin went behind the desk and poked him with his gun. No response. He grabbed a bushel of hair and gently moved his head up. It was as loose as a rag-doll's. His neck was broken.

Colin checked the body temperature – still warm. Without a word, he laid the head back gently onto the desk and gave Derek the sign for eminent danger. They waited for a few minutes, listening. They heard some noises from the room they were supposed to check. Derek moved forward, Colin followed at a safe distance.

They waited patiently in the corridor, their guns at the ready, silencers mounted. They weren't surprised when the door suddenly burst open. Derek and Colin shot simultaneously. A small dark clad figure, stopped in his tracks and crumbled to the floor. Derek checked the man before picking him up – two holes in his forehead and a couple more in his chest. The door had swung to so he kicked the door open fully and shoved him back into the room – no response from within. The man's feet acted as a doorstopper.

Colin, known for his persistency, motioned Derek to wait. He knew there could be someone else in the room out of sight. That would place them at a disadvantage. In a field battle a hand grenade would have sorted out this problem, but they didn't want to draw any attention to this little skirmish. After a few more minutes Derek gave the sign to give up. Colin negated. He'd just shaken his head when there was movement in the room. A black clad figure ran forward spraying the doorway with bullets from a Kalaschnikov. He got the same treatment as his pal.

Derek stepped over the two bodies and went in. He removed the drawer from the desk and laid it aside. He reached in at the opening and removed an envelope that was stuck at the back.

They left the way they'd come, silently and watchful, their guns now hidden but within easy reach, making their way back to the safe house. A change of clothing and weapons was now necessary, but before that they had a fax to send to John with the information inside the envelope. Their next important visit was to the Necropolis.

Passau – Wednesday afternoon, 31st August

It was a hot day. Henri and Gertrud lay in a barn-loft. They were peering out through a hay-lift opening that overlooked a wide expanse of cultivated fields and a farm, situated on the North East outskirts of Passau where the lorry with the dirty bomb was supposed to be.

'You see those armed men, Gertrud?' asked Henri.

'I can see one, but where are the others?' she replied.

Henri explained to Gertrud where the guards were placed.

'Oh, yes – I can see them now. But they don't look as though they're very alert do they,' she exclaimed.

'It's their job to protect the farm buildings, especially the one in the middle where the lorry is, or was last time I was here,' said Henri and added,

'Don't be fooled by what you see, Gertrud. Those guards won't hesitate to shoot without asking questions.'

Henri explained about the farm, bought a couple of months back by the Nazi group who still call themselves secretly *the Vikings*, chosen because of its ideal position near the city purely for use as a dirty bomb site on *zero day*.

Both traversed the scenery through their binoculars whilst Henri pointed out the guard's positions and laid out his plan.

'There are four guards outside, Gertrud, and another four inside and maybe a few more.'

He laid his binoculars aside and touched her on the shoulder. She dropped hers and turned to look at him.

'Listen, I'll creep up on each one of those outside in the order I told you. You stay far enough away. Once I've got the first one, who looks the easiest, I'll give you a signal like this,'

Henri gave off two soft whistles.

'Okay, Gertrud?' he asked.

'I've got it, Henri,' she replied, adding,

'What're you going to do to them, Henri? Are you going to kill them?'

'No, Gertrud – there are plenty of ropes and an old shirt we can tear up and use for gagging that I saw on our way in. They're lying in the corner near the pitchfork down below. I'll knock them out and tie them up. I'll give you a gun once we've got the first one,' he said.

Gertrud nodded, her eyes now glowing.

'You'll have to keep watch whilst I tie them up,' he added – looking at her sharply to see if she understood the importance.

Gertrud nodded, enthusiastically. She was glad Henri wasn't going to kill them.

'I'll go into the house on my own though – two of us would be too risky, besides, you're not used to this sort of cloak and dagger stuff,' he said, smiling – not wanting to hurt her feelings. He paused for a moment and added,

'Once it gets dark we'll get moving.'

That was Gertrud's signal. She put both hers and Henri's binoculars aside and rolled Henri over onto his back. She kissed him gently on the lips and moved her hand down to undo his belt.

Henri signalled her to stop by shaking his head and adding,

'Sorry, Gertrud, not now – I'll need all my strength for what lies ahead tonight. We ought to take a nap in turns now. We've a good few hours to go, you know.'

With that said, he rolled back over onto his stomach, picked up his binoculars and continued to watch.

Gertrud understood – she made herself comfortable and closed her eyes.

Henri's first target was sitting idly throwing pebbles at an unseen target in the dark. He crept up behind him and with one well aimed karate chop – knocked him out. He whistled. Gertrud came to stand watch whilst he gagged and tied him.

The procedure was the same with the other three guards. Gertrud was thrilled – this was a new adventure for her, especially seeing it all went off perfectly.

The house was more difficult. He thought it wasn't enough just cutting the telephone cables, because they'll all have cell phones. One call and the lorry would explode, set off by remote control from somewhere else, maybe through a cell phone attached to some sort of mechanism acting as a detonator. He knew enough about their methods – he'd been their best recruit and bomb maker. He was glad the gun had a silencer. He'd have to get into the house, play it by ear and hope his senses don't let him down.

He went in by the back door through the milk kitchen. A good choice – obviously a door that until recently had been in regular use and well oiled – on turning the handle and pushing it open not a sound did it make.

He had three throwing knives in his neck sheath and the gun with a silencer he'd taken from one of the outside guards. He'd only use the latter if he'd no other choice. He slipped into the main kitchen and as luck would have it, a Nazi was sitting at the kitchen table with his back to him. As with the others outside, his karate chop fell short of breaking the guys neck. He grabbed his hair before the head could hit the table. He cursed inwardly as the chair scraped horrendously over the floor tiles. A voice from the next room shouted out,

'Be quiet you ass. I'm trying to sleep.'

Luckily it was a curse that didn't require an answer and it gave him a good idea where his next target was. He quietly gagged the kitchen victim and tied him up real tight.

He went silently through the ground floor of the house putting another three out of action. He cursed again to himself at the tiresome task of tying them up.

Upstairs was slightly different. The stairs were old and the wooden steps worn and creaky. Anybody upstairs was now possibly warned. He decided he might have to use his gun. He reached the top of the stairs. There was only one way he could go and that was to the right. Four rooms led off to the left from the landing. At the end was another door to the right. He knew it led up to the loft.

He knocked at the first door and waited. Those who were sleeping upstairs in more comfortable rooms would be superiors and would expect anyone to knock first – Henri knew.

'Come in,' said a husky voice. Henri noted his victim was still half asleep and knew now where to point his pistol.

He opened the door and turned with his pistol arm raised towards the position he reckoned his next victim would be. The guy's eyes were closed again – he was half asleep. He let out a cry of indignation when Henri's gun jabbed against his temple,

'What the hell..!'

In a swift movement, Henri withdrew the pistol and gave the guy a sharp, devastating blow with his fist – targeting the weakest part of the guys jaw. That took the pressure off long enough to get him gagged and tied up. The next two rooms were empty. There was only one left in the last room.

He recognised the person lying on the bed from the Viking training camp – a nasty piece of work. He was not displeased to be confronted with this one. Fritz was his name – had been particularly keen on seeing Henri broken during training and went out of his way during torture exercises. Henri had been extremely hard on himself and held out to most of the exercises, only up to the point where that guy had tried to put his penis up Henri's arse. Helga had admonished him for resisting. Henri told her she didn't know what she was talking about. He'd nearly killed the guy for trying. Maybe he would now.

'Hey, you stinking bum-fucker, remember me?' he shouted.

The guy blinked his eyes open a couple of times, maybe thinking this was just one of those weird exercises.

Henri's mouth contorted into a wide grin – all his teeth showed like a skull without lips.

'Okay, you arse. Up out of that bed and sit on the edge, feet on the floor, and make it real quick, before I decide to put a bullet in your head,' said Henri, his voice sharp, cold and real mean.

Fritz pushed his eiderdown aside and in one swift movement his feet were glued to the floor.

Without waiting for a comment, or to glut, Henri shot him in both kneecaps. Fritz went chalky-white and gasped for breath. He grabbed his kneecaps and held them, groaned and doubled-up on the floor, hissing barely discernable curses and obscenities. After a while he got over the initial shock and cried out,

'Why, Henri, why?'

Henri replied,

'You know why, you bum-fucker! Now not another peep from you, you bastard – roll over on your stomach and put your hands behind your back.'

Fritz obeyed immediately. There was no messing about with Henri Walker when he had that mean look in his eyes. Henri tied him up and on last thoughts, tore a couple of strips off the bed-sheet and bound them around the guy's kneecaps. He didn't want him to bleed to death. Fritz was moaning and whimpering as he left him, trussed up like a turkey.

He retreated down the stairs cautiously – looking and listening. He reached the bottom and waited for a few seconds. Satisfied there were no signs of other assailants, he moved back through to the main kitchen and the milk kitchen and quietly into the dark night using the well-oiled door as his exit.

He made his way stealthily to the middle barn, or so he thought. The chirping of crickets ceased abruptly. He stopped in his tracks immediately and waited, listening and searching the dark intensely. After a few seconds the chirping continued. He carried on towards the middle barn – this time a little quieter. His senses detected cigarette smoke near the barn. More guards, he thought – probably in the barn.

The door to the stalls was ajar. He went through the stalls and walked towards the low wall separating the stalls from the barn. He went forward, bent-down, until he could see through into the main part of the barn. The lorry was there. A guard was sitting smoking a cigarette with his back to the wall, only ten metres away from Henri's current position.

How stupid thought Henri – maybe I should just leave it up to this guy – he'll burn the barn down with all that hay around. No, he decided – he didn't want the dirty bomb going off too near Passau. He moved a bit nearer – just behind the guy, and stood up slowly to his full height and leaned over the wall.

Again, as with the others, a well aimed karate chop between the neck and shoulders put the guard out of action. He jumped over the low wall, picked up the burning cigarette and put it out. As with the other guards, he took the trouble of tying this one up too. He searched the guard for the lorry keys and finding them, went to the driver's cabin, unlocked the door and after checking the cab for booby-traps, climbed in.

He looked through the small back window. He perceived barrels of radioactive waste – dismantled radioactive x-ray parts, sacks of various fertilizers and others he couldn't decipher. The cases of TNT, fuse and charging device are probably at the back. That's where a booby trap will be too he thought. Blowing up this lot would cause a radioactive fall-out and kill a lot of people immediately and a lot more on a long-term basis. If blown up in a town the size of Passau, it would make it unliveable – another Chernobyl.

He left the driver's cabin, made his way to the back of the lorry and unlocked the double doors. Holding the right-hand door firmly, he ran his fingers gently down the inside, feeling for any trip-wires. He found one on the bottom of the door-locking lever. He checked the length of the booby-trap wire. It was long enough to open the door to get in sideways. He secured the door from opening any further and climbed in. Once in, he defused the booby trap. The dismantling of the fuses from the automatic relay card was very tricky because he didn't want whoever held the triggering device to know it'd just been made redundant. Let them think they've destroyed Passau when they press the button. He rewired the circuit replacing the cell phone with his own to be used as the triggering device. Only Gertrud knew his number. He produced a piece of wire from his pocket that he'd found next to the old shirt and ropes and cut off a suitable length of copper wire that he twisted into shape. He didn't have a soldering iron, so he had to make do with chewing gum to join and fix the wires to the circuit card. When he was finished, he went over to the barn doors and opened them wide. He stood at the side for a couple of minutes and gave two short whistles for Gertrud who was out there, in hiding. A few minutes later she joined him.

She hugged him fiercely,

'Oh, Henri, I was so frightened something would happen to you.'

He calmed her down by patting her back and saying,

'It's nearly over Gertrud, nearly over. You'd better give me your cell phone, I'll need it if I have to detonate the bomb earlier. I've just used mine for triggering the bomb,' he said.

Helga handed him her cell phone.

'Let's go get Helga shall we,' he said, a glassy look in his eyes.

They took the lorry and drove over to the *Viking* training camp, thirty-five kilometres, due west. Not a word was spoken. Gertrud had tried when they started, but he shook his head and said,

'Let's not talk, Gertrud. I have to concentrate.'

He didn't want to talk to anyone, he was so sick of *the Vikings* and their plans to help destroy the world. Thoughts of Helga and her sister Frieda misusing him really aggrieved him and made him feel depressed. He'd have to pull himself together.

He thought about Helga's place. Helga lived on her own in a house outside the perimeter fence of the *Viking* training camp compound. Her garden led directly onto the camp separated by a high wire fence topped with an overhang, interlaced with barbed wire. The garden was well concealed by trees and thick shrubbery, an ideal hide for the lorry later on, he thought.

They parked in a hiker's parking lot near a wood, about 500 metres from Helga's house. He gave Gertrud two of the guns he'd picked up from his victims. He had two pistols in his pockets – one had a silencer.

They walked directly through the woods and reaching Helga's house, took up position in the back garden behind some low bushes. He motioned Gertrud to lie down. He did the same. They watched Helga move about in the kitchen. The lights were on in the living room – the patio door slightly ajar. He waited until he was satisfied she was on her own. He tugged Gertrud's arm motioning her the time was ripe. They got up and moved over the lawn to the terrace. He slid the patio door open gently, enough for them to enter.

Their plan was – Gertrud would position herself on this side of the door to the kitchen. He would sit down on the sofa facing the kitchen. He didn't want to pounce on her in the kitchen as there were too many shining surfaces where she may see his reflection and grab a knife or something – he wanted her alive. Should Helga make a move back into the kitchen then it would be up to Gertrud to grab her. They took up positions.

Helga heard something moving in the living room. She opened a kitchen drawer, extracted a small revolver and made her way into the living room. She stopped abruptly in the kitchen doorway. Helga thought she was seeing a ghost,

'Henri – oh my God! You're supposed to be dead,' she cried, and rushed suddenly forward towards him.

She stopped in front of him, the arm with the gun, hung loosely at her side.

Having moved so fast towards Henri, she missed seeing Gertrud on her way in who now closed up behind her and grabbed the arm with the gun. She twisted the small revolver from Helga's hand. Still holding her in a vice-grip, she shouted,

'Get down on your knees, you bitch.'

Helga obeyed and dropped on her knees. She had no other choice because Gertrud was twisting her arm to breaking point. Henri went over to the bay windows, shut and locked them and let the blinds down. He went over to Helga and bent down. He grabbed her blouse collar on both sides with his hands and pulled her up on her feet. He ripped the blouse apart and pulled it down over her shoulders and off her body. He did the same with her skirt. He got out his special knife and with one quick movement, cut off her bra without leaving a scratch on her body.

'Let's go,' he said, motioning her toward the front door.

'But what have I done, Henri? Why are you doing this to me?'

'You misused me, Helga and I'm gonna misuse you now,' he said, coldly – adding,

'Where're your car keys?'

'On the hall stand,' she stuttered – her voice now shaking with fear.

Gertrud shoved her towards the door. He opened it and checked the outside.

'Okay, you make one sound and you're dead. Let's move,' he said.

He drove – Gertrud sat in the back with Helga, her gun stabbing into Helga's ribs. A couple of minutes later they arrived back at the lorry, when it dawned on Helga what that meant. She began to remonstrate,

'Oh, no Henri, you're not going to blow me up. Please, I'll do anything you want, anything. I'll have sex with you and please you with all your desires. Or maybe you want to watch while I have sex with Gertrud? Or maybe you would like to have a threesome? Or do you want money? I've got a lot of money in a bank in Switzerland, you can have it all,' she pleaded.

Gertrud shot questioning looks at Henri – his eyes responded with a faint gleam – his facial contours changing, his loins were bulging a bit too. He said what they were both thinking,

'Okay, Helga I'll let you live if you give me the money details. I'll send Gertrud here to your bank in Switzerland. Once she gets the money she'll ring me up, then I'll take you with me to the other side of the woods and let you go and that's a promise. Now the details please, and don't forget if Gertrud doesn't call, then I know she's been arrested and you're gonna die a very painful death. Remember Fritz? I'm gonna start like Fritz always ended up doing,' he said, trying to scare her, knowing he would never in his life do it. He'd probably just put a bullet in her head. What Henri didn't know – he'd just given her a shock with those words about Fritz. That's exactly what her Nazi father had done to both her and Frieda since they were kids – bum fucking.

'Oh, and another thing – any of your buddies come by then I'll be obliged to blow this lot up including you and me,' he said, laughing, knowing he wouldn't hesitate.

'Okay, Gertrud, let's put some blankets on the ground and tie her up, so she doesn't get funny ideas.'

Henri tied Helga's hands behind her back whilst Gertrud tied both feet together.

'You'd better be off, Gertrud. Oh, and don't ring me up on my cell phone number – it'll blow us all up!'

'Oh, Henri,' she said, rushing over to him, hugging him and kissing him hard on the lips. You do trust me that much Henri. I love you Henri, you know that?'

'Yes, I do, Gertrud.'

'Let's do it in front of her Henri,' she said, excitedly.

'Better not, Gertrud. Let's wait until this is over. I need to stay awake,' he said, pointedly.

'Oh, well – later on then,' she said, disappointment sounding in her voice and showing on her face.

'Ah, well then – I'll be on my way,' said Gertrud, shrugging her shoulders.

She put her arms around Henri and hugged him very tight. She gave him a kiss that told him she was full of longing for him. She shouldn't have done it because Henri got one of his big hard-ons. Gertrud drove off in Helga's car.

Helga had been quiet for some time, but now she only had Henri to contend with. She'd always managed to wrap him around her little finger,

'Got a hard-on Henri? Want me to fix it? Come on Henri – I'm on heat too now. Let me kiss it for you and cool it down.'

It was too much for Henri. He pulled his pants off and waved his dick in front of her mouth. She kissed it and pulled it into her mouth. He was in frenzy – he wanted more.

'Untie my legs, Henri and pull off my panties.'

He didn't budge. She could see he was contemplating.

'Look, put your hand under my panties and feel my pussy. I'm all wet with excitement,' she said, invitingly.

He couldn't resist anymore. He moved his hand down her body and over her breasts. He stopped suddenly at her nipples. This was the first time he could remember Helga with raised nipples. Maybe she likes it hard – sort of brutal! He moved his hand down under her panties. Helga *was* wet with excitement. He took out his knife and cut the ropes holding her feet together. He pulled off her panties and moved her legs apart. He licked her clitoris with the tip of his tongue. Her pussy smelt musky and her secrete gave off an inviting salty taste in his mouth.

'Oh, Henri, more – Henri – ah..!' she moaned and writhed with her backside – moving her pussy upwards and towards him.

He knew what damage Helga's legs could do, especially with his head between her legs, so he withdrew it and with one movement, turned her over onto her stomach and penetrated her pussy from the rear. He went in deep, thrusting slowly and feeling her heat. Before he came he experienced Helga's orgasm. It was a real flooding and left barely enough room for his sperm that followed shortly after. When he was finished, he tied her feet up again. She made no move to resist.

'Henri, do you know, that's the first time in my life I've had an orgasm. What a pity it's under these circumstances,' she said, letting out a slow saddened sigh.

He put a blanket over her and moved to a safer distance. They had a long wait.

It was five in the morning when he heard a dog barking. He grabbed Helga and put her in the lorry. He shoved the blankets in after her. He stretched himself and decided to have a pee at the side of the lorry when a man with a dog came by. Luckily they were in the woods where dogs have to be on a leash.

'Morning,' said Henri, nonchalantly to the stranger as he approached.

'Morning,' came the reply.

'Ah, well, I guess I'll have to be on my way again,' said Henri, loud enough for the stranger to hear and made for the cabin door.

'You'd better not be caught here parking by the police, you know. This parking place is only for hiker's cars,' said the stranger – his dog was growling.

Henri nodded and said,

'I know, but the others were all full.'

Henri didn't wait for an answer – he got into the cabin and drove off – his destination – Helga's garden.

He parked the lorry in the garden – under the trees and well hidden from sight and carried Helga back into her house.

'I need to go to the toilet, Henri,' she pleaded.

'Allright then, I'll undo your legs, but no funny business.'

He undid the ropes tied around her ankles and accompanied her to the toilet.

'I'm so sorry Henri, but I have to do a number two,' she said with a touch of real pine in her voice.

'Just do it. I'll wipe your bottom afterwards,' he said, reluctantly, and stood there waiting.

'You really would, Henri!' she declared, sounding astonished.

He stood in the doorway and remained quiet until she was finished. She flushed the toilet with her elbow, got up from the toilet seat and remained in a crouched position until Henri had wiped her bottom. Henri fetched a fresh air spray from the windowsill and sprayed the room. He placed her on the bidet and let the warm water run. He soaped his hand and wiped her bottom with his warm soapy hand, going through from the front between her legs. The warm water from the bidet washed most of the soap away. He helped wash the rest away using his hand from back to front rubbing her pussy lightly in the process. Helga was in ecstasy.

'More Henri more,' she cried.

He stopped, pulled a towel from the rack, lifted her off the bidet and laid her on the floor where he dried her like a baby. When he was finished he said sharply,

'Stay where you are, Helga.'

He pulled his pants off and washed his dick and parts. He turned Helga over onto her stomach again and poured some baby oil over her back and bottom. Henri had never before been so aroused. He rubbed the oil over her back and down between the insides of her legs – moving up slowly – reaching her pussy to massage her clitoris lightly. His hands moved over her bottom and downwards again, inside her legs and up again over her pussy, continuing until she was really moaning. He stuck his thumb in her pussy and massaged her clitoris with his fingers, moving his thumb slowly, in and out. Helga came with such an impact it surprised him.

'More, Henri, more,' was all she said.

He massaged her more for a while until she came again before he stuck his penis in. It was such a size it hurt. This time he moved slowly, trying to penetrate as far as he could. With one hand under her stomach, to the front, he continued to massage her clitoris. She pushed her head back to be kissed and he forgot completely she was his prisoner. She'd forgotten too. They kissed in frenzy, half from the side with Helga's neck strained as far back as she could, her lips pouted to the side and her tongue out, exploring. Helga managed to turn around. She pushed him on his back and moved onto him, her arms still tied and held above her head. She put them over his head and used the back of his head and neck as a fulcrum. She moved in rhythm – not the Helga he'd known. They both came at the same time. It was Henri's first and Helga's fourth time. Helga wanted more. She bent down and kissed away the last of Henri's sperm. She moved the fingers of her tied-up hands over his penis and started to move it up and down until it was fully erect once more. She got onto him again and they somehow ended up in the butterfly position. They had found a position where the woman takes over – a dangerous position where the penis could break. Helga did it with such energy and enthusiasm, he said to himself he's definitely going to let her go later on. She kissed him passionately, moving her tongue inside his mouth and biting his lip gently. Helga came again, this time her voice was louder, her cries almost continuous. He got on top, then from the side and ended up in the rear position again. By the time he came Helga was ready for more, but he couldn't. Helga lay back on the floor. By now, her hands were nearly loosened from the bonds. She spoke,

'Henri, look my hands are nearly free. My feet are no longer bound and I haven't tried to escape. Would you believe me if I said I wouldn't try anything until Gertrud gives you a ring?'

Henri wasn't sure about anything anymore. He'd just had the best sex of his life.

'Okay, Helga – I'll let you get dressed. Then we'll have breakfast.'

An hour later they were sitting at the breakfast table, smiling at each other openly – satisfied, after fantastic sex and a good breakfast. Henri wished Helga had never had anything to do with the far right group. He forgot the past – all the bad moments, the killings, the torture. He realized she was that sort of a person – a masochist and hadn't known it. That was what it was all about with Helga and her sister Frieda. Maybe they had the same bad experiences in their youth as did he and Gertrud. Probably misused by a parent or other grown-up and brainwashed by *the Vikings* on top.

They were just clearing up breakfast when they heard a helicopter hovering over the woods where he'd parked the lorry the night before. The sound came nearer. He decided they had to move. He remembered Helga's BMW motorbike he'd noticed in the garage the night before.

'Okay Helga, let's get some motorbike gear on and leave. You can stay here if you like – it's up to you.'

'I'm coming with you,' she burst out, 'I don't want to be blown up.'

It was 8.50 am. – only minutes until the bank opens he thought. Drive for half an hour and stop to have a rethink. They put on motorcycle gear and went into the garage through the adjoining door in the kitchen.

The helicopter came nearer and flew over the camp. It hovered for a couple of minutes over Helga's house before it banked and flew off towards Passau. He waited until the helicopter was far enough out of hearing before he steered the BMW out of the garage in low gear and up the side road and out onto the main road where he accelerated and changed gears appropriately feeling the power and exhilaration. His thoughts were running in many directions. He was confused by the change in Helga. If they noticed the lorry from the helicopter it won't be long before the police surround Helga's house so maybe he won't detonate the bomb after all. He didn't want any policemen killed. Maybe he should stop right now and make that call – at least get rid of that *Viking* camp. What was he going to do with Helga? Gertrud wouldn't want her with him, or would she. After all, she did say she wanted to have sex in front of Helga, so there must be something she'd noticed about Helga he'd missed before. No, he thought – when Gertrud rings and everything's okay, he'll call the police and tell them about the dirty bomb and the booby trap in the lorry – yes, that's what he'll do, and tell them who's responsible.

They had travelled twenty minutes when Gertrud's cell phone rang in his pocket. He pulled over to the side of the road.

'Hallo, Henri – I've got the money. See you in Munich,' she said, excitedly.

'Hi, Gertrud – that's great! Listen, I'm bringing Helga with me to Munich. She's damaged goods too, I reckon – maybe we can have a threesome,'

Helga looked at Henri and smiled shyly. He added,

'And we'll split the money three ways, what do you say?'

'I don't know what to say, Henri. If you say she's okay, then I won't say no to a threesome, I'd be delighted. I'm getting all heated up thinking about it. The money is no problem either. I'll see you both in Munich then, Henri,' she said, the emphasis of longing underlining her statement.

'Looking forward to it too Gertrud,' he said, pressing the off button and grinning with great satisfaction.

They climbed back onto the motorbike. Helga snuggled closer to him than before. Her hands moved down to his crotch where she felt something big that wanted to break out. He drove to the next village where he stopped at a public telephone booth and made a short 110 call to the police informing them about the lorry, the dirty bomb and those responsible all tied up in and around the farm. He took a northerly farmer's track cross-country to another village and from there he had decided he would criss-cross on small country roads before joining the Autobahn to Munich.

Haifa – Wednesday evening, 31st August

The Arab waited patiently for Gustav Bormann at the Ben Gurion arrival terminal. His fear of Bormann was greater than his hate, like most of his fellow Arabs who had anything to do with him. Being on a job with him was like having one foot in the grave. It was worse than being with Abu Mousab Al-Zarqawi, with whom he'd had many a skirmish with US troops in Iraq.

Gustav Bormann saw him and nodded his head slightly in recognition, as he walked towards him. Two other Arabs took Bormann's luggage that the Nazi torturer and killer dumped in front of them. Without exchanging a word, they left the cool building and made their way quickly through the devastating heat to an awaiting car, a big black German limousine that immediately pulled out as the doors were shut.

Caleb Gold and his team of five cars stuck with him all the way to Haifa, changing cars to avoid getting blown.

The limousine stopped at an apartment block in the *Wadi Street* – near the German colony in Haifa, not far from the docks.

Frieda Schulz was not expecting his company and shuddered in fear when she heard the door open and he, above all people, came into the front room followed by four Arabs. She already had her rucksack packed and was waiting to be led back over the border, thinking she'd accomplished her mission successfully.

'Didn't expect to see me so soon, did you Frieda?' Bormann said, icily.

Frieda was so stricken with fear at his sight – she couldn't manage a reply.

'I see you've got your rucksack packed. That will save me some trouble.'

He turned to the Arabs and said,

'Get her and tie her up.'

Frieda woke up from her panic attack and screamed, 'Help, help,' as loud as she could, until one of the Arabs put a filthy, sweaty hand over her mouth to stop her.

'Now let me see,' said Bormann, 'what was it I promised you if you failed?'

He didn't wait for her answer because the Arab still had his hand over Frieda's mouth.

'Dear, dear! She doesn't know it yet, does she – poor girl. Failed again, hasn't she. Blew up the wrong woman too. What a pity,' he said, *tut-tutting* and shaking his head.

'Besides,' he said, 'you've used our organization for a personal vendetta in trying to kidnap and kill those German and Israeli youths.'

'But I was ordered to do so by *Abu Mousab al-Zarqawi*,' she managed to cry out, after she got a bite at the Arabs finger.

Frieda's eyes looked at him pleadingly. She tried to say something but only muffled sounds came out. The Arab was now holding her mouth tighter. No chance anymore of getting another bite. Bormann came over to her and pulled out a long thin knife.

'Make her stand, and you others, strip her,' he said.

The Arab holding her pulled her up and the other three ripped her clothes off.

'What a lovely figure you have, dear Frieda, and such an ugly face to go with it – let's see what uncle doctor can do to make both parts meet in ugliness.'

Using his stiletto, he cut a swastika across her stomach, just as though he was using a ballpoint pen. With that done, he gave an order in Arabic. One of the men stuck tape over her mouth, but not before she got out a final cry. She put all her strength into it.

Caleb Gold and his men had taken up position in a private flat across the road. He now gave the order they'd been waiting for,

'Okay men, let's get over there and put an end to this and remember, make sure we get that woman and Bormann alive – I'm not too worried about the other thugs.'

The Arabs dragged her over to a side door. They nailed her to the doorframe by driving two ten centimetre long nails in, one at each wrist. Frieda fainted after the first nail was driven in.

'Now wait until she's conscious before you rape her,' he said coldly.

The first Arab was pulling his pants back up – the second one was in the process of raping Frieda, even though blood was running down her body from the wrists and cuts, when the door burst open – Caleb Gold and his team arrived just in time to stop further raping and cruelties.

Two Arab thugs were standing near Frieda, waiting for their turn. All four thugs were put out of action for good. Bormann was totally unaware he'd been followed from the airport. The first time his guise had been blown. He sighed inwardly, knowing he was a fool to have believed the Israelis wouldn't recognise him. He was arrested and transported to a special police building not far away. Caleb's men weren't too particular about the way he was handled on the way there.

Frieda was taken to hospital where she was given a tetanus injection and one to counteract the shock. Her wrist wounds were cleaned out and bandaged – local anaesthic jabs applied along her stomach cuts that were then stitched-up and bandaged.

'How is she Doc?' asked one of the men from Caleb Gold's team.

'She'll be okay! She's in an extremely good physical condition and if the nails weren't rusty, the wounds should heal fairly quickly. The muscles have taken most of the damage but the sinews are still intact. The psychological damage is a different matter. I want to keep her here under observation for a few days, just to be on the safe side. She'll be needing physiotherapy, once the wounds begin to heal.'

'Okay, but you'll have to put her in the secure section. She'll need round the clock protection.'

'Okay,' said the doctor, 'I'll get that arranged. You'd better let her sleep for a couple of hours before you start questioning.'

They led Bormann into a special room with no windows, only artificial neon lights that cast more grey to the otherwise dark grey walls. A table and four chairs were the only items that broke up the monotony of the empty room. Bormann kept his mouth shut. He held his Nazi head high, as though he was saying,

'How dare you, I'm of the supreme Arian cast, you lowly creatures.'

Caleb Gold gave an order. Two of his men shoved Bormann onto the only chair with armrests and tied him up. Caleb moved next to Bormann and pulled out a long, slim, shining metal box from the table drawer and opened it, holding it a few centimetres away from Bormann's face.

'Know what this is Bormann?'

Bormann looked at the contents and saw a long syringe and

a number of ampoules. He said nothing but his eyes showed recognition.

'We don't need you to talk to us willingly, Bormann, because we know you'll only tell us lies. This little ampoule injected into your vein, however, will be enough to extract the truth, don't you think?' said Caleb, wickedly.

Caleb turned back to the table and laid the syringe box onto the top. He extracted an ampoule, sawed the tip off and inserted the syringe needle, drawing the liquid out into the syringe and pressing the air out until only liquid spurted out. He tied a rubber tube above Bormann's left bicep and patted the arm looking for a suitable vein. He disinfected it and inserted the needle. He loosened the rubber tube and proceeded to inject the fluid watching Bormann closely.

He'd only injected half the fluid when Bormann started to shake, his eyes opened up like gob-stoppers and foam emerged from his mouth.

'He's bloody allergic,' cried one of his men.

Caleb pulled the needle out immediately, but it was too late. Bormann's head fell onto his chest. The body jerks gradually receded until only an occasional light jerking of the feet and arms occurred.

Caleb couldn't find a pulse beat, so he hit the alarm button and called the doctor.

They were too late. Either Bormann was allergic, which Caleb doubted, or whoever had swapped the truth drug ampoules for poison had made him an executioner. Whatever it was that killed him was of no interest anymore. In this particular spec ops world, it's now a case for the body disposal team.

Thursday morning, 1st September

Caleb Gold paid a visit to the doctor in charge of Frieda. 'Morning doc, how's our patient? Ready to talk is she?' asked Caleb Gold, expecting a positive answer.

'Well, not really. She's still in shock. I've given her some painkillers. You can have no longer than half an hour,' he said, earnestly.

'Okay, Doc. That'll be fine,' said Caleb, knowing a half-hour can easily lead into an hour. If the Doc had said, ten minutes then he would have put her condition down as a little bit more serious, but half-an-hour!

Frieda was awake and aware of her situation.

'Good morning, feeling better today are we?' Commented Caleb, not really expecting an answer.

'Yes, thanks,' replied Frieda, 'and thank you for saving me from that sadist, although I don't really know if you're going to be any better,' she said, sadly.

'Are you ready to talk, Frieda?'

'You know my name?'

'Oh, yes – and a lot of other things about you too,' he replied, confidentially.

'Well, are you ready to talk?' he repeated.

'Yes, I think so, but I have a question first,' she said.

'Go ahead,' said Caleb.

'Do you really think I'm safe, here?'

'Well, it's not Fort Knox, but we are in a secure hospital area and you are being protected round the clock,' he answered.

'Okay, that's a fair enough answer from your point of view, but let me tell you, we have a lot of your people on our payroll and that doesn't make me feel good at all.'

'Then how do you feel about telling us who they are so

that you can be more assured of your own safety?' He answered.

'What's in it for me if I become a witness for the State of Israel?'

'That's not for me to decide, I'm afraid,' he said.

'Well, that's the end of our conversation for today, isn't it,' she answered cockily and closed her eyes.

Caleb left the room and made a few phone calls.

An hour later he went back to Frieda's sickroom. She seemed to be sleeping. Her head was turned towards the far wall.

He went over to her bed, approaching it on the far side and got a shock. Her eyes were staring into nowhere – a big dark purple hole marked the entry path of the bullet that had penetrated her skull right in the middle – between her eyes.

His phone call request must have gotten into the wrong hands. Frieda had been right in her assumption after all.

Haifa – Thursday evening, 1st September

Olaf must have felt like a king last night. His arrival was preceded with great expectations – rewarded when our little group, consisting of Chris, Steve, Carla, Paula and myself, met with him. We'd already digested the information from his fax that Derek and Colin had sent from *Tyre*. He presented us with more general information about the border area and the site south of *Rmaich*, including the position of our particular cave and two other caves. There had been no mention of other specific caves, so we were quite surprised. I told them we should keep that information to ourselves. Chris and I had agreed it was time we told the others in our small group about the mole. I thought this was the right moment,

'I've some bad news too, I'm afraid. We have a mole,' I said, bluntly.

After a few moments silence and some dumb struck looks, Steve jumped in to fill the pregnant pause and asked,

'Who's your suspect, John?'

'Its John Barnes, isn't it,' said Carla.

'Blimey, you're right, Carla,' said Chris, 'but how did you suspect him?'

'Well, it was after you told us about EPISCOPE, the Vatican Secret Service, who are no other than the Opus Dei. You see, I have great admiration for anyone who's not a Jew who can read the old Hebrew Torah and can quote the New Testament like the back of his hand. When he puts fanatical thoughts and interpretations to some of the texts, that's when you find out if he's a religious freak or if he is purely interested in bible archaeology,' she said and added, 'I was going to talk to you about it, so I'm glad it's come up now.'

'Well, folks – now we all know – Chris and I have other information that point to him too! What I propose, is we give him slightly changed information to handle, to make sure, whoever's payroll he's on doesn't interfere with our mission,' I said, adding, 'and when we go for it we'll have to keep a very close eye on him. Oh, and another thing. I think we should reduce our morning group to this little gathering, including Olaf, of course.'

I smiled at Olaf who I realized was still with us.

'Don't mind me, I'll try and pick things up as we go along,' he said.

'Okay,' said Chris and took over,

'Our lads had some luck at the Necropolis. I'll try and make it as brief as I can. First of all they had to make some bribes through their host in *Tyre* to visit the Necropolis in the evening. Their host even managed to arrange a guide, a Lebanese archaeologist, who led them directly to the only sarcophagus in question from the scanty information we provided. Now, the assumptions we made, or should I say John, made, were partly correct. The top of the sarcophagus only had the inscription:

Temple of the soul is God שִׁמְלִי יָהֲוֶה

They were a bit perplexed because there were no other readable clues on the outside. Colin Hughes had a brilliant idea. What about the top of the sarcophagus from the inside? Their guide had a bag of tools with him. He'd been instructed to open the sarcophagus if necessary. Except for one stone that was sand stone, the rest of the sarcophagus was marble. He loosened the sand stone and pulled it out. The sarcophagus was empty but on the inside top were a number of engraved Hebrew inscriptions that read as follows:

חֲצוֹת. מֵעָם יָם גָּלִיל עַד צֹר

וְכַלָּה חִיץ שְׁלִישִׁי חֹר יָמִין

Translated into English:
Half way from Sea Galilee to Tyre trade route third Cave Southside.

Now if we put all the other information we've got:
- The coordinates and exact location of the cave Olaf got from that corporal
- Gravestone's conclusion gathered from the information from various documents that Paula has certified as Gravestone's
- Papers hidden in the lining of the suitcases from Zuckenic himself or maybe Anna or Martha
- The fact the German woman Frieda was looking for a cave in the same region and showed the corporal the copy of an ancient map
- Our meagre success so far with the Ark Code and the
- Newest information from the sarcophagus, we get the following picture:

Collated information in English:
My – sarcophagus – half – way – from – Sea – Galilee – to – Tyre – trade route – third – cave – fortress – south side – proclamation – establish – testament – genealogical tree – Jesus – blood-brother – exchange – open area (terra continens) or (barren fields)

Some of it makes sense, other bits we may have to leave out because they seem to confuse. It is possible to juggle it about a bit. Maybe when we have more time we'll find the answer using the Ark Code. For the time being, I think we'll leave it as an incomplete picture. What we should do now is make a trip tonight to find out if we're on the right track and see what's in that cave. What we've also looked at is a bible map of the area at the time of Jesus' crucifixion. The trade route described is the route used by the early Christian pilgrims from *Tyre*, who attended some of Jesus' preaching. Jesus used it too. He was also in *Tyre* and *Capernaum* near the *Sea of Galilee*. Both towns are at each end of the trade route described. The holy apostle Peter's house was in *Capernaum* too and *Rmaich* is almost halfway between *Tyre* and the *Sea of Galilee*.

Now for some good and bad news – I'll pass you back to John.'

I paused, and swigged down the last of my tea,

'We had a message this morning concerning Bormann – we talked about him at great length last night. Olaf was right – it was Bormann he'd seen at the airport. Bormann was arrested last night, just as he was caught torturing Frieda Schulz, the German woman for failing to kill Paula. She'd also been crucified and raped.'

'Oh, my God,' exclaimed Paula and Carla almost simultaneously.

'Bormann was poisoned by an insider in a special police establishment last night and Frieda was shot dead in her sick bed within the special secure area of the local hospital a few hours ago by an unknown assailant, who appears to have access into the secure medical wing,' I added.

'She must have seen her killer then,' Chris said, and sighed.

'They must have had a tip, too,' I answered.

'Well, they really deserved to die for what they've done and the next one is Bolkow, that's for sure,' said Paula, viciously.

I took over again – no one commented on Paula's vengeful remark,

'Okay, Chris and I will make arrangements for us to visit the cave tonight. I think a small team mainly of a commando nature would be best. I'll let you have a look at the Hebrew inscriptions, but don't leave them lying around, and give them back to Chris as soon as possible. Well, let's wish those who go tonight, good luck.'

Many voices arose to the words *'good luck'*.

I gave Ben a call and took him up on his promise of guides into the Lebanon. He said he'd ring back. I needed to go to the loo, and then I'll have to make plans with Chris for tonight. Paula grabbed me as I was coming out of the loo.

'John, I expect you'll be going with the commando group?'

'Your guess is right, Paula. I have to.'

'Be careful, won't you,' she said.

'Don't worry – it'll be a quick in and out job, as I see it. More like a recce, just to see the layout and maybe enter the cave and have a look around. If it gets dangerous we'll pull out. I just hope our guides see it that way too.'

'Why's that, John,' she asked.

'Well, it's well known the Israeli army enjoy the excuse of asking for heavy support even when they have small skirmishes. That's the last thing we want. They'd probably blow up the cave and the surroundings, that's if they haven't already been disintegrated before now.'

I paused, put my arms round her, gave her a big hug and a kiss, and said,

'I'll see you later, darling. I have to make arrangements with Chris for tonight.'

Paula wouldn't let go until she'd responded with a long sensuous kiss. That brought me back to my senses and to reality – asking myself – what the hell am I doing, going to violate a dangerous border, armed and ready for battle.

Ben rang back and gave us directions where we had to report to.

'Good luck, John!' he said, 'You're mad, if you ask me,' he added.

'That's exactly what I was thinking myself Ben. Sure you don't want to join us?' I asked jokingly.

'Not on your life, and watch your back, John.'

I took that as a sane warning. You never know who's going to turn traitor next in this game. Especially when there's a lot at stake.

I went looking for Chris and found him yelling his head off.

'Where's that fucking sod, JB?'

Nobody seemed to know.

'Last I saw of him was last night on the terrace, Chris,' said Dick Knight.

'Hasn't slept in his bed either,' commented Mike Jones.

'Bloody hell, Mike – why didn't you tell me? Maybe he's been knocked off by someone,' said Chris.

'I was just going to tell you, but you're always so darned busy,' retorted Mike.

'Probably done a bunk, if you ask me,' said Bob Turnkey.

'For Christ's sake what the hell's got into you lot?'

'JB's no good, Chris. Reckon he's been bought, the way he's been acting the last few days,' added Bob Turnkey.

'Okay, lads, out with it – what's been going on?' I asked, butting in to the general mass conversation.

'Been on his computer late, night before last. I watched him through my night-glasses. Looked like he was on the Internet. You said we weren't allowed to. I had a look at the log in the morning. Seems he'd deleted it. I thought maybe he was having a chat with his loved ones, or something. Wished I'd reported it – sorry everybody,' said Bob Turnkey, slightly anguished.

'Well, that puts us in a bit of a predicament doesn't it,' said Chris angrily.

I butted in, not wanting the lads too disturbed. Chris can get very obnoxious.

'Okay, lads, thanks for telling us – we'll have to cut our losses. Maybe he's done us a favour, so don't worry about it,' I said and grabbed Chris by the arm.

'Let's go and have a talk, Chris.'

We went through to Paula's part of the building and made ourselves comfortable in the huge living room.

'Okay, Chris – he hasn't got Olaf's coordinates and our latest from *Tyre*. He may have Gravestone's conclusions but that won't bring him far enough. Whoever he's with, they may have information we don't possess, so we're going in there early tonight at dusk. Hopefully they'll not be there that early. We'll lay booby-traps in the first two caves once we've recced our cave. That should give us a slight advantage if they do appear. I just hope they know nothing about our third cave. What's your opinion?'

'Well, I think we should leave here latest 2 pm this afternoon. Find our military contact and get orientated with the area and the map. Counting us two, we should take at least two men, John. Less than that's too risky.'

'Okay, Chris, but who's going to take charge here if you go?' I asked.

'What about Olaf?'

'Come on, you can do better than that!'

'I know exactly what you're saying, John. You want me to stay here?'

'You're darn right. We don't have anyone else with your leadership qualities and organising talent, and we have to keep up our vigilance too. Don't forget, Paula's still a target.'

'I can see you've decided to take Olaf then, am I right, John?'

'Well, he knows the area and I want to give him a chance of getting his self respect back, you realize that don't you, Chris?'

'No hard feelings, John, I understand. I'd better have a look, see who's best at booby-traps, hadn't I,' he said, with a twinkle in his eye.

That's my Chris, I thought.

We entered *Zone V* just short of the border and introduced ourselves to the Major in charge of our particular sector. He was very jovial and made a few sidelines about Rambo tactics. He was enjoying himself I could see. We were more than well armed – ready for the worst. What the Major didn't know was why we were interested in the other side of 'no man's land'.

In the evening, we made our way to the foremost post, where we parted from our guides. As dusk approached, we went down a path behind a low saddle, unseen from the Lebanese side, until we reached the bottom. Keeping under a long stretch of sheer rock on the Lebanese side, we made our way along the valley. We reached an open area where we had to climb up a path at a 60-degree angle towards an ancient fortress, where, according to the information from the Major, only a few stones remained. From what we'd seen in daylight, there was a path that led off under the summit, below the fortress. Well, not really a path, it was more like a goat's track. We had our night-vision headgear down. After a half-hour's walk, stopping occasionally to listen, we reached the junction to the goat's path.

I smelled cigarette smoke from above and gave a signal to stop. We heard some voices for a few minutes that faded away on the summit. We carried on towards our goal. After another hundred metres there was a small inlet into the mountain. I gave the order to secure both sides of the path on either side of the inlet. I went forward towards a huge boulder that appeared to have fallen from above. That was exactly where our cave should have been. There were many smaller boulders heaped around it.

I looked up automatically to see if there were any more loose rocks above us, a bit cumbersome with the helmet and other gear. I tried bending my back but that was no good either. I gave up and climbed over the smaller rocks until I got behind the biggest boulder that was over 2 metres high. There was a man's sized gap behind it and some of the smaller stones had filled it up a bit. I managed to squeeze down behind the big boulder.

I was face to face with an opening in the rocky mountain, covered by an old grey cloth that crumbled when I tried to pull it down. There it was, our cave.

I signalled up to Olaf, who was standing at the top of the boulder, to join me. We had a strict agreement – no talking. My men had shown Olaf the basic British hand signals before we left.

I entered the cave to make room for Olaf to climb down and join me. I now had my night-vision goggles on. I motioned Olaf to stay at the entrance and made my way slowly towards the back of the cave. I studied the walls on either side for any signs or writing – nothing. There were three small, 30 x 30 centimetre cubbyholes that had been hewn into the rock at the back of the cave. I looked at each one carefully. The third one was at the back where the cave started to narrow and seemed different. I touched the rear of this third cubbyhole, running the palm of my hand over it. I knocked on it lightly and went back to the other two, doing the same. I had made a major discovery – the back of the third cubbyhole was hollow. I went to the front of the cave, tugged Olaf's arm and motioned him to come with me. It was contrary to what we'd planned, but I wanted him to share this discovery with me.

I showed him the first cubbyhole, knocked on it lightly, then did the same to the second one and gave him the thumbs-up at the third one. I pointed at him to knock on it gently.

Olaf knocked on it very gently and nodded his head eagerly. I put my hand over his mouth just in time to stop him yelling hurrah! I got my field knife out, placed it in the centre and stabbed it into the back, causing my knife arm to reverberate. It didn't budge – just scratched the surface. I tried the edges. That was it. I scraped the edges free and prised it out. It was a square piece of copper and wood about five centimetres thick that had been fitted into the back a long time ago and covered with clay and dirt.

I dislodged it and pulled it out. The back of the cubbyhole was hollowed out. Inside was an old urn sealed at the top. I reached in and lifted it out gently, thinking, was this the thing we're all looking for? I handed it to Olaf who held it fondly, looking at it from all sides. I took it from him and put it in my rucksack that had padded sides. I motioned Olaf to go back to the front of the cave. I waited until he was far enough away before I picked up the cubby-hole cover – comprising wood and copper and looked at both sides carefully – no sign of inscriptions or indentations. I decided to take it with me, just in case. I placed it carefully in the back compartment of my rucksack that had even better padding. I joined Olaf and gave him the sign to leave.

We went back outside and climbed up over the rocks and into the clearing. I gave the thumbs-up and the signal to retreat. I discarded my initial plan of placing booby-traps in the other two caves. No unnecessary risks now – maybe we've got what we came for.

The return trek was swift. Even so, we were just as careful as we'd been on the way in. We reached the end of the saddle, near the top, on the Israeli side – safe from the sight of any Lebanese border patrols, where we joined the Major and his small detachment. He grinned his head off and said,

'What, no fireworks, eh!'

He'd no sooner said that when a barrage of gunfire and explosions occurred on the other side, a bit farther off from where we'd been. I thought automatically of the first cave. JB and his cronies have tried the first cave and probably met up with the wrong people.

The Major said gruffly,

'Let's go.'

Not bothering to hide our smirks, we followed him up over the top and on towards his small camp and our vehicle.

Two and a half hours later, we were back at Paula's. The four of us were grinning so much, those who were waiting in the kitchen let off a loud hoorah! Paula made to jump into my arms. I was holding my rucksack in front of me, my arm through the shoulder straps.

'Careful, Paula, it's in here,' I said, admonishingly.

'Oh, my God,' came from Paula's and a few other mouths.

'I think Carla should be the one to handle this,' I said.

Carla was sitting at the end of the table eating a sandwich.

I placed my rucksack carefully onto the table near her. Carla's eating stopped. Half a sandwich hung from her mouth. I opened the rucksack and lifted the urn out gently and placed it in front of her. She pulled the rest of the sandwich from her lip and put it back on the plate. She took a big swig of herb tea and wiped her mouth with the back of her hand. Her eyes were wide when she asked,

'You want *me* to open it?'

I smiled and nodded my head, saying,

'You're the archaeologist, Carla – you know what's to be done.'

'Then we'd better do it professionally, hadn't we. I suggest you put it in a safe place for the night and we'll do it in the morning. We have to photograph it from all sides, weigh it and every bit of the seal, wax, cloth or dirt, has to be carefully removed and placed in special containers,' she said.

Many disappointed oh-s! and ah-s! were to be heard, so she added,

'It's a bit like forensics, you know. I'm sorry, but that's the way it's done.'

'That's okay, Carla. We appreciate that. We'll do as you say then – tomorrow!'

Under many eyes that were saying, come on just open it up – I picked it up again, replaced it carefully in my rucksack, and left the kitchen with Paula, Chris and Olaf in my wake.

'Mum's got a safe behind the *Gauguin* copy in the living room. Let me open it for you,' said Paula, excitedly.

We went into the living room. Paula lifted the painting off the wall to reveal a fair sized safe.

'Now turn your backs please, whilst I dial the combination,' she ordered, laughingly. Nevertheles, she waited until we'd all turned around.

'Thank you,' she said, and returned to face the safe and dial the combination.

We heard a click followed by the movement of the safe door.

'Now you can turn back! John?'

I handed her the precious urn, which she placed in the safe, closed the door and spun the dial.

'That's that, until tomorrow. I hope nobody gets the idea of burgling tonight. Maybe I should put the alarm on, eh!' she said, jokingly.

I had a hunch that the cubbyhole covering was more important than the urn. My instinct told me not to disclose my possession as yet.

Later that night as I lay in Paula's arms – she was stroking my balding head and kissing me occasionally, she said,
'You know something, John. Apart from that guy, what was his name?'
'You mean JB,' I said.
'Yes, that religious freak, as Carla defined him. Yes, well you know I really like your *bunch* and even that German, Olaf.'

It was an early breakfast for everyone. The enthusiasm in the air was suffocating. My only hope was they wouldn't be disappointed.
Carla knew she was the most important person that morning. She wouldn't say a word at breakfast. When she was finished she stood up, looked at me and said,
'See you at Paula's in 15 minutes John, Chris!'
I sympathised with her. She'd taken over a big responsibility and didn't want to make any mistakes.
We were all waiting for her. Paula had extracted the urn from the safe and put it on the table. Carla examined it and made a few notes. She picked up a camera and began taking shots from different angles. Olaf obliged by holding it up for her as requested, with and without a ruler. The two of them seemed to get on very well. Carla used a very fine knife and cut off the top part of the seal in one piece, which she put in a small plastic container. She wrote something on the cover. She did

the same for the rest of the seal. In the end we had six small plastic containers with the contents of the seal. The big moment had arrived. Using two long tweezers she pulled out a piece of rolled papyrus and laid it on a thick cotton cloth.

The papyrus looked to be in a very good condition, or so it seemed to me. Carla addressed us,

'Ladies and gentlemen, I'm afraid I've got a disappointing statement to make. This papyrus is not two thousand years old. From the state it's in and from the type of seal, I would put it around the year three hundred AD.'

'Bloody hell,' said Chris, 'a bloody goose chase,'

'No it isn't, Chris. It has a purpose, you'll see when we open it. There must be a reason for having taken so much trouble to hide this document in the first place. I'm now going to try and unroll the papyrus. If I see it breaking at any point, then I shall have to stop. We will then have to pass it on for conservation treatment. Paula, do you have a dustpan and brush – I just need the brush?'

'Just a minute, I think I know what you need,' she said and went out into the hall.

She came back a few minutes later holding a small brush.

'Yes, just what I need,' said Carla.

She pushed the handle of the brush gently into the hollow of the rolled up papyrus to use as a stabilizer.

'Olaf, dear, would you take the tweezers and hold the end of the papyrus – not too tight, but tight enough to hold it when I open the roll.'

Olaf did as he was told.

'Okay, Olaf, are you ready?' she asked, sweetly.

Olaf grinned and said, 'I'm ready any time, Carla.'

Carla grinned too and said,

'Okay folks, let's see what's written on this little piece of history! Oh, Paula, could you get me two long books for weights once we've opened it?'

Paula brought over two fairly heavy looking books.

'Lovely, dear,' said Carla, and began to open the Papyrus.

When it was fully opened, three words were clearly visible in Greek writing. Carla translated them into English – they read:

Jesus' Testament – kept safe

Many thoughts went through my mind – disappointment... I was a young lad again – getting a pair of socks for Christmas instead of the new bicycle I'd so wished for... it's obvious though that Jesus did leave something behind... I believe we're on the right track... maybe a deeper investigation and re-evaluation of our clues may bring more light to the matter... I wonder if the cubbyhole cover holds any clues... Looks as though we're finished here for the time being.

There were many comments to be heard that day. Disappointment underlined most conversations. I rang up Ben Goldmann and passed on the news of our discovery.

'Don't be too upset, John. I think you all did a splendid job and the message is really a sensation. You do realize Jesus did maybe make a Testament of sorts or maybe even a hint towards his brother or the other disciples. It doesn't matter which of them carried out his will. Whoever it was did their job well. Bye the way, I hear there was a shootout on the Lebanese side of the border, glad you weren't involved. It seems though one of your men was found dead, together with an American Vatican Monsignor, Henry Bush, two Italians, five Germans and two other Brits. Apparently Lebanese authorities captured a seriously wounded Italian who states he belongs to the

Vatican Disposal Department and says he has diplomatic immunity. Bye the way, what was your man doing with that lot, John?'

'Oh, he was just a mole or someone who got misused by a religious cult. A great pity really. He was a brilliant analyst.'

'Ah, well, at least you're alive and have found a woman at last. Maybe you'll settle down, eh, John?'

That had sounded more like an order than a question, I thought.

'You never know, Ben. I never thought I'd find such a love again after Anna. Maybe you should try it!'

'Maybe I should, John. Oh, and don't forget to return the heavy stuff I lent you, will you?'

'No, I won't, and I'll never forget your help Ben. I can't tell you how grateful my men and I are for your support. Thanks a million, Ben.'

'You're welcome, John. Pop in before you go back over, I have an important matter to discuss with you.'

'Okay, Ben – see you in Tel Aviv.'

I rang off thinking, what the hell's Ben got to tell me. My main thoughts now, were what to do about the cubbyhole cover. Maybe I should have declared it and got Carla to examine it. Something, maybe it's me being careful or just canny, tells me not to disclose my cubbyhole cover find – not to the present company. Maybe I'll take it with me and have some different experts examine it – perhaps an MRT scan...

Haifa – Friday, 2nd September

We were all gathered at the breakfast table waiting for an announcement I was about to make. 'Morning ladies, morning lads,' I said, giving my best smile of the month, 'you probably realize why I've called in this meeting.'

Some low murmurs passed around the table.

'We've tasted a little bit of success and I'm proud of you all, including Paula, Carla, Steve and Olaf. It has definitely not been easy and some of us have had their share of travelling around and sleeping in strange beds.'

A few of the lads grinned at that statement, Paula too. Noticing her smile, I realized what I'd just said and returned the smile. This time it was a real genuine Colgate one. I let the smile dwindle before I carried on.

'We've had our share in losses too, so if you'd indulge me, I'd just like to hold a one minute silence for Ian Stewart, Martha Stern, Martin Cole, Professor Gravestone, Janet – the American student and our saddest loss of all – John Barnes, who was one of us and either sold out to Opus Dei or was just another brainwashed catholic. Please stand up.'

Everyone stood up and held their heads bowed.

After the one-minute silence, Derek Montgomery, who has a beautiful tenor, sung to Ian Stewart's favourite Scottish song that just happens to be mine as well,

Ca' the yowes, tae the knows,
ca' them whaur the heather grows,
ca' them whaur the burnie rows,
ma Bonnie dearie.

That was the chorus, to which I joined in with my baritone. The song caused a lot of tears not only from Paula and Carla.

'Well, folks I'm sorry to have to say this, but for the moment our involvement here is over. We have some unfinished business waiting for us in the UK and Germany. Oh, and don't forget to pick up your pay cheques and your flight tickets from Chris. I'm pleased to say *the Agency* has been extremely generous.'

I looked at Chris who was grinning from ear to ear. We were both pleased our budget had been hardly touched and had decided to split the rest with the lads.

'Your flight is not due until Tuesday so you can have a spree either here or anywhere else, but be in Tel Aviv for the flight. Go easy with the booze too. Anyone not on the flight won't get the extra bonus that's awaiting you in Berlin. Anyway, once again – thanks everyone.'

I sat down. Most of the lads thumped their fists on the table, some of the others clapped.

Chris started organizing the lads for different chores. Paula and I left the kitchen and headed for her mum's part. I had to add some notes for my end report to *the Agency*. That is if Paula lets me. I'll have to word it so that our mission here was mainly dealing with Frieda's lot, which isn't far from the truth.

Berlin – Tuesday, 6th September

The departure was heartbreaking – Paula was in tears all morning. It was like a final farewell. She wanted to accompany us to the airport but I had to decline – I hate farewells at railway stations and airports. I promised her I'd be back once I'd got everything settled in

Europe and then I'd stay with her until her Mum arrived – then we'd go to cold London. I told her of my plans to quit my job at *the Agency* but somehow I didn't seem to be getting through to her.

Our return flight to Berlin was mostly held in silence. Whilst we waited in the departure lounge cafeteria at Ben Gurion, some of the lads were saying they'd like to go back to Paula's place someday. I took that as a great compliment for her and thought I must tell her when I call her up tonight.

It was well into the night when we arrived at Berlin Tegel. The *bunch* spent the night in the airport hotel – I went to my flat. After the last booby-trap scare, I wasn't sure about my hideout. Besides, we were too dog-tired for any messing about. Paula wasn't in when I rang her up.

Next day we found the hideout just as we'd left it. No more booby-traps and nothing missing. One of the lads suggested JB must have been the booby-trap layer. He was the only one who hadn't been there when we discovered them and he'd been on duty the night before, so he'd had enough time to place them. Someone else suggested he might've been the one who knocked off Gravestone because it was strange only Gravestone's notebook was missing and JB had obviously known about it. A lot of heads nodded in agreement.

I placed the cubbyhole cover in a secret compartment of my safe. One day soon, I'll have it examined. For the present I've had enough of treasure hunting.

I got Chris, Jack the Ripper and JW to accompany me to the safe house. Jack and JW remained in the main part of the house to secure it from intruders.

I showed Chris into the concealed room where I had a double computer mirrored system that had been logging and transferring every interactive movement and every *bit* of information Jack had made in his computer system in *the Agency* Headquarters – his so-called secure system he believed was impervious to any hackers or Trojans. I'd arranged that before Ian was killed and Martin was declared missing.

I could also enter his system from here at any time, using a special super-user code I'd embedded in his kernel.

'Bloody hell, you ingenious git,' he blurted out, once I'd explained the situation to him.

'Well, fuck my old boots,' adding, *'John, John the piper's son,'* accompanied by a little jig, ending in a spin turn.

I interrupted him.

'It wasn't *John*, Chris – it was *Tom, Tom, the piper's son.*'

He ignored me.

'Anyway, looks like we're gonna find some baddie info, eh!'

Without another word, Chris rubbed his hands and sat down at the terminal.

'Dear, oh, dearie me!' he said after four hours of searching.

I'd been watching his skilful and pointed searching, picking out the important bits. Ben Goldmann had warned me about Kenneth Woodward before I went to Ben Gurion Airport, when I looked him up as he'd suggested. He warned me implicitly to be very careful. I thought he'd been implying my rendezvous with Elsa. This looked a lot more dangerous.

That bastard Woodward's been working with those sods, those bloody traitors from MI6, the ones we called EUCLID. He's the boss – the planner. The ones that conjured up the 9/11 and Iraq plot, I noted, sadly – guiding the Al Qaeda cells to target the WTC and implanting false intelligence.

'You sure no one can trace this little set-up, John! What

you've got is more dangerous than a hydrogen bomb – bloody hell! Your boss Jack Orlowski and Kenneth Woodward from the Mossad are in on the same game, John. This is real bad. I hope we don't get a bloody nose from this lot. Look I'll make a couple of copies to be on the safe side. You take one and I'll take the other. On second thoughts, you'd better send one to Paula as well and tell her to get it to Ben Goldmann, he'll know what to do. I'm sure I don't at the moment,' he said, seemingly at a loss for further comments.

'Maybe Charles Cross can help out. I think it's worth a try,' I said, hopefully.

'I don't know, John, I have a funny feeling about that guy. I wouldn't trust him, not with this lot. It's above him, that's what it is,' he said, adding, 'he'd probably give it to his next higher superior who may happen to be on the wrong side.'

'Hmm,' I murmured, 'I'm not so sure about that, Chris.'

'It's your neck, John, but I advise you against it and that's a sound warning from a friend.'

'Okay Chris, I accept that and I'll think about it,' adding, 'Do me a favour though. You send the copy to Paula. If it's coming from you she'll probably call out the Israeli National Guard,' I said, and smiled at the thought.

'I'll do that John. Now give me a half-hour to pick out the best pieces to copy.'

Heathrow – Wednesday evening, 7*th* September

I arrived at Heathrow with Chris. He said he'd some private business to attend to. He wasn't very talkative during the flight. Knowing Chris, I reckon he was working out something complicated and didn't want to be disturbed. We said quick goodbyes – we had return flights the next afternoon.

I went home and stopped at Clive's on my way up.

'Ah John, you, em, have a visitor – a lady. She said you'd be here shortly.'

'What's her name, Clive?' I asked.

'Oh, em, sorry John, I've forgotten.'

'Well, what's she look like?'

'Oh, about forty, brunette, blue eyes. Has a beautiful figure, John. If you get fed up with her, send her down to me will you?' he said, jokingly, with a touch of hope in his eyes.

'Hmm,' I said, 'you seem to remember her looks well enough. Anyway thanks Clive.'

Can only be Helen, I thought. What's she doing here? Of course, Charles must have told her. I rang him up from Berlin this afternoon. I must have a rethink about Clive having the keys to my flat – can't have him letting half London in with all those treasures around. Maybe I'll just speak to him gently, after all, it's bloody difficult finding someone reliable. I'll just remind him not to let in any strangers – that should probably do it.

I opened the flat door and was overwhelmed by Helen who threw herself at me. She kissed me on the mouth, sticking her tongue in and giving me the feeling she wanted me badly. I managed to free myself and put my bag down. I wasn't really in the mood.

'Hello, John,' she said sheepishly.

'Hi, Helen, this is a surprise!' I said.

'I couldn't help but come, when Charles told me of your arrival this afternoon. You know if it hadn't been for that shooting at my place..'

I interrupted her, 'I know Helen, I had the same feeling,' I said unashamed.

'Let me take your coat off, John, and come into the lounge,'

Helen took my coat and jacket and laid it on the hallstand. She hooked her arm in mine and led me into the lounge. We stood at the sofa in front of the fireplace. Helen put her arms around me. Her perfume and the touch of her silken dress aroused me. I let my hands explore her back and her round bottom. I could feel the thin slip she was wearing underneath. I pulled her dress up and let my hands wander down inside her panties. She began to kiss me and undo my shirt. I unbuttoned the front of her dress and pushed it over her shoulders and onto the floor. She opened my belt and pulled my trousers down. My underpants followed. She became erratic and wanted to get on top. I let her.

An hour later I was exhausted. She wanted more but I needed a break.

'What a pity,' she said, 'I was just starting to get underway.'

She got up and said,

'I need a drink, what about you, John?'

'Eh, yes a scotch will do, with just a little water, thanks,' I said and started putting on my clothes as she went over to the bar.

She came back over with two drinks in her hand, still naked.

'Not going somewhere, are you, John?'

Something about the tone of her voice irritated me. Somewhat dominating, I thought and remembered. She'd once been a policewoman.

I took the drink from her without answering. Something was wrong here, but I couldn't figure out what. I took a sip of my whisky, thinking she's picked the wrong bottle. After the third sip I cottoned on. She'd put something in my drink.

I woke up with a horrible headache. I felt like heaving up and couldn't move. My eyes wouldn't focus on the surroundings. I heard a blurred voice saying,

'He's coming to, Ken.'

Ken I thought, not that Ken. Where's that nympho. I realized I was still duped and confused. After a while I managed to get a few words out,

'I need a glass of water,'

I got my glass, more like a bucket of water they threw in my face, pouring the rest over my head.

My eyes began to focus on the individuals in the room. Charles Cross, Kenneth Woodward and my old friend and buddy Yankee Doodle Jack Orlowski and another man I didn't know. My senses must be boggled – I was seeing the young woman who'd been at Ian's funeral leering at me, her nose seemingly out of proportion. What the hell's she doing here? What's Charles doing with this lot? As it began to register, my heart sunk. Charles of all people, and I'd told him all about his fellow traitors. He's warned them all and they've managed to avoid being arrested, solely through me trusting Charles. How could he, the blasted traitor and how could I have been such a fool.

'Yes, he's awake now,' said the unknown man.

'Hello John, I must say, you've caused us a lot of trouble you know,' said Yankee Doodle.

'Tell me Jack, how come these professionals put up with such a slob like you, eh?' I said, provokingly and what's she doing here,' I asked, nodding my head in the direction of the young woman.

My voice didn't sound too impressive at all, a bit squeaky I thought. I'll need more bass next time, I think.

'Enough of that, John,' said Charles.

'You know what we want and we'll end up getting it so maybe you should be helpful and give it to us now. I promise you a quick bullet, otherwise Ken here, says he's got a big bone to pick with you about a woman called Elsa, so he won't be as nice to you as I am, or I'll leave you to Eileen, here, ex IRA, who's very good at torturing. Now how about cooperating?'

'Sure, Charles, what do you want to know. After all I've never held any information back from you have I,' I answered cynically, my thinking gradually clearing enough to realize the spot I was in.

'That's what we want to hear,' John.

'But, before I start, how about a few answers first, eh?' I asked.

'Go ahead, John, there's nowhere you can take the information, so I don't see why not,' replied Charles, who seemed to be in charge.

'Who killed Anna, Ian, Martin and Martha, and why?' I asked.

That was the cue for the young woman who couldn't withhold herself.

'I killed your fucking wife, you bastard – you and your SAS

unit were responsible for the death of my father in Belfast when I was only a baby. His name was Sean O'Connor. I was only a teenager when I swore to my mother on her deathbed, I'd get the officer-in-charge, where it hurts most,' said the young woman,

'I'm Eileen O'Connor. I did it with the help of an ex-Stasi officer who Jack arranged, she added, spitefully.'

Silence.

'What were you doing at Ian's funeral?' I asked.

'Oh, that! I was visiting Jack and he thought it would be amusing for me to play the part of Ian's courtesan or be mistaken for a relative. That was a laugh, wasn't it Jack?' she said, turning to look at Jack who was grinning smugly, obviously enjoying every minute.

'You should have seen the inquisitive looks on your faces when your lot gave condolences to me – a stranger to the deceased,' she said, laughing hysterically.

I didn't wait for her to finish her maniacal performance – I repeated my question,

'What about the others, who killed them?'

'Well John, it's all rather complicated,' replied Charles, 'but, you see, I had to give the unfortunate order for Martin's disposal. Jack Orlowski reported in that Martin was on to us. He didn't report directly through *the Agency* but used the old MI6 channels where we had the best informant you could think of, John Scarlotti. That was obviously a dangerous situation for Jack. Martin must have been on to him because he didn't report through *the Agency* channels. The taking out of Ian and Martha is another story, I think Jack should tell you, he'll enjoy that,' he added, with a cynical grin on his face.

How could I have trusted this man, I thought. I twisted my head to look at Jack Orlowski, who was fidgeting,

'Eh, ah, em,' he said, clearing his throat.

'You see, John, you are such an idiotic patriot to your country, you can't see further than your nose,' he said, and giggled.

'Get on with it,' snapped Eileen O'Connor, who obviously had some power over Jack, or didn't like Jack's praise of me being a patriot.

'Yes, well, we have an alliance with a powerful group of business magnates who have influence over most political groups in the world.'

'You mean Nazis,' I replied.

Jack ignored my comment and carried on in his southern drawl,

'It was during one of our many meetings the subjects in question came up. You see the Jewish woman was too well informed about our group and of our alliances. She must have gained the information, partly herself, and also with the help of Ian Stewart, who happened to have followed me on more than one occasion and was spotted. Ian Stewart passed his knowledge on to Martin, so it was really Ian's fault we had to kill Martin,' he said, gleefully.

I thought, if only my hands were free!

'All we had to do was to have a word with their leader Heinrich Bolkow, who arranged for one of his Nazi groups, *the Vikings* to undertake this pleasant task and swoop-de-whoop, it was carried out exactly at the time and date we chose,' he said, sadistically.

'You creep Jack – and you paid tribute to him with an oration I wrote for you. How low can you get – eee…git – you slimy Yank,' I said, the bile forming and wanting to spew-up – hopefully with enough power to hit Jack. It didn't – just stayed in my stomach and remained wishful thinking.

'Now we've been more than cooperative John, how about telling us what you know about us?' asked Charles.

'That's easy. That greenhorn at your side has documented all your comings and goings and holds a complete worldwide membership list. The only name not on the list is yours, which obviously distinguishes you as their unscrupulous leader,' I took a deep breath and carried on, 'Jack is so sure of himself, he thinks the system he set-up is safe from hackers and Trojans. Well he's wrong, 'cause I smelled a rat long before and re-generated his system and have been logging every movement of your organization your meticulous buddy here has passed on through his so-called secure system. If you're wondering where it is, then that's easily answered. It's in one of *the Agency's* safe houses in Berlin and if you want to check to see if what I'm saying is true, then I'll give you the address-code and super-user password to get into the system.'

I took another deep breath, I felt really wonky even sitting down, tied up as I was. I gave them the code and password. The other man left the room.

Five minutes later the other man came back and said something to Charles.

'Well, John – you're as much the professional I always thought you were. Pity about your weakness for women, though,' he said, and smiled sickly.

Ken butted in,

'Let's finish him off, now.'

'No, not until we find out if he's deposited the information elsewhere. According to our computer expert next door, a large amount of highly sensitive data was downloaded yesterday,' said Charles.

'Well, I sent a copy to MI5, to Mossad Headquarters in Tel

Aviv and deposited one in Berlin with instructions for you to be arrested for my murder, should I happen to pass away unexpectedly.'

'I've had enough listening to this bullshit,' said Jack – his southern drawl now seeming more nauseating than ever before.

'I say let's do what Ken's just suggested. Let's kill him here and now. Each one of us gives him a bullet somewhere and Ken is allowed to finish him off.'

'That's just what I would expect from you, you little American twerp, you..'

I didn't get any further. Jack shot me in the kneecap, or so I thought – well it felt like it.

'Enough of that Jack, Ken – let's have a break. Let's go next door and think this over,' said Charles.

I had gathered all my reserves together for that bit of dialogue. Now, I was ridden with pain and nausea, and completely exhausted. Besides the drugs were still in me – darkness descended.

I was awakened by a friendly voice. It was Chris. I thought – this is a pleasant dream,

'John, wake up. Wake up, John,'

On and on it went, just like when you wake up after an anaesthetic when the nurse calls you back to the living.

I eventually came to my senses. The room was full of police officers. A pretty dark-haired policewoman was examining my knee. She was bent down, her bum nearly on the floor, resting on her heel – one knee on the floor, the other pointed upwards. I could see her white knickers. Now I knew I was back in the world of the living and my mind and body were returning to active modus. Well, what a bloody shame though, I thought – missed all the fireworks.

Chris was standing apart talking to an Assistant Commissioner. He interrupted his chat and came over when he saw I was fully awake,

'That was bloody close, John. How's his leg, officer?' he asked.

'Just grazed, doesn't even need stitching. I've put a bandage on it. Sorry about the trouser leg, though,' she said, standing up and smiling.

I thought – you could do it all over again, dear. I looked down at my baggy trousers. One leg was ripped up above the knee and a blending white bandage was wrapped around the knee. Glad I was wearing baggy ones tonight, I thought, even though it was a women's night. I giggled inwardly – thinking, thank goodness for baggy trousers – they'd helped put Jack's aim off.

'Where are the baddies, Chris?' I asked.

'Been taken away, John.'

'Pity, I just wanted to tell that shit Jack, he can't even shoot properly,' I said and giggled.

At first it was high-pitched, then it became a hoarse laugh. I continued to laugh my head off at Jack the twit and my baggy trousers. Chris joined in and a few others too. The policewoman had hysterics and had to hold herself on my shoulder. Others who thought it was weird in such a situation to laugh just stared and withheld. When we'd finished, I asked Chris,

'Don't tell me Chris, it was your intuition this time and you had me followed, right?'

'That's right, Jack. I got a team organised and became very worried when some guys carried a bundle out of your apartment block. We followed them here, so I called for reinforcements from MI5. That's about it, John. Oh, we arrested Charles' sister Helen too. Will you be making charges against her, John?'

'Under the circumstances, I'd rather not. I'd prefer to keep my personal life out of this as much as I can.'

'I'll see what I can do then,' said Chris, 'and for Christ sake, John, be a bit more choosy in the future when you have a one night stand!'

Bloody cheek, I thought. Wasn't Helen the one that got me going? I noticed the young policewoman was grinning all over her face and her eyes had that glazed, I wouldn't mind about one either, look.

London – Thursday morning, 8th September

I made breakfast, placed everything on a tray and hobbled into the lounge. I made myself comfortable on the sofa and poured myself a cuppa. I switched on the telly and watched the 8 o-clock news. The reporter was babbling about one of those periodic multi-vehicle accidents, this time involving a lorry, two cars and two government vehicles near Hendon. I was just about to switch to another channel when the reporter began talking about the people involved,

'*...four Special Branch officers and a senior police officer, AC Charles Cross, who was accompanying an important senior member of the ISIA and a member of the Israeli diplomatic corps. All seven persons were killed outright. The bodies have been recovered. New Scotland Yard has just issued a statement regretting the loss of one of their best men and....*'

I switched the telly off and sank back onto the sofa. Bloody hell, they hadn't taken long in getting rid of them. I thought – this is a field day for the press. It won't be long before the government releases a big political story about this event, then bury the assassination, if it was true! Who's responsible – went through my mind? My first suspicion went to John Scarlotti, who, according to Chris, apparently took early retirement a few days ago. I wouldn't put it past Ben Goldmann and the Mossad either. Ben had maybe meant something else when he warned me about Kenneth Woodward. Then there was my own organization too – maybe not wanting a scandal of this nature. Tony Blair's team is not very popular at the moment either. Another scandal this size would have broken his back, especially the roots and nature of the organization Charles belonged to and their obvious involvement in getting the government to intervene in Iraq. Of course, there is always the CIA to consider!! I'm glad to be going back to Germany, able to leave this mess behind. Then on to Israel once we get Bolkow and his cronies. Elsa and Paula – which of the two do I decide. After all, a durable relationship depends on many parameters and both seem to be even on points.

I had just got my baggage together when the telephone rang,
'John, oh, John! Have you heard the bad news. Ken was killed in a car crash in London,' she cried out.
'Yes, I know. I'm sorry, Elsa,' I said, although I'd only been guessing. I paused for piety's sake, 'but how did you find out, his name wasn't broadcasted?' I asked.
'I had a phone call from Ben Goldmann. He expressed his condolences and had the cheek to ask if I wanted to bury him,' she said, and added, 'he's just been killed and that's all he thinks about.'

'He's just doing his job, Elsa. Jews have to be buried as soon as possible, mostly on the day of death or the day after. It's their custom, so don't be angry, eh!' I said.

'Well I told him I'm not interested. He said he'd arrange for the burial in London tomorrow or the day after. Said something about identification being difficult because he was badly burned.'

'John, what's going on?'

'It was just a car accident, Elsa, so don't worry. Look I'll give you a ring from Berlin this afternoon. I was just about to leave for the airport when you rang.'

'Okay, John – until later then, bye.'

'Bye, Elsa.'

Well things are happening real fast.

I said my thanks to the policeman on protection duty at my flat door and told him he wasn't needed anymore as I was now on my way to the airport.

I met Chris in the departure lounge, he had that *"I know"* look about him.

'Hi, John – how's you're leg?' he asked, grinning.

'Hi, Chris – it's allright – only a graze – another scar to add to the others. This one will remind me of that skunk Jack Orlowski, I guess – well, for a few weeks at least.'

Chris laughed.

'Bye the way, Chris – thanks for not listening to me and for getting me out of that nasty situation,' I said.

'Bollocks, John,' he muttered.

'Have you heard the news?'

'Yeah, but only about Charles Cross – I can only guess who the others were.'

'Your guess is right. Kenneth Woodward is another of the

victims. Had that verified through Elsa who rang up this morning. Says, Ben Goldmann asked her on the phone if she wanted to bury him,' I said.

'Bloody, hell, John. That's cheeky ain't it?'

'Not really, don't forget he was Hans's father. Maybe Ben wants to avoid giving him a hero's burial in Israel, after all he was the European Chief of the Mossad, and it's not out yet that he was involved in the 9/11 intelligence agencies' conspiracy. Anyway, now we can concentrate on getting Bolkow. I've asked Olaf to stay on with us. He may be of invaluable help. Perhaps through some of his old contacts with the BND.'

'We'll see, John. We'll see.'

Berlin – Thursday afternoon, 8th September

I finished writing my preliminary end report for *the Agency* board meeting, now relocated to take place in Berlin. I gave a detailed version of the unscrupulous organization Jack Orlowski belonged to and finished by adding my resignation following the completion of the job I'd set out to do – bring the last person on my list involved in the death of Ian Stewart and Martin Cole to justice. I added a postscript:

"I have a vast amount of information showing that Jack Orlowski misused the Agency and the European Headquarters in Berlin for his own heinous purposes. He was a member of a world wide criminal organization."

I needed that, should the board refuse further funding. I sent it off as an email to the *director of the board, Sir Thomas Phillips*.

I don't really trust all those *fellows on the board,* but I had to show I still held some mighty strong cards.

My next task was the promised call to Elsa.

'Hi, Elsa,' I said softly.

'John, oh John. I'm so glad you called. I had a long talk with Hans. He doesn't believe what I told him about his deceased father. You know – what you told me in Israel! Maybe you can convince him, John.'

'Well, maybe he just doesn't want to hear the truth, Elsa.'

'Perhaps, I hadn't thought about that,' she said and added, 'When are you coming down South, John? Hans has left for university, you know. He starts studies on Monday.'

'That's a pity, Elsa – I'd liked to have spoken to him. Look, I have important business to do first but I'll try and get to you within the next couple of days. I may not be able to manage it until Monday, though.'

'But you'll still come, won't you, John?'

'I promised, Elsa! I'll give you a ring beforehand, okay?'

'Oh, John, of course! I'm so looking forward to seeing you again. Take care.' 'You too, Elsa,' I replied, warmly.

My feelings for Elsa and Paula conjugated, unsure, or simply not ready for decision-making. If I'm not careful I'll end up losing both.

We had a meeting early that evening in my hideout. Our subject was Bolkow and the Nazi renewal of power. Olaf stood up and addressed us,

'Let me say something, lads. I've made a few enquiries about the far right, especially Bolkow. His organization has no alliances with the current Nazi political parties. Bolkow's lot just use them to spread their filth, fear and terror. They do have an alliance with Al Qaeda though, that's for certain – yet here again only to suit their own purposes. We're dealing with a revival organization called ODESSA that John already pointed out to you. It's just the name that has the ultra-right touch, most probably picked by Bolkow who was one of the founder members. Of course there are some nasty Nazis involved, but this particular organization doesn't purely consist of Nazis. We're dealing with powerful companies who have worldwide networks – their aim is to take over world control. They've a global trading company in *Zug*, a district with the lowest Swiss taxes they use as a so-called *World Trade Centre*. What I've also been able to obtain, is information pointing to a bunker system in Switzerland. Apparently Bolkow is hiding out there,' Olaf said, adding, 'and don't forget, Switzerland is a neutral country.'

'Neutral, my foot,' said Jack the Ripper,

'There are as many Nazis in Switzerland as there are in Germany, and that's a fact.'

Mike Jones piped up, 'Let's still go get 'em!'

'Yeah, let's get 'em,' came from a few others.

I butted in,

'I would much prefer to lure him out, but I'm afraid from what Olaf told me at lunchtime, he's dug himself in – he's not moving.'

'What sort of place is this bunker system, Olaf?' asked Colin Hughes.

'It's an old atomic bunker in the mountain range of Toggenburg in Switzerland, only 40 Kilometres from Lake Constance as the crow flies. They've a number of observation posts that to the untrained eye look like real weekend Swiss chalets, of which hundreds are to be found in the area,' answered Olaf. He made a grimace and continued, 'It's impossible to get into the bunker system. However, I've made some enquiries through old friends in the BND. Apparently they've had their eye on the group for some time. It would be next to impossible to get the Swiss authorities to arrest Bolkow. But some good news – the BND has identified the heads of the organization by observing Bolkow over a longer period. The group we've named ODESSA meet on a regular basis every three to four weeks at the Hotel Steigenbühler in Davos. Their main cover is new economic trading ventures with the world's major global player countries and some of the 200 less important countries. We still don't know if there's a connection with EUCLID. That's the group of agents from intelligence agencies responsible for using Al Qaeda that led to the 9/11 disasters and the falsification of Iraqi WMD information. ODESSA should have met last night. It may be a coincidence they didn't, but it could point to a link with EUCLID. Maybe the arrests in London and the subsequent killing of the EUCLID leaders in the multi-car crash upset their plans a bit,' said Olaf, finally, before he sat down, having said his say.

'Bloody hell, Olaf – we should have been on our way to Davos directly after lunch,' cried Chris.

I butted in.

'Don't panic. Olaf's friends are staking out the hotel. They've an agent in the building working as a staff member who says the group's re-booked the *Rotary Salon* conference room for tomorrow afternoon.'

Chris retorted,

'Yes, that's all very well, but do we know for sure that Bolkow's going to be there too?'

'Good question Chris,' answered Olaf, 'we don't know for sure. Apparently he's not usually on the list, but my friends reckon there's a good chance he'll be there tomorrow. The agent has been told there will be an extra guest coming tomorrow who has to be treated extremely well.'

'Well, that could point to Bolkow, couldn't it,' I declared, raising an eyebrow – questioning for further support to my suggestion – no reaction.

'We'll just have to take the chance then. If we don't get him tomorrow then there's always another day, ain't there lads,' said Chris, a big grin showing his eagerness and will to persuade. Some of the lads nodded their heads, ready for a new adventure and the prospects of more dough.

'Okay, lads – then that's settled, we'll be leaving for Davos tonight,' I concluded, grinning.

Chris added,

'I've some lovely ideas what we can do with them when we get them,' he said wickedly.

'I'll bet you do,' replied Derek Montgomery.

I'd another call to make – an acquaintance from the Old Soviet KGB. Juri Kalinkovski, ex member of department IX, responsible for the personal security of Russian government VIPs and property protection. He supported the *Alpha group* that refused to storm the Russian White House in August 1991, which was a great booster to his career. He has his own private security company now – organising the travel and protection of Russian businessmen and their families – mostly when they're abroad. Just before I took retirement, he even offered me a very lucrative job with his private company. It was more like a return favour for saving a young rich Russian couple in *Gaschurn,* Austria, that were being attacked by a small group of Nazis who happened to have caught my eye. The couple had managed to slip their bodyguards and were slightly drunk too. But not drunk enough to recognize the help

I gave them. I scared the Nazi youths off by pepper-spraying two of them and catching the third one with a nice back handed slice under his nose. I escorted the young couple back to their hotel. It turned out – the young man was a Russian oil-multi worth billions. I bumped into the couple again at a reception held in the Russian Embassy a week later in Vienna. Juri Kalinkovski escorted them in personally. The entourage consisted mainly of bodyguards. The young couple saw me when they entered the reception room and rushed over to greet me, leaving the bodyguards totally off-guard. I got a hug from the young guy and a big lipstick kiss on the cheek from the young woman that she was rubbing off with a paper tissue when Juri joined us. The young guy explained to Juri that I was the person who'd saved them in *Gaschurn*.

Juri was all over me at the Embassy, like a rash – said I saved his face. Implored me to join his company on the spot. After many Vodkas and persuasive words I managed to wave off until the Russian Ambassador came to my rescue. I reckon I would have had liver cirrhosis by now if I'd joined his security travel company.

Juri still owes me that favour though. Maybe he can help out with a small transport problem – I know he has a fleet of aircraft and helicopters at his disposal. I gave him a call.

Davos – Friday, 9th September

We arrived in Davos in the early hours of the morning. Olaf's two friends had arranged temporary accommodation in a hay barn. Unfortunately, we won't have time to enjoy the beautiful scenery on a mountain hike or eats in a five star restaurant, or even experience the night life mixing with the rich and famous in one of the exclusive night clubs.

Chris, Olaf and I went over to meet Olaf's ex-colleagues.

Olaf introduced us to Kurt Blessing and Christopher Manning from the German BND. After the customary shaking of hands and polite smirks, Kurt Blessing spoke,

'Gentlemen, I think a snatch, in or around the hotel, is out of the question. The hotel security department have a highly advanced technical surveillance and protection system, well trained security personnel and CCTV cameras on every corner inside and out. All security personnel are armed. Special locking and alarm systems top it off. Otherwise it wouldn't get used for G8 meetings, would it,' he added, smirking.

Chris muttered something. I gathered from his *visage* he wasn't too happy how things were running for us. Kurt carried on speaking, 'However, we've arranged some vehicles for you should you want to try and snatch Bolkow on his way back to his bunker. I'd like to point out if you get him, we'll arrange for his border crossing into Germany where he'll be tried by a German court. What do you say?'

I thought if we said yes, then we could have the vehicles *and* their support. What we do with Bolkow is another matter. To save the day, and our faces before this pointed gun I said,

'Well, Kurt, I think that's a splendid proposal but what if some of the other participants of that conference just happen to fall into our trap too, and what happens if there's a shootout. We haven't any weapons?'

Christopher Manning grinned and said,

'We've thought of that. There are enough weapons, plus extra ammunition in the vehicles.'

'Well then, that's a proposition we can't refuse, eh, lads?' I said, trying to save the day.

No comments from Chris. Olaf was obviously ashamed at the way we were being treated. The BND were leaving us to do the dirty work. If it's successful, they get the goods and the glory. If it doesn't, then we have the casualties and possibly great difficulties with the Swiss authorities – maybe even jail – *c'est la vie*. I added,

'We need communications equipment too, and could you possibly fit two of the vehicles with a flashing blue police light, a *Blaulicht* – and one of those police hand-stop, lollypop signals, I think they call it a *Polizei-Kelle* in Germany!'

'All the equipment you require for an operation of this type has been distributed to each vehicle.'

'But you can't possibly have known we'd need the blue lights and lollypop signal,' I protested.

'Well, that's the way we'd have done it,' said Christopher Manning, smugly.

'Okay,' I said, forcing a grin, 'we'll do it your way, but we'll decide on the tactics and where. You keep out of it until we have our man. Oh, and add two RPGs to that list,' I said, nearly adding *basta*, 'and I don't think they should be a big problem, as the Swiss RPGs are renowned to be among the best in the world.'

It was a lousy day for a take – raining cats and dogs. I sent Chris, Derek and Colin out with Christopher Manning for the handing over of the vehicles and to check the inventory – a Land Rover with a fixed blue police light and three SUVs. I got Chris to keep Christopher occupied and get him back into the hay barn on some excuse. I needed the other two to check the vehicles for tracking devices and I didn't want any onlookers. They would probably follow us anyway but maybe they might just get lost, or their own vehicle may not even start. I was more concerned with the *after*, than *before* the take. Derek came back.

'Okay, Jock there's all we need, even two Swiss police uniforms,' he said and laughed.

I thought that was splendid, it would make our task easier. I went over the route with Olaf and Chris. Olaf reckoned our only chance was between *Klosters* and *Gruesch*, because after that they would be going for a longer drive on the Autobahn E43, then branching onto the E60 and past *St. Gallen* where they would then turn off onto smaller roads towards Bolkow's bunker. I let him explain. His idea was we would have to try and force them to drive into one of the sightseeing parking lots along the route using the police lights and signalling disc. I took over and suggested stopping Bolkow right at the beginning of his return journey from Davos. That would be the least suspect. Davos is known for the frequenting high society with their drugs and drink, so a police check outside of town wouldn't be suspect.

'That sounds all right, John, but what if they don't stop and what do we do with him, or them afterwards?' asked Chris.

'Good question, Chris – well, if they don't stop, we'll have two vehicles ahead to block the road, and they'll be facing one of our RPG's won't they! The question, what do we do with him or them afterwards is simple. I'm not going to hand Bolkow over to the Germans. Because of his age, he'll never go to trial in Germany. He'd then live on to further his cause with those other heinous devils. No, I've got a better idea,' I said and dropped my cookie.

'All we've got to do, is get him to the helicopter pad at Klosters. I've arranged for a Russian Kazan, VIP type Mi-17 to pick him up and fly him to an unknown destination where he'll exchange the comfortable helicopter for an uncomfortable journey back to the Ukraine. That's where he helped murder those thirty thousand odd Jews and that's where he should be put on trial.'

'Bloody hell, John – that sounds superb! You've been busy ain't ya,' said Chris.

'Yes, as a matter of fact I have,' I replied and turned to Olaf, 'I know this is asking a lot, but being a Black Forester it shouldn't be too difficult for you to impersonate a Swiss policeman. I really do need you in one of the police uniforms,' I said bluntly, knowing he wouldn't say no.

Olaf nodded but didn't reply. Obviously he'd accepted the half-order and was already going through the impersonation in his mind.

Colin, JW, Jack the Ripper and myself were in the lead vehicle waiting near the Hotel for Bolkow to arrive – also to check other guests. Two other vehicles were parked discreetly, 800 metres away, just past the congress centre and near the junction to the Hotel Steigenbühler. Their task was to relay information on all arrivals and to leave ahead when the time came. It would be a long wait.

We registered two German limousines that arrived together. I recognised Bolkow's butler Heinz next to one of the drivers. Due to the rear windows being tinted, we could only make a guess as to the amount of people in both cars, so we put them down to at least eight people. Of further interest were one Austrian, a number of Swiss and a Saudi limousine with diplomatic plates. I gave the order to concentrate on the two German vehicles.

It was getting dark when we saw the first of the suspect vehicles leave. The two German limousines were the last to depart – time for action.

Two of my men were in Swiss police uniforms. One was waiting at the beginning of a car park in the middle of the *Wolfgang Pass,* only about five or six kilometres outside of Davos, ready to move out into the road and wave Bolkow's vehicles in when he gets the signal from us. The other policeman, Olaf, was standing in the car park just behind the jeep with the flashing blue light. Both SUV's were further up near the car park exit.

We followed at a safe distance and gave our signal. As Bolkow's limousine approached, my policeman stepped out into the middle of the road and waved both cars into the parking area with the police hand-held lollypop that illuminated in the dark. We tailed in behind them. Olaf, in police uniform, was standing behind his jeep waiting. The two limousines stopped. The road policeman made his way quickly into the car park, passed our SUV and approached the two limousines from the rear. His hand was near his gun, his holster catch off. Olaf went forward to the first vehicle and tapped on the driver's window, making a hand movement for the driver to let his window down. Olaf asked the driver in perfect Swiss German for his papers,

'Guten Abig, Fahrzeug Kontrolle! Ihre Papiere bitte!'

Olaf took the driving licence and car papers from the driver and flashed his torch over them. He bent his head down slightly towards the driver and told the driver it stinks of alcohol from the car and asked the driver if he'd had anything to drink,

'Es riecht nach Alkohol in ihrem Auto. Haben Sie Alkohol getrunken?'

The critical moment had arrived. My men were now in

position, ready to attack if necessary. The driver looked at Olaf and grinned. Olaf saw the movement of the second passenger just in time. He dived towards the ground as a bullet singed the hairs above the left side of his face. He rolled away to the rear.

At the sound of the shot, our RPG man moved out from behind our foremost SUV and aimed at the front limousine.

As Olaf was rolling towards the rear, my policeman who was behind the two limousines moved out, ran forward, and opened fire. Two perfect shots and the driver and his front seat colleague were put out of action. My men came out from all sides now.

I approached the rear car. That's where I expected Bolkow to be. I had two of my men on both sides of the limousines. The front vehicle couldn't break out because their driver was incapacitated. The rear vehicle was too close to the front one and would have to reverse first to break out and our SUV was directly behind it. They wouldn't make it under a barrage of machine guns and an RPG that would at least rip open the front and engine even if the limousine was armoured. The two vehicles were trapped.

'Okay,' I shouted in English, 'you lot in the front car – stay put.'

I moved over to the rear limousine and shouted.

'Right, you lot in this car – get out real slow and leave your weapons in the car. If anyone comes out and I find a gun on him I'll shoot him in the balls,' I said, and wasn't really sure if I would, but the way I was feeling I thought I might just do that. Just in case one of those types had called back to Davos for help, we'd have to move fast. They got out.

'Hands up and on the car – feet apart – get moving you bastards,' I said.

We rubbed them down real quick – searching for objects and sent them off on a little hike. Bolkow wasn't in this vehicle. The result of the rubdown and car search gave a collection of cell phones, knives and guns. Maybe we'll get valuable information from the cell phones later.

I moved over to the front car where we went through the same process. Apart from the two in the front who were wounded, only Bolkow and Heinz his butler were in the back seat. I waved my gun at them to get out. Bolkow swung his legs smartly onto the tarmac and tried to stand up like a real proud Arian. Heinz followed. I went over and said,

'This time you're not going to get away you Nazi creep.'

I gave an order,

'Tie and gag this one up real good and get those two wounded out and well away from the cars,' I ordered, 'and then let's get the hell out of here.'

I sent Heinz the butler over with the two wounded men after they'd been rubbed down. If looks could kill I would have died on the spot. The hatred spewing from Bolkow's reddened eyes was devilish.

Petrol, two small incendiary tubes, and the two limousines were ablaze. So far so good – we got the hell out of there – in convoy to *Klosters* and the helicopter pad. We arrived there twenty minutes later.

I let out a sigh of relief as I noticed our back-up vehicles that I'd summoned there yesterday. They were parked and pointing in the escape direction near the entrance to the narrow road leading to the helipad. I'd reckoned our chances of getting stopped in the SUVs as being high, as we only had the choice of one exit road leading to the Autobahn from *Klosters*. We'd have had great difficulty explaining our bogus uniforms and weaponry if we got caught in the BND vehicles. Standing near the helicopter was my friend Juri, grinning like a Buddha. Near him was his usual entourage of bodyguards.

'My friend, John,' he said, as we got out of the car and went towards him. His big hand shot out for a shake and the other enclosed me in a tough embrace.

'So you've brought my country a nice present, have you,' he said, and eyed Bolkow.

'As promised, Juri. I only hope justice is done,' I said, solemnly.

'Oh, I shall certainly make sure of that, John,' he said, and grinned, showing rows of gold teeth.

'We've got no time for Vodka, this time, Juri. Maybe next time we can celebrate, eh?'

'Sure, John – until next time,' he said, still grinning.

Juri went forward to his helicopter followed by his entourage holding Bolkow in the middle – a monster, as depraved as they come, rivalling Hitler and Stalin.

We waited until the helicopter was in the air with its human cargo before we made our departure down the lane and a quick change of vehicles.

Once we were on the Autobahn I relaxed and turned to Olaf – I felt in need of a few answers,

'Tell me Olaf,' I asked,

'Was that justice or was it destiny?'

'I don't really know, John. For us Germans it means no bad press about harvesting Nazi criminals. There are still a lot of them alive that are not being prosecuted by the judiciary system. *Let sleeping dogs lie* is the main motto and *it's such a long time ago* is another, or to the neighbours of most known Nazi criminals – *he's such a nice gentle old man!* The German judiciary system has never been denazified, so what do you expect! Bolkow deserves to be punished by those he caused so much death and sorrow, if that's what you're implying, John. If I'd my way I think I'd have blown them all up for what they're planning to do to the world.'

I didn't bother to comment – enough had been said. Fortunately all four vehicles had valid Swiss Autobahn *vignettes* – otherwise the Autobahn police could have stopped us and we didn't want to be registered anywhere near Klosters.

We made our way back over the border to Friedrichshafen in Germany where I said goodbyes to my *bunch*. They were booked on a flight to the UK – each with a very big bonus cheque in their pockets.

Olaf gave his friends from the BND a call and informed them where they could pick up their vehicles and weapons. He didn't mention Bolkow as I'd asked him to give Juri enough time to get him well out of judicial reach of the BND. Olaf was about to carry on to Munich to placate his friends from the BND. I hadn't told him, but I shall be on my way to Buchenberg soon where I'll stay a few days with Elsa. After all, a promise is a promise.

'Tell me Olaf,' I asked, 'I always wondered what it was Hans' friend Robert thought important to mention?'

'Robert, let me think. Ah, yes, I think I know. It was about some guy from *Burgberg* who threatened Hans once and is known to be a member of the Nazi Party, the NSPD,' replied Olaf.

'So that was it,' I said, knowingly.

We said our goodbyes. I waved Olaf off and waited until he was well on his way before picking up my rental. But first of all, I tried giving Paula another ring. Her mailbox answered once again. I drove off along the road – Lake Constance on my left and the distant mountains of Toggenburg darkening the horizon behind it. Many pieces of the puzzle have fitted and now I'm on my way to Elsa to carry on where we left off at Freiburg. Maybe I'll stay longer than a few days at her place, who knows, but I still have to go to Berlin to sort things out with *the Agency* and my hideout. Then there's another matter – check out the messages and telephone numbers from the cell phones we picked up from Bolkow and his cronies. Perhaps next week I'll go on to Israel and Haifa and Paula. It's going to be difficult to decide, which of the two – Paula or Elsa?

Black Forest – early Saturday, 10th September

Buoyed by the success of the last mission, I drove happily towards my next destination – Elsa's Black Forest dwelling in Buchenberg, singing to a song on the radio, *'don't worry, be happy.'*

My thoughts went to Paula. A pity she wasn't in when I phoned. I detest leaving messages on mailboxes. I'll try again when I stop to freshen up at my favourite South German drive-in at Engen and have a bite to eat – not bad food for an Autobahn restaurant.

My mind wasn't that preoccupied not to notice the car that pulled out of the airport car park and stuck with me on the B31. I registered a total of three cars on the major road between the airport at Friedrichshafen and Ueberlingen that were possible tails. Being the only direct major road along Lake Constance between Friedrichshafen and Ueberlingen, I wasn't particularly disturbed, just a wee bit uneasy.

After a few moments of weighing-up the situation, I decided to test my suspicion by turning off the direct lake route, the E54 at Ueberlingen and taking the overland route higher up. Bingo! Normally, the lower route, the fastest and most direct would've been taken, not the case here. I was now fully alert. Maybe it wasn't such a good idea going to Elsa's. It would only endanger her. Perhaps the three cars belong together, which I doubt very much. They were seven-up. Maybe the word's out and I'm still on somebody's hit list. It wasn't hard to figure out who that might be – Bolkow's lot out for revenge. Okay, I thought, now my suspicions have been confirmed I'll have to get back to the major road – the lower one along the lakeside. Although the upper road is normally frequented with traffic, there is still a danger of being pushed off the road and annihilated at some quieter spot. I accelerated well above the speed limit of 100 kmh and drove like a madman to the next junction where I turned left and took a side road back towards Ueberlingen, only a few kilometres away. I noticed at least one of the cars that also accelerated, but kept behind me at a safe distance. Back in Ueberlingen, I turned onto the E54, where I felt relatively safe for the moment – plenty of traffic. I let the speedometer needle drop back to cruising speed.

I gave Olaf a couple of calls and had to make do with his mailbox. Fortunately, my hired car was a BMW. I reckoned I could get at least 260 kmh out of her and seeing the Autobahn is extremely busy, I should be able to get to Engen safely enough.

I turned into a parking space near the entrance and walked in briskly, making my way to the cafeteria bar. It was just before 11 am, so I managed to get my order in for a continental breakfast and a pot of coffee. I kept an eye on my rear view through the mirroring behind the glass shelves. No sign yet of my tails. Looks like they're sitting it out in the cars. I gave Paula another call and left another of my countless messages in her mailbox. Maybe I'll have to contact Carla. She might possibly know where Paula is. I hope nothing serious has happened to her. I've put away my first thoughts of having a shower and shave at the drive-in, realizing the risk from my tails.

I tried Olaf again.

'Ja, Ertl,' a deep voice answered.

'Olaf? Thank goodness! Don't you look in your mailbox? I've left you two urgent messages,' I whispered, sliding off the bar stool and moving a couple of metres away from the bar counter.

'Sorry John, I've just picked up my cell phone from security at Pullach. You know I had to give them a debriefing. I've just turned the darn thing on,' he said, his voice changing from apology to anger.

I ignored his reprimand.

'Listen, Olaf – I'm on my way to see Elsa. She wants to talk to me about Hans and now I've spotted at least three tails, seven-up. I'm currently at the Engen drive-in on the Autobahn E41,' I said, trying hard to avoid my nervousness escaping with the vocals.

'John, John! That's a weak excuse if ever I've heard one. Can't leave the women alone can you. Must have a bad conscience too, not even a word either, me being Elsa's brother and all that,' he said, crossly, adding,

'Listen, I can put your mind a little bit at rest. You've had the BND tailing you since leaving the airport. They're real mad at us you know, especially with me, as I did nothing to stop you – giving Bolkow away to the Ukrainians. It was only when I spoke with my ex-big boss, Horst Henning, and underlined the political implications, that I was let off the hook,' he said, with a sigh of relief.

'Well, that's good news, Olaf. I feel as relieved as you do, especially regarding one of the tails. Maybe they'll keep the others off my back. Concerning Elsa – she told me not to tell you – said you'd only worry again and be mad at her,' I said, knowing it wouldn't help, no matter what excuse I tried to give him. Even the truth hurts sometimes. I've already told him – let your little sister go her own way and don't molly-coddle her, you'll only smother her – it never gets through to the big brother.

'Hmm,' he said, 'you know you'll only hurt her in the end, John. You don't know German women enough to understand them. Elsa's not a one-night stand, you know. She really is infatuated with you, maybe even in love, I don't really know for sure. Besides, you've got Paula to consider. Now, she really is in love with you and, she's got more to offer than my little sister, Elsa,' he said, triumphantly.

The waitress put my breakfast tray on the counter. I nodded and gave her a broad thanking smile.

'Listen, Olaf – I'm not so sure you understand Elsa's needs anymore. I'm not going to go into any detail on the phone but I'll say this – Elsa is 42 years old and she needs me at the moment and I'm going to be there for her. Maybe she'll change her mind later on, after all, maybe I'm too old for her, but I can give her the secret desires and love she's missed or craved for,' I said, swallowing hard, knowing my feelings for Elsa were deeper than I thought, the more I started to think about Olaf's reprimanding dialog. I pictured Elsa for the moment – her charming personality, her short blond hair, blue eyes and sparkling nature. I could see those eyes looking at me fondly and even her inquisitive looks sometimes, trying to grip the situations at hand. I could see her slender hand, tucking and smoothing her hair behind her ear, unconsciously, when we spoke. It was her spontaneity too, and the sound of her voice..

'John, John?' Olaf was shouting into his mouthpiece.

'Sorry Olaf, just in deep thought – I'll be at Elsa's for the next few days or so. Then I'll be moving on to Berlin to settle my affairs with *the Agency* and then on to Israel, okay?'

'Go to hell, John, you're messing up my sister's life.'

I started to reply and found myself speaking to a *toot-toot-toot*. Olaf had cut the conversation.

I ate my breakfast leisurely, finishing off with an extra pot of coffee, thinking, where's Paula. I left the drive-in at 12.15 pm – no sign of my tails. Back on the autobahn, I put my foot down.

I entered the sleepy village of Buchenberg just after 1 pm, turning off the one and only central road, down into the valley, making my way towards what they call, the *Mueckenloch*. In days gone by a swampy area, hence *Mueckenloch,* meaning *midgets hole,* now well irrigated, but still some midgets and bloodthirsty horseflies.

Elsa's place was on the rise on the other side of the valley. A peaceful haven situated in a nature reserve area, surrounded by woods and small fields and a wee burn gurgling its way, twisting and turning, at the bottom of the shallow valley. I shoved the gear into second, taking my feet off the pedals gently, letting the engine take over control. The BMW purred steadily along a gravel road – an avenue of birches and fir trees on either side. I put my foot back on the accelerator and branched off to the left on a steep climb, a *cul-de-sac,* at the end of which stood Elsa's cute little Black Forest house.

I cut the engine and sat in the car for a few moments, enjoying the silence and solitude that surrounded the house, woods, and gardens.

I opened the door silently and listened hopefully for the sounds of nature, damning my tinnitis and the droning of a jet far above – completing the furthermost apex of its circling before gradually reducing height to land at Zurich, Kloten airport. No signs of Elsa. Her car wasn't there either. Maybe I'm too early, I thought.

I removed my bag from the boot, went up to the front door and rang the bell. No answer. I tried the door handle – the door gave way, so I went in. I dropped my bag in the hall and called out,

'Elsa, Elsa! Are you there?' No answer. Ah, well, I thought. I might just as well take that shower and have a shave before Elsa arrives. She's probably out shopping. I took my bags upstairs and left them on the landing, taking out fresh underwear and clothing. I had a shave first, and searched my toilet bag for toothpaste. Blast, I couldn't find it – must have left it somewhere. I opened the bathroom mirror cupboard and borrowed Elsa's toothpaste. Putting it back in the cupboard, I noticed two razors on a shelf and two toothbrushes in a glass. That's strange, I thought, as I closed the cupboard again. Olaf doesn't live here and Hans has gone back to university. Maybe it's Hans' and he's just forgotten it or maybe Olaf does stay here occasionally. I had a long shower, letting the water hit my head longer than necessary, trying to clear my thoughts.

Things have gone real fast over the last few weeks. I let my mind go through many channels and pipes – alleyways and crossroads, finding the loops, checking out and picking up the leftovers – realizing that I still had a few unaccomplished tasks to complete.

I changed into fresh clothing, slapped on my favourite *Chanel Platinum Egoiste,* and made my way downstairs, into the living room and slumped down on the sofa. I was asleep immediately.

I felt something descend on my lap and opened my eyes to find Elsa smiling wickedly at me. No chance to say hello, she pressed her lips gently on mine and poked the tip of her tongue through, searching for mine. I let her find it and tickled hers too. She pulled her head back and laughed. Her blue eyes twinkled. It was her turn to make love to me. She kissed my eyelids and bit my ear teasingly. She moved her hands up behind my head pulling it towards her and kissing me hard. I moved my hands up behind her back. She pushed them back and opened her blouse, undoing her bra. With a quick jerk, she pulled it out, dropping it aside. She took my hands and moved them up onto her breasts. They were firm and white, like a young teenager's, and warm to touch. Her nipples were stiffened, her longing great. I kissed and caressed them with the tip of my tongue then moved my lips upwards towards her neck and earlobe. She got off my lap and leaned back, shaking off her blouse. Her skirt was next. She undid the side clip and standing up – let it drop to the floor – she had no knickers on. She pulled me up on my feet, undoing my shirt and trousers, it seems, all in one go. I was surprised too, at the amazing speed with which my underpants were whipped down and off. She reached up and put both hands on my shoulders, pulling them down and whispering in my ear for me to sit down on the carpet. I complied and had my back resting against the sofa. Elsa moved in...

It was a long and exhausting evening. Elsa was making up for lost years and I gave myself fully to her striving for more, her inexperience and her need to explore the realms of lovemaking fully. It was exultancy pure and I enjoyed it to the utmost. The naivety and love we exchanged for each other surpassed all other earthly pleasures – even the sex I'd had with Paula was no comparison. This was what love was about too, I thought. It's a great difference between just having sex and having sex with someone you love. Some women think that way, I've been told – you should only have sex with the woman you love.

It was getting dark when we untangled and Elsa suggested we go out for eats. It must have been the rumbling of our stomachs that brought our hunger to her ears.

Before we left, Elsa switched the light on in the parlour and locked the door, turning the lock twice.

'I always lock up at night. Funny isn't it. Leave it open during the day and lock it up at night,' she said and giggled, 'Olaf is always cross, you know, when I leave it open,' she said, as she took my arm and swung it gently in time with our pacing, like a teenager, as we walked over to my car. Elsa was really happy, that's for sure.

We managed to get eats in the *Schappelstube*, a good *non-haut cuisine* restaurant. The quality and service surpasses most of the other restaurants and guesthouses – extremely clean and the personnel very friendly. As a Scot, I'm exceptionally pleased when the conditional parameters meet my utmost satisfaction, especially the main parameter – reasonable prices.

We ate mostly in silence, enjoying each other's company – passing smiles of devotion and lust. Elsa seems to have exchanged her withdrawn provincial manner for a livelier mundane one, I thought. She must have read my mind.

'You know something, John!' she said, when we'd finished eating.

I nodded and smiled, waiting for her to continue. She took a few slow sips of red wine and holding the bulb of her glass in the cups of her hands, her eyes sparkling and her elbows resting on the table, said,

'Let's talk about us. You know, you've changed my whole worldly outlook on life. I'll never be the same person again. It's not that I'm unhappy, I'm just a little bit confused. I don't think our friendship would last a longer relationship, you're much too dangerous a man to have around. You've too many scars from the past and anyway, to put it bluntly – you're a fantastic lover but you're too much a ladies man and the age difference would estrange us as the years pass.'

I watched her closely during this transfer of words, each one hitting the target brutally. Her hands left the glass, one hand stroked her hair back behind her left ear, then both hands shot up in the air, the fingers intermingled and the palms stretched upwards – the strain of telling the truth being too much to just sit there, eye to eye, and talk coolly. It has obviously been bothering her and I think I know the reason. Olaf has told her about Paula. Her last words caught me like a sledgehammer hitting my solar plexus. My *para sympaticus* and *sympaticus* nerves were having a battle – paralysing everything. I couldn't swallow the saliva building in my throat, awaiting passage – blocked entirely. The actions with her hands told me she still wants me, but under her conditions, whatever they are. I think I know. She wants me to surrender unconditionally. Retire from active duty and become a one-woman man. She watched me expectantly, almost pleadingly. I knew that look – I'd seen it once before when Anna had asked me to leave the BIS and take up a civilian job. Maybe I'm too old for all this, or she's not the right woman. I may be a lot older but that shouldn't make a difference with real love. I don't like a pointed gun held against me but I also hate hurting anybody. Elsa's just added a deep wound. I always feel like I'm sort of, only forty or so. Never paid much attention to my real age. Always thinking – it's what you feel like and can do, and I reckon I could still take on any youngster. Another thought occurred. Elsa wouldn't be holding a gun against my chest if she didn't have an alternative. That was it I thought, remembering the extra shaver and toothbrushes.

'You've found a younger man Elsa – someone who'll always be there – someone who has a regular job from seven to five and has his slippers in the stair cupboard? You know I could never compete with that,' I said, sadly, yet wishing somehow I could.

'Well, as a matter of fact, John, I *have* an admirer. It's purely a platonic friendship and I'm not sure at all now, if I want to carry on with him. You really have upset my worldly outlook, you know.'

'I'm sorry, Elsa, but I think it was Hans' disappearance that brought me back into your life. I apologize sincerely if I've confused your feelings but you know, deep down I love you more than you could ever imagine. I've often thought about that song *love hurts* over the last weeks and I confess, it really does hurt. Maybe the thought of being much older than you hit the right button. I guess I'm out of your reach and thought I was only good for fun. That's why I've never gone further,' I said, looking at her hopefully, knowing I was telling the truth.

'Oh, John, I'm so sorry. I didn't mean to be so cruel. I thought you were playing with me – one of the many women in your life. I thought I was paying you back for playing with me when I said that about your age. Oh, John,' she said, and took both of my hands in hers,

'I've always admired you and fell in love with John Jameson the first time he came to visit this area with Anna. When she was murdered, I was so sad for you and would have fallen into your arms then, if you'd wanted me to. Oh, John, I do love you so much. It hurts me too, you know and it still hurts, knowing you have another woman waiting for you in Israel. That is what hurts most,' she cried, the tears now running down her cheeks.

I leaned over and kissed some of her tears away. I changed chairs and sat next to her.

'Elsa, you are the first woman since Anna. I've never been able to even think about going to bed with another woman before you. Anna's memory always seemed to disrupt any advances going further than a flirt. I don't know what happened to me after being with you in Freiburg, but it seems to have triggered something amiss in my life. Listen, I know German women don't usually take the initiative when talking about feelings, they seem to accept things as they come. As you didn't give me any hint of loving me so deeply, I assumed **I** was the one night stand!'

Elsa smiled at my last words.

'Was that so,' she said, wickedly, sniffing her nose and laying her hand briefly onto my lap, letting it run down slowly, then pulling it back.

'What are you going to do now, John. Now we've shown we are meant for each other?' she said, her blue eyes spelling love and looking long and quizzically, hoping for the right answer.

I knew this question would come sometime and I was somehow prepared. At some time I had already played this serious scenario in my mind.

'You're German and I'm British. I'm a globetrotter and that eases the matter a little but also complicates it. I've a flat in Berlin that is fortunately only rented, but I also own a factory complex there as well where I'm building a boat. I'd like to keep that until the boat's finished. I own an old flat in London – a family heirloom. The contents are priceless and should really be in a museum, but I gave a promise on inheritance to keep and cherish them and the flat. I've unfinished business to see to in Israel and that means I shall have to see Paula. I have unfinished business in Berlin too, with the ISIA. I've handed in my notice, but I still have to bargain with them about my gratuity. Then there's Hans. What will he say, what will his reactions be? Where would we live. Would you want me to stay here, or would we live in London, or retire to some island in the Canaries or the Bermudas, or just move about? You see, Elsa, it's all very complicated and I don't know how you'd react if I had to work on my boat, or spend some time in London. Would you accompany me, or let me go on my own?'

'A lot of questions, John – I'm not a demanding woman. I've never had a man at my side so I don't know what it's like – you'd have to help and guide me. I don't think I'd be jealous, I'm passed that, but I would end our relationship if you went womanising once you'd settled for me. I would love to accompany you and do things together and help you if I can. I want to feel you and be near to you, to enjoy happy moments together and be sad when sad times fall. Hans loves you like an Uncle, you know that and he will never forget what you did, organizing his rescue. Olaf has always seen you as a brother. I know he curses over you occasionally, but that's only normal. Jesus, John – this all sounds like were doing a business deal. Let's cut it, I don't like the way it's going,' she said, vehemently, 'Maybe we should get one of those old fashioned marriage mediators to handle this,' she added, giggling.

'Let's go home Elsa, we can carry on the conversation in the living room, if you like,' I said, grinning impishly.

'You mean the bedroom,' she replied, giving me such a sexy look.

Deep down though, I had an unpleasant feeling – who do I choose? Elsa or Paula, knowing I really love them both!

Klosters, Switzerland – early Saturday, 10ᵗʰ September

Along with Richard Teufel, leader of the Nazi Party Germany and three remaining bodyguards – Bolkow's butler, Heinz Krieger, left the police post in Davos angered and confused. That English *Schweinehund* and his *Bande* had kidnapped his Fuehrer. He was mad at Teufel for his egregious handling of the matter, allowing his Fuehrer to be taken without a real fight, and letting their cars be set ablaze. Teufel's delitescent motives were only too apparent – he obviously wants to take Bolkow's place.

'Listen, Krieger,' hissed Teufel, as they turned the corner on their way to an associate to pick up a car he'd arranged, 'once we get to our Toggenburg headquarters and find out where that English agent is...,'

Krieger butted in, 'You mean the Scottish agent John Jameson,' he said, showing his superior knowledge and eagerness to please.

'Yes, Jameson,' said Teufel, turning to Krieger annoyed and sneering at him for the interruption.

'I want you to take two men and go after him. In the meantime I'll try and find out where they've taken Bolkow,' he said curtly, turning his head abruptly to the front and walking ahead swifter. That meant – no further discussion on the matter.

Krieger trailed behind. He was disappointed. Not only did Teufel not call him *our Fuehrer* any more, thought Krieger, fuming – his crooked sneer was telling its own tale too. He wouldn't be too interested in finding Bolkow, that's for sure. Maybe he just wants me out of his way, so he can take over control.

Toggenburg HQ – Saturday 10th September

Bolkow's butler, Heinz Krieger, drove in anger from the Toggenburg headquarters. His thoughts were still clouded with remorse at the kidnapping of his beloved Fuehrer and angry at the low response for revenge from Richard Teufel.

'Two extra men,' Teufel had sneered. 'That's all you'll need for ridding us of one man.'

His destination was a small village in the Black Forest called Buchenberg where he will annihilate the cause of his misery.

'Put those *scheiß* cigarettes out you bums,' he shouted furiously – glancing through his rear mirror at the two sneaky individuals sitting in the back.

Maybe he'll go back and kill Teufel once this job is done. The thoughts of killing Teufel brought him to another idea. He was the only one, apart from Bolkow who knew the code for setting the fuse-timer for the huge pile of explosives laid throughout the HQ. The explosion would destroy the Toggenburg complex completely. He smiled, content that he, the smallest rat in the nest, was the most powerful.

Black Forest – Saturday night, 10*th* September – Elsa's place

Elsa's head rested on my shoulder as I drove the three kilometres from the *Schappelstube* to her house. We passed the guesthouse *Krone* in a sharp left bend, then up a slight hill and turned right shortly after, onto the narrow road that led down into the valley towards the *Mueckenloch*.

Just as we were about to leave the rise, Elsa sat upright and shouted, 'Stop!'

I braked immediately. On the other side of the small valley was her house.

'John, I can't see any lights. I know I left one on in the parlour. It can't be Hans and you told me Olaf was in Munich. Anyway, he wouldn't dare come to my place knowing you're with me,' she said, annoyed.

'Maybe the bulb's gone, Elsa. But to be on the safe side, is there any other way we can approach your house – maybe from the top, on the other side?' I asked, lightly – trying to appear calm.

'Well, we could make an approach from above the *Muehllehen*. If we left the car there, we could go by foot along a farm track that runs parallel to my house. From the track it's only a hundred metres to the house down the side of a field,' she said encouragingly.

I smiled, thinking how professionally she'd accepted the situation. I felt uneasy though, realizing our only weapon of defence was my SAS close combat training, my eyes, and my sense of smell – my hearing was useless.

'Look Elsa, we may be worrying about nothing but I think your idea is splendid. Once we get to the last 100 metres though, I would ask you to take cover in one of the adjoining fields until I check the house and surroundings, okay?'

'Yes, John, of course,' she said, the concern wrinkles now disappearing from her face.

At this time of night not many cars travel these extremely narrow country roads. Maybe only those going home or the wily drunks avoiding the major roads and eventual police controls. We turned back and went around the village on side roads. I turned the lights off and shoved the gear into second as we travelled down a steep lane, gradually approaching the *Muehllehen*. I parked the car near one of the buildings and cut the engine. We stayed in the car for a few minutes. I motioned Elsa to remain silent. I began to wonder if I was doing the right thing. We were sitting ducks for anyone with rifles and night vision. No, I thought, this whole damn thing's too risky. An alternative abode had occurred to me instead of the possible risk of going to Elsa's place. I turned towards Elsa and was about to tell her, when two figures carrying rifles emerged from a farm track just ahead of the building where we were parked. Fortunately they didn't have any night vision gear on otherwise we'd have been goners – the heat of the bonnet would have given us away too. They could be local hunters on their way home, but I didn't want to bet on it.

I slid down under the steering wheel forcing my head down to the side, at the same time shooting my arm out and forcing Elsa down too. Having grasped the situation immediately, I was glad she didn't ask silly questions. Fortunately, the two figures didn't come down our lane. They must have disappeared behind a building and over a field leading to the ruins of the *Waldau* castle. Both our heads were still down and looking at each other.

'Elsa,' I whispered, 'just keep your head down for a few more minutes. I've been thinking it may be too risky going to your house. I've thought of a better place. We'll wait a few more minutes then make a move towards the town of *Hardt*. You don't happen to have Olaf's house keys by any chance?'

Elsa grinned, despite the situation and nodded, whispering,

'Yes, of course, I have them on my main key ring. Why didn't I think of that before – *Mensch!*' she said, cursing herself.

After waiting another five minutes I started the car and without further ado, set off on the narrow road, up the hill towards the guesthouse *Moenchhof,* hoping, whoever was after us wasn't blocking the narrow road. Having passed the guesthouse, I turned on the lights and proceeded towards *Hardt*. From there, we carried on to the town of *Sulgen*. On entering the town, we went down a steep hill to some traffic lights and turned off onto the road where Olaf had inherited a house from an uncle.

It was strange being in Olaf's house with Elsa who was hanging onto my arm. Anna's ghost still hovers in my memory and maybe it lingers in these quiet rooms. Uncanny, I thought – it was as though I was trespassing. Maybe it was just the ancient building or Olaf's reprimand. It was one of those nights where you've had enough and just want to snuggle up and be glad of the other's company. Love is a natural phenomenon, I thought, and even though sex is a part, it's not always a necessity.

We woke up to a radio in the living room blasting morning music from the South German SWF4 musical request program. Each request announced by the friendly voice of Michael Brannick.

'Looks like Olaf's back, John,' she said shyly and stretched her arms behind her.

'Sounds like it,' I replied, looking at her and grinning. I stroked her hair and ran my hands down to the nipples showing through her thin t-shirt. I stroked them and let my hands move up her arms.

She gave me a quick perk on the lips and said, soothingly,

'Not here, John – Olaf's too prude. He wouldn't condone it.'

With that she wriggled out of my arms, moved off the bed and disappeared into the bathroom. I swung my feet onto the floor and stood up. I stretched my arms. My fingertips touched the ceiling. I put on my clothes and went into the living room where Olaf was sitting like a moron at the dining table laid for three.

'Morning Olaf,' I said cheerfully.

No answer.

'Look, Olaf, I'm sorry we jumped your private sphere last night, but we had nowhere else to go. Elsa's place was staked out with armed men and I wasn't going to risk her getting hurt,' I said, hoping I still sounded apologetic.

Still no answer – Elsa was standing at the door – she moved into the room.

'Now who the hell do you think you are Olaf – are you my brother or are you the hotelier of some cheap hostel who doesn't have any manners?' she yelled.

Olaf took his napkin from his lap and shook the crumbs off onto his plate – folded it up neatly, and laid it aside. He got up quietly and made for the door. At the door he half turned and said,

'Just put the dishes in the dishwasher before you leave.'

It couldn't have been more dramatic because the radio commentator interrupted the music with a news flash. Olaf stood in his tracks with his hand on the door handle. He turned and looked at us aghast, as the information poured out,

'*We have some new information about the shoot-out near a*

house in Buchenberg last night. Official sources say that three gunmen were waiting to allay the owner of an isolated house and were accosted by members of the German security forces. Two of the assailants were killed and one was seriously injured. A member of the security forces was slightly wounded. Our hospital correspondent reports it was only a flesh wound. The wounded assailant is still in a critical condition. He is in the intensive care unit of the central area hospital at Villingen. The circumstances surrounding this incident are not yet known. A spokesman for the security forces reports that the gunmen opened fire when ordered to lay down their weapons. Some neighbours report it may have to do with the house owner's son, who was recently kidnapped by Arab extremists in the Palestinian autonomy area. We will interrupt our program with more news as it comes in. And now..'

Olaf went over to the radio and switched it off. He turned to both of us and said,

'I'm so sorry, Elsa, John. I didn't know. How can you possibly forgive me. Come here Elsa,' he said.

Elsa went over. Olaf took her in his arms and wept like a baby. I retreated discreetly to the terrace outside.

We sat on the terrace that overlooked *Sulgen* and talked our hearts out. I realized too, my tails had really been the BND or German security forces working with the BND. Olaf went into his study to take a phone call. When he was finished he came back outside where Elsa and I were sitting, hand-in-hand on a Hollywood swing, swinging gently to and fro.

'Looks like your presence is urgently required in the *Villingen* hospital, John – the wounded assailant is Heinz

Krieger, Bolkow's butler, and he's asking for you. The doctors don't give him much chance of survival. It's your choice, John. No one's forcing you,' he said.

'Of course I'll go. I'd never ignore a dying man's last request,' I said.

Elsa pressed both hands over mine.

'I'll go with you, John,' she said, sweetly.

'That's settled then, we're all going,' said Olaf, adding,

'We'll have to get a move on, though and don't forget, I've been given official status from *Pullach*, so don't answer any questions even if they're from the German CID or other security organizations. I'll speak to them, okay?'

'Okay, Olaf,' I said.

Elsa made a face behind Olaf's back that made me laugh. Olaf shook his head, obviously used to it.

I was allowed into the intensive care unit, accompanied by a German CID man and Olaf. Elsa had to stay outside.

Heinz Krieger was very pale. His eyes caught mine. He made a slight movement of his head, an obvious indication for me to come closer. He said something inaudible so I put my ear closer to his mouth.

'Thanks for coming Herr Jameson,' he said, in between wheezes.

Still acting the polite butler type, I thought, or maybe that has always been his role in life.

'What did you do with my *Fuehrer*, where did you put him,' he wheezed, his voice gradually dwindling.

I thought – Heinz will be leaving us shortly!

'I sent him to the Ukraine with a friend of mine, an ex KGB man, Jury Kalinkovski,' I said, hoping that would haunt Heinz in hell.

'You fool, Herr Jameson, you foo..,' he said, his voice dwindling off and a smile appearing on his face.

His eyes looked kindly at me as he managed out another word, 'thank yo...'

Alarm beeps were now sounding on the monitors.

I wonder what favour I've done him, I thought. Maybe my coming – good manners, though – exellent qualities for a butler!

A doctor and two nurses ran into the room, shoving me aside and taking over their patient – it was too late. One of the nurses dragged the heart defilbrator trolley over.

'No need for that any more,' said the doctor, shrugging his shoulders as he switched off the life saving equipment and ran his hand over Heinz's eyelids, closing them for good. He looked at his wristwatch and wrote something on the patient's record sheet. He turned towards us,

'That's it, gentlemen – take your leave from Herr Krieger by all means, but don't stay too long, we need the bed,' he said, turning around and swishing out of the room without further ado – normal daily routine ahead and no room for sentiments. There are some jobs, I thought, where sentiments could make you redundant.

Olaf was very kind, and let us stay at his place in *Sulgen* – said he had a lot of work to do in Pullach. Seems they were very impressed the way he's been handling things lately and have given him a freelance job and temporary security status plus his own office. Olaf had been especially chuffed when I handed him the cell phones we'd gathered on our Swiss outing. The addresses and telephone numbers included a number of foreign statesmen. One in particular had been called frequently – none other than that of the Russian Prime Minister.

I stayed a few more days, trying Paula's number when Elsa was out shopping. Seems Paula's mailbox has packed in, all I get is an indefinite dialling tone. Carla isn't answering either. I tried Ben, but he hasn't been available and his beetroot secretary is not good at lying – something's afoot, I thought. My bad conscience made me think perhaps Ben had a hand in this and maybe told Paula about Elsa. Or maybe Paula is a Mossad agent after all. Many scenarios passed through my mind. Foremost – Paula is punishing me for Elsa. There's one thing I've never been able to come to terms with, and that's jealousy and bitchiness.

I began to think of Ben. He gets my gall up with his moral apostle attitude towards me regarding women – bloody moron. He's never really forgiven me for marrying his half-sister Anna. I guess he's been right to a certain point in blaming me indirectly, now I know it was Eileen O'Connor who murdered Anna because of a personal vendetta involving the death of her IRA father in Belfast during a skirmish with my SAS group and Republicans. The hell I thought, I'd never been with another woman since Anna's death and Elsa was my first. Then there was Paula and my one-night stand with Helen. What the bloody hell does this guy expect after such a long time – bloody purist. He seems to know a hell of a lot. Too much for someone who sits back and pleads ignorance and piety. I know it from experience – it's those who keep a low profile who're the most dangerous. I recall the enormous difficulties I experienced with Anna being a Jew and I being a catholic. No, it wouldn't work, not with a jealous woman – not now! I guess I was foolish voicing my love for Paula. I think I'll go back to my old outlook on women – generally loving a woman without telling her. It's the easy way out and avoids getting hurt – *c'est la vie!* Having a bad conscience though, upsets the inner balance, so I'll have to get Chris to check out Paula in Haifa – make sure nothing's happened to her too. Thinking about checking Paula out made me decide to give Jan Hellstern a call,

'Ja,' a male voice answered.

'Is that you, Jan?' I asked.

'Yes, John – didn't expect to hear from you again, I must say. What is it this time?' he asked, sounding annoyed.

'Did you come across a Jewish woman called Paula Zuckenic, Jan. It's of vital importance!' I said, urgently.

'Hm, you should know better than to mention names on the phone John, but allright – yes, I do happen to know her. She was BG's best protégé – she should have become an actress – she's that good. Does that answer your question, John?'

'It certainly does, Jan. Thanks, and sorry for the disturbance.'

I rang off without waiting for his comment. My pulse was doing double-time. It all fits in now – her visits to the museums – obviously to hand over information and fetch new instructions. The place in Haifa is probably a Mossad safe house or a retreat for employees. The whole thing's been steered by that bastard Ben Goldmann and I've been really and truly duped like a greenhorn. Maybe in the end they were just after Bolkow or even JC's testament. Perhaps her tears were real when I left her in Haifa. She knew the reason why. She had her orders. She'll never be happy again, though. I know, because I took similar orders years ago to leave off a woman I'd fallen in love with – a young Jamaican woman from South London called Veda. Apparently she didn't fit into the establishment scene at the time. I was forced to tell a story of lies or carry on with her and look for another job. I've never forgotten her to this day, mostly because I lied to her.

Two days after the shooting incident I left for Berlin.

Berlin – Tuesday, 13th September – ISIA Board Meeting

I'd sent my preliminary end report by email last week to Sir Thomas Phillips, the director of the board and was anticipating a frosty reception – I was touched by the friendly greeting I received from the ISIA board secretary.

'Mr Jameson, how nice to see you again,' she exclaimed, politely.

'Hi, Jasmine, nice to see you too,' I replied, and meant it.

She was one of those types of secretaries who are nice to you even when passing on bad news.

'Sir Thomas was outraged the way you've been treated. I'm to express his deep regrets about the bad handling you received from Jack Orlowski. He wishes to see you in the board meeting,' she said, chuckling, 'It wouldn't surprise me if he offers you a position on the board,' she added, smiling, 'I'm sure we'd all be delighted here in Berlin. You have a big family of admirers here, you know,' she added, blushing, 'would you like to freshen up before the meeting? You can use my private room if you like,' she added, fluttering her eyelids. 'You must be tired just having got off the plane.'

Well that's an invitation I won't refuse, I thought and I could do with a freshen-up. Besides, nobody I know has ever been invited into Jasmine's private room.

'I'd love to, Jasmine,' I said, putting on my best bass, 'I've just got off the plane and could do with a freshen up.'

Jasmine moved out from behind her desk and walked a couple of paces to a cupboard. She opened the cupboard door and dialled a combination. The door swung aside to reveal the entrance to her small secret apartment.

'Make yourself at home, Mr Jameson,' she said, smiling.

'John, call me John, please,' I said, and bowed politely.

'Why, that's nice, John, I'd love to,' she replied, and added,

'Just close the inner door – the outer door shuts automatically. When you want out just open the inner door. Oh, and if you feel tired you can have a rest on the couch, the board meeting is not scheduled to finish within the next three hours. I must go now, bye,' she said, still smiling, with a slight touch of wickedness around her mouth.

Maybe she was thinking of staying but couldn't leave her desk unoccupied, not with a general board meeting in full progress.

I brushed my teeth and took my time with the shower after having my second shave of the day. I donned fresh underwear from my night bag and slapped a dab of my favourite after-shave on my chin and neck before I put on my white shirt, closed the cuffs and slipped back into my executive type dark suit. I like wearing a tie. I find it adds that extra bit of elegance, or as some women put it – manliness.

I stepped through the door back to reality. Jasmine gave me an appreciative nod and smile. Standing next to her was Michael Johnson, Sir Thomas' right hand.

'John, welcome back. You've certainly been in the wars, haven't you? Read your report.'

I held out my hand.

'Nice to see you again Michael – how's your squash arm?' I added, knowing full well he hasn't played squash since he bashed his racket and broke his arm on the squash court trying to beat me.

'Still the same, John – haven't played since. Arm's still not up to it,' he replied, sadly.

'Maybe you ought to train the other arm – ambidextrous, eh,' I suggested.

'Good God no, not the other arm as well, certainly not,' he replied, laughing.

'Anyway, John,' he added heartily, Sir Thomas would like you to present your last findings to the board and he specifically said, don't leave anything out just to save a few faces.'

'Okay, Michael, I'll follow you in,' I declared, ceremoniously.

Sir Thomas was more than pleased to see me. He stood up when I entered the room, the other members following suit. I became embarrassed with what followed. Sir Thomas started and one after the other the board members clapped their hands until they were all clapping. The clapping stopped when Sir Thomas stopped. What followed was a moment in my life I relished – I received thanks and appreciation for doing a dangerous job, which is not usually the case. I was overwhelmed, but canny enough to recognise the manipulation – aimed at winning me over once more. But this time my mind was made up.

I gave my final report to the board members, leaving nothing out and going further than I'd initially intended.

White faces and occasional gasps gave vent amongst the members during my horrendous tales. Shouts of, *'shame on them,'* or *'bloody traitors,'* passed some worthy mouths on the mention of names and their particular roles in the international plots and murdering. I left Jack Orlowski to the end giving many members food for future thoughts by ending with, *'where there's one, there may be others.'* Once again I was applauded until Sir Thomas sat down. Without further ado, he came to the point,

'John, we would like to invite you onto the board. What do you say?'

I thought, Jack had been on the board too. That disgusted me, 'Thanks for the offer, Sir Thomas, but I'm afraid I'm not the right person. I'm a field agent at heart and have other plans. What I would suggest, however, is you employ me on a freelance basis. Whenever you require my expertise, just give me a call. That way, I can lead a fairly normal life, I hope,' I said, and smiled.

'Well, that sounds like a damn good idea, eh?' said Sir Thomas, his head moving in a half circle, pretending to look for approval from the board members and nodding his head at the positive response and the occasional, *'hear, hear.'*

'Well, I think we can accept that, John, it's a fair offer under the circumstances. Of course we'll double your salary, and since you saved the organization from being eliminated I think we can afford 1 million Euros imbursement for yourself and fifty thousand Euros for each of your companions. I believe you call them your *bunch,*' he said, ending the discourse by adding,

'And once again, gentlemen – thanks to a courageous and loyal John Jameson.'

'Hear, hear,' came loud and clear from the board members who were all smiling.

Sir Thomas stood up and began clapping. The others followed – it went the rounds again.

I realized my polite dismissal immediately and was at the door by the time the clapping round was ended by Sir Thomas. I left the room without further ado, feeling elated. Sir Thomas had been very cautious in not mentioning the damaging data I'd collected. He knew damn well my offer to stay as a freelance ensured my silence, at least for the time being. The generous pay-off on their part was a bonus to secure it. One day he'll want a chat about the data, no doubt. For the moment, it stays in a safe place as a measure for my personal safety and wellbeing.

I wasn't too keen on a visit to the main ISIA HQ building after the board meeting. Maybe some of the staff that'd been loyal to Jack Orlowski would think I was relishing the moment of victory. There were many good agents there too, so it would be out of place. I'll have to give it a few more weeks.

Exhausted, I went to my Berlin flat. My neighbour with the Persian cat was all over me with questions. I took my mail and thanked her, leaving her frustrated with all her questions unanswered and entered my flat.

I undressed quickly and threw myself on the bed. For the first time since Anna's death, I felt depressed. I was torn apart. I felt Paula's presence and longed for Elsa's company. Tomorrow, I shall go back to Buchenberg and stay with Elsa. We have a lot of planning to do, among other things.

Moscow – Saturday, 18th September

The transport plane landed on a military airport strip just outside Moscow, restricted for normal commercial aircraft. As the plane rolled towards the hangar, Heinrich Bolkow laughed inwardly. What a day for the Russian FSB and of course for me, Heinrich Bolkow, he thought. He had great difficulties trying to withhold his joy when he saw Juri Kalinkovski at the helipad in Klosters. That fool Jameson thought he was handing him over to the Ukrainians for trial. Juri Kalinkovski, ex KGB and now a freelance member of the FSB was a good friend from old days in the KGB Villa at Dresden. Heinrich remembered those days well. His first *Fuehrungsoffizier* from the KGB, Vova, met him on numerous occasions, and not far away had always been his personal back up, Juri. He laughed out loud.

Juri looked over and grinned. He could guess what Heinrich had to laugh about.

The plane taxied around to face the hangar. The engines were trimmed down low and finally cut.

'Time to leave *Genosse* Stern,' said Juri, clapping Heinrich on the back and laughing his head off.

He'd been so used to his guise as a *Jude* that for a moment Heinrich reacted to the name on impulse and stood up instantly.

Juri's laugh was bolstered, pleased at the reaction to his quirk.

Heinrich scowled, but took it without insult. It was really meant as a compliment he realized – after so many years holding out his guise with those stupid Jews. But not long now and his old friend Adolf Hitler will finally have his main wish come true. He stepped out of the plane onto the mobile steps and was surprised when a small detachment of soldiers, a guard of honour, came to attention. He reached the bottom of the steps where he was greeted by no other than his old *Fuehrungsoffizier* from the KGB, Vova, who was now President of Russia. He remembered him well. With the help of his own organisation, Bolkow had passed on valuable information to him about the Euro fighter.

Vova gave him a brotherly hug and shook his hand viciously. He was smiling, which is not often the case. Heinrich knew the cause.

'My dear friend Heinrich, welcome home,' he said heartily.

'Thank you, Mr President, thank you – I'm so glad to be here,' said Heinrich.

'Let us take the parade, shall we?' said Vova and without further ado both men made their way towards the guard of honour – Vova with his arms swinging and striding with the unmistakable gait and bearing of an experienced and well trained FSB officer.

The officer in charge gave the command, *'present arms,'* and waited until the President and Heinrich marched along the front row of soldiers before he fell in behind. Heinrich Bolkow, Nazi criminal, turned Soviet spy, is being given the honours. At the end of the row, both men stopped and turned to the officer who saluted. Vova nodded in salutation followed by Heinrich Bolkow. Both men turned towards a waiting limousine. As they reached it Bolkow stopped and turned to Vova. With a slight grin he addressed the Russian President, *'Die Sonne geht im Osten auf.'*

Vova laughed and said, 'You still remember your first identification password, Heinrich,' and repeated it in Russian patting him on the back, '*Со́лнце встаёт на восто́к*'.

They climbed into the limousine and left the military airport followed by a large escort of motorcycles and armoured vehicles.

'Tell me Heinrich, are the bombs placed?' asked Vova, as their vehicle turned onto the main road towards Moscow.

'Yes, Mr President, we have one 5Kt bomb well placed in Tel Aviv and the other in Tehran,' replied Heinrich.

'Then we will just have to wait until the time is ripe, won't we,' said Vova, and laughed quietly, pleased with Heinrich and his own devilish plan.

'What about the search for JC's testament?' asked Vova, suddenly.

'Well, it wasn't found but we know now one exists or has existed,' replied Bolkow, 'we are still pursuing the hunt. It is only a matter of time before we will have it, I am sure,' he added, smirking.

Vova nodded and smiled, contented with the way things were moving. Vova thought he had planned well. The West is dependent on oil and gas. He will make them more dependent and then one day, he or his successor will set off the first atomic bomb in Tehran. The second bomb in Tel Aviv will follow the next day. Of course, a barrage of rockets coming from the appropriate direction will disguise both bomb detonations. The havoc and war in the Middle East will last many years, he is sure and will give him his biggest opportunity to cripple the Western governments. The oil flow from the Middle East will freeze indefinitely. He had all the strings to pull and whichever one he pulled would mean one more step towards world domination and the end of the super powers USA and China, and their alliances. They would have to dance to his tune. Then would come his biggest triumph. He would produce the Testament of Jesus Christ and the Christian religions would crumble, and hopefully, also the Western governments. Vova laughed demonically.

Heinrich guessed what he was laughing about and joined him.

('Absence of evidence does not constitute evidence of absence')

Appendices

JESUS OF NAZARETH

Fact not Fiction

Let us go back in time to try and describe the atmosphere that may possibly characterize the Jewish people of Palestine towards the end of the third decade AD. Without a doubt, it can definitely be said that very strong political and religious Jewish nationalistic elements existed. Jewish leaders of either element were allowed a certain amount of freedom of speech.

Prior to his taking over of the administration, Pontius Pilate had been warned of the fanaticism with which the Jews practised and protected their religion. He had his own plans and discarded the warnings of his predecessor. Due to his hence clumsy handling of the administration, the public dislike of the Romans was at its highest level. To top things off, the holy city of Jerusalem and with it the Holy Temple, were put wholly under the jurisdiction of the Procurator. This caused continuous upset for most Jews. The Roman Emperor tried in vain to respect their religious feelings to a certain extent, but his officials had the daily task of maintaining the Roman law – at the same time, governing a people they did not understand – much like the occident and Arab world of today.

The fanatical and puritan views of the Jews at the time were in fact very extreme. Their strong religious belief was the primary motive that gave momentum to their nationalistic striving for power. In their eyes, the Romans were not only political adversaries – they were foremost enemies of the Jewish religion.

Bear in mind, that during the public ministry of Jesus, Palestine was a border region on the Eastern frontier of the Roman Empire. The desert area of the Nabatean Kingdom stretched to the South and East. It centred in Petra but extended northwest to the Mediterranean and North to the vicinity of Damascus. To the Northeast was the Parthian Empire, which in 40 BC had attempted to control Palestine and still constituted a threat to Rome's mastery. Because of the forces near Palestine that required watching, and rebellious spirits within the country that were continuously plotting to throw off Roman control, Rome was constantly on the alert against invasion or uprising. Hence, the charge that Jesus was trying to make himself King (Luke 23:2) was something that was taken seriously.

The only direct contact with Roman territory and forces was to the North. Not far to the Southwest lay Egypt, constantly in communication with Palestine and securely under the control of Rome. But the Nabataeans were the break in the land link connection with Syria to the North.

It was the responsibility of the Roman governors in the more stable province of Syria to exercise supervisory control of Palestine in critical times. Palestine was definitely under their protection and watchful oversight. A vivid illustration of this occurred in 36 AD. Pontius Pilate, the Roman procurator not only of Jerusalem but also of Samaria, Judea and part of Idumaea, was under suspicion of acting unwisely in crushing a Samaritan disturbance, and Vitellius, the Governor of Syria, deposed him and sent him back to Rome for trial.

Most people think of first-century Palestine as a strictly Jewish country. The facts concerning Decapolis lead to general correction of this train of thought. The word "Decapolis" is Greek. It combines the words *deka (ten),* and *polis (city)* – referring to a federation of cities marked by Hellenistic organisation and culture. The original league of ten cities probably came into being under Roman protection after Pompey took over the region in 63 BC.

The earliest mention of Decapolis is in the Gospels (Mark 5:20, 7:31 – Matthew 4:25), (Josephus' *Wars of the Jews* (ca 75 AD)), and (the *Natural History* of the elder Pliny (ca 77 AD)). Pliny lists the cities as follows: Damascus, Philadelphia, Raphana, Scythopolis, Gadara, Hippos, Dion, Pella, Gerasa and Canatha. Ptolemy, a second century writer, names eighteen cities (Greek probably wasn't his best language or it had a hidden meaning).

During the Ministry of Jesus, there were approximately 20% Hellenists (Greeks) in Jerusalem. This has been verified through archaeological excavations and documents. The Jews regarded them as heathens even though some Hellenists became faithful followers of Jesus. Against the background of this cultural clash between Hellenistic and Jewish elements, we must understand the situation during the ministry of Jesus. The visible challenge to Jewish faith and customs probably does much to explain why the Pharisees were so strict in the observance of their ceremonial laws. It also added to the fiery spirit of revolt that the Zealots showed against the Romans. Many Jewish patriots felt that Roman power, which supported Hellenistic influences, was directed against both their liberty and their entire way of life. Palestine had become a battleground of two cultural worlds. Jesus could not have been ignorant of the Hellenistic forces. If he shunned them, then he must have done so deliberately.

Jesus of Nazareth began his ministry – the effective teachings and miracles, during the term of office of Pontius Pilate (26 – 36 AD). His historical data – time and place of birth, his upbringing, etc., which modern biblical historians are largely interested in, remain mostly in the dark and/or, cannot be verified. Even his year of birth cannot be determined exactly. For a reconstruction of his life we depend mostly on the New Testament and Flavius Josephus.

The first Christians, for their part, were not primarily interested in his life history, but in his proclamations and deeds. Therefore, biographical references result mainly from a certain pre-understanding of the nature of Jesus' work.

It can be determined from the few New Testament statements that Jesus was probably born during the last reigning years of Herod the Great, therefore before the year 4 BC. Whether indeed his birthplace was Bethlehem, as some texts indicate, is by no means certain and cannot be verified. The only thing that is certain is that Jesus spent his youth in Nazareth, a tiny village in the barren mountains of Galilee that only had one well for the entire village. This has been proven both archaeologically and historically. This would make it a fairly small community from the ecological perspective. Nothing more can be said, or is known, about his youth and this fact raises many questions.

Early Christians were obviously less interested in his birthplace and childhood. When they reflected on his life, then it was mainly about the facts themselves and the conclusions, but not about the correctness of historical dating. That was generally the case concerning Jesus' historical data. It was only important to them how he appeared, what his actions were and what he had to say. Not when and where he appeared. At the time of Jesus, Jews generally reached maturity, according to the law, at the age of thirty.

According to Luke (3:1), Jesus' public appearance began in the 13th year of the reign of Emperor Tiberius. As the reign of Tiberius was 14 – 37 AD, then Jesus' first public activity can be set to the year 28 AD.

The reading of the synoptic gospels (Mark, Matthew and Luke) give the impression that Jesus was only active for one year – first in Galilee and after that in Jerusalem, with a spell of abstinence in the desert for 40 days. On the other hand the Gospel book of John suggests that he was active for at least two years. Other information points to his being active for three years from the age of maturity at thirty until his crucifixion.

The flimsy statements don't make a good impression – therefore are definitely insufficient for any clear, historical-archaeological decision-making. Unquestionably, Jesus was mainly present in Galilee, where one of Herod the Greats' sons, Herod Antipas governed. Jesus' presence was mainly on the banks of Lake Genesareth, in the adjacent countries in the East and the Roman province of Syria.

What strikes quite puzzlingly, is that the bible texts make no mention of Jesus appearing in important cities such as Tiberius or Sepphoris, to mention but a few that were in the region also fairly near to Lake Genesareth. Evidently he had a preference for the open country and smaller towns and villages. That's where he appeared. He announced that with his coming, the beginning of the Kingdom of God began – one should convert, purify his heart and long humbly for God's justice. The Galileans – renowned for their religious zeal – were generally devotional listeners to his words, although they misinterpreted the words of God's healing nature in their strive for nationalism.

Without any miracles, Jesus would no doubt have remained

a sand corn in the desert of history surrounding the Christian faith.

NOTES ON JAMES – JESUS' BROTHER

(Fact not Fiction)

According to the New Testament, Mark 6:3, it is proclaimed that Jesus had four brothers: James, Joseph, Judas and Simon, all residing in Nazareth. It is also mentioned that he had sisters as well. We'll not go into the question of whether they were half-brothers and sisters or cousins, as some have tried to suggest. Suffice to say – Mark describes them explicitly as brothers (dictionary: – sons of same parents), adopting the general description for brothers and sisters. Mark's notes were written in Greek. He was an assistant to the holy apostle Peter.

As with the Jewish religion, James as Jesus' brother believed that he, being the next eldest family descendant, dynastically followed as the new religious leader after Jesus was crucified. As with Mohammed in the Islamic religion, it is regarded that direct descendants may speak in the name of the prophet. The New Testament speculates this was not according to Jesus' testament, because normally, one of the Apostles would have been his choice. If this was indeed the case then the question arises why was James not his choice because it was generally normal Jewish practice at the time. Bearing in mind that the New Testament is not speculative then where is Jesus' testament?

Compare also Mark 3:31-35 where Jesus was not interested in meeting his mother and brothers who were waiting in the crowd outside, when their presence was made known to him. This fact relays a general unimportance regarding a dynastical follow-up, as he points out that all *brethren* are his brothers and sisters.

On the other hand, James became the most ardent follower of Jesus and a central figure of the Christian faith in Jerusalem – supported by Paul *(letters)* and Luke *(in the Apostle history)* for the period of the 1st and 2nd decade after Jesus' death. This could point to him having followed normal Jewish practice.

It is not proven that James became a follower of Jesus purely post mortem. We know that Jesus possessed the divine light. We can therefore assume that he grew up with at least some of his brothers and sisters, in particular with James, the second eldest, in a somewhat peaceful and heavenly atmosphere. Therefore, James *would have been* a follower of Jesus' teachings and an utmost believer in his brother Jesus. This is most probably based on brotherly love and the knowledge given by his mother Mary, that Jesus was a Prophet and only secondarily as a dynastic follow-up. It would have been only natural for him to follow Jesus' footsteps after he was crucified.

When the holy apostle Peter visited Jerusalem from Rome he was only the number two. It was James who took the prerogative, presuming the right to direct all proceedings.

In the introduction to James' letters, James is referred to as the brother of Jesus and the leader of the Jerusalem Jews.

It is speculated that Peter distanced himself from James's Christian path, which had fixed Semitic basic roots. Peter and Paul's travels and the Roman influence were pointing in a different Christian direction, which was to include heathen followers and eventually discard the Semitic roots. James' profile was old-fashioned for many and he was a stubborn and stout Jew at heart.

It was difficult for most Jews raised in Judaism, to understand the new Jewish Christians, who still visited the temple, yet mixed and practiced Christianity with heathens.

Even some of the Jewish Christians were upset about that too, as they had always hoped that Jesus would restore Israel and free it from the heathens, although Jesus in his preaching, had maintained that the Kingdom of God had begun and there was no reason to rid Israel of the Romans.

For most followers 20-30 years after Jesus' crucifixion, it became clear that there would be no Kingdom of God for Israel. Even though Paul, in a letter 20 years after Jesus' crucifixion, still maintained that the Kingdom of God for Israel would be coming. That letter coming from Paul, one of the biggest supporters of the Christian faith for Jews and heathens makes one wonder what changed his mind.

James headed the *Council of the Apostles* in the year 48-49 AD in Jerusalem. Under obscure reasons, he was stoned to death in the year 62 AD.

James was also a hindrance to the followings of the later New Testament, where Jesus was not supposed to have a brother.

The main problem of the Christians of the first generation was, that they always hoped that Jesus would return.

Bearing in mind the fact, that Jesus was able to read, it can be assumed that he possessed the ability to write. The question: who he had chosen as his predecessor lies unanswered when the fact remains that he was quite aware that his brother James, as the next eldest family descendant, would dynastically take his place – unless of course he had provided for this possibility by writing a **testament**, declaring one of the Apostles to assume this holy task, or he was just a normal human being with gifted healing powers who just hadn't bothered about any kind of testament.

The Role of Archaeology in the Study of the New and Old Testament

General archaeology as a science, is based on the excavation, deciphering and critical evaluation of records of the past and is no doubt a perennially fascinating subject. It can teach thinking skills, problem solving, and it enhances cooperative learning. It is also an excellent way to promote cultural awareness, which leads to an understanding of multicultural societies. Studying the past allows one to study and project the consequences of human behaviour and decision-making. For the most part, archaeologists work in teams with other archaeologists or with archaeological students.

Of even greater interest is the more restricted field of Biblical archaeology. It deals with the excavation, deciphering and critical evaluation of ancient records of the past that touch directly or indirectly upon the Bible and the messages contained therein. Biblical archaeology has become a growing attraction, drawing the attention of numbers of enthusiastic investigators, students and theologians when many are looking for data verification and not just hearsay.

THE BIBLE

Various archaeologists and historians have excavated numerous historical locations in the places described in the Old Testament in their search for verification. Some began to realize this was extremely tedious and unrewarding in many cases. As a result, the cry by many historians and archaeologists over the last decade has been, to do more research on the original biblical texts. Since then, many false interpretations from Aramaic and Hebrew to Greek and many other languages have come to light. It has been agreed by many theologians and historians therefore, that neutral experts should be allowed access to all early Christian documents held by the Vatican and elsewhere in order to revise them.

THE BIBLE – TORAH CODE

(A theory)

There has been speculation as to whether the 3,300 years old text of the Old Testament was ever written by man at all. Various references have been made in the past that the Torah has a secret code. A Rabbi Bachya made the earliest record to a Torah code in the thirteenth century. He wrote that the code begins with the first *Bet* of the book of Genesis and skips 42 letters between each successive letter of the four-letter code *Bet Hey Resh Dalet*, which indicates the average length of the lunar cycle. Amazingly it does so to the accuracy of five decimal places. Jeffrey Satinover discusses a full explanation of this in his book *Cracking the Bible Codes*.

Recent research using high tech computers have been made by a number of experts over the last couple of decades. The research reveals concealed Torah data describing events of history that have indeed taken place. Can it be true then, that the Torah, written 3,300 years ago, conceals a code of certain events that were to happen thousands of years later? This is authentically explained by Barry Steven Roffman in his 2004 book *Ark Code* – Searching for the Ark of the Covenant using ELS *(Equidistant Letter Spaced)* Maps from the Bible Code, including many other references.

    Book details   ARK CODE
                                ISBN 0-9616306-4-7
                                By Barry Steven Roffmann
                                April 2004

GLOSSARY

Abteilung S	Department S (S for sonder –> Special)
Abtel	Liqueur
AC	Assistant Commissionner
Agent Recruitment & European Operations dept.	– see codename Melucha
Al Qaeda	Arab terrorist organisation grounded by Bin Laden in Afghanistan
APAM	Mossad abbreviation for ongoing ops in security dept.
Ark Code	Also known as Torah code – means using ELS to find secret messages using coding in the Torah
Ark of the covenant	– coffer, chest or vessel containing tables of Jewish law
BIS	British Intelligence Service
Biskotchos	Crispy, salted biscuit rings
BKA	Federal Investigation Branch (Bundeskriminalamt)
BND	German Secret Service (Bundesnachrichtendienst)
BRD	Germany (Bundesrepublik Deutschland)
BT	British Telecom
Castlerobin	Name after a booby-trap bomb that was placed outside an Orange Hall at Castlerobin, near Belfast, on September 9th 1971 in a wooden box. The bomb disposal officer who tried to move the box

	was killed. An anti-handling device, micro-switch, if moved more than a fifteenth of a centimetre was incorporated into the ignition circuitry.
CCTV	Closed Circuit Television
Chai	tea
CI	Counter intelligence
CIA	Central Intelligence Agency
CID	Criminal investigation department (Kriminalpolizei)
DA	Double agent
DDA	Double-double agent
Diamond	Codename for Mossad secret communications dept.
Ebionism	Christianity is still climbing out of its Jewish shell. Jesus was a Jew and groups like the Ebionites insisted a person had to be Jewish to be his follower. They believed in Christ but saw him as the Jewish Messiah.
Echelon	Israeli codename for NSA – electronic eavesdropping – telephone – Email
ELS	Equidistant Letter Sequencing ELS – reference: Barry Steven Hoffman – Ark Code – ISBN 0-9616306-4-7 April 2004
ENT	Ear Nose & Throat
EU	European union
EUCLID	Name of group comprising intelligence organisations involved in 911.
EPISCOPE	Vatican Secret Service also known as Opus Dei – after same object as John's group

FAT	File Allocation Table
FBI	Federal Bureau of Investigation
Fighter	Mossad terminology for non-Mossad agent who fights for the Mossad behind enemy lines
FIO	Field intelligence operator
FSB	Russian Secret Service, formally KGB
GCHQ	Government Communications Headquarters
GDR	German Democratic Republic previously East German communist government
General Security Service dept. –	see also codename SHABACK
GITMO	US – Guantanamo Bay Prison – Cuba
GMT	Greenwich Mean Time
Gnosticism	Adaptation from Greek philosophy – the world is miserable, a cesspool of ignorance and suffering and it's not even really our world. We came from somewhere else and salvation is finding our way back.
HAARETZ	Israeli newspaper
Halvah	Sesame and honey bar
HEU	Highly enriched uranium
HQ	Headquarters
ID	Identity
IID	International Intelligence Director
IRA	Irish Republican Army
ISAAC	Internal security administrational access computer
ISIA	International Security Intelligence Agency set up after 911

JIC	Joint Intelligence Committee
Jihad	Islamic –> holy war
JSIC	Joint Services Intelligence Committee
Kalaschnikov or AK47 – assault rifle originally of Soviet design favoured by terrorists	
KGB	Cold War days – old Russian Secret Service
Kidon	All Mossad executions are carried out by Kidon
kph	Kilometres per hour
LAN	Local area network
Liquidation dept – see also codename Metsada	
LKA	Criminal Investigation Group (Landeskriminalamt)
Marcionism	Made a point of eliminating even the smallest speck of Judaism from their Christianity. Their success was enormous. The new faith dominated parts of Asia Minor and influenced it elsewhere for hundreds of years
Melucha	Main Mossad dept. for recruiting of agents and secret ops in Europe. They use foreign nationals as agents
MET	London Metropolitan Police
Metsada	Mossad dept. responsible for the Fighters and Hit team groups. Fighters = non–Mossad fight behind enemy lines. Kidon = liquidation groups (teams), killer or hit units
MfS	East German Secret Service (Ministerium für Staatsicherheit)

MI5	British Security Service (internal security) does certain CI functions overseas. Main job – protecting British secrets at home from foreign spies and to prevent domestic sabotage, subversion and the theft of state secrets
MI6	British Secret Intelligence Service. Main job – collecting information overseas and other strategic services. MI5 and MI6 are controlled by the JIC.
MSU	Marine Support Unit
Mossad	Name for the Israeli Secret Service
Mossad Annihilation Team – also known as Kidon or hit team	
Mossad Communications Department – also known as Diamond –>codename for Mossad secret communications dept.	
MP	Military Police
Nakam	Israeli organisation set up after WWII to find and kill Nazi criminals (self–justice)
NFPÖ	National Freedom Party Austria (National Freiheitliche Partei Österreichs) – right wing
NSA	National Security Authority (American Military Intelligence also known as Echelon –>codename for the NSA world wide electronic eavesdropping – telephones – emails)
NSPD	National Socialist Party Germany (National Partei Deutschland)
NSY	New Scotland Yard
NVD	Night Vision Device

OCU	Operational Command Unit
ODESSA	Code name for German organisation that helped 18,000 Nazis SS escape justice. Also code name for Bolkow's group – links to Al Qaeda and other worldwide organisations intent on taking over the world.
Opus Dei	Extreme Secret organisation of the Roman Catholic Church
PAHA	Israeli specialist analyst department (Pailut Hablanit Ovnet) responsible for analysing information on terrorists
PDS	Leftist Socialist Party Germany (Partei des demokratischen Sozialismus)
PM	Prime Minister
RPG	Rocket Propelled Grenade
RRT	Rapid response team
RUC	Royal Ulster Constabulary
SAS	Special Air Service
Sayanim	Israeli Secret Service –> sleeper
S–Bahn	City District Railway
SBG	Saudi Bin Laden Group
Security Operations dept. – see also codename APAM	
SHABACK	Israeli General Security Service – equivalent to FBI
SIS	Special Intelligence Service
Signal Intelligence Units – also known as 8200 –>codename for Elint and Sigint units of Israeli Secret Service	

Sleeper	Non–active secret service agent living a normal life, in a normal job who can be activated as required (see also Sayanim)
SO	Special operations
STASI	East German State Security (Staatsicherheit)
Supt	Superintendent
SUV	Special Utility Vehicle
Terrorist Analysis dept. – see also codename Paha	
Trümmer-frauen	WWII – women who cleared away debris after the bombing and helped in the rebuilding of Germany
U–Bahn	Underground Railway System
UK	United Kingdom
UN	United Nations
US	United States
USA	United States of America
Vesper	German sandwich meal
VW	Volkswagen
Watchers	MI5 officers – visual surveillance and identification of individuals presenting a security risk
Wikinger	German right wing youth organisation called The Vikings
WMD	Weapons of mass destruction
WTC	World Trade Centre
8200	Elint and Sigint units of Israeli Secret Service

BOOK CHARACTERS

Surname	Chr. Name	Place/Setting
Abdul-Saad	Akram	Saudi Investment Group Oleyan
	Abraham	Jacob Weizmann's chief
	Ali	Merchant in Sur, Lebanon
al–Zarqawi	Abu Mousab	Bin Laden's right hand in Iraq
Allthorpe	Clive	Ex barrister – John Jameson's concierge in London
Anderson	Markus	CID Berlin – loaned to ISIA, RRT on Ian's murder case
Atkins	Tom	Head of SO MI6
Bailey	Maureen	Duty officer MI6
Barnes	John	Member of bunch – ex analyst specialist/programmer also religious freak
Baum	Hans, Joachim	NFPÖ
Bennett	Jill	Joan Miles's staff officer
Blessing	Kurt	member of the BND – German Secret Service
Bolkow	Heinrich	SS criminal – takes over identity of David Stern after WWII
Bormann	Gustav	Assistant to Heinrich Bolkow in the Atomic Bunker
Bush	Henry	Vatican Monsignor – head of Opus Dei in Vatican
Cole	Martin	ISIA – Head of ISIA

Cross	Charles	Assistant Commissioner – SO – New Scotland Yard
Cross	Helen	Charles' sister
Daley	Jack	Chief Inspector – OCU
Davidson	Ari	Head of Mossad
Dearcove	Richard	MI6 Chief
	Dion	known as Goldmouth – Greek philosopher & orator
Dietrich	Holger	German Attorney General
Docherty	Sir Miles	JIC
Donaghue		Father Donaghue – Irish priest
du Fries	Jacqueline	ISIA – FIO
	Elena	Elias' fiancée
Ertl	Elsa	Olaf's sister
Ertl	Hans	Elsa's son
Ertl	Olaf	Pseudonym Karl – ex BND Agent – Elsa's brother
Fadl	Elena	Elias' fiancée
Fadl	Maria	Elena's sister – nurse
Fenton	Chris	Freelance – SO eqpt
Feldhausen	Robert	Hans Ertl's friend from Buchenberg
Ferguson	Ian	British Intelligence Corps – Hans' classmate in Damascus – Arabic studies
	Fritz	Sadistic trainer at Viking camp
Füller	Christian	Vicar of the Nicholas Church in Leipzig

	Gertrud	known as big tits – Henri Walker's girlfriend in rehabilitation House Abax – Bad Dürrheim
Ghazi Nour	Muhammad	Mahmud Trading inc., Rotterdam
Gholam	Munir	Lebanese businessman – BLG
Gold	Caleb	Mossad surveillance chief
Goldilocks		Mosssad code name for surveillance object – Elsa Ertl
Goldmann	Alda	Ariel Zuchowski's (Anna's father) partner
Goldmann	Ben	Son of Ariel Zuchowski and Alda Goldmann – Anna's half–brother
Goldsmith	Golda	Kenneth Woodward's sister
	Graham	Special ops driver NSY
Gravestone	Alistair	Archaeologist
Grossman	Joshua	Assistant to head of SO, MI6 – Tom Atkins
Gurion	Sarah	Jacob Weizmann's wife
	Helen	Charles Cross's sister
Haddock	Dave	Chief Superintendent – SO anti–terrorist dept NSY
Harburg	Jochen von	German Foreign Office
Hayward	June	the Agency –ISIA
	Hellion	Mathematician at Secacah responsible for coding
Hellstern	Jan	ex Mossad agent
Hellwig	Johann	Leipzig Social Centre organisation committee

Henning	Horst	member of the BND – German Secret Service
	Hermes	Messenger and agent in 67 AD
Holzbein	Helmut	Detective Chief Supt, CID Eastern Central Command
Holgerlein	Detlef	Board member of German International Corporate Bank
Holzhaus		Chief Inspector SO, Leipzig
Huebber	Hermann	Council chairman–protestant church in Germany
Hughes	Colin	Member of bunch – ex analyst specialist/programmer, ex Royal Marine Commando
Hughes	Pat	Chief Inspector MET
Hughes	Colin	member of bunch
Idris	Achmed	Landlady's son at Hans's digs in Damascus
Idris	Hussein	Brother of Achmed's deceased father – retired Brigadier of Syrian Army
Jack the Ripper		Nickname for Jack Ripple – member of the bunch
Jacobs	Moshe	Friend of the Sterns – Jeweller in Leipzig
Jacobs	Sarah	Moshe's wife
	Jacob	Mossad Surveillance officer Tel Aviv
	Janet	Student – Paula's flat in Haifa, Rehof Jafo Street
	Jessica	Student living at Paula's flat in Haifa, Rehof Jafo Street
	Jock	Nickname for John Jameson

	Judith	Cook – Haifa
Jameson	John	ISIA – Chief of FIO Dept. SO
	Jasmine	ISIA – secretary to the Board of Directors
	JB	Nickname for John Barnes – member of the bunch
	JW	Nickname for John Wilson – member of the bunch
Jones	Mike	Member of bunch – ex analyst specialist/programmer
	Josephus	also J. Flavius – takes over JC's map & ltr – testament
Kalinkovski	Juri	Personal Security Enterprise – ex KGB
Kamal Kassas	Mustafa	Swiss Bank International
Kraus		Middle–aged Nazi – member of The Vikings
Krem	Albert	Priest at boarding school who misused Henri Walker
Krieger	Heinz	Butler at Aunt Hera's
Knight	Dick	Member of bunch – ex analyst specialist/programmer
Kuhn	Regina	Doctor – Psychiatrist who treated Henri Walker
Laden	Bin	Arab terrorist born in Saudi Arabia (world's most wanted person)
Lenders	Stephen	Director General of MI5
Lorenzi	Fabio	Opus Dei assassin
Macmillan	James(Jimmy)	MI6 – MI5 coordinator
Mai	Karin	Aid worker and co–driver – Villingen – relief goods

Maier	Herbert	Doctor in charge of parole committee – Henri Walker
Manning	Christopher	BND dept. chief
Mathilda	Sister	Catholic nun working in dangerous inmates dept
	Mousa	Ali the merchant's nephew – Sur (Tyre)
	Omar	Syrian Army driver
Miles	Joan	Deputy Director forensics NSY
Montgomery	Derek	Member of bunch – ex analyst specialist/programmer, ex Royal Marine Commando
Neukirch	Ralf	Assistant to Heinrich Bolkow in Atomic Bunker
O'Connor	Eileen	IRA terrorist – daughter of Sean O'Connor – killed in Belfast
O'Connor	Sean	Father of Eileen – IRA terrorist
Orloff	Isaac	Deputy chief of SHABACK – general security service
Orlowski	Jack	ISIA – Dept. Chief SO–anti–terrorist dept
Phillips Sir	Thomas	Director of ISIA board
Putin	Waldemar	Russian PM
Rannick	Michael	German SWF4 radio commentator
Rapp	(Frau)	Owner of Café Rapp in Buchenberg
Reaves	Bill	ISIA – Security Guard

Ripple	Jack	Member of John's bunch also known as Jack the Ripper
Rothman	Steve	Computer expert Haifa – specialist for Ark Code
Rubinstein	Carla	Professor – biblical archaeologist expert – Haifa
Rubinstein	Elias	Head of PAHA – analyst dept (Mossad)
Sadeh	Hakim	Achmed's Uncle – civil engineer – mother's side
Said	Rashad	Colonel – Syrian Secret Service
Salomon	Judith	Mossad operator in Metsada dept – Sarah=colleague
Sawwaf	Paarviz	Syrian Education and Culture Minister
Scarlotti	John	Director of MI6
Schmidt	Hermann	Lorry driver – Villingen – relief goods
Schmidbauer	Albert	Professor in charge of Psychiatric Hospital Rottweil
Schneider	Albert	Land surveyor from Passau
Schneider	Frederick	Jesuit priest – restorer working in the Vatican
Schneider	Silvia	Albert Schneider's wife
Schulz	Frieda	Classmate of Hans in Damascus – Arabic studies
Schulz	Helga	Henri Walker's social worker – not related
Schwarz	Moshe	Head of APAM – ongoing ops in security dept (Mossad)

Silvermann	David	Head of Mossad Metsada Dept – executions
Simpson	Sheila	Han's classmate in Damascus – Arabic studies
Simpson	Susan	ISIA – Orlowski's secretary
Skorzeny	Otto	SS Officer – founder of ODESSA – helped 18,000 SS escape justice at end of WWII
Stahl	Dieter	SO duty officer – German CID Stuttgart
Stein	Hera	Golda Stern's sister – Leipzig
Stein	Jacob	Mead of Melucha – Mossad recruitment dept
Stern	David	Young Rabbi – Leipzig
Stern	Golda	Wife of David Stern Leipzig – maiden name Stein
Stern	Martha	Ian's girlfriend – Jewess from Leipzig – involved with Jewish/Palestinian freedom movement. Real name Zuckenic – took on name Stern
Stewart	Ian	ISIA – FIO
Teufel	Richard	Leader of the Nazi Party Germany
Turnkey	Bob	Member of bunch – ex analyst specialist/programmer
Van der Falk	Gerard	ISIA – FIO
Van Gelders	Henrich	Hans' classmate in Damascus – Arabic studies
Walker	Henri	Multiple personality disorder – killer

Weis	Heinrich	Fire Brigade Commandant – Leipzig
Weizmann	Jacob	Doctor – analyst specialist for Mossad PAHA dept
Willis	Douglas	CNN Reporter
Wilson	John	Member of John's bunch also known as JW
Woodward	Kenneth	Hans' father – European Chief – Mossad ops
Woodward	Elias	Son of Kenneth Woodward – Hans's half–brother
	Yasmin	Elena's distant great Aunt
Zuckenic	Ephraim	Husband of Sarah & father of Martha – famous archaeologist
Zuckenic	Martha	Daughter of Sarah and Ephraim – takes on name Stern
Zuckenic	Paula	Daughter of Ephraim's sister Sara – doesn't marry
Zuckenic	Sarah	Maiden Name Stern – Anna and Martha's mother
Zuchowski	Anna	Sarah Zuchenic(Stern) marries John Jameson – gets murdered
Zuchowski	Ariel	Anna's father – divorces – Kibbutz with new partner
Zuchowski	Sarah	Maiden name Stern – Anna and Martha's Mother – re-married – Zuckenic

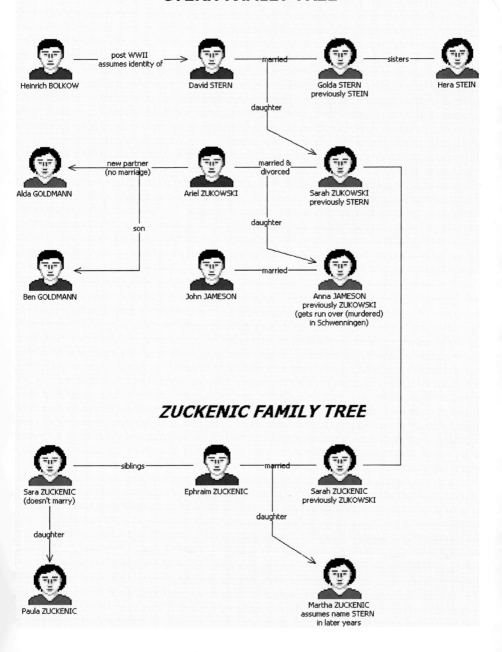